Christopher Ransom is the author of internationally best-selling novels including *The Birthing House* and *The People Next Door*. He studied literature at Colorado State University and worked at *Entertainment Weekly* magazine in New York, and now lives near his hometown of Boulder, Colorado.

Also by Christopher Ransom

The Birthing House
The Haunting of James Hastings
The People Next Door
The Fading
The Orphan

BENEATH THE LAKE

CHRISTOPHER RANSOM

sphere

SPHERE

First published in 2014 by Sphere
This paperback edition published by Sphere in 2016

1 3 5 7 9 10 8 6 4 2

A CIP catalogue record for this book
is available from the British Library.

ISBN 978-0-7515-5131-0

Typeset in Caslon by M Rules
Printed and bound in Great Britain by
Clays Ltd, St Ives plc

Papers used by Sphere are from well-managed forests
and other responsible sources.

MIX
Paper from
responsible sources
FSC
www.fsc.org   FSC® C104740

Sphere
An imprint of
Little, Brown Book Group
Carmelite House
50 Victoria Embankment
London
EC4Y 0DZ

An Hachette UK Company
www.hachette.co.uk

www.littlebrown.co.uk

To Kamuran
who takes care of his people
and travels without fear

In spring of youth it was my lot
To haunt of the wide world a spot
The which I could not love the less –
So lovely was the loneliness
Of a wild lake, with black rock bound,
And the tall pines that towered around.

But when the Night had thrown her pall
Upon that spot, as upon all,
And the mystic wind went by
Murmuring in melody –
Then – ah! then I would awake
To the terror of the lone lake.

Yet that terror was not fright,
But a tremulous delight –
A feeling not the jewelled mine
Could teach or bribe me to define –
Nor Love – although the Love were thine.

Death was in that poisonous wave,
And in its gulf a fitting grave
For him who thence could solace bring
To his lone imagining –
Whose solitary soul could make
An Eden of that dim lake.

EDGAR ALLAN POE, *The Lake*

The Storm

Born of an ancient river and dammed by man, fighting for survival, Lake Blundstone lies sprawling, stretching, endlessly reshaping its borders in north-central Nebraska. The state's name is derived from the Otoe Native American *Ñí Brásge*, or flat water, given to the Platte River system that feeds Blundstone. The lake earned a reputation as a sailor's paradise, thanks to winds that almost never cease. But when cooler pressure fronts roll down off the Rocky Mountains onto the long runway of the Great Plains and collide with opposing warmer fronts, paradise is no more. Stalks of grain are crippled, windmills become helicopters, barns are shorn of their siding. On a lake with over one hundred and thirty miles of shoreline, thunderstorms can turn treacherous in minutes, unleashing tornadoes that haul skyscrapers of water into the sky.

The Mercer family have been vacationing at Lake Blundstone every June – peak season for the storms – since 1979, this being their fifth trip. Which is to say, the Mercer family have been very fortunate.

Until today.

*

Raymond Mercer, still proud of turning eight three weeks ago, begins the morning with a cheese Danish and tumbler of Tang while his parents sip their coffee around the picnic table at the center of Mercer Base Camp up on Admiral's Point, the sand bluff overlooking the small bay on one side, the real lake on the other. The camper, the Ford Bronco towing it, and the fourteen-foot catamaran's trailer hitched behind that, together form a semi-circle around the family fire pit and lawn chairs, giving Raymond an unspoken but very real sense of security in what has become their humble vacation home.

Raymond's twelve-year-old sister Colette, who goes by Colt, is across the plateau, brushing her teeth and washing her sun-streaked blonde hair under the old well with its orange iron pump handle. Their big brother Leonard, fifteen and always looking for an excuse to practice driving, has buzzed off on the small Honda mini bike Dad salvaged from a yard sale for seventy-five dollars and restored in his workshop. Sometimes Leonard lets Raymond ride on the back as they jounce along the bumpy dirt trails through the tall weeds, nicknaming this one Turtle Lane, that one Bullsnake Row, the native animals basking up an appetite before seeking shade during the hot midday. Raymond is still tired from the fireworks celebration they shared on the point last night, so he doesn't mind that Leonard left without him.

By eleven, everyone is down on the beach, the lawn chairs set up, water toys spread around, Warren's transistor radio pulling in oldies from towns unknown. Always the protective mother, Francine applies sunscreen to Raymond's nose and shoulders before they all head out on the sailboat, the Aqua Cat's yellow pontoons cutting through the cove's calm green with its suspended flakes of brown algae and out into the deepening blue. Warren drops anchor and lets the kids swim under the trampoline deck, hauling Raymond up between the pontoons only to launch him out once more like a cannonball.

By afternoon the Mercers are spread out, playing or lounging in their own private reserves within the larger resort. Francine is inside the camper preparing turkey, apple and Swiss sandwiches while Warren fusses with some new project he's cooked up this year – augmenting the ceramic grill, mounting a new sun shower system to the camper shell. Leonard is out fishing from his inner tube, Colt is reading her book back in her tent and Raymond is playing with his toy soldiers on the crumbling slopes of the sand cliffs, throwing clods at infantrymen.

Tiring of his war games, he carries his bucket down the beach in search of toads. Night is the best time, when the heat drops and the insects come out, but sometimes the day brings a surprise. He ventures as far as he is allowed but finds no toads.

A little girl in a yellow swimsuit appears, walking with her own plastic bucket. She has blonde hair like Colette's and she's younger than he is, six or seven at most. She is alone but for the dog at her side, a bulldog mix of some sort, muscular under a cinnamon coat. The dog pulls a little steel cart with two knobby rubber wheels like the ones on Raymond's dirt bike back home. He watches the dog keeping step with her, gradually understanding it is

3

not a cart but a custom, dog version of a wheelchair. The animal's head is wide, with powerful jaws and a white spot on his muzzle. He looks happy, lips pulled back, tongue hanging to one side, jowls catching the breeze. The tail wags in odd half-swings that make Raymond's heart ache.

Now and then the girl plucks something from the beach. She holds her find before the dog's muzzle and his ears perk up, he sniffs with little interest, and she drops it before moving on.

Bored or thirsty, the dog trundles away, the braces of his two-wheeler clanking across the thick beach and down to the water, where he laps up some of the lake. He wades in until his chest meets the surface and his wheels are submerged to the axle. He drinks, then retreats, front legs U-turning him back to dry land, where the smooth cinnamon turns into a coat of spikes that shrug off a glittering mist. The dog stares across the lake for a moment, ears tucked low over the thick round of the skull. He sniffs, guarded, waiting for something.

A few steps later the girl halts in surprise, reaching cautiously, taking the new find in her small hand. She studies it closely, then looks up, noticing Raymond for the first time. She smiles and waves to him.

Raymond waves in return and the dog makes a practiced pivot with the vehicle, the uncoordinated hind legs prodding at the small dunes. The powerful chest and front legs compensate with a sudden stampede, hauling the buggy, its tires fanning little roosters of sand until the dog is close to galloping. When he reaches her side the dog is panting, stumbling, offering his services once more.

The girl lowers the new thing and the dog sniffs it once, then barks at it, backing away, tail curling. A succession of barks comes deep from his chest, warning her.

The girl pats the dog's shoulders and smoothes his pointed ears, then looks to Raymond. They are closer now, but not close enough to talk. The sunlight is white around her small shape, her tiny dark shoulders and wet blonde hair. She holds up her find for him to see, but all he makes out is a speck of green or blue between her fingers, like a rough or blocky gem.

Raymond doesn't know what to do, what she expects.

She tilts her head, as if just now noticing something about him that puzzles her more than the gem. The dog looks to Raymond and barks again, cheeks loose, the tongue a little gray surfboard bobbing between coral spikes.

She sets the object in the sand, smiles at him once more, then turns and heads back up the beach, the bulldog in his buggy keeping pace at her side.

Only after the two of them disappear around the next bend in the cliff does Raymond understand she left it for him.

'What time is it, Dad?' Raymond likes to ask, having lost his sense of time and sometimes the ability to recall which day of the week it is.

'What do you care?' Warren always responds. 'You got somewhere you need to be?'

The hours melt. The days blur. Warren likes to brag that after three days at Blundstone he is so detached from the

5

real world he forgets his phone number at the office. It is a place and a mindset that distracts even prepared people from the encroaching storm. Including a little boy lost in the construction of a sand castle.

The sky darkens by the slightest of shades. At the far south end of the lake, inside the pretty stacks of white cumulus, gray thunderheads gather like a hidden fighter squadron. The tame breeze Raymond has come to take for granted picks up so gradually, he thinks nothing of his mother's straw hat tumbling down the beach. Every sand castle needs a moat, and he has been careful to dig one out near the water line. The first few flecks of rain are no more noticeable than a splash of lake.

Fleas bite at Raymond's eyes until he realizes they're actually grains of sand kicked up by the wind. Covering his face, he crawls into the shallows to rinse off, only to be greeted by waves pouncing up to his chest, knocking him on his back. He is on the verge of tears, betrayed by this beach and the water that has only ever been his friend, and then his mother is shouting, running toward him, and he is too shocked to cry. She yanks him up so fast he thinks he is being punished.

The two of them scramble up the powdery cliff, through a cutaway path. The howling wind is almost indistinguishable from his mother's panicked breathing. On the bluff, a point of knee-high weeds and yellow flowers, one of Raymond's green Incredible Hulk flip-flops is shucked off and the weather is like something from another planet.

The camper door is slamming itself against the fiberglass sidewall. The picnic table is upside down. The lawn

6

chairs and an entire row of clothing that had been strung out to dry are twirling across the field. Leonard's little motorcycle is lying on its side, leaking gas. Across the field, a Park Ranger's truck speeds along, horn honking, its brown door badge running with dirty water as if melting. Everywhere the rain is cutting at them sideways, mixing with clouds of sand grit that stings Raymond's bare back.

Raymond's mother shoves him inside the camper, drawing the fiberglass shades down over the window screens. She orders him to stay put, then leaps out once more, latching the door, running toward the boat ramp. Raymond remembers that the boat was beached around the corner, on the other side of the point, and his father is probably scrambling to secure it now. Where are Colt and Leonard? He doesn't know, but they are bigger, stronger, and Mom and Dad will make sure they are okay.

The camper has a refrigerator, stove, bathroom, kitchen galley, room for five. It must weigh a couple thousand pounds and sits on leveling jacks, but is now rocking as if the lake has already crept up over the cliff, hellbent on taking Raymond away.

He hops over seat cushions and counters, moving from window to window, trying to see his family. 'Mommy,' he whines, the fear in his own voice adding another layer to the dread coiling inside him. The fiberglass shields leave only shapes and shadows, sealing him inside a bubble of deep gray light. He imagines himself locked inside for days, weeks, a boy cut off from the world, coasting hundreds of miles away, flying or floating until they find him in another state, Ohio perhaps, or Texas, and he will be a

7

hero, the brave kid who survived despite it all. He is old enough to entertain such visions of heroism, and young enough to shudder at the real possibility of being stranded.

He remembers the window beside his bunk, the raised bed at the rear end of the camper. He scurries up and tucks himself cross-legged into the pile of his sleeping bag, hunched over, peering out. The perch affords him his first aerial view of the lake, which sprawls outward from the beach some forty feet below.

The water that was just an hour ago a large, safe, slightly rippled lagoon now looks like a raging sea. The waves come in a tumbling broken puzzle of white-capped chop, ridges and angles of charcoal-colored water tall as his father and wide as a school bus. Though the camper is still warm from the morning heat, Raymond pulls on his hooded sweatshirt and stuffs his hands in the front pockets. For a long while he cannot move, cannot avert his eyes. He is mesmerized by the raging lake, the low dark sky, the whirling devils of sand racing by.

There is no sign of his parents or siblings, but maybe they have all taken shelter down in one of the tents. Or they are just a few feet away, hiding in the Bronco. Or maybe they got lost, wound up ...

Drowned.

He stifles a panicked sob and looks away. The lake is too scary, too ugly. What else does he have up here in his bunk? There is a strange book Leonard gave him for Christmas last year, a comic with panels and illustrations of freaks and freak accidents. *Ripley's Believe or Not!*, a sort of greatest hits anthology of the early comics. Raymond digs into it now, focusing on the man who lived with the railroad spike through his skull, worms able to regenerate their own heads, the baseball pitcher who was struck by lightning during the game and finished it, maniacal Nazis, Sasquatch sightings, creepy mummies, abnormal pets, and even the ads for toys and novelties he has seen a hundred times – it's all deeply fascinating in this moment. Anything but the storm.

The reading, the warmth of the bunk, the dark afternoon sky, the hissing wind and rumbling waves ... eventually the combination lulls him to sleep.

He dreams of nothing.

Raymond wakes untold minutes or hours later, not feeling rested or afraid, only irritable that he is still the only one in the camper. If any of his family returned, they decided not to wake him. The view through the window is as gloomy as before, but the rain seems to have softened and the wind, while still gusting, is no longer strong enough to rock the camper. He dares himself to go out and look for them, but he does not trust his sense of the storm. The waves continue rumbling from center lake to beach rim in a constant, staggered formation, a cauldron of raw natural energy expending itself in all directions.

And then he sees them, down there in the water, and it is enough to make him disbelieve his own eyes. First there is Leonard, and not far away the blonde hair and bright green one-piece swimsuit that belong to Colt. They are diving through the waves, moving away from the beach. Raymond shouts, 'Hey!' as if to warn them, but of course there is no way they can hear him from inside.

Dad is chest-deep and hurling himself parallel to a pair of waves that threaten to overtake him. Only at the last moment does his father curl against the swell, arms churning as if to claim someone from drowning as the wave bears him up and shoves him toward the beach. Ten feet he rides it, twenty, more . . . his father is laughing, braying like a fool, and finally Raymond understands.

They are not panicking. They are not trying to save anyone. They are playing like big kids in the deep end of the pool. Raymond has been in here for hours, worrying, and they are out there *having fun?*

Raymond has never heard the term 'body surfing' but he grasps the concept now. One after another they take turns wading out, dodging rollers, pointing and waving each other on before replicating the move his dad made. They look like seals, all noses and bellies, until the waves break down and leave them tumbling in the sand, and one by one they leap up to do it again.

Mom is a little ways down the beach, closer to the point, waist-deep between swells. She steels herself, then points her hands and dives into a monster, vanishing for a five count, then pops up again, hair flying, and Raymond can almost hear her laughter from up here. He's not used to seeing his mother throw herself into dangerous situations, and it is disturbing.

They left him out, as if they have discovered a magic they want only for themselves. They didn't think to invite him down, or decided he was too small. He knows he is pouting, acting like a baby, but still. He stays, watching them splash and dive and ride their way back in. Over and over, a seemingly endless cycle.

Off to the right, within shouting distance of his own family, another has decided to enter the fray. Raymond recognizes them vaguely, a mother and father and their teen son, the parents heftier than his own, the son taller than Leonard but skinny, frail looking, all ribs and boney chest. They have been camped a few hundred feet down the point and seem poorer than his own family, who are not wealthy by Raymond's own knowledge of such things (his father is always reminding them how hard he works to afford things like the used Aqua Cat, the rebuilt mini bike and the camper that Uncle Gaspar found for them at a wholesale auction). But this other family doesn't have any such recreational vehicles, used or not. They don't even have a propane grill.

What they have is one humongous, ugly green canvas tent, a sagging beast that took them most of a day (and a lot of cussing and yelling at each other) to set up. A few ratty lawn chairs, and a rusted-out white Chevy truck that looked like something out of an after-school special reminding kids of the dangers of hitchhiking. Raymond had seen very little of the family, except for a few passing glances on his way to the outhouses half a mile down the dirt road. The wife in her wide flappy orange-flowered swimsuit with a tutu or ballerina thing around the waist, her ankles thick as the roll of toilet paper she carried in one hand. She's wearing the same kind of beach outfit down there now, knee-deep in the surf, petrified.

The dad has a beer-wagon belly, thick arms, moss-like hair

11

on his back, and he too is a mass of white flesh everywhere but for his face, which is lobster-red. He's not so much surfing as trying to batter the waves into submission, it seems. He might be laughing but it looks like he is yelling, roaring each time he flops into the center of another roller.

Though the sky seems a shade lighter now, silvery gray with cracks of sun, the water itself has darkened beyond gray-blue, as if the lake is not ready to give up the storm just yet. The strangest thing is how much darker it is in the shallows, where the water should be lighter brown. Way out past the bay the blue seems held back by a border, some kind of barrier unaffected by the rolling waves.

Raymond's unsettled gaze is drawn back to the teen son from the other family, who has hacked his way farther out than any of them. He bobs vertically for a moment, cupping his mouth to the lake, and Raymond wonders if he is drinking it. But then the boy glazes over, suddenly tired, and the word 'drowning' floats through Raymond's mind once more.

Another crooked wave rises up behind the boy, and he springs to life. His skinny white arms wind around and around as his legs chop into the wave. Somehow the narrow length of him turns into a ski and he shoots forward, spine arched, riding the gray edge faster and faster, until the last possible moment. Just when it seems the wave is about to throw him against the cliff wall, his body jack-knifes and crumbles into a pile of limbs, slapping him to the beach.

Raymond tenses, convinced the boy just broke his neck.

But the kid unfolds and rises again, excited and shouting. His mother looks frightened as the boy stomps along the beach, bends over, takes two fistfuls of wet sand and begins slinging it at the surf before charging back in.

The mother slips and falls as if pulled under by the current, some kind of undertow – though Raymond has never felt such a thing here. Several waves ride over the spot she was standing in and she does not come up once they have passed. If she doesn't know how to swim, she's in big trouble.

Somehow Raymond knows they all are.

The father tromps back out, spitting water and hitching up his cut-off jeans, which are now laden with dark sand that runs off in syrupy streams, and he seems to be coughing or choking. He staggers, legs cutting into the almost black shelves, slapping around like a man who has lost his hat or gone blind.

The head-banging teen son points to where his mother vanished, jabbing with his finger, and Raymond is almost certain the boy is laughing.

At last the mother pops up out of the water, on her feet and closer to shore, swept back to her original knee-deep position. She stands tiredly, shoulders slumped and head down. She doesn't move as the waves slop against her hips and up to her chest where – Raymond can see this clearly and is shocked by her lack of awareness, then ashamed to notice it at all – one of her breasts has flopped out.

Her husband, who seems only curious as he trudges over to her, leans in close as if trying to recognize her, and then slaps her across the side of the head so hard the woman reels sideways, stumbling in a circle to right herself. She does not look up or cry out or run away. Her shoulders slump once more, and Raymond is glad that her hair obscures her face. He doesn't want to see her expression, or the blood that must be leaking from her nose.

With no further exchange or provocation, the husband socks her again, this time with what appears to be a closed fist.

Raymond looks away, a sick thrill and equally repulsive hot shame making his entire body quiver with a new kind of fear. His own family are staring at this other development in dumbstruck confusion.

The teen son hops and surges toward his father, and Raymond assumes the kid is about to grab the big man, shove him away from the poor woman. But the son does not defend his mother or attack his father.

Lashing out like a boxer, the boy punches his mother in the stomach.

The husband seems unaware of the violence his son just perpetrated, or that his son is there at all. He reaches for his wife's neck as she folds over, catches her, raises her upright once more. He slaps her twice and then his meaty fingers are sinking into her windpipe. He is soon strangling her with both hands, and behind them, leaping around like a joker in some deranged king's court, the son screams at the sky.

Raymond is hiccuping his way through tears and unshackled terror by the time his own father collides with the fat man, shoving the son down in the process. Leonard is not far behind, and even Colt looks ready to fight, to defend this poor woman.

14

The dark water churns, and their limbs splash and claw through the shrinking waves. The lake is so dark now, he can't see their arms and legs beneath the black surface. The lake appears to be cutting them in sections, swallowing them.

The top of someone's head bobs up, only to be submerged again.

Raymond's dad slams a forearm down on the other dad's collarbone, again at the base of his neck. The murderous hands release the wife, who falls face first into the lake and does not attempt to get up.

The teen son leaps onto Warren's back, but Leonard is there, yanking the kid by the legs, dragging him away from the mess before the kid can get a good grip.

Colt screams at all of them. Raymond's mom screams at Colt, telling her, he imagines, to get away, get back.

Chaos reigns. Bodies swarm and crash. Another rogue wave moving almost sideways douses the two men, and just when Raymond is prepared for all of them to clash in a frenzy, the melee ends.

All three of them, the mother, father and teen son, are rolling in the water. They look like drowning victims Raymond has seen on TV. His dad drags the huge man up to the beach. Leonard follows suit with the teen son. Colette and Mom work to pull the mother by the legs into the shallows.

Because the camper is set back from the cliff's edge, Raymond's view does not extend to the first ten or twenty feet of beach directly below, nor to the hill and cutaway path his mother led him up a few hours ago. The last thing he sees is his father bending over one of the bodies, as if preparing to attempt mouth-to-mouth, then Colt's wet blonde hair running away, down toward the point. At last, all of the legs, shapes, people, his family and the other, are out of sight. Gone.

Raymond sits, stunned, crying. For a long while he cannot move. His young imagination is flooded with horrible possibilities and outcomes, working to fill the void they have left in the wake of their violence.

The winds taper off. The sun breaks through the clouds. The rain thins and slides away, leaving only a sunset mist. The churning lake becomes a pattern of smaller swells, the gray fading to a welcome deep blue.

It's over now.

Raymond slides down from his bunk, legs weak, stomach sour, and pads his way to the camper door. His feet feel lopsided, and when he looks down he understands why. His right foot is still in his Incredible Hulk sandal, the left is bare. He pauses, hand on the doorknob, thinking about the frightening race up the cliff with his mother, the whirling sand on the point where he lost it. First he will find his sandal, then he will go look for them, feet protected from the sand burrs and sharp sticks.

That's what Leonard would do. Right?

But he can't bring himself to open the camper door. The knob won't turn in his hands. The frosted window has turned deep gray, deeper than the lake when the storm was at its worst, and he knows that an unnatural night has fallen on the other side.

He holds the doorknob, torn between two important

needs. One is to find his family, make sure they are safe. The other is to stay inside, hidden from the bad people, the tricky storm, the descending darkness. He remains stuck for a long time, until time itself loses all meaning and his fears take full ownership of their host.

Eventually, something else opens the door for Raymond Mercer, prying it from his stiff young hands with heart-stopping force.

Nothing is ever the same after that.

Invitation

Summer used to be Ray's favorite time of year, but this one is beginning to make him wonder if he would be better off spending the remainder of his warm seasons much further north, in Canada or Alaska, a place one imagines the weather or a grizzly bear being the encompassing problem. Where everything is reduced to the moment, make fire or die, his blood or yours, pure survival.

Existence down here in civilization is not so dire, at least not in his daily dealings, but it is more complicated. He can't stop feeling depressed by the trivial outpouring of everyone's status updates, even as he grows numb to the real tragedies playing out across the world. He takes solace in researching a new set of kitchen knives and ordering limited runs of denim from Japan, but his anxiety returns before the packages arrive on his doorstep. Two years shy of his fortieth birthday, Ray has a strong suspicion that he is merely killing time, consuming things, contributing nothing of value, presenting a forgery of the self for his lack of understanding of the man he has in the meantime become.

These are bitter thoughts, he knows. Bar thoughts, the

kind that make a man reach for another drink on another July afternoon, spreading his fuck-me-it's-Tuesday mood across his usual corner booth in Pescado Rojo, where the air conditioning is strong, the beer cold and it's just a little easier to keep the bad news chilling in the meat locker of the mind. The Rojo is one of several restaurants his father owns, and one the old tiger has not visited in more than a decade, the last time either of his parents visited Ray here in beautiful Boulder, Colorado, where weed is legal but glaucoma and Birkenstocks have not been cured. At the outdoor patio end of the cantina, sprinklers are misting patrons reluctant to return to the office, the bartender is squeezing his way through a mountain of limes, the psychedelic desert and doom sounds of Calexico permeate the afternoon.

Not a bad place to work, or pretend to. This corner booth, unofficially recognized by the staff as his office, is a place to show up, and as such it may be the only thing holding him together.

The first blow came in early May, when Ray lost his primary investor in the business venture that was to be his stand of independence – escape – from the family's wealth. For going on six years now, Mercer Hospitality, the retail and travel arm of the larger corporation, has been paying Ray ninety thousand per year to consult with the managers and operations personnel at various restaurants, flower shops and a furniture franchise. Ray's job description has something to do with recommending local and online marketing strategies where he sees potential to increase revenues, and what he has to show for his diligence in this free-range capacity over the past eighteen months is a series of coupon ads in the university daily and a 'snarky' culinary blog whose entries leave him feeling almost as fraudulent as his paycheck.

The weird part is, no one seems to mind he has become a wastrel. Despite the quarterly updates being funneled back to his father via Gaspar Riko, Mercer's Corp's head of legal affairs and Warren's *consigliere* since both men came home from Vietnam, Ray has not heard from his CEO-father in almost seven years. He clings to his last measure of pride, refusing to petition the family treasury for a seed investment even as he survives on its maintenance.

The second knock was perhaps less troublesome in the long run, but no less insulting in the short. Ray hadn't realized that he didn't love Pam until she announced she had met someone in the Bay Area, was moving in with them in three weeks, this thing she and Ray had shared for the past two years was over, lifeless, they both knew it. He had known their relationship was not meant to last, but he still found it difficult not to take her warm, apologetic and terribly logical severance as a verdict on his value in the scheme of her life, and to females in general.

'I'm so relieved,' he'd told her during that final dinner. 'It's for the best, absolutely, you deserve the right one. We all do,' and he meant that. After, he walked Pam to her car, hugged and cheek-kissed her goodbye, laughing at one of their old jokes and wishing her all the best. But inside he was twelve again, heart-stomped by Tracy Valdez, who had said only 'you're not very mature' before roller-skating away to take Brian Leiderman's hand at Wheels Rink before Ray could finish unlacing his skates.

Well, adult Ray consoled himself, at least summer is here. Long days to spend indoors, cranking the air conditioning, binging on a TV series about people leading awful (but awfully exciting!) lives.

Then the drop-dead heat of July came beating around, and with it Uncle Gaspar. The Mercer family lawyer broke their quarterly schedule and paid Ray an early visit, bushy gray eyebrows wiggling with mischief, bad thing #3 issuing from between his elderly-cherub lips.

'Now there's a man who looks like he could use a vacation,' Gaspar announces, finding Ray in his booth and clapping his hands with a Scoutmaster's glee. 'Pack a bag. Meet at the old camping ground. Your father will handle the rest. Food, supplies, equipment, gear, fireworks. You know how he loves to prepare for the eventualities. Your siblings are already on board. Just make the drive. Wednesday, ten days from next.'

'Have you lost your mind? Has he?'

'Bring Pam. How is Pam these days? She always wanted to meet the whole clan. This is your chance to—'

'Pam's gone.'

'That's, well, quite unfortunate. Can she be salvaged? Your father is still hoping for a male heir. From the next generation, of course.'

'Can she be ... forget it, Gaspar. Pam's out. I'm out.'

The lawyer grins and wags a finger.

'Tell Warren and Francine I'm busy. Better yet, that I refuse.'

'Mm. No.' Gaspar glances at his watch.

'Excuse me?'

'You cannot refuse.'

'He talks to his board of directors more often than he bothers with me. Leonard is MIA and Colt sends a card at Christmas. I'm supposed to jump at the chance to spend a week pretending I still have a family? Roasting marshmallows at some redneck paradise in Nebraska? Does he really believe that's going to happen? They won't miss me, Gaspar. And that's a fact.'

Gaspar leans back, scratching his formidable belly, as a bus boy delivers his usual ice water hold-the-ice. He swirls the glass but does not drink from it.

'It is a funny thing, you know. People in Colorado, they want a beach vacation, they fly down to Cancún, Puerto Vallarta, all the way the hell out to Hawaii, and for what? Paying thousands just to sit on a beach, swim in the ocean, soak up the sun. But Blundstone, this is only six hours away. The water is clean, far safer than the ocean. And the sand is like something stolen from Thailand. As with that South East Asian delight, anything goes at Blundstone. Or so it was, back in the day. Before the secret got out. In the seventies, those first few years when I stumbled upon it and convinced your father to give it a go, there were maybe one or two park rangers for the whole lake. Forty miles of beach on each side, a thousand places to camp and start fires and race your boat, roll a dune buggy, spend the entire day in the nude. Lawless. People did it too, they did everything out at that lake. We knew a family, they caravanned out onto one of the sand points with about two dozen campers and tents, maybe seventy people in all. Put on a bacchanalia of a wedding that lasted four days and nights. Dance floor, hallucinogenics by the trash bag, couples swinging from tent to tent like owl monkeys, and when it was over more than a few of them claimed to have seen God. Can you imagine such a thing being allowed these days? Of people even trying? Well, the times they are a-changed. But family tradition lives on, yes?'

'Good closing argument, counselor. I'm not going.'

After a long, uncomfortable silence, Gaspar removes his tinted spectacles, revealing moist eyes ringed red with grief.

'He didn't want any of you to know until you were together, out there, but ... Your father's heart is failing. Inoperable. Valves are too weak. He waited too long, and now even Labor Day will be a stretch, the cardiologist tells me.'

A dizzying heat pulses up through Ray's neck, pressing behind his eyeballs.

'His last wish,' the lawyer says, hushed as a priest. 'To spend one more glorious afternoon with his family, on the soft sands of Lake Blundstone. It was his, you know. It was always his. He called it *the Big Lake*. With that gleam in his eyes.'

Ray blinks.

'My read on this? The trip is what's keeping him going. He's swimming to the shore, and once he reaches it, there will be nothing left.' Gaspar smiles forlornly. 'The Big Lake. You see?'

Ray nods, bested as well as ashamed.

'Good. Because everything is at stake now, Raymond.'

Gaspar rises from the booth. 'Everything your father built, including his family. It's a fortune and a life, and who knows how we all walk away.'

Ray watches Gaspar do just that, exiting through the darkened cantina, out into the white glare of sidewalk. Ten days is not enough time to prepare. A hundred would not be. He will not be able to do it alone. He is afraid of what his family have become, what his father will make of his youngest child. Ray does not want to wake up the little boy, the one who was abandoned, locked inside of a suffocating camper all night while a terrible storm took his real family – the one he loved and thought he knew – away.

But that was thirty years ago. He is an adult now, and all hope has not been lost. It's a Tuesday, almost four o'clock, and he is in his father's restaurant. Salvation may be a stretch, but there is one thing in the bar that never fails to soothe his nerves, a narcotic more potent than any drink.

Her name is Megan.

The Waitress

Megan has been a server at Pescado Rojo for about fifteen months, and from the first time she waited on him, taking his usual order of lobster mole enchiladas and a sweaty bottle of Negra Modelo, Ray has sensed, in his slumbering ardor, that she is so much more than a waitress. She is the secret longing he has refused to admit to anyone. A workplace *what-if* he allows himself to indulge only when she is serving in the sections that do not include his booth. The strangely satisfying trade-off to admiring her only from afar being that, in her immediate presence, he can blame co-worker etiquette for his fear of rejection even as he suffers like a monk.

The clock sweeps over 4:00 p.m. Her shift begins.

Her tanned bare ankles and the smooth calves above a pair of bright yellow flats are the first thing he sees, and the jolt causes him to quickly look down.

'Hey, Ray.' Megan swings a hip on her way to clock in at the wait station terminal, pausing as she ties the strings of her red apron behind her waist. 'Whatcha workin' on today?'

He counts to three or five, until he senses his blush has begun to fade, then looks up from his laptop as if too concerned with marketing budgets to have registered her presence until now. So many thoughts are swirling through his head that for a moment he cannot respond. His father's heart. Pam's goodbye. The investor who walked off the deal. Loss, loss, loss, and now the trip. None of those things matter during the uncomfortably long seconds he peers into her dark brown eyes, noticing as is his custom and secret pleasure the coal crescents under them, her inner brightness and friendly smile contrasted with the deeper shade suggesting a misstep or two with Eros. Some episode of heartbreak that stained her with traces of wisdom. Something of the tired scullery maid in her today. He is aware of the thread of chauvinism threading through such an observation, and he is aware that, even though it is she who serves him, he would gladly spend the rest of his life doing whatever she asked.

Clearing her throat, Megan affixes two ballpoint pens to the pouch at her hip. 'Ray? You a little lost there, buddy? You look like someone just told you your dog died.'

This remark is close enough to reality, he can't hold back a dark laugh. Out of bravery or desperation, he finds himself breaking whatever it is the monks agree to.

'Actually, someone sort of did. But that's not – listen, do you want to sit down for a minute?'

'Yeah, of course. What's wrong?' She slides into the booth, bouncing her gaze from table to table, in case any are waiting for her to wait on them.

'This might take a few minutes,' Ray says. 'If Rafael gives you any grief, tell him I borrowed you.'

She flashes a nervous smile. 'All right.'

'Can I get you something to drink?'

'Isn't that my line?'

'Not today.'

'Oh. Sure. Iced tea?'

Ray is up to fetch the pitcher kept at the station near the hall to the kitchen. He scoops ice, pinches two tall glasses, carries everything back to the table. He pours, first for her and then for himself.

'Thanks.' Megan takes a polite sip, then a series of longer swallows. 'It's hot out again.'

'More?'

She shakes her head. Waits. So . . .?

'Right, so, I don't have anyone else to talk to. And I know we barely know one another, even though you see me in here four or five times a week, but I feel like I can talk to you. Or maybe I just want to. Whether there was, ah, someone else or not.'

Megan seems less perplexed by this mess of an opening than he had any right to hope for. She almost says something, then tucks her lips between her teeth.

'You always seem grounded to me,' he says. 'Like whatever it is, it's all under control. Like you know something the rest of us don't. It's comforting.'

'I don't know about grounded,' Megan says.

'No? Then what's your secret?'

She stares into her glass, offers a listless shrug.

'I'm sorry,' he says. 'I didn't mean to cross whatever line

exists, if there is—no, there must be some kind of line. We don't have to do this right now.'

She looks up, frowning. 'No, it's okay. It's just throwing me off a bit. We always say hi and talk, but we never *talk*, you know?'

Ray nods.

'You're always so polite to me,' she says. 'So formal. I was kind of starting to worry that I remind you of some . . . or I annoyed you?'

'No. Megan. In fact it's just the opp—'

'Sometimes when you work with people for a while,' she interrupts, 'it's so easy to start thinking you know them. Like, you have this relationship. Not *relationship*, but it's this *thing*. Quiet, but there, and things are being spoken even when nothing is. But it's also like, what if it's all in your head? You know?'

Ray can only manage a nod.

'But now we're talking, like normal people,' she continues, 'and I don't mind telling you something about myself. The change just threw me off, that's all. So. You want to know why I'm waiting tables at thirty-five, right? Why am I coasting?'

'I never thought that. Okay, maybe I used to. But I know about coasting. It's hard. Maybe harder than putting yourself into something that matters.'

'Until you give it everything and the "it" on the other side decides it doesn't want your everything. Then coasting becomes very appealing.'

'I must be working my way up to that part,' he jokes.

'Yeah, well, I had a high-pressure corporate job a few

years ago,' she says. 'And maybe one day I will again. There was a guy, but we were too young. We should have ended it about three years before we did. I tried to pretend he wasn't worth feeling so bad about. But suppressing all that gave me panic attacks. I tried therapy, taking the meds, I read all these books. In the end, I just decided to give myself a break. Drive around the country. Care less about what other people want from me, do what sounds good for a few months. Eat more chocolate. Pathetic, right?'

'Has it helped?'

She considers, but not for long. 'I certainly don't regret the past few years.'

'Then I think it's amazing,' he says. 'That you did that for yourself. In fact, I envy you.'

Megan squints at him. 'You should never say that about someone you don't know very well.'

Ray nods. 'Fair enough. But I still want your advice.'

'People say that . . .'

'And never take it,' he finishes.

Their eyes meet in accord. She sips more tea. And then Ray leans forward, elbows on the table, and tells her everything that's gone wrong lately. About his father's approaching end. This sudden trip. Pam, whom Megan has seen many times in the restaurant but not for a while. About the loss of his primary investor. The sense of doom following his every move.

Does he sound needy, a lost cause begging for a life preserver? It's possible, but it doesn't feel this way. Raymond feels as if he is talking to an old friend and, he tells himself, this is all he was hoping for. A brief connection. Someone

29

on the outside to look in and understand. To console, if not advise, and lacking all else to simply bear witness.

Along the way, studying the tapering fullness of her lips and the shape of her shoulders beneath her lilac-blue peasant blouse, he hears a voice inside calling himself a liar. The voice knows what he is really hoping for is to bring her along, on the trip or maybe just into his dying vision of a life, the one he has been feeling slip away, an existence of coupledom and harmony, home and love and sex and hosting dinner parties and Sunday morning coffee breath, children. Is that too much to hope for?

'It is a little strange,' she tells him near the end. 'But all families are a little strange, aren't they?'

'Mine's more than a little.'

'I think you should go,' she says. 'Just make it your trip too. Whatever that means.'

'I wish it was happening six months from now,' he says, voice nearly cracking. 'If I was really lucky, that might be enough.'

'For?'

Ray exhales. Might as well go all in. 'After six months, if I'd played my cards just right, you *might* be my girlfriend, and if I begged and pleaded, you might consider going with me. I wouldn't have to sneak away from them by myself, with no excuse. I'd just say, Megan and I are going for a romantic walk on the beach. My father would be so proud. And I would ... wow, listen to me. Now, *that* was pathetic.'

Megan is quiet, blushing, and he's sure he just scared her off for good.

Then, eyes holding his, 'Maybe we shouldn't wait. Sometimes when you coast too long, you miss out on something that could have been ...' She stops herself, shakes off the idea with a laugh, looks away. 'I was just thinking how hilarious it would be if we pretended I was your fiancée, or girlfriend, whatever. That would show them, right? This could be helpful for you, or terrible? But no, it's not something I would want to do alone, either.'

Ray is stunned, then elated, then scared. 'Why would you do that?'

'I miss being around families,' she says. 'Mine are no longer with me.'

'Your mother and father?'

'I had a brother too.'

He is afraid to ask how, when. 'I'm sorry.'

'Me too.'

He does not know how to proceed. She smiles, letting him off the hook.

'It was a *long* time ago. Look, I think you're making this a bigger deal than it needs to be, but I'm just a waitress who hasn't had a vacation in three years, so you probably shouldn't take me too seriously.'

'I would love to take you seriously,' he says, his mouth turning dry. 'But I really can't ask you to do this.'

'I think you already did, Ray.'

'I thought you asked me.'

Megan grins. 'Hey, do you guys have a boat? I know how to water-ski.'

'Let's hope so.'

*

31

There are many reasons Ray cannot sleep the night before departure, and of course Megan is the chief among them. But she has also become a sort of psychological Calamine lotion, pretty and pink, soothing every burning irritation and itchy concern about the family reunion trip. So what if he hasn't seen his siblings in eight years and the last go round ended with Colt in howling tears, Leonard in jail? Why fret over discovering just how much his parents have deteriorated; they lost interest in him before he graduated high school. Megan will be there.

But it all seems too convenient. There must be an angle he can't see . . .

Stop. Accept a little good fortune. You're due.

Around five he drifts into an approximation of sleep, fluttering between states. His dreams are illuminated by white sun, carpeted with blonde sand soft as flour, and jeweled with deep blue lapping wavelets stretching beyond any realistic horizon, a body of water that is impossible in Nebraska. The sand is scorching the bottoms of his feet, he has been walking the beach, burrs catching between his toes. He has been walking for hours and hours, possibly for days, and there is far too much sand. He walks miles of it, staring at the sand, and when he next looks up, the lake is gone.

There is only sand. A barren wasteland of blinding hot sand in all directions.

He is lost, alone, left for dead.

The beach begins to fracture, the sand swirls around and around . . .

Calypso music, digitized and abrasively loud, filters into

his half-asleep dream and he opens his eyes, feeling as though he has not rested for weeks.

He turns off his cell phone alarm. The screen clock tells him it's 6:30 a.m. He is to pick up Megan in thirty minutes.

After a quick cold shower and another brushing of the teeth, Ray collects his weekender bag from the den. He takes a final inventory, making sure he has everything to see him through the five-day camping trip:

5 T-shirts. 2 shorts. 1 jeans. 3 pair socks. 5 underwear. Swim trunks. A pullover sweatshirt. His battered Paul Smith sneakers, a pair of leather flip-flops. Toiletry kit. Ibuprofen. Five thousand in cash. A baseball cap. The rest – food, first aid, tent, sleeping bags, every tool imaginable, beverages, GPS, enough gear to occupy a Middle Eastern capital – his father will supply, regardless of his health.

Ready?

No. He doubles back to the den and sets the duffle on his desk. Crouches before the bottom right drawer, unlocks it with a small key. Removes the steel safe box, sets the three dials to the proper code, pops it open. He unwraps the oil-softened, faded-orange Dark Horse Tavern T-shirt in which it is kept, inserts one of the two single-stack magazines, flicks the safety on, off, on again, and then rewraps the Colt M1911 .45 single-action his father gave him when he turned twelve, the sidearm Warren carried through Vietnam and Laos, and digs the bundle into the bottom of his duffle.

Now he is ready to pick up Megan and ferry the two of them five hundred and eighty-three miles north-east, thirty years back in time, to sands Ray has not walked since he was a boy and they were a real family. Together, harboring no secrets.

Safe.

Cover Story

It is a time machine of sorts – their means of transport – as well as another gift from his father. Warren gave Ray the two-tone maroon-over-creme 1978 Ford Bronco for graduating high school, but it had already been imprinted with so many memories throughout Ray's childhood, his thirty-eight-year-old son still cannot bring himself to think of it as his own.

Prior to handing the keys over to Ray, Warren had the original-matched paint job reapplied, had the 6.6-litre motor rebuilt, installed thirty-three-inch off-road tires, sealed the floor in new rubber, upholstered the interior in new saddle leather, wired in a CB radio, added a second fuel tank, giving them nearly seventy gallons capacity, and outfitted the rig with the full-size spare, a first-aid kit, flares, a toolbox, roof rack, jerry cans for more fuel and water. The glove box still holds Warren's old nylon tape case containing Glen Campbell, Cat Stevens, Supertramp, Bread, The Beach Boys, Jan and Dean, and a dozen or so other artists from the old man's heyday.

Ray debated leaving the Bronco in the garage in favor of

taking his newer and much more sensible Honda Pilot, not least because the Bronco – and Ray's careful preservation of it – felt a bit too much like a desperate appeal for his father's approval. But in the end, he could not deny the old man this acknowledgement to tradition. He had been embarrassed when he arrived to find Megan standing on the curb at the address she had given him, one bag and a small cooler filled with beer on the sidewalk, shorts and a fleece shirt, flip-flops, her hair pulled through the back of a purple Rockies cap. She seemed reluctant to open the passenger door, as if he'd rolled up in a van with a disco ball inside.

'Everything okay?' he'd asked, once she recovered and hopped in.

'Thought I left the stove on inside my apartment,' she said. 'But I'm good. Cool truck, by the way. How come I've never seen it down at the restaurant?'

'Gas,' Ray said, shifting into drive. 'The mileage is obscene.'

'Oh,' she says. 'That makes sense.'

'So, what's our cover story?' Megan asks as they pass through Sterling, about an hour from the Nebraska state line. The towns seem to be shrinking, the grain elevators rising. The terrain is prairie weeds, pink rocks, scraggly green brush, and long intervals of cottonwoods clustered near the lazy brown rivers. Occasionally the quartz and mica in the gray sun-starched highway twinkle in the heat.

'Cover story?' Ray turns down the radio. Even the high-

36

powered classic rock stations out of Denver have become garbled with static. Soon they will be left to choose between sermons, demagoguery and crop reports.

'Our history,' she says, sitting up in the Bronco's passenger seat. 'How we met, our best dates, favorite restaurants, where you proposed, our song. You know, our story of *us*.'

Proposed! 'Oh. I guess I kind of forgot we were really going to play it that way.'

'I have tons of ideas,' she says, a child eager to begin Twenty Questions. 'I've been mulling it over for the past three days.'

Ray cuts his eyes at her, frowning.

Megan reaches over the big plastic console and slaps his arm. 'Don't be so serious, or I might step out of character.'

'No, no, we wouldn't want that.' It had not really occurred to him to take the whole girlfriend or fiancée thing so literally. 'You're doing me a big favor. I don't care if they know the truth.'

'You don't want me to be your girlfriend?'

Ray twitches, opens his mouth in protest.

'I'm kidding,' she says. 'We're just friends, right? I work for you, too, but—'

'Yeah, about that.'

'I know, I know. I am here of my own free will.'

He looks at her. 'I hope you really feel – I hope you *know* that.'

'I do.'

'Good.' Ray fidgets with the ventilation gates.

'Okay, how about this,' she says. 'Let's make up a story,

because what else are we doing for the next – how far did you say this lake is?'

'Another three hundred miles. At least.'

'Right, five more hours of corn,' Megan says. 'It will pass the time. When we get there, you can play it however you want. Tell them you picked me up hitchhiking or we eloped, whatever, and I'll follow your lead.'

This relaxes him. And he is curious to hear her vision of it, this make-believe romance. It's one way to learn more about her, and isn't that what he wanted?

'All right,' he says, opening a bottle of water. 'We met at a concert at Red Rocks. Wilco, two years ago.'

'Wilco? Blech. Depressing.'

Ray sighs. 'Okay, you pick the band.'

'My Morning Jacket?' She leans back and rests her heels on the dash.

'Nicely done.'

She claps. 'You saw me in the parking lot and decided to chat me up?'

Ray grins. 'No, you were two rows ahead of me. I was watching you do that swaying dance for half the show, wondering what your name was. Then those drunk girls from Aurora edged into your space and when you pushed back, a fight broke out. You were about to get tossed, but I smooth-talked the security guards.'

Megan spreads her palms across the windshield, opening the imaginary stage curtains. 'By the time they busted out Mahgeetah during the encore, I decided to pull your arms around my waist.'

'Your hair smelled like rain.'

'Aw.'

'And cheap beer.'

'Hey!' Megan slaps his arm again.

'I didn't mind.'

'You offered to walk me to my car, but we decided to wait for the parking lot to empty out. We were the last two people sitting in the amphitheater.'

'I asked for your name and phone number,' Ray says. 'But you said no, let's agree to meet here again next year and see if it was meant to be.'

'And I said no way. I'm hungry, let's go get late-night diner food.'

'For which I was secretly relieved. The only thing open at that hour was a Denny's.'

'I had Moons Over My Hammy,' she says. 'That actually sounds good. I want that now. Do they have a Denny's out here?'

'I can't remember,' Ray says. 'But I do remember that I had at least two kinds of breakfast meat, three eggs, and four cups of coffee.'

'Ugh, so full. What are we gonna do about my car? We left it at Red Rocks.' She is speaking as if they are back there now, in the booth.

'You shouldn't drive this late. I'll take you back in the morning.'

'That's sweet, but I don't crash at strangers' houses.'

'I'm not a stranger. You can trust me. I'll sleep on the couch.'

'What if you can't trust me?' she says.

'Then that will be too bad.'

Megan laughs but does not look at him, just as he is not able to look at her. To look now would break the spell.

She opens her own bottle of water. 'We were inseparable for eight days and eight nights, though we had done nothing more than kiss and hold hands.'

'We did everything. Went to the movies. Ate long brunches. Ducked into record stores. On the seventh night I cooked Indian food for you.'

'I lost the bet,' she says. 'I didn't believe you could cook like that, but it was delicious.'

'I had the advantage. Working in my father's restaurants. Wait, what did I win in the bet?'

'Winner got a back rub.'

'No guy wants a back rub,' he says. 'But all right.'

'On the seventh night, we drank too much wine and confessed things to one another.'

'Oooh,' Ray says. 'This is getting intense.'

'We knew what was happening. We'd both been through enough bad relationships. This time we were going to be honest from the beginning, no matter how scary the truth turned out to be.'

'I told you I had never been in love. I felt like such a freak, I was beginning to wonder if something was wrong with me.'

'You're the first guy I opened myself to in almost four years.' Megan looks out the passenger window, and he can't tell if she realizes she slipped into the present. Or maybe it wasn't a slip. Either way, something has hit close to home. He's got to find a way to lighten it up.

'I never told anyone about my business plan, my dream,' he says.

'But you never could keep a secret from me?'

'Sad but true.'

She watches him expectantly. 'I knew it was going to be brilliant and ...'

Ray is more nervous now than the last time he pitched an angel investor.

'When I was a kid, there was this old barbershop in town, Stan & Ollie's. A real old-school hole in the wall. My dad used to take me and we'd get our haircuts together. A whole cross-section of Boulder's natives gathered there – real estate people, bartenders, mechanics, cops, the mayor. They had an old radio playing hits from the fifties, there was a beer cooler, and a huge jar of caramel lollipops for the kids. Sometimes my dad would sit with the owner, this old guy Fred, and they'd play checkers at the little table in the corner. Guys kept their own shaving mugs on the rack in back. It was like a club, with open membership. All men of goodwill were welcome at Stan & Ollie's.

'And that got me thinking, a few years ago,' Ray continues. 'What's a haircut now? For men it's an errand, a chore. Women have salons, day trips to the spa, a pedicure, massage. Guys lack the imagination, so it's basically a strip mall chain where they mangle your hair, or a sports bar to watch a ballgame. But the wives don't like that, the husband running off to go drinking with the boys, leering at waitresses, and you can't take your kid to a bar.'

'Some people do,' Megan says.

'And when you talk to couples now, with two working

parents, what do you hear? There's never enough time. Mom and Dad are going a hundred miles per hour, always tired. The kids are shuffled from school to sports to lessons to homework to bed. It never stops. And it's all broken out, separate.

'But what if there was a place where fathers could take their sons … sure, there would be barber chairs, hot towels, straight-edge shaves, all old school but with modern stylists. But so much more. Hi-Def TVs showing sports from around the world. No bar, but a soda fountain, a billiard table, checkers, chess, a fireplace, air hockey—'

'Free wi-fi?'

'No wi-fi. No internet. No video games, but maybe skee-ball or a mini basketball court with Nerf hoops and a real parquet floor. The idea here is human time, not tech time. Being present, holding a conversation, making new friends. And the best part is, while this is aimed at fathers and sons, moms are happy too.'

'Because she gets a break from the kids,' Megan says. 'And from her husband. While the boys are out pretending to be men, she has time to do her yoga, go shopping, get the massage, take a nap.'

Ray nods along. 'And she can't be mad, because what's her husband doing? Spending quality time with his son, not throwing back beers at Hooters, but really being there with the kid. Everybody wins.'

'I love it,' Megan says. 'It's genuine. There's nothing like that out there now. You can market this to special events, private parties. Oh! And you have to have a section for the moms and the sisters, little takeaways to say thanks for letting the boys be boys. A bucket of single roses, three bucks each. Scented candles, toy bracelets and candy necklaces, anything that says we were thinking of you.'

Ray is beaming. She understands it, believes it. He always feared it was a little too male, too exclusive. It needed a woman's touch, and now here's precisely that.

'I quit waiting tables,' Megan says, 'to help you finish the decor, the marketing campaign, balance your books. But only if you agreed to make me a manager.'

'You contributed so much, I had to make you a partner,' he says.

'We stayed up all night painting murals on the walls. I finally got to use my art degree.'

'The walls, yes. Ernie and Bert, Muhammad Ali, Frank Sinatra, Superman. The heroes.'

'What about the name?' she says. 'It's got to have the perfect name. Something that captures the goodwill and neighborhood vibe, a little old school but not too old-fashioned, because this is the new twist on that.'

Ray takes a deep breath. 'This isn't set in stone, but the one that keeps coming back to me is Brothers' Lounge.' He swallows. 'Because we are all brothers. Men of all ages. Friends, grandfathers, fathers, sons.'

'Good,' she says after a moment of consideration. 'But not "Lounge". Just *Brothers*, no apostrophe. It's simpler, humbler, sounds less like a bar. It's not obvious at first, but the people who experience it, they'll understand, and that's exactly the word-of-mouth cachet you want with this.'

'Brothers.' Ray tests it out, seeing the sign above the door. 'Brothers.'

She raises her eyebrows, nodding hopefully, yes?

'It's perfect.' He can't stop smiling. 'You're ... that was something.'

Megan grows quiet, looking worn out. Neither of them can add to it now. They went too fast, ending on just the right note, and there is nowhere to go but down. He wants to keep reliving it with her, all the restaurants and road trips and holidays and arguments ending in make-up sex, new adventures and their favorite movie, late nights in the backyard, wine and stars, and long Saturdays spent hiking, shopping, meeting each other's friends, laughing, kissing, bringing home chicken soup on sick days, so much more to bring to life. He feels he should lean over and hug her and tell her it's all going to be okay, it's not too late. But there are many miles to go, and maybe the ability to ride in companionable silence is another test for them, for anyone.

The miles roll by.

The next time he looks over the console, Megan is leaning against the window, eyes closed, mouth open. He turns the radio off, trying to hear beneath the drone of the tires and the hot wind bracing the cabin the quiet of her breathing.

Two Families:
One Alive, the Other …

They conquer the hundred and eighty miles on I-76, which merges with I-80 and crosses over into Nebraska. Then the next hundred miles or so along I-80 until they reach the town of North Platte, where they stop at the Whiskey Creek Wood Fire Grill for a lunch of baby back ribs, slow-cooked chicken, and sides of cornbread, coleslaw and macaroni.

Over lunch they discuss Ray's memories of the lake, what little he has retained of the five summer trips from his early boyhood. The view from the dam, when they were driving in, the ritual of their father telling them to look all the way down the lake, you couldn't see to the other end, but if you concentrated hard enough you could make out the curvature of the earth. And Ray always did, seeing the great bend and feeling somehow that his father had done it for them, remaking the whole earth into a knowable place, this small kingdom that now belonged to them.

Campfires. Kites in a dogfight. His sister Colt's darkening

legs and back. Leonard snorkeling, spear-gunning a carp, its brutalized scales falling like coins in the shimmering gold shallows. The fireworks tradition that evolved for the last night of the trip. Rows of tents strung together with clothes-lines and jet skis and inflatable toys during those years when the water was low, exposing two hundred feet or a quarter mile of beach instead of the usual fifty feet or so, inviting small shanty towns of families and wild singles to sprout up, mingle, party, borrow each other's tools, digging someone's Jeep from a sand bog, form various alliances and grievances before packing up and heading home, never to see one another again.

The sand. Fine blonde sand that worked its way into everything, your clothes, your tent, the food, the sleeping bags, your hair and teeth. It followed you home and stayed with you for days.

Is he really going back there? Is that even possible?

'We better get back on the road,' Ray says, tensing now that the history has circled closer to the missing pieces. The waiter returns with the bagged leftovers.

Megan looks disappointed, almost suspicious of his abrupt end to the nostalgic descriptions. But she follows him to the Bronco without further comment, and they follow Highway 83 northbound, right up the middle of the Cornhusker State. A few miles later, her feet propped up on the dash, she finds another angle into it.

'So, how long has it been since you've all gotten together?'

'Six or seven years,' Ray says, knowing it's been more like ten. 'Does that sound like a lot?'

'Depends on why,' Megan says. When he does not take the bait, she asks, 'What do your siblings do now?'

'Last I heard, my brother Leonard was living in Seattle, making a living at poker. He was always very smart but has an addictive personality. There were a lot of problems with drinking, drugs, but I think he got through that phase. Or traded it for gambling, little side businesses here and there. He once bragged that he had hidden almost eight hundred thousand dollars from the IRS. I have no idea if that's true because, among other things, Leonard is a world-class liar. You can't trust anything he says. But if you know him well enough, you can read the subtext, so it's almost like hearing the truth.'

'Sounds like quite a character,' Megan says. 'Were you close, as kids?'

'I was always kind of in awe of him. Scared of him, but I looked up to him a lot, too. He could be very resourceful, in his own weird ways.'

'Like what?'

'When Leonard was in sixth grade, he sewed a pair of gloves out of mice hides.'

'Mice hides?'

'Don't ask me where he got the mice. He changed for the worse around high school. He always liked to prank me, and I didn't mind, until the pranks turned nasty. He hid my bike from me for a whole week one summer, which made me cry every day. Once, he tied me to a tree and took target practice with his bow and arrow. He used to wear three-piece suits to high school, even though he only showered about every third day. He had rock-star hair and was basically an asshole to everyone, which sort of made it equal and not all that offensive, if you knew him well enough. It was just his way. Girls loved him. By the time I was thirteen, Leonard was living in Paris, then Budapest, Mexico City for a while. We grew apart. I always thought he would wind up in jail or stabbed in an alley.'

'And you have a sister, right?'

'Colt.'

'Your parents were into horse racing or something?'

'Short for Colette. It was how I said her name when I was too young to pronounce it, and I guess it caught on.'

'I'm imagining a tall blonde,' Megan says. 'Queen of the prom. Or a real tomboy.'

'Neither, really. She was average in a lot of ways, sort of a late bloomer. She was brilliant, but never wanted to stand out. She played the nerd for a few years, but there was never a pattern with her.'

'She's older too?'

'Four years ahead of me. She was in the house until she turned twenty, and then she announced she was going to the East Coast, skipping college because she already had a job lined up. She got into ad sales with a tiny cable channel when she was in her late twenties, convinced the owner to sell her a minority stake, then sold it for a small fortune about five years later. Last I heard she was engaged to a banker named Simon.'

'Wow. Successful woman. Sounds like she takes after your dad.'

'My dad was just a hustler, a natural salesman. Mom saved him from a lot of mistakes. It was her idea for him to buy the first company, a failing mini chain of flower shops, something he knew nothing about. But she showed him how to turn it around. After that it was just a run of deals, investments, partnerships, the booming nineties.'

'And your parents, they left Colorado too?'

'Soon as I finished high school, they set me up in one of the rental houses and headed south for Miami.'

'It must have been difficult, your whole family leaving.'

'Most kids go away to college. It was like that for me, except the reverse. My family left my hometown, but in another way it was like they never left. His lawyer, an old friend of the family, Gaspar – you've seen him in the Rojo?'

'Older man with the bushy eyebrows and gray suits?'

'That's him. He and my father were very close, room-mates from college. They served in Vietnam together. The story is, my dad saved his life over there, and a few years later, Gaspar pulled a bunch of strings to get my father his first real business financing. They go through these battles together, like an old married couple. After my folks moved away, Gaspar became the company's lead counsel and my dad's presence out here. He used to take me to lunch once a week when I was in school, ask me if I had enough money, how my classes were going, were there any girls, all that. He was like my uncle, a mentor, and something of a spy. My father's eyes. And between him and the whole Mercer business thing scattered around town, my parents were never really gone. I saw them almost every time I drove across town, you know?'

Megan looks pensive, lost in thought.

'What's wrong?' he says.

'It's just a little too … how we both had these distances in the family. I had an aunt that looked after me, and she still keeps tabs.'

'What was it?'

Megan's voice flattens. 'My dad was drunk. He was driving us back from a Thanksgiving celebration at my aunt's house in Colorado Springs. My brother and I were sleeping in the back seat. I never found out what my mom was doing, if she was awake or not. If they were arguing about something. It doesn't really matter. We went through a guardrail and rolled down a big hill. At the bottom, I was thrown out the station wagon's rear window. I broke my collarbone, my arm, some ribs, and had a punctured lung.'

'Jesus.'

'No one who stayed in the car survived. Well, my mom for two days, but that was just a technicality. Her brain functions … I spent five weeks in the hospital. My aunt was there around the clock. After a few days I figured out why she was the only one. She didn't have to say the words. I knew.'

'How old were you?'

'Almost six.'

'I'm sorry. No child should … Jesus Christ.'

'I wish I had been a little bit younger,' she says. 'Or a lot older. I don't know. Maybe it happened when it was supposed to happen.'

Ray thinks about that.

'I'm lucky I had my aunt.'

'She must be very special to you. What's her name?'

'Vicky. Not even a real Victoria, just Vicky.' Megan smiles. 'Isn't that the perfect name for a crazy aunt? The kind who lets you get away with whatever you want?'

'Sounds about right,' he says.

'At least you get to see them again soon,' Megan says, as if they have been talking about his family all along. 'Even if it's awkward or difficult. At least they'll be there. Something as important as family should be confirmed once in a while, I think. Because you never know what you're going to regret.'

'Yes.'

Megan keeps glancing at him, and he knows she's coming to it.

'Was it some kind of falling out, or did you all just sort of drift apart? I can't tell if you know and don't want to talk about it, or if you really don't have any idea.'

All at once he feels very tired. He wants to pull over, find a hotel, and watch a lot of free HBO.

'Sometimes I think it all started with our last trip,' he says. 'Other times it seems like maybe that just fed into the dynamic we already had. It drove me crazy for years, and then I tried really hard to stop thinking about it. I never imagined they would decide to go back.'

Megan clamps the tip of her straw between her teeth.

'The lake,' Ray says, realizing he owes her the truth, while there's still time to back out. 'I was eight that summer, when the bad things happened out at the lake.'

Exit Camp

Abandoned, eight years old, Raymond sits stunned and crying over the violence he has just witnessed. More frightening that the physical assault, the bodies rolling in the waves, is the question of what it all means. He has been given a glimpse of something far too adult and cruel – things he never imagined people doing to one another. A darkness has stained his world, the purest place in it. For a long while he cannot move, his imagination flooded with horrible possibilities, working to fill the void they have left in their ugly wake.

His family hurt, killed. The other family tying his mother up with rope. Leonard running and hiding in the trees while the big man chases him with a knife. The storm raging on and on all night, for days, stranding him here forever …

But the winds do taper off. The sun does break through the clouds. The rain thins and slides away, leaving only a sunset mist. The churning lake becomes a pattern of smaller swells, the gray fading to a welcome deep blue.

It's over now.

Raymond slides down from his bunk, legs weak, stomach sour, and pads his way to the camper door. His feet feel lopsided, and when he looks down he understands why. His right foot is still in his Incredible Hulk sandal, the left is bare. The storm took it. He pauses, hand on the doorknob, thinking about the frightening race up the cliff with his mother, the whirling sand on the point where he lost it. First he will find his sandal, then he will go look for them, feet protected from the burrs and sharp sticks.

That's what Leonard would do. Right?

But he can't bring himself to open the camper door. The frosted window has turned deep gray, deeper than the lake when the storm was at its worst, and he knows that an unnatural night has fallen on the other side.

He holds the doorknob, torn between two important needs. One is to find his family, make sure they are safe. The other is to stay inside, hidden, safe. He remains stuck for a long time, until time itself loses all meaning and his fears take full ownership of their host.

Until a dark shadow two times the size of a real man looms on the other side, then presses itself against the window. A fist that sounds like a mallet begins to pound on the camper door, sending vibrations of anger down into his hand. Raymond wants to let go and run, but there's nowhere to go. Whatever it is will catch him in here, batter him to death and throw his body in the lake.

The knob turns. The fist slams the door once more before the knob is pried from his stiff young hands with heart-stopping force. Raymond screams –

53

His father steps in, kneels and clamps one hand over his mouth.

'Quiet, son,' Warren says. 'It's all right now. We're safe.'

Instead of following his father into the camper, the others stand around the fire pit, silent shadows in the night that is almost morning. Warren leads him outside, where he sees Colt and Leonard and their mom. Everyone is here, together, alive. But they do not rush to him in apology or explanation. Even his mother does not hug him. No one speaks. Raymond's family looks too tired to speak and, even in the dark, he can tell they are avoiding looking him in the eyes. He begins to ask the questions – Where were you? What happened? Why did you leave me for so long? – but they do not answer. Something heavy in their silence in turn silences him.

Colt's shoulders bunch up and she coughs out a single, sore-throated sob before covering her mouth and turning away. Raymond has the impression someone told her not to cry, no one is allowed. He takes a step toward her and Leonard catches him by the arm as Mom and Dad close around Colt. They walk her into the camper, and Warren nods at Leonard as if passing some kind of secret code, then shuts the door.

'Mom, wait—' Raymond begins.

'No,' Leonard says, tugging him away from the camper. 'Colt's staying with them tonight. You're with me in the tent.'

'What happened,' Raymond says when they are a safe distance away, crossing the point. The moon is nearly

54

full and there is plenty of light for them to make their way across the field and down the boat ramp, into the trees. Leonard shakes his head, shivering. 'Come on, Len. You have to tell. Why did those people – what was that?'

'You saw? What part?'

'In the water, the fighting. After that I couldn't—'

'Two park rangers came and took those fuckers to the hospital,' Leonard says. 'We had to answer a lot of questions. Don't worry about it. It's over now.'

'But why'd they do that? That man punched—'

'They were drunk. Or sick.' Leonard won't look at him, and he sounds brokenhearted. 'It doesn't matter. Some people are just bad news.'

'But what about the other family? Where did—'

'Will you stop?' Leonard hisses. 'Enough. We're gonna get some sleep and then first thing in the morning we're going home, so please. Shut the fuck up, all right?'

Raymond doesn't speak the rest of the way to the tent.

After falling back on his sleeping bag, Leonard drops into a profound, rigid state of unrest. He looks like some kid who's been beaned in the head with a baseball, eyes rolled up, the whites agitated. His hands curl stiffly over his chest like claws, as if warding off something creeping towards them. Even without the moonlight reaching into the tent's dark center, Raymond can see that his brother's arms are raked with red scratch marks, his fingers caked with grainy soil and mud.

The same kinds of marks and dark stains are on the rest

of his family, when they come back for him two short hours later, in the darkness of earliest morning, informing him the trip is over. Now. Get in the truck.

It's time to go home.

Getting Lost

None of it – from that first unruly wave that struck him in the chest to the silent, alienating ride home in the Bronco – has ever sounded as suspicious, off-kilter, and just plain *wrong* as it does today. Telling Megan everything he can remember, Ray feels like a fool, and one who is guilty of delivering incriminating testimony about his family.

'I probably made it sound worse than it was,' he says, attempting to downplay, though he knows it's too late for that. 'You have to remember, I was a kid. Being left alone was pretty damn scary, but in the end, what really happened? My dad interrupted a domestic abuse incident and got a bloody nose for his efforts.'

Megan has no response. She didn't say much through the entire story, especially after the part about the husband trying to strangle his wife in the waves.

'I'm sorry,' he says. 'I should have told you all about that before we were four hundred miles down the road. It's not too late to turn around. If you don't feel up for this, I totally—'

'They never talked about it,' she says. 'Not the next day or for weeks, years later. They never sat you down and explained it? The subject never came up at the dinner table?'

'I'm sure they did discuss it, but never around me.'

'That doesn't seem strange to you?'

'Obviously they should have handled it differently,' Ray says. 'But I think you're getting at something else. They were hiding something. They lied to me. Whatever it was, there was a lot more to it.'

Megan stares at him and nods. *Duh.*

'And you think I never considered that?'

'Then what do you think really happened?'

'You heard the story. You now know as much as I do.'

'I wish I had a cigarette to go with this beer,' Megan says, unfastening her belt and pivoting in the seat. 'You want one?'

'Not yet, thanks. But if we don't find that turn soon, I'm going to need something stronger than beer.'

Megan plops down and opens the can of ale with two fingernails. She drinks deeply and stifles a burp with the back of her hand. 'Excuse me or not but too late.' She shoots him a quick smile. 'So, the park rangers who got involved. Leonard said your dad went for help? Or did they just show up?'

Ray blinks several times. 'My dad took Leonard's little Honda to the general store at the end of the lake. It was closed but there were a few houses down there. He banged on some doors until somebody let him use the phone.'

'Why didn't he take the Bronco?'

'There were trails through the woods, short cuts. The bike was faster.'

'I'm not trying to interrogate you,' Megan says, pulling on the beer again. 'But why didn't he call the police? And wasn't the motorcycle out of gas?'

'He did call the police. Or the rangers did. The police came later and took them off to jail. Or the hospital first, then jail. Whatever. The gas was leaking, not empty, obviously.'

Megan purses her lips, shakes her head. 'Did you see the rangers when they came back to the camp ground? The police? Anyone?'

'I was locked in the camper, like I said.'

'But you had the windows. You would have seen lights, right? Sirens, something at night? Heard the engines, all the commotion?'

Ray is aware of his jaw clenching. 'The other windows had fiberglass storm shades. Even with the sun out, which it wasn't, you couldn't see more than blurry shapes, shadows. The only real window was facing the lake. The rest of the camp ground was behind, where I couldn't see a thing, and I was scared out of my mind, all right?'

'Sorry. Don't get mad,' she says. 'Here, have some beer. It will help you think.'

'I don't need help thinking,' Ray grumbles as he reaches behind her seat and digs a beer from the cooler. He pops the top, hesitates. 'It was green. I remember that.'

'What was?'

Big slug of beer. 'The ranger's truck. Pale green with a brown State Parks badge on the doors.'

'So you did see it that night,' Megan says.

'Or when it was still light out, before the storm. I don't know. Oh yeah – the ranger was an old man with big shoulders and a yellow mustache. Brown uniform, cowboy boots. A real hardass Nebraskan. His thumbs looked like horns.'

'Horns?'

'I remember being scared of them. The skin of his hands was chapped, spotted. Fingernails were yellow, cracked, sharp. They made me think of horns, like you see on an old sick goat.'

'Wow. Sounds like you remember a lot now,' Megan says. 'That's good, right?'

'You know what? To be honest, I could have seen that ranger and his truck days before, or on another trip, anytime. I can't remember anything about what happened on that trip in the days and hours before the storm hit. It's entirely possible my memory is filling in the gaps because I'm trying to explain something that I can't really explain.'

'But—'

'I told you everything I know! Why would I lie to you? To scare you? Impress you? I agree, it's huge mess, it ruined my family, and that's all I know, okay?'

Megan has managed to avoid recoiling from him, but she looks pale, hurt.

Neither of them speak for a few miles.

Ray sighs. 'That wasn't cool. I have no right to be angry with you. I spent a long time trying to forget the whole thing, but the closer we get to this stupid lake … I'm sorry.'

60

Megan reaches over and runs her fingers through his hair, massaging the back of his head. 'I'm sure there's a perfectly rational explanation for all of it. I shouldn't have pushed so hard. Whatever happened, I believe everything you said, and I'm sorry you had to go through that.'

'I appreciate that. But I'm not sure I believe what I said.'

'No one in his right mind would make up such a story, especially not for some girl he's taking on a road trip back to where it all happened.' She studies him thoughtfully for a moment. 'Unless he was a real psycho, planning to cut her into pieces and dump her in the lake.'

Ray laughs. 'Oh, that reminds me. Next time you turn around for another beer, would you please hand me that machete under the bench seat?'

'Mister Romantic.'

'I try.'

Megan watches the scenery passing by, then consults her phone. She thumbs the screen a few times.

'Uhm … did we miss a turn? I feel like we've been on this highway too long.'

Despite driving the past hundred and however many miles since lunch, eyes on the road as he told her the story of the storm, he realizes now he has not really been seeing the road at all. He sits up straight, cracks the window to let some fresh air blow over his face and takes in their surroundings. How long as it been since they passed one of those giant sprinkler trains arcing over the rows of corn or soybeans? It's greener up here, with more woods and fewer farms, nothing quite familiar. Then again, it's been thirty years since he made the journey. The land changes. Towns grow, or shrivel up and disappear.

'Yeah, maybe. Shit. I really don't want to arrive at night, bumbling along the beach looking for Camp Mercer, trying to set up the tent in the dark. Please tell me we're still west of it? I know the lake is east of Highway Eighty-Three, and we haven't turned, so ... Right?'

She swipes the screen of her phone a few more times, and Ray allows the Bronco to decelerate. There is no one behind or ahead of them as far as he can see, which is pretty far considering the road is flat and straight for miles and miles.

'No, keep going,' Megan says. 'If we stay on this for about another twelve miles we can head west, or sort of south-west, down along Highway Twenty for about thirty miles. That should take us to One-Eighty-Three, and from there it should only be another fifteen miles or so.'

Ray sighs. 'How confident are you with all that?'

'Pretty confident.' Megan holds her phone up for him and wiggles it. 'See?'

'I don't know why it matters. It might be better for both of us if we wound up in Idaho.'

'Here it is,' Megan says, pointing to a distant exit ramp. 'Take that and go right.'

He does. A while later she tells him to take another right, then a left, and two hours later the sun is setting and they are still lost.

On a whim, Ray takes an unnamed county road. It's paved but not well. It will probably lead to a dead end, or a dirt road that deposits them on a farm. But he is gambling on the possibility it will pop them out of the vortex they have become stuck in, maybe even onto one of the lake's entrance roads. He pushes the Bronco up to seventy, then eighty miles per hour as if trying to force the answer.

Ten miles tick by. Fifteen. Twenty.

Thirty-one miles after the last turn, a few dilapidated barns give way to a row of small white houses, then a pale brick building that might once have been a post office. Is this a town? Ray didn't see a sign. But any business will do at this point. Dusk has turned the lawns a shade of green close to black, the sidewalks are empty and Ray's back hurts. They need to ask for directions and get back on track before this turns into a real problem.

'Brace yourself' are the first words Ray has spoken in approximately forty minutes. 'I think it's time to meet the natives.'

Megan starts beside him, which in turn startles him right back. He didn't even know she was sleeping.

Folklore

Shaking off her second nap of the trip, Megan doesn't bother asking where they are. Shit All Middle of Nowhere, USA, is usually self-explanatory.

The only option turns out to be a truck stop, diner and gas station combination. One of the older independent ones, with wood paneling and only two street lights in the small cracked parking lot. The inside is brighter, the row of vinyl counter seats visible from the pumps where Ray parks to top off the tanks. They have enough fuel to go another two hundred miles, but he doesn't want to take chances on how long it will take them to get unlost.

He pays the girl at the register in the convenience and souvenir section, wondering what all the plastic trinkets and Cornhusker paraphernalia are supposed to help you commemorate. She might be sixteen or twenty-two and she looks unhappy and used to it.

'Say, do you know if we're close to Blundstone Lake here?' Ray says. 'My friend and I got a bit sidetracked.'

The girl seems to mistrust the hundred dollar bill he gave her.

'What lake is that?' Her voice is lightly rasping, deeper than it should be.

'Blundstone,' Ray says. 'The big one. We must be within fifty miles of it.'

'Lots of lakes 'round here,' the girl says, depositing his bills and coins in a pile before turning around to slip a pack of Pyramid brand cigarettes from the rack above. For a moment Ray thinks she is going to hand him the smokes, until she peels the cellophane seal, flips the cardboard top, whacks the base against her wrist, and one springs forth at the same moment her tightened mouth duck-bobs for it. 'Never heard of Bunson,' she mouths around the prize.

Ray is tempted to ask for a map, but he doesn't see any and what's the point? Google may not have scoured the entire planet yet, but a thirty by four-mile reservoir could not have escaped their satellites and roving cameras. The girl probably hasn't traveled beyond the county line.

'Thanks anyway,' Ray says.

She forgoes any further acknowledgement in favor of setting fire to her coffin nail.

He finds Megan seated at the counter in the diner area, watching an older woman, sixty and smoothly stout under her mustard-yellow waitress top and the white tablecloth smock, blending up a vanilla milkshake. The smell of Salisbury steak hangs in the air, the curtains, the fibers of the trampled carpeting. A couple of truckers are siphoning coffee and scratching strips of lotto tickets at the end of the counter, comparing sums lost and gained and, possibly, the manner in which their lives have been altered. A whiteboard above the heat lamp counter informs patrons the special of the day is *Andie's Pork Cutlet Spighetti w/roll and coffee $4.75*.

'Here ya go, darlin',' the waitress says, placing a tall glass of milkshake and the steel-bucket of preserves beside a straw and spoon. 'Anything else for ya?'

Megan turns to Ray, 'You want something?'

'Did you ask her?' He can feel the woman's heartland smile turn on him.

'Do you know how we can get to Blundstone Lake from here?' Megan asks the waitress. Her name tag is located near her collar and reads ANDIE.

Andie's smile shrivels into a pucker. 'You two come down from Minnesota?'

'Colorado,' Megan says. 'We're meeting some family out there for a few days.'

'I wouldn't be so sure about that,' Andie says. 'No one in your party musta called ahead, talked to Game and Parks?'

Megan looks at Ray. Ray shrugs. 'What's the deal?'

'Blundstone been closed going on two years now,' Andie says.

Ray picks up Megan's milkshake straw and taps out a little beat on the counter. 'Closed? How does a lake close?'

'No longer open to the public,' Andie says. 'No campin', no fishin', no swimmin'. And probably no huntin' neither.'

How about fiddlin' and drinkin' and screwin'? Ray would

66

very much like to ask. *Do they still allow that? And when does the albino boy with the banjo appear?*

Instead, 'There must be some mistake. I'm sure my family would have checked.'

'If so they mightn't uh passed it on to you,' Andie says. She is refilling a silverware tray, puttering as she continues to offload the bad news with repressed delight. 'I know 'cause my brother and his dipstick buddies used to go out every weekend, but not no more.'

Megan looks to Ray. 'Maybe we can call someone.'

'How far away is it?' Ray asks Andie, ignoring Megan.

''Bout forty minutes, right up the road. Won't do you no good, though, unless you plan on gettin' fined out the kazoo.' Why does this sound like a threat? Why would this middle-aged waitress care?

'Why did they close it?' Megan says.

Andie lines up the nearest three napkin dispensers and begins to stuff them with freshies. She looks at them again, considering something.

'Come on,' Ray says to Megan. 'This is silly. We'll take our chances.'

Clank. The waitress bangs one of the napkin dispensers on the counter.

Ray and Megan jump, glancing at one another.

'It's not silly,' Andie says. 'Big-B used to be a decent place for families. Safe, clean, affordable recreation. Then all the idiots from Colorado, Wyoming, and them college kids from over Lincoln come along. Seems people can't just appreciate something nice in nature. They got to ruin it with their trash and reckless behavior.'

67

'Is there more?' he says. 'Or is your moral outrage the only thing keeping us from enjoying our vacation?'

Andie sighs, leaning against the counter. 'You know what, young fella? Maybe you'd be better off headin' right on over to that lake. Have yourself a real good time and see what comes of it.'

Ray holds her contemptuous gaze with his own. He knows he's being a jerk, but he's tired of driving, tired of being lost and tired of this woman. Something in her corn-pone delivery feels too over the top, even for rural Nebraska, as if she is putting on an act for no other reason than she doesn't like their Colorado license plates. Something in her eyes ... not so much anger as a deep coldness. A deadness. He wonders what made her this way.

Megan clears her throat. 'Don't listen to him, Andie. We're just tired from being on the road all day. It would help us to know if there's some kind of danger. Ray's family might already be out there and we need to make sure they're okay.'

'Some kind of trouble,' Andie says to Megan, smirking. 'How about drownin's, boats sinkin', campfires out of control. Sand cliffs eroded, fallin' in on kids. People with too many firearms, shootin' each other over a missing beer cooler. Date-rapers. Fishermen goin' out, never heard from again. That do it for ya?'

'More than most lakes and state parks, is what you're saying,' Ray adds, his curiosity piqued.

'Bill Parson was here he could tell ya. He's been sheriff this county goin' on forty years, seen a lot of grief over that lake. Hunnert and fifty or more is what he says.'

'That sounds like a bit of—' Ray manages before Andie cuts him off.

'*Reported*. Those are jus' the ones reported dead or missing. Not counting unreported and injuries.' Andie busses the ketchup and mustard bottles. 'Water is tainted. Wind like the devil. Too much sand. Who's idea was it to put so much sand all the way in here, in Nebraska? We don't need it, I tell ya. Makes decent people act out.'

'Oh, for Christ's sake, what are we talking about here?' Ray says. 'Spring break hooligans? Alcohol and general stupidity make decent people act out, not sand.'

Andie turns to Ray, and her expression suggests she has just about had it with his smart mouth. 'Tell you a story. My niece was out there with her fiancé years ago. They decided to go swimming in the middle of the lake. Was a calm day, not a cloud in the sky. She hadn't been drinkin', nor her beau. They turned the motor off and dropped anchor. Wind come up fierce, boat got turned around. Somehow the outboard got started up, which shoulda been impossible because the ignition key was in her fiancé's swimsuit pocket. All but cut Lila in half, the prop did. Teddy had to make two trips to get all of her back into the boat.'

'Oh, my God,' Megan says.

Andie's not finished. 'Storm picked up fast on the heels of that, he's screaming back to Daley's, the full service camp ground on the east side because that's the nearest way to get her out to a hospital, but the boat capsized less than a quarter mile from the docks. And this on the side of the lake where the wind's at its weakest, hardly ever see whitecaps that close to the land. Lila went back in the drink. Teddy got caught in the bowline and drowned. The whole mess wash up at the dam two hours later.'

It takes Ray a moment to process this. What's missing.

'Someone else was with them,' he says. *A survivor. Or else how would anyone know the whole story?*

'Their son,' Andie says. 'David. He was seven. He hung onto the boat and rode the storm out, by the grace of God, though there ain't much God left out there.'

'Was David hurt?' Megan's hands are clutching at her chest.

'Doctors can't find a thing wrong, except he hasn't spoken a word since they found him. He's legal age now, still won't make a peep.'

All at once, Ray's legs feel weak. *That's why you get irritated*, he hears Pam saying, long ago during one of their arguments. *Because you know I'm telling the truth and it scares you. I get it. You don't need to apologize. I just wish you could recognize it and save us the bickering.*

'—sorry to have taken your time, and for your family,' Megan says.

'There's a hundred stories just like that one,' Andie says. 'Go on home now, honey, with or without this one.' She thumbs in Ray's direction. 'Keep away from that ugly puddle.'

Ray flips a ten-dollar bill on the counter. The two of them return to the Bronco in subdued introspection. Megan looks satisfied in some way, her curiosity tantalized. Ray wonders where his father is right now, and how much

70

of this the old man has heard before. What he knows, what they all know and never told him.

Outside, the sunset has marbled the sky deep purple, soon to be black.

The Gate

Megan agrees to drive so that Ray can dial various family members, all of whom should be on the road or at the lake by now. He has mobile numbers for Colt and Leonard, but no idea if they are current. He won't bother trying his parents. Francine and Warren rarely answer calls, reaching out only through one of the company exchanges. Besides, Gaspar Riko is the one who put Ray on this mission which is quickly evolving into a goose chase, and Ray is anxious to give the family's *consigliere* an earful.

Ray's phone shows three signal bars of reception. He dials Leonard and gets nine rings before cutoff, with no voicemail, only a dead disconnect. He dials his sister. Before it can ring, a mechanized voice informs him the number is no longer in service.

Gaspar is up next. The lawyer's mobile rings through to voicemail, and Ray says, 'Gaspar, we're lost, but that's my fault. We just talked to some locals who seemed pretty sure Blundstone is closed, and has been for two years. If that's true, guess what? That's *your* fault. Call me back immediately.'

Ray dials Gaspar's home office and leaves a similar message on the lawyer's service there, capping this one off with, 'I find it hard to believe no one knew about this, the way you and my dad like to plan ahead, so what the hell? No one else is answering their phones. You better hope my ailing father isn't lost too. If something happens to him, *that's on you.*'

Stabbing the phone off, Ray opens another beer. Megan is sipping another as well. They have not seen a police car or any other car since leaving the truck stop and things are looking darker and more barren than ever. He is angry and in another way relieved. Now they can blow this whole thing off and go home.

'You okay?' Megan asks.

'You think I went too far, throwing my dad's illness in Gaspar's face? Or, I guess, the voicemail version of his face?'

'I couldn't say. I don't know what your relationship with him is like. From what you said earlier, I thought he was this kindly old uncle figure. But that didn't sound like you trust him very much.'

This observation catches Ray off guard. 'No, I do. At least, I can't think of a reason not to trust him. There's just something about the way he's been hovering around my family for so long. It's an old friendship thing with my dad, and business, but there's some other piece I've never understood. Sometimes Gaspar acts like my dad works for him, not the other way around.'

'But he wouldn't purposely send everyone to a lake he knew was closed, right?'

73

Ray stares at the deep gray strip unfolding before them. It's not a highway, just a straight and narrow country road. A chubby pile of gray and black fur comes up on the right shoulder. A raccoon. He decides against pointing it out, since most women in his experience don't like to see or hear about roadkill.

'I don't know why I took it out on him,' he says. 'Why I'm so agitated. It's like I spent the past ten days preparing myself for this trip, sucking it up and trying to take it for what it is. Probably my last chance to spend time with my dad, and a nice chance to be with you, if nothing else. But soon as I get my head around it all and feel ready to embrace it? We're lost and no one's answering the phone. It's standard dysfunctional Mercer operating procedure all over again.'

'I think I found the last road in,' Megan says, looking adorably gung-ho behind the Bronco's thick, leather-wrapped wheel. She tucks her clutch foot under her other leg to raise herself higher in the deep captain's chair. 'We're like fifteen minutes away from your camp ground, or at least the point thing you mentioned.'

'Admiral's Point? Really?' There is no sign of the lake in any direction, though of course it's hard to tell now that night has fallen.

'You guys probably would have come in from the west, not being lost like we are,' she says. 'We went around the lake's north end and now we've circled back. Unless your dad got lost once or twice, this wouldn't look familiar to you.'

'You really want to do this?' Ray asks. 'Or are we doing it just to say we tried?'

Megan gives him a sympathetic look. 'I think you let that woman in the diner get a little too far under your skin.'

Ray is beginning to think his traveling companion knows him better than he ever suspected.

'I could tell you didn't believe her at first,' Megan says. 'But something near the end got to you. The thing about the boy who lost his parents?'

'That, and her whole song and dance, warning us to stay away. She was bullshitting us, obviously. Probably has nothing better to do with her life.'

'That's exactly what I thought, at first,' Megan says. 'But why make all that up?'

'What she said at the beginning, before she launched into the accident,' Ray says. 'Idiots from Colorado, Wyoming, people spoiling nature, getting drunk and naked. Typical locals. Half of them feed off tourism, take pride in their attractions, and the other half resent outsiders and want everybody to go back where they came from. It's not logical. It's just human nature. Some people are more territorial than others.'

Megan doesn't seem convinced. 'I agree that there was an element of that. But that's what bothered me. The whole locals versus outsider thing felt too rehearsed. Something we would expect. But what if it's kind of a double-fake?'

'I'm not following you,' Ray says.

'Tell the truth in such a cornball way, it feels like a ruse, the thing we've come to expect. We scoff, keep on going. Meanwhile, it also happens to be true.'

Ray shakes his head. 'That sounds like a lot of conspiracy and performance art for an ordinary waitress at some truck stop. More likely, she hates the lake because something *did* happen to her family. It was their fault, but they're dead, so who can she blame? Outsiders. Spring-breakers. Whoever happens to remind her of the pain it caused.'

'Do you think . . .' Megan begins, 'I'm not trying to play psychologist, but maybe that's why you two didn't like each other. We reminded her of that bad time in her life, and she reminded you of whatever happened with your family?'

'God, I must sound like such a traumatized little brat,' Ray says.

'I think you love your family, and whatever happened that night, and in the years that followed, hurt you. Not so much because of what actually happened, but because it pushed you all apart. There's nothing bratty in that, Ray.'

He sighs at length. 'So, what do you think? Two hundred deaths at some lake. Boats gone wild. Wouldn't that have been some kind of national news?'

The speed with which she responds suggests she began formulating her theory miles ago. 'Not if they were spread out over the years. Say the accidents seemed unusual to the locals, but not enough for the bigger trend to catch the attention of CNN. Also, if there was some kind of weird angle to the worst ones, you know how that plays. Some hysterical guy calls the newsroom and tells a story about how aliens stole his wife, he kind of ruins any chance of someone believing the woman disappeared, even she did.'

'Right,' Ray says. 'They think he's a crank and move on.'

'And he is a crank, because there are no aliens, but what if he killed her himself?'

'Eventually people notice she's gone missing, they investigate, the husband gets the murder rap, case closed.'

'And, meanwhile, no one ever bothers to look into that other thing, the extra detail, the unexplained whatever. If that can happen once, why can't it happen a hundred times?'

'Why does it matter?' Ray says. 'Aliens don't exist.'

'Do we really know that?'

'Are we talking about aliens?'

'I'm making a point,' she says.

Ray has another pull at his beer. Up ahead, closer to the lane paint than before, another dead raccoon appears. It's the country. Not much traffic. Lots more wildlife. Ray can't decide if the math makes sense.

'Then what is it?' he says.

'My point is—'

'No. I mean it sounds like you actually believed her,' Ray says. 'So, fine. Let's pretend something *is* out here. What could it be?'

'Oh God, that's gross,' Megan says.

Another raccoon appears, this time in the middle of the opposite lane, stretched out on his belly, little forepaws aimed ahead, a smear of black fluid from the head pooled over the white line.

'Third one I've seen in the past twenty minutes,' Ray says. Whatever was attempting to breach the surface of his memory has vanished again. He checks his phone. No messages. No reception bars. How often does that happen anymore? The whole country has been networked. Most of Nebraska's hog farmers probably have smartphones by now, and demand solid reception.

'Okay, this is getting sick.' Megan points across the dashboard, to Ray's side of the road. One, two, three, and some fifty feet ahead, a fourth dead raccoon.

'What is this? Raccoon town?' he says. 'Aren't there any other animals out here?'

'Why hasn't someone cleaned them up by now?'

'We haven't seen a police car for hours. No road crews, no other cars since we left that town. I'm thinking no manpower out here means one very closed lake.' He pauses. 'But that doesn't mean the waitress was telling the truth.'

'Do you see something out there?' she asks, rolling down her window.

Night air blows over him, warm and thick. The scent of grass and trees and something fainter, dryer, like hot pavement. Or sand. There would have to be a lot of sand for someone to smell it, right? Across the field, a density in the darkness suggests a tree line. For the first time, he experiences a tingle of the familiar.

'Slow down a little. Keep an eye out for a small building, like a tiny log cabin.'

They pass another raccoon, no more alive than the others. Its snout is aimed toward what Ray senses to be the direction of the lake. He is pretty sure that all of the raccoons died facing the lake, as if they were on their way to it and something – not a vehicle – stopped them in their tracks.

For a moment he imagines the two of them driving through a barrier of some sort, an invisible line that, once crossed, will kill them instantly, sending the Bronco careening off into a field or culvert where they will be found days later, the empty beer cans blamed for their tragic deaths. The secret Blundstone conspiracy preserved.

Megan decelerates, setting her beer in the console's cup-holder. Ray leans forward, neck bristling in anticipation. A pale skirt of gravel opens to the highway on her side. 'Should I?'

'Yes.' It's a guess, but it feels right.

They curve left and roll down a dirt lane at perhaps fifteen miles per hour. Small rocks and bits of gravel pop and ping from the tires.

'Turn on the brights,' Ray says, then reaches over the wheel to do it for her.

The road and the fields of tall grass on both sides whiten, expand, and reveal a flurry of moths and other flying insects.

'What now?'

Ray sets his hands on the dash, leaning in anticipation. 'This always took a while, as I recall. It's probably no more than three to five miles to the lake itself, but it felt like forever. Dad always went real slow towing the boat and the camper in, like he wanted to torture us with it, draw it out.'

'That your cabin?' Megan says.

Off in the field, maybe a hundred yards away but moving closer as they round a bend, is a structure not much larger than a tool shed, its wood siding faded from a deep maroon to a bleached, pinkish red.

'Looks like it. That was a ranger's ... well, I want to say office, but that's not right. It was a little check-in station, with an emergency phone, a map on the outside wall, and a drop-box you could leave a payment for the permits or fishing licenses. Pull over and aim the lights at it.'

'What for?'

'Maybe there's a map. This might be Admiral's Point, or we might be way the hell over on the wrong side of the lake.'

Megan brings the Bronco to a halt, reverses a bit and turns into the shack until the headlights illuminate the box. The windows have not been cleaned in at least a year. The small door at the rear seems to be hanging open. A bit of senseless graffiti has been scrawled across the siding, a bunch of black lines covering a splotch of yellow.

'Oh Jesus!' Megan whispers, ducking.

'What?'

'Somebody's inside.'

Ray's skin retracts and adrenaline splashes into various channels, informing him just how much tension he's been repressing for the past thirty minutes. He doesn't see anyone inside or around the dilapidated outpost, though. Nothing moving through the high grass. He is beginning to relax when his eyes catch on a solid form behind the dirty window and – yes, sir, one human shape. A body, standing tall inside the shack.

'Oh, that,' he says, shuddering.

'What *is* it?' Megan is still whispering.

'It's okay, no problem. We haven't done anything wrong.' Without thinking, Ray leans over and mashes the Bronco's horn. The bleat seems deafening.

Megan slaps his arm away. 'What the hell?'

'If someone's in there at this hour, they should know they have a visitor.'

'No one should be in there at this hour!'

'We have the Bronco,' he says. 'If someone comes after us, we can run them over.'

'Or leave?'

Megan keeps her head down. Ray watches the window. The shape isn't moving. He can't see a face. Maybe the outline of shoulders, a patch of a brown shirt or jacket, but not much more, and it's difficult to be sure what he is looking at due to the grime on the window. He honks the horn twice, pauses, then once more, laying on it for a good five count.

'Ray, stop it!'

Nothing moves, inside the shack or out.

'That's either not a person,' he says. 'Or it's a dead one.'

Megan gasps, and he considers going for the gun in his bag, but he doesn't want her to know he has brought along a firearm, unless they have a true emergency. This isn't that. Yet.

'Be right back,' he says.

She seizes his arm. 'You are not even.'

Ray rests his hand on hers. 'Megan, come on. Now you're letting that lady's stories get under *your* skin. There's nothing in there, especially not some psycho waiting to kill trespassers.'

81

'Then why are you going?'

'Because we need to know. Where we are, I mean.'

Before she can protest again he slips out the passenger door, leaving it open. There is only one way to do this, he reminds himself. Boldly and without hesitation. He marches right toward the shack until he is within ten feet or so, watching the window the entire time.

'Hello? Hey there!'

No one responds. The bodily shape seems fuller now, but it does not move.

He cuts left, toward the rear of the tiny building, to the door, which is indeed ajar. The Bronco's bright headlamps cut through the shack, through another window, and continue across the field beyond. He knows when he opens the door, he will be able to see everything inside quite well enough and this is in no way comforting.

He reaches for the doorknob, then retreats. Too close. Instead, he toe-kicks it open and steps back. For a moment it feels as though his hair is literally standing upright, flying away from his skull as his face burns in anticipation.

'Hey, hey!' he barks, jumping back as the shape turns and starts coming for him, twisting to life like a mobile stirred by wind. The skin is desiccated as paper, its eyes hollow, the rest stuffed with sand that trickles from its mouth.

Ray freezes, exhales. It's not a person, dead or alive.

It's a dummy. A man-sized doll made of burlap or rough cotton, stuffed with something lumpy. Someone took the time to dress it, giving it an old brown button-up shirt with

82

a collar and epaulets. Its stubby, socked feet are hovering above the floor and the neck is snugly cinched in a coil of rope. No hangman's knot, just a simple loop of yellow nylon cord, leading up over one of three wooden beams buttressing the tiny building's short A-framed roof.

The face is utterly blank, and all the more disturbing for its lack of human features. On the shirt's chest area, someone has used a black marker or few dabs of paint to draw a crude badge, not quite a star, more like the forestry symbol with its rounded bottom and three points at the top. Ray steps a little closer. In small letters above the emblem is the word 'badger'. No, that's not right.

Ray takes another step, then one more, until he is standing half inside the outpost.

It says,

BADRANGER

The only other things in the shed are a few empty wooden shelves built into the wall, some loose wiring up near the left window, probably where the phone used to be, and a concrete floor with a drift of dead weeds and dirty sand blown into one corner.

He forces himself to look at the bad ranger dummy one more time just to make sure it's still a dummy. Of course it is. It's only that the longer you stare at it, the more it begins to resemble—

A horn *honks*, and Ray jumps, his heart lurching into a painful beat as he slips in the gravel and almost falls on his ass. He is panting and his armpits are soaked.

He looks at the Bronco, where Megan is waving wildly

out the driver's window. Well, enough thrills for one night. No. Don't look back.

Don't. Just go.

Ray walks back to the truck very casually, the urge to look back and make sure it is not following him excruciating to resist. He puts on a smile for her, climbs in and shuts the door.

Megan is goggle-eyed, waiting for the report.

'Empty,' he says. 'Let's go.'

'That wasn't empty. I saw you jump!'

'Tell you later.'

Megan doesn't budge.

'It's not a body, all right? Some high school kids pulled a prank, is all. We're close now. I want to see if the others are here.'

'Why won't you tell me?'

'Because then you'll want to see for yourself and I don't want to waste any more time,' he says.

Megan begins to reverse back onto the dirt road. 'Promise you'll tell?'

'Sure.'

The dirt road winds through half a dozen more corners, and a deeper line of trees makes itself known on Ray's side. Tall cottonwoods with rough trunks, their white seedlings drifting on the night breeze like thick, malformed snowflakes. The lake is there, he knows, right on the other side. He has a sudden unquenchable urge to see the lake at least once, to confirm that this piece of his childhood is not a bad dream or a buried family secret, but real.

Real, and only a lake.

A final rise takes them up and the road plateaus. They are on the point, the very same land where the family used to camp, and soon he will see the well with its old orange-painted iron handle where Colt used to brush her teeth and Ray used to drink until his head ached from the cold on those hot summer days. Close, so close, he swears he can feel the lake in his veins, in his bones.

Megan brakes hard, the Bronco's fat tires sliding on the gravel, and Ray spills his beer as he throws a hand up to keep from slamming into the dash.

'What the—?'

She points directly ahead.

He had been gazing off toward the grass and trees and didn't see it. Now he does. It's difficult to miss, even at night.

Two pairs of thick steel arms arching over the road to meet in the middle, the spars plated with metal sheets painted bright yellow, with heavy steel chains looped and padlocked in three places. In the center a square red sign at least four feet by four. The words on this sign were not painted but manufactured, with studded steel grommets that all but sparkle in the headlight beams.

BLUNDSTONE STATE PARK – LAKE – BEACHES –
ALL FACILITIES CLOSED TO PUBLIC
NO EXCEPTION!!!
VIOLATORS WILL BE PROSECUTED TO
THE FULLEST EXTENT OF THE LAW
MINIMUM PENALTY OF $10,000 AND 1 YEAR IN JAIL

They stare at it for a moment that stretches well beyond the time required to absorb the message.

'Wait,' Ray says. 'Does that mean we ain't allowed to do any campin', huntin' or fishin'? I can't tell.'

Megan laughs, raising her beer. He opens a fresh one and their cans clank together. 'Cheers,' she says. 'We made it,' he adds. They drink.

'What time is it?'

Megan looks at her phone. 'Eleven twenty-two p.m.'

It feels like four in the morning, and Ray is not the least bit tired. Nervous, scared, wired, a little drunk on beer and road motion, yes. But not tired.

He looks at his traveling companion. She is grinning, asking the question with her eyes. Do they dare? He leans over the console and she meets him halfway, until he is close enough to catch the scent of her skin and the summer night in her hair. They are steps from the lake, her lips only a breath away. Their eyes hold.

He wants to cross the line but is afraid. She will have to choose.

'Let's do it,' she says, pulling away from him as she shifts the Bronco in gear.

The Beach

They edge the Bronco around the gate, into the field, then back onto the road, and a minute later they are still alive.

The end of the road becomes a concrete boat ramp descending approximately ten car lengths. Megan brakes at the top, the headlights shining down into a bowl of sand and short trees, some of them growing sideways, in tangles and gnarls, as if trying to smother each other. There is no sign of water.

Ray gets out and manually locks the front hubs. Back in the cab, he shows her how to shift the beast into four-wheel drive.

'Why'd you do that?'

'Lake must be down this year,' he says. 'This is actually good. Now we don't have to walk around looking for them. The sand is thick but we have big tires and the worst ruts are usually only about a foot deep. The rest is firm.'

'But it seemed like such a good idea at the time ...' Megan sing-songs.

'We're not going to drive off a cliff or down into a

sinkhole,' he says. 'Think of it as driving across a big park-ing lot, just a little softer.'

'Right,' Megan says, unfastening her seatbelt. 'Your turn.'

'If you insist.'

They trade places, crawling over and under each other. Ray reverses to engage the hubs, then shifts into drive and they roll down the ramp, leveling onto sand that rocks them gently from side to side, back and forth, in a mushy rhythm. Ahead, there are black dust-tinted ripples in the sand, and taller ridges or drifts, but no tire tracks like he remembers. No one has been here for a while. Months, two years, maybe longer.

Tree growth is spare, the kind of saplings that thrive now only because they are not weeds submerged under ten or twenty feet of lake, with small yellow and green cir-cular leaves like aspen. The rest of the beach in every direction looks like a blonde-brown moonscape. The Bronco acquits itself well, and Ray remembers his father doing exactly this, in the same vehicle, telling them how going a little faster, closer to twenty miles per hour instead of five or ten, actually keeps the wheels from sinking in. Ray juices it a little and soon they are squirming, cruising, almost hovering over the ridges and berms.

'It's like a sleigh ride in summer,' Megan says, waving her arm out the window.

The cliffs are little more than gradual slopes now, the natural erosion having taken the edges off of the thirty-and forty-foot columns that used to rise and fall up the coastline.

'I'm keeping close to higher ground until we figure out where the water line is, just to be safe,' he tells her. 'Sometimes we used to stumble into weird mud bogs, or small lagoons, with about two feet of water and something like quicksand at the bottom. But not real quicksand.'

'Um, yeah. Let's not drive into one of those.'

He veers in a broad, side-to-side pattern, scanning with the headlights. No sign of other campers, either. Nothing but the sparse trees, yellow flowers, deadfall branches dried like bones in the occasional shell-fragmented mud bog gone dry. And lots of sand.

They follow the beach this way for a couple of miles and Megan yawns. Ray realizes this is silly. The lake is over thirty miles from end to end. They could drive like this all night without finding his family. He slows, cutting toward the water, which has to be out there in the darkness somewhere.

The Bronco rocks and digs through the softer berms and then bites and stutters like a car on a dirt road through the flatter, hard-packed ridges. The air cools as they gradually move deeper.

As much to himself as to her he says, 'I'm kind of tripping over here.'

'What is it?'

'I just really grasped the fact, we are driving *under* the lake. I mean, this used to be water here. A lot of water. My family sailed across this land. We swam up there.' He points to the roof of the Bronco. 'At least thirty, maybe fifty feet above where we're sitting now, Colt and Leonard and

I were hanging off the back of the sailboat, dragging our legs through what is now bird-level. Isn't that wild?'

'It is. Really something. But I feel like we're wandering kind of far off the—'

The Bronco bounces hard, cutting her off. Ray shakes his head angrily as the steering wheel jerks through his palms. Something rough back there, like running over a fallen log. The sand is hardening, turning jagged. Through the windshield there is no sign of water.

'Unbelievable. Lake must have gone down fifty to seventy vertical feet,' he says. 'We're at least a mile from the point. Half the lake could be gone.'

Megan throws up her hands. 'What if there is no more lake?'

Ray grunts, pushing the Bronco harder, anxious to find the water line, as if needing to prove something to her. The truck slams through a series of dried ruts. Megan spills beer on the floor.

'Sorry,' he says, but does not ease up on the gas pedal.

The Bronco revs, the hood dips, rises, and a few seconds later they are airborne, weightless and falling over a drop whose bottom they cannot see. Ray's stomach knots and he holds his breath as they levitate from their seats.

'Ray!' she hollers, raising a hand to keep from hitting her head on the roof-liner.

'Hold on!' as the nose dives.

The truck comes down hard, throwing them against their restraining belts before springing them back against the seats. The steering wheel shimmies violently for a few seconds, and they bite through a final thick dune before levelling off. Things are eerily smooth for half a minute. He glances at the speedometer and sees that they have somehow reached forty-five miles per hour.

'Ray! For God's sake, slow down!'

'All right!' He lets off the gas and slaps the wheel.

'Can we please stop?' Megan says. 'Now?'

'What for?'

She gapes at him.

He turns into a patch of deep sand and lets the Bronco plow itself to a halt. Shuts off the engine, the lights. His heart is pounding. His legs feel like rubber and he is furious. He closes his eyes and breathes through his nose. The engine ticks and the smell of something burning comes from under the hood or chassis.

'Hey. You okay?' Megan rests a hand on his shoulder and he flinches. 'Easy there, guy.'

Ray blinks a few times. Forces himself to smile in apology. What are they doing out here? Why is he driving down an empty beach? The whole trip collapses in his mind. He wants to be home, alone, not with her, not responsible for this woman, who is really just a stranger, isn't she? What could she possibly see in this excursion? Why did he think he could—

'Ray? Why don't we get out and stretch our legs. Take a break, hm?'

He doesn't want to get out of the truck, but realizes he's scaring her. 'Yeah, good idea. All this driving.'

The sand is insidious, filling his sneakers after only a few steps. He twists an ankle, stops, sinks to his knees.

91

Not tired. Just a little car woozy. He rakes two fistfuls of the powdery warmth and rubs them together.

'Do you have a flashlight?' Megan calls from the back of the Bronco. 'I don't want to wander off in the dark and trip over a log or something looking for the ladies' room.'

He stands reluctantly and joins her at the tailgate, using the key to power the rear window down. He opens the toolbox his father left behind and removes a pistol-grip flashlight with something like five thousand candle power. Pulls the trigger and aims the beam across the sand, away from the truck, scanning back and forth. The flashlight's deep, defined cone of bluish white light reaches fifty times farther than the truck's headlights. It's like a beacon from a lighthouse, a thing that could bring down a plane. He searches and searches, walking around the truck, scanning in every direction.

'Come on, you bastard,' he mumbles, unclear whether he means the lake or his father. 'I know you're out there.'

'Uhm ... Ray?' Megan is waiting for him to hand over the light.

Sand, gradients of sand sloping down, down ... and then blackness. Smooth, shiny blackness. Is that ...? Yes! Six, seven hundred feet away, beyond the next down-step, a black shiny surface, roughened by breeze.

He feels rescued, vindicated. 'Megan, c'mere. Look.'

She walks over to stand with him, leaning against his shoulder. 'Aw. It's still here. Now give me that thing before I wet my pants.'

Ray surrenders the flashlight. Megan tromps off to a

92

cluster of bushes, too short and bare to hide a person, but better than nothing. She shuts off the flashlight. Ray looks away, knowing she deserves privacy, even if he can't see her. The moon is out, but his eyes are struggling to bring the landscape back into focus.

A minute or two later, the light clicks on and comes bobbing back toward him. He sees feet in the sand, and the light sweeps up to his face, into his eyes, blinding him. It's like being stabbed with a beam of raw headache.

'Hey, watch it.'

The white glare shifts beyond him, stops. He can't see her. The circle dances wildly, closing on him, and shuts off. He is plunged into total darkness.

'Megan, what are—'

A body slams into him. One arm shoves, jerks him sideways, a hand clamps over his mouth. Hot breath on his ear.

'SSShhhhh!'

This does not sound like Megan. Megan should not be this strong, acting crazy.

'Whuh—' he manages, and then he is being dragged to the ground.

'Be quiet!' Megan growls in his ear.

He has only a couple of seconds to be relieved it is her.

She speaks very quietly, and he knows she is trembling. 'We're not alone.'

'What?'

'I saw them.'

'Where? Who?' He turns, trying to see her beside him, but her face is just a dark shape.

'Down by the water. There's a bunch of ... not even

sure they're people. Almost like … dozens of them, all dressed in white.'

Ray feels as though he has entered a dream, one that began when they crossed into Nebraska and won't end until things have turned stranger and stranger and—

'Standing there, facing the lake,' Megan says. 'When the light hit them, they all turned around. They saw me, Ray. They know we're here.'

The Tent

After the short span of paralysis that follows, Ray reaches for the spotlight and Megan snatches it back.

'Are you crazy?' she whispers. 'We're not doing the little ranger shed again. We have to get back in the truck. Now.'

She pulls him up and they scramble into the Bronco.

'Don't slam the door,' she says.

Ray latches his as softly as possible and sinks down in the driver's seat. He can't see anything beyond the first fifty feet of empty darkened beach, not without the headlights.

Slowly, Megan leans forward until her hands rest on the dash, her chin above, forehead almost touching the glass. He watches her for a minute, sceptically. But the tension in her hands and shoulders is real.

'What are we supposed to do now?' he says, keeping his voice low but not yet willing to give into a whisper.

She sits back. Blinks at him.

'Do you want me to drive us out of here?' he asks. 'If so, I have to turn on the lights. It's too dark. Smashing into a tree or the cliff would really not be good right now.'

'What if they're still there?'

'The water is pretty far. Even if you did see some—'

'I know what I saw. They turned around, Ray. All together, at the same time. They had faces. And their faces were like masks. Those milky, see-through masks only bank robbers and serial killers use.'

Ray doesn't like the way that sounds. Worse than the masks is the idea of them all turning in unison. He rubs his mouth. 'That's not what I meant. I'm saying, I turn on the headlights. You aim the spotlight out the window. We take a good look. Count to five, ten at most. If those things are still there, we get a better idea of who's screwing around out here.'

'They were *not* regular people.'

'Okay. A better idea of who or what. Bottom line, they're either dangerous or they're ... well, what do you propose? You saw them. You tell me.'

She looks at the windshield again. 'Turn them on. It's going to drive me crazy if I don't know.'

'Before or after I start the engine?'

She chews her lower lip. 'Before. But be ready to move.'

'Okay.'

Megan covers her face and makes a moaning sound.

'Hey, it's going to be all right,' he says. 'We're safe in here. I have ...' But should he tell her about the gun? What if she hates guns, judges him for bringing it? Thinks he's paranoid or dangerous?

'What?' she prods.

'A hammer in the back. For staking a tent. Plus tire irons, tools. No one's going to hurt us. I promise.'

She nods.

His fingers begin to twist the ignition tabs.

'Wait! No engine, you said.'

'I have to turn on the accessories for the lights to work.'

'Oh, right.'

Ray twists the key two clicks. He pulls the headlights knob. A cone of beach turns golden white, but does not extend very far. There's nothing within its reach except for sand, weeds and hazy darkness on either side.

'The spotlight,' he says.

She turns, staring at the passenger window, which is solid black. 'I'm too scared to roll it down.'

'Shine the spot on it first.'

Hesitantly, she raises the pistol grip and squeezes the trigger. It clicks, reflecting back at them, turning the entire cab bright white. Megan yelps, jumping out of her seat, and Ray gasps in reflex at her sudden movement.

Megan fumbles the light over to him. 'Turn it off! Off, off!'

He does. 'All right, all right. Calm down. I forgot about the reflection. I'll do it.'

He rolls his window down before she can compose herself and delay some more. Nothing on his side. He sweeps the light in his left hand, carefully studying the terrain until the beam is pointing straight ahead. It's harder to find the water from inside the Bronco. He leans out the window, rising from his seat. Lowers the beam and peers above it, then to each side.

'Can you see it?'

'I think I see the lake, but it's not as shiny now. The surface. It looks farther away, but I'm not even sure I'm looking in the right direction. Where were you standing?'

'I don't know.'

'In front of the Bronco? To the side? Your best guess.'

'Behind and to my side, I think. But facing front, like we are now.'

Ray shifts the spotlight farther right, then left, trying to follow the edge of its beam. His feet slip on the floor-mat and he sinks down, then pushes himself up again. Can't hold a good position. He plants his left elbow on the door sill, gets his right foot under his weight, and in the process the spotlight tips forward, slipping from his hand.

Falling outside, onto the beach.

'Oops.'

'You dropped it?'

He looks over at her, then gestures toward the windshield. In the sudden absence of light, it appears pitch black now. Their eyes haven't compensated yet.

'Are you going to get it?' Megan asks.

'Kind of have to now.'

'Hurry.'

Ray sighs again. Pats along the door until he finds the latch. Pulls it, shouldering the door open with a loud creak. He looks down as he lowers his foot between the widening wedge of sand below. The spotlight is tilted backward, pointing under the Bronco, toward the rear end.

His sneaker touches down in the sand and he keeps one hand on the door as he slips out, bending over. He reaches for it.

White light flashes behind him, and Megan screams. Ray spins, falling backward. The back of his head knocks against the door's inside panel before his butt lands on the beach. In the split second before the door rebounds, he sees the entire cab of the Bronco lit up as if thirty spotlights popped on at the same time, from inside.

Megan is thrown back against her seat as if being electrocuted, mouth open, bathed in laboratory white. Her scream shuts off before her mouth closes.

The strobe blinks out, its power ricocheting through his eyes, back into his brain in diminishing flares as his head thuds in the sand.

He blinks away a small wave of dizziness, scrambling to his feet. He is still on one knee when something heavy and wide thumps hard down on the Bronco's hood and Megan screams again. Ray jumps back as a black sheet of something incredibly fast and liquid glides over the windshield, the roof, and over the rear end.

He ducks, grabbing for the spotlight with both hands. Snags it, swings it up by the nylon cord, finds the grip, pulls the trigger. He chases the black shape around the rear end of the Bronco, stabbing the beam in every direction as if the light were a weapon.

'Ray! Don't go!' Megan shouts.

There's nothing out there, anywhere. No animals. No footprints. He raises the spot, arcing it through the air above, at the sky. But he knows it wasn't a bird, not even a huge one, like a heron. It was just a wide black smudge, of something faster than any animal.

'Ray!'

'Coming!'

He runs back, hops in, slams the door and rolls up the window.

'Lock the doors!' she cries. 'All of them!'

He palms the metal tee on his door. 'The tailgate is manual. I have to go back out.'

'No fucking way,' Megan gasps.

'What was that?' he says, looking over his shoulders, through the windows.

'I don't care. Just go. Start it. Get us out of here.'

He does, and Megan bursts into tears.

An hour later they are still inside the Bronco, parked up by the cliffs, beside the only cover they could find – a low but wide shrub of some sort. Megan has stopped crying but looks entirely wrung out. After racing off in a blind panic, they argued for at least fifteen minutes about where the boat ramp should be, driving aimlessly. Up and down the beach, back and forth, in circles. It was her idea to stop, before they ran into something else or became more lost than they already were.

He found the shrub, and she helped herself to another beer. She drank most of it in three long swallows, one hand pressed over her heart. His own was still beating in time with the sore spot at the back of his head. He tried asking her for more details, what she saw and felt as it hit the hood, but she only shook her head. Not yet.

Now they sit in silence, watching, checking the windows, but not with the spotlight. Megan took it away from him, scowled at it, then threw it into the cargo bay. He represses a yawn, knowing she will not let them sleep here.

'Tell me about something else,' she says. 'Just talk. About anything except what just happened.'

Ray tries to summon a happy memory. 'I miss the toads. There used to be hundreds of toads on the beach at night. We would collect them in a bucket. Toads the size of softballs, little babies like a pencil eraser. But they're gone now, I think. Something drove them away—'

'*Ray.*'

'Sorry. I didn't mean to.'

'Did you keep them?' she asks. 'Take them home?'

'No, we always released them a few hours later. My mom was afraid we'd get warts, but we never did.'

'Maybe it was reflections in the water, some trees,' Megan says, changing the subject. 'A bunch of high school kids having a rave or something. That's possible, right?'

Ray frowns. Is she trying to talk herself out of what she saw? Of course she is. He has been too. Trying to find a rational explanation for the black thing, the one that moved like an anti-spotlight but somehow managed to bang the hood like a giant bat before lifting off again.

'Sure,' he says. 'It's late. We're exhausted. All these little details are piling up. We're probably imagining things, blowing it all out of proportion. We should go to sleep for a few hours, look for my family in the morning. If they're not here, we'll find the boat ramp and head home.'

'Fine, but not here. I can't sleep here.'

'When you're lost in the woods, aren't you supposed to stay put until you regain a sense of direction? We can't do that at night.'

'Pick one direction and go for a mile or so in a straight line. We can handle that, right?'

Ray starts the truck. 'I can fold up the back seat and you can stretch out in back for a while.'

Megan nods. 'Thank you.'

He turns the Bronco away from the cliff and they begin to roll. 'Headlights okay?'

'I guess.'

After a mile or two of the straightest line he is capable of, they dip into a low valley, then rise again to find themselves facing another series of cliffs. They seem familiar, and Ray banks the Bronco left, heading (he believes) in the direction of the boat ramp. Megan doesn't comment, and they trundle along at a moderate clip for another ten or fifteen minutes. He is watching the sand, looking for their earlier tire tracks, but so far there is no sign of them.

Megan sits up straight, then rolls her window down and leans out, watching something far off to their right.

'Whoa, what's with the newfound bravery?' he says.

She points toward three o'clock. 'Turn that way.'

He does. 'What is it?'

'Somebody's camping, a really big set-up. It looks like the circus came to town.'

Ray follows her extended arm like a compass needle, until the headlight beams slowly bring it into focus. A tent the size of a small house appears, with rooms and additions, an awning staked over a makeshift porch of lawn chairs and other piles of equipment. There is at least one vehicle nearby, a big truck, maybe some umbrellas planted in the sand and some other odds and ends strewn about, but they are not close enough yet to make out the details.

'Is that them?' Megan asks.

'Probably. No one else would be crazy enough to camp out here.'

Ray slows the Bronco to a walking pace. With all that's happened since they found the entrance road, he has forgotten to prepare himself for the moment. The reality of seeing his family in the flesh. The relief that would follow far outweighs his earlier misgivings.

'I don't see any people,' she says.

'It's late. They must be asleep.'

Twenty yards and closing. The tent is boxy, tall, the canvas a faded gray or light brown. Steel poles and ropes all around, a wind chime of some sort hanging off one corner. It's quite a contraption, and a settled one.

The truck is white, a weathered model from the seventies, the panels over the wheels rusted out. A trailer is attached, the kind of open flatbed with wood walls for hauling hay or lawn equipment.

'This can't be them,' he says. 'I don't see my father or Leonard driving out in that, and Colt wouldn't be caught dead in that tent.'

Ten yards off, Ray turns the headlights away from the camp site.

'We can't give up yet,' Megan says.

'Can't shine our brights into their tent. It's rude.'

They circle the front, the truck, the half-dozen lawn chairs scattered around, keeping a polite distance. The lawn chairs are old, with fraying webbing of yellow and green nylon, the kind that itch your bare legs and fold up like a mousetrap if you fail to sit down just right or weigh more than a hundred pounds.

'Any movement?' he asks.

Megan frowns, glancing at him and back to the camp ground, trying to find a way to voice some concern.

'What's wrong?' he says, slowing to a halt. The camp site is behind them.

'Does any of this stuff look familiar to you?'

'No.'

'Really? You better look again.'

Ray leans out his window, peering intently at the spread, then back to her. Megan is chewing her lips nervously. Scared.

'What am I missing?' he says.

'The story you told me . . . ' She waits for him to finish the thought. 'The other family?'

For a moment Ray's mind simply short-circuits. He has no idea what she is referring to. And then some kind of wishful ignorance mechanism fails and everything clicks into place.

Big ugly tent, faded gray, but very well might have been green.

Beaten white truck.

Ratty lawn chairs.

A bunch of gear that looks like it's been sitting in the sun for thirty years.

104

'No ... no way.' He yanks the shifter into reverse. The wheels dig hard, throwing sand in all directions as they circle once more. He lands the headlamps square on the tent. He studies it for a moment, then edges alongside it. 'Holy shit.'

'Maybe it's a coincidence,' Megan says in a rush. 'Same kind of tent but some other family.'

'That'd be a hell of a coincidence,' Ray says.

The front flaps of the tent are clipped shut with a few clothespins.

'What's the alternative?'

'The family that almost drowned in the storm decided to come back to Blundstone the same year my family did. Or they never left.'

'What the hell is happening out here, Ray?'

Ray has no answer for her. He is thinking about the gun in his bag again.

Megan crosses her arms. 'You want to walk over there in the middle of the night and wake them up, don't you?'

'My family is missing,' he says. 'They should be here, and they are not here, unless they're in that tent or there is some kind of other ridiculous explanation. Either way, you see, we don't have a choice.'

Megan shakes her head.

'You can wait in the truck,' he says. 'I don't expect you to be a part of this.'

He reaches for the door and she stops him, taking hold of his arm.

'Wait,' Megan says. 'If someone comes out and it's not one of your family members, we're leaving, driving out, right now. No excuses.'

'Okay.'

'And try calling out first. Politely. Before you exit the truck.'

Ray nods. Rolls down the window.

'Hello? Excuse me?' Then a little louder. 'Sorry to wake you, hello!'

No action. No lights inside.

'Hello?' Megan tries. 'Anyone home?'

They sit. They wait. There is no response.

Ray bursts into laughter.

'What's so funny?'

'This! Right here! What the hell are we doing, shouting at an empty tent?'

'Leaving. We're leaving, Ray.'

He turns once more to yell through the window, and his voice halts in his throat.

The flaps of the tent's front door bowl open and a man rises up, taking two quick steps over the sand before stopping. He is tall, hulking, and one of his arms is twice as long as the other. The deep voice carries clearly in the night.

'Get out of the truck,' the man says, and Ray realizes it is not his arm. The man is holding something long and slender, raising it to his shoulder. Bare shoulder, bare chest, bare everything. 'Now, before I burn the two of you down.'

Twenty paces away. Stark naked and aiming a rifle at them.

Ray is paralyzed, his spirit lifting out of his body. The man walks, the barrel tip and the larger black eye of the scope steady and looming larger with each step.

'Do what he says, Ray. Exactly what he says.'

Slowly, Ray twists his neck and looks back.

A phosphorescent green dot has settled at the center of Megan's throat.

Pleased to Meet You

They stand side by side on the dark and endless beach, holding hands. Megan's breathing is irregular but quiet. Ray does not feel himself breathing at all.

During the past terribly magnified minute or so, while they went about sliding from their seats and joining on this side of the Bronco as they were told, the man has been walking toward them, toes inching along as if balancing on a rope in the sand. The green dot has been shifting from one to the other. Ray keeps trying to think of some clever way to get to his father's pistol in the bag in the back of the Bronco or, barring that, something clever to say to stall this madness and begin the process of talking their way out of it. But clever has decided it wants no part of this situation.

'Don't be brave,' Megan whispers.

Ray squeezes her hand a little harder.

The man is stocky but ill-defined, and deeply tanned. What Ray mistook for bald is actually a scalp turfed with gray stubble about the length of the man's five-day beard. The chest and thighs are mostly hairless. The man appears to lack even a shred of embarrassment or self-awareness, as if he were some form of primate for whom clothes are an unnatural nuisance, tried once at someone else's urging and long ago discarded. The eyes are somehow hugely open and calm, lake-water-black, the sum of it all giving Ray the strong impression of an executioner.

'Who told you?' the man says in a moderate, almost sleepy voice.

Ray's lips part but the words do not come.

'Was it Portland Lance? Baby-Tree? Who's paying your fare?' The man is four or five steps away and the rifle is aimed at Ray's chest. The green laser sight has gone out, or settled between his eyes. 'This is a nice place to bury someone, so if you come to collect,' the man says, 'you might want to rethink that.'

'We're not,' Ray says. 'I don't know those people. We're lost.'

'Bull, bull, bullshit.'

This odd statement sounds weirdly familiar to Ray. And: Portland?

'We're looking for his family,' Megan says. Ray is impressed with the clarity and control of her voice. 'We're just camping, I promise you.'

The man takes two more steps. He lowers the rifle, gazing at her, then back to Ray. For the first time, Ray sees the man blink.

'Ray?' the man says. 'That you?'

Ray's entire body slackens. His mouth is quivering with fear, gratitude, relief. And then a lot of anger.

'Leonard,' he says.

'Holy shit. That's my goddamn brother! Get over here,

you sonofabitch. I almost shot you!' And then the naked man is laughing, holding his big belly and laughing like a hog fed up on rotten corn.

'Oh my God.' Megan releases Ray's hand and staggers away.

'You fucking asshole,' Ray says. 'A gun—?'

He stomps over to his big brother, slaps the barrel aside. The rifle falls in the sand and Ray punches Leonard in the mouth. 'You stupid shit!' He kicks Leonard in the shin as the big man buckles to his knees. 'Sick bastard!'

'Enough!' Megan shouts.

Leonard is still laughing, holding up one arm to ward off more blows. He spits blood into the sand. 'I thought you were someone else!'

Ray kicks his brother in the kidney, but the fight is leaving him. He is too relieved to carry this any further, and, no matter how well deserved, there is something unseemly about kicking a naked man in his middle age.

'Who else would be out here, you fucking maniac? What's wrong with you?'

'I got people,' Leonard says, catching his breath and wiping blood across his forearm. 'Looking for me. Debts. Lots of … debts.'

Gambling losses, Ray thinks. The IRS. Drug dealers. It could be anything, anyone, and this is no surprise. His brother has probably screwed and swindled more people than he's shaken hands with.

'You almost shot your brother and … his girlfriend. You *slob*. What the hell are you doing with a gun and no clothes?'

110

Leonard struggles to his feet, wheezing, and Ray realizes his brother is not well. He used to be skinny, wired on cigarettes and risk. Now he is bloated, gray, pathetic. Whatever Leonard has been doing with it, life has given him what he deserves.

Leonard looks at Megan, who has mustered the courage to rejoin them. 'I'm really sorry about that, miss. I didn't mean to scare you. Leonard Mercer.'

He offers his hand as if he were dressed in a suit and tie, and things only turn weirder when Megan steps forward to shake it.

'Megan, and you need to be more careful.'

'I'll make it up to you, darlin'.'

'No, no,' Ray says. 'Don't make up anything to anyone.'

'Look at you, with a woman and all. I always thought you were half gay.' Leonard throws an arm around Ray. 'God damn I missed you, Ray-Ray.'

'I have clothes in the truck,' Ray says, pushing his brother off him. 'And what the hell? You saw the beast and thought you better pull a gun on us to be sure?'

Leonard stares at the Bronco. 'Why would I think that gas pig belonged to you?'

'It's been in our family for over thirty years.'

Leonard blinks earnestly. 'Are you sure?'

'That's Dad's Bronco, Leonard. You grew up in it. Is there anything left of your brain, or did you fry every last cell?'

'Ray, I don't remember the names of my three ex-wives. Well, Sheri, but she was a special case. She had these toes like—hey, why are you driving Dad's truck?'

'He gave it to me when I turned eighteen. I brought it out of hiding for old time's sake, which is starting to look like the dumbest thing I ever did.'

Leonard scratches his chin, contemplating in the moonlight.

'Clothes!' Ray says. 'Put some clothes on, for God's sake!'

Megan laughs.

'I'm on beach patrol, the natural way. You should try it.' Leonard smiles at Megan. 'There's no one out here, kids. We own this fucking pond.'

'Are you sober?' Ray asks.

'What, you mean in real life or just right now?'

'I guess it would be too much to hope for both.'

'I haven't had a drink in fourteen years.' Leonard's chest swells with pride. 'Only drugs go in this body are my two Cs – the cholesterol meds and lucky Cialis. I'm old, Ray. Older than I ever thought I'd be.'

Ray is almost but not quite moved by this lament.

'Do you know whose camp site this is?' Megan says, gesturing at the green tent.

Leonard smiles. 'It's rather Spartan, but that's how I roll. Got a blacklight inside. You like it?'

'You brought that?' Ray says. 'The truck too?'

'Who else you think? Colettey and her little brat?'

Megan looks to Ray for an explanation.

'Not now,' Ray mumbles to her, disturbed. His brother either thought it would be funny to recreate that family's – what were their names? No one ever told him – camp site in period detail. Or, far worse, Leonard somehow managed to acquire their actual tent, truck, and all the rest. Is that even possible? What chain of events would have had to transpire to allow that?

Leonard appears offended. 'Something wrong with my gear?'

'Something wrong with everything about you,' Ray says. 'Where's Mom and Dad? They make it or are we stuck here with you?'

'You know how the old man is.' Leonard retrieves his rifle. 'Got here at five this morning. Did it all himself. Right down to the last bungee cord and welcome mat.'

'Colt brought who?'

Leonard nods. 'Sissy had herself a roll in the cabbage patch a few years ago. Kicked out a little blonde version of herself. I think its name is Sienna. No, Sierra.'

Ray has a niece, and no idea what to make of the news. 'So it's Mom, you, Dad, Colt, Simon and Sierra?'

'Simon wised up and booked it home to London,' Leonard says. 'Come on. Camp's all set up, just down the beach a ways. I'll walk you to it.'

Ray glances at Megan. Another long walk down the beach? No thanks.

'Just tell us where to go, Len. We'll take the truck.'

'You can't drive in there,' Leonard says. 'You'll wake up Mom, and we don't want that. She's in a fragile state. Besides, it's only a couple hundred feet. Right back in the trees, safe from the wind. Got to watch out for those storms, you know.'

Leonard bobs his eyebrows at Megan.

'Put some clothes on first,' Ray says.

Leonard nods and slips into his tent.

Ray turns and hugs Megan. 'I'm so, so sorry.'

'It's okay,' she says into his chest. Her shoulders are concrete with tension.

'No, it's not. You should press charges. I might.'

'He seems kind of sweet.'

'Nice to know you still have a sense of humor. Say the word and I'll take you home. Like, now.'

'I just want to lie down.'

'All set?' Leonard steps from the tent wearing a pair of baby blue skivvies and a yellow trucker hat, nothing more. The gun is no longer with him, so all things considered it's an improvement.

Megan laughs. Ray laughs with her. There is no other way to deal with it.

Mercer Base Camp

Only once inside the small compound Warren Mercer has constructed in the last twenty-four hours do Megan and Ray understand how they could have driven past it three or four times. From the broader beach out where Leonard has set up his homage to the glories of white-trash past, the view of the sand hills which occasionally sharpen into cliffs is like a wall. But up close, on foot, the breaks in the wall become evident, sections set deeper into the bluff revealing gaps and crevices that even in daylight would only be visible up close.

Ray also knows none of these hidden crannies would be accessible if the lake itself were not half drained, underfed and otherwise evaporated. The narrow channel Leonard walks them through, which opens into an entirely 'new' campable area the size of a grocery store parking lot, used to be underwater. The basin floor is hard-packed sand, shrubs, human-high weeds, and smaller dust-gray dunes, all divided by bare walking paths and thickets of willow. The journey into it is a disorienting maze, until the path of tiki torches begins to lead them into the heart of Mercer Base Camp.

Somewhere in the center of the hills on two sides, and a sheer dark brown cliff on one more, is a round clearing that appears almost man-made, as if their father had sent in a team of landscapers to clear the ground weeks in advance. The circle is illuminated by a perimeter of ten or fifteen more torches and a small fire in the stone pit at its center. Set back against the cliff, positioned under cover of what will be the daytime shade, are a black Land Cruiser and polished silver Airstream trailer (the parents), and a small red tent beside a pearl-blue Audi Q5, which Ray guesses belong to his sister.

It must be after 2 a.m., a little late for saying hello to the rest of his family, and this is fine. He and Megan are bone-tired, dizzy from driving and a lack of dinner and the scare Leonard gave them. They are also dehydrated, sliding into an early hangover after the four or five beers they each consumed. Ray knows all they both want is to be left alone with a bottle of water and a bed. Or beds. He is not sure what the arrangement will be.

'The old man's already braced the trailer and sunk the dead man anchors for the tents,' Leonard says. This is his second allusion to the storms, Ray notes. His memory must not be quite as poor as he has made it out to be. 'The rations are packed in three fish storage lockers cooled with solar gennies. Everything is military crisp, secured, inventoried, bungeed and otherwise un-fuckable without the captain's say so, as you will discover in the morning. You're back in the woods a bit. Dad wanted you out here but I told him baby bro might want his privacy. You always were the special case.'

'Sounds fine.' Ray is too tired to care if this is supposed to be an ominous reference to the past or just another insult.

Leonard leads them to the right of the vehicles, down a suggestion of a trail through a tall stand of dead cat tails and furry green weeds. There are no grasshoppers, their absence reminding Ray of those summers when they caught dozens the size of Matchbox cars, hard as bark and full of spit.

'You seen any wildlife out here yet?' Ray asks. 'Toads? Box turtles? Anything?'

'Not so much as a horsefly,' Leonard says. 'They know. The animals are always the first to know. And the first to get the hell away, to flee the real danger. Telling us something, but do we ever listen?'

Megan looks at Ray pointedly.

'See anything else?' Ray asks. 'Anything weird?'

'Like what?'

'White lights. Black shadows moving too fast. Something hit the truck a little while ago, then vanished before we could put a light on it.'

Leonard looks back over his shoulder. 'Moonlight does funny things out here. Wait till you try and fall asleep. Hear the sounds.'

'What sounds?' Megan says.

'Whispers. Quiet music like horns underwater. It's no big deal. Just the stuff of nature we're not used to. You get used to it.'

After another hundred steps or so, at the base of a fully mature cottonwood, they enter another clearing, this one only the size of a two-car garage. Three tiki torches add some light, enough for Ray to see the brown parachute tent, which looks like something from the future, a Mars habitat with capacity for four, with iridescent window screens, a door tall enough for them not to have to duck through, and two coolers beside the plastic welcome mat. Ray fixes on it, heart aching over his father's extraordinary attention to detail, adding new touches every summer, the pride he took in revealing some new gadget or accoutrement each day of the vacation. As kids they teased him, rolled their eyes at his showmanship. But after being away for so long, Ray finally understands. His father did it because he was a soldier, has always been a gear freak, yes, and it satisfied some internal need for order. But it was also maybe the best way the old man knew to articulate his love for his family.

'Water, beer, juice, soda and fresh coconut meat's in the blue cooler,' Leonard says, running the beam of his Maglite over the iceboxes. 'Fruit, muffins, protein bars, live aloe and first-aid kit are in the yellow one.'

Leonard unfastens the tent door and holds it open for them like a bellboy. Megan wipes her feet, and Ray follows her inside.

A lantern hanging from the ceiling casts soft white light over a double-bed-sized air mattress raised up on some kind of bamboo frame. The floor mat is also bamboo, and they leave their shoes beside a cotton hamper with bamboo dowels for hanging towels, clothes, swimsuits. On one side of the bed is an atomic clock on a small foldable nightstand of military canvas, and somewhere a fan is

118

humming with a soothing whisper effect. There are no sleeping bags, only fine cotton sheets and one fleece blanket folded back sharp as a trouser cuff, and two pillows encased in matching plum cotton.

'I think I saw this hotel in a magazine,' Megan says.

'Mercer style,' Leonard grumbles. 'You'd think all these years the old man's been away he'd have lost his touch, maybe tried to do this on the quick and easy. But it's like the opposite.' He faces Ray, shaking his head, marveling. 'It's like he's been saving it up, Ray. Planning and scheming for decades, preparing for our return. He's outdone himself this time. It's a little spooky.'

'It's just Dad being Dad,' Ray says.

'Or Colonel Kurtz.' Leonard chuckles. 'Wait'll you see the inside of the Airstream. That's a hundred thousand dollar rig, *before* he turned it into his own little space station.'

'I need something cold,' Megan says, slipping out of the tent.

Ray studies his brother. 'What's with all the gear, Len?'

'Dad's a hardware fanatic. A survivalist, you know—'

'No. *Your* gear. The tent? That truck? Lawn chairs – seriously, what are you trying to pull with that stuff?'

'I've had it for years. What's your problem? Hey, did you bang this girl yet? She looks like she could—'

Megan returns with two cartons of coconut water, handing one to Ray. She also has a fresh pear in hand, ice-cold and dripping from the cooler. She presses the fruit to her forehead and her mouth falls open in relief.

'Well, I guess I'll leave you two kiddos to it,' Leonard

says, winking at Ray. 'See you in the morning. If you're still here. Brunch is served at nine. Big announcement will follow, I imagine.'

'How is he?' Ray says, solemnly. 'How's Mom taking all this?'

Leonard looks up at the tent's ceiling, distracted by a white moth fluttering its way toward the lantern, battering itself in a frenzy. Is he surprised? Ray wonders. Does he know what's happening out here? Leonard scratches his bare chest and then meets his brother's gaze.

'You heard the Hungarian creep. He's dying. Mom too. They're both dying and there's not a damn thing we can do about it. Everything is beyond – well. I've outstayed my welcome. 'Nighty-night.'

With that, Leonard makes his exit.

Mom too? Did he just hear that? Ray can't absorb any more bad news today. He seals the tent door and turns to Megan.

'So ... one bed,' he says.

'Are you all right?'

'I'll sleep on the floor. Just spare me one of those pillows.'

'Stop it. Come here.'

He takes a couple tentative steps. She takes a deep bite of the pear and then sets it on the nightstand.

'It's okay,' he says. 'I'm fine. I'll be fine down here.'

Megan touches his face, her fingertips cold from the pear. She kisses him once on the mouth, then looks up, gazing into his eyes.

'How will we ever fall asleep?' she says. 'After all that.'

Ray can't think of an answer, and she doesn't wait for one.

Watching him with an unreadable expression, Megan crosses her wrists at her waist and pulls her T-shirt inside out and drops it. He doesn't think it's lust or longing, or even duty. It's more serene, a matter decided long ago. She unfastens her shorts and lets them fall to her ankles and he is trying very hard not to stare at the silken black front of her panties and her pale white skin behind them. The black bra seems to drape itself across the nightstand. She pulls him down, until they are both lying back on the surprisingly firm air mattress, legs hanging over the side.

The sheets are cool. She pushes a pillow under his head.

'Megan ...'

Her hair falls over his chin, his eyes. She kisses him again. Stares into his eyes for a moment, then slides down, pushing his shirt up. She lingers over his navel, kissing, pushing her hair to one side. Her hands are hot, dry.

He watches the lantern, where the surprise moth has fastened on the cage of light. He can't find his way into it, a way to hang on. She is giving too much, and he worries there is pity in it. He slides from under her and pushes himself to his feet. She rolls onto her back and looks up, eyes low and studying. Waiting.

'You don't have to,' he says, though this is not precisely what he means. 'Everything is out of control. I don't want you to feel like ...'

Megan rolls onto her stomach in reply, or as though he commanded it. Her middle back dips and her shoulders rise as she clutches a pillow under her throat. With one hand she reaches behind and pushes her underwear down, first one side and then the other, leaving them in a place halfway, the band of black silk stretched across the soft of her knees. The heart-shaped pad above the twin contours of her bottom is porcelain-white, beaded with sweat. The backs of her thighs furred in patterns that seem unnatural and also too natural, vestiges of a previous animal life.

Her hips slide against the mattress, forward and back. She is explaining something about herself. Or about him.

'We were inseparable for eight days and eight nights, though we had done nothing more than kiss and hold hands.' She looks over her shoulder, not at him, but in his direction. The wind coming through the screen smells of sage. She rolls onto her back again and stretches her arms above her head. 'But we were so tired of not feeling what two people are supposed to feel.'

Ray's legs are empty. The day has taken it all from him. He feels the tent rolling forward as if on a platform. He kneels on the bamboo mat, one hand under her hip, the other flat on her belly.

'And on the ninth night we let go,' he finishes. His mouth is closest and he begins that way. She is salted. He buries himself. He buries everything in her skin and hair and warm breath, until he is blind and no longer knows where he is, how she came to be here with him, or why he exists at all.

Night Swim

On every vacation he can remember, Ray never seemed to be able to sleep past dawn, when the first light is still its deepest blue. He has never known whether it is the excitement of being some place foreign and all the new sensory input, or the fact that so many vacation days entail lots of walking, swimming and drinking beer in the sun. Something always drags him to sleep earlier than usual and rouses him that much sooner, a rediscovered thing in him wanting to make the most of the next day which, on any vacation, is one of a very limited number.

This morning, their first at Lake Blundstone, is no different. Ray wakes before the sun, which seems miraculous given the ordeal that was yesterday. More than twelve hours in the truck for a trip that should have taken only seven. The stress of being dislocated and lost. The multiple scares and strange sightings since arriving, culminating in the confrontation with the armed madman who turned out to be his brother. And finally, permeating every waking moment since she agreed to join him on the trip, the idea and presence of Megan.

The hope and excitement and wanting to be at your best that comes with spending so much time with someone you barely know and are attracted to. It's exhausting. So much pent-up emotion, a fraction of which was expended in a sexual encounter that Ray cannot, in his first waking moments, find a label for. Whatever it was, he does not consider it a one-night stand, nor the kind of earned true love they fictionalized in the Bronco. He has no reference point for what transpired between them. The closest he can come to framing it is as a much needed release between two people who had been circling one another long enough to feel safe.

The tent is still dark. He rolls over, his body stiff, intending to wrap his arm around her, not to wake her but only to let her know he is here. He reaches, his shoulder sliding on the choice cotton sheet, and he is greeted by a mattress vacancy.

Where could she have gone? And why, at four or five in the morning?

He steps into his leather sandals by feel. Her running shoes, the purple Nikes she changed into when they reached the beach, are no longer beside them. She probably slipped out to pee. And yet he can't help feeling something is wrong.

Leonard? Ray wouldn't put it past his deranged older brother to find a way to lure her back down to the beach. If not explicitly to seduce her, a ruse Ray cannot imagine her falling for, especially after what they just shared, then possibly out of sheer loneliness, wanting someone to regale with his bullshit stories of danger sought and death

124

narrowly escaped. Leonard is a lonely man, now more than ever.

So many weddings and holidays past, Leonard would show up with a new girlfriend (or fiancée or wife), the young lady more often than not harboring an abusive past and purportedly thriving in her current exotic career (stripping, importing 'medicinal' marijuana, tattooing D-list celebrities, etc.). But he hadn't brought one on this trip, and in his stag attendance Leonard would require careful observation. *I don't drink anymore*, Ray can hear his brother whispering as he leads Megan down the path, back to his obscene tent, *but this is a special occasion. I'll have a sip or two while you tell me how you found yourself tagging along with my brother. He's weak, you know, which can be endearing, for a little while.*

Ray is outside now, circling the tent, their camp site, and the cooler pre-dawn air and dark shapes of the trees and brush only sharpen his concern. Maybe it wasn't Leonard at all. Maybe she ventured out to pee or take a walk and some other kind of trouble found her. Maybe, and this could happen very easily, she got lost.

'Megan,' Ray calls out in a heavy whisper. But why is he whispering? His parents are sleeping inside the Airstream, which is parked at least a hundred steps away. They won't hear him. 'Megan,' he calls again, in a speaking voice that seems both inadequate and too loud. '*Megan.*'

He forgot to bring a flashlight but is already nearing the larger camp site, where the hind end of Colt's Audi sits orb-like and dusty on the edge of his path, and his eyes are adjusting to the retreating darkness, the sky a moonless and misty indigo above and a lighter shade of denim far to the east. He studies the sand for footprints, and there are plenty, but he has no way of knowing if they are from last night or more recently, or if they are even hers.

He gets lost in the maze of weeds and finds himself at the base of the deep brown cliff, turns back, and a short minute or two later emerges out onto the beach proper. A hundred yards or so to his left stand Leonard's tent, the white truck and the Bronco. The other direction is a dark plane of sand sloping directly to the water.

This is strange enough to stop Ray in his tracks. He could swear that the water line had been, as of four hours ago, at least half a mile from their camp site. They'd driven a good distance before running into Leonard, hadn't they? At least two miles up the shore and another half-mile inland.

But here it is, the black surface with the first gloss of morning light, and, though he can barely feel the delicate breeze on his bare arms and chest, Ray can see the tiny jewel-like ripples of the water only a short walk from where he stands.

We got disoriented, he thinks. The beach might extend half a mile or more in some places, but there could very easily be inlets and nodes reaching much farther up. This is logical, but something deeper inside him feels threatened.

Don't be stupid, Ray can hear Leonard saying, in his boyhood voice. *It's only water. And sand, and a few fishy things clinging to their habitat.*

Ray is about to head toward Leonard's own bizarre stunt

of a habitat when something down by the water glimmers, fetching his gaze, halting his feet in the sand. Something moved, didn't it? Something silvery, upright, like a piece of the moonlight that walked on water, onto the shore. One moment it is thin as the edge of a glass pane, the next fuller, like a person but not a person. And people are not phosphorescent. They do not twinkle.

He remembers Megan's description from last night. Faces. A row of them, white bodies standing on the shore, turning to stare at her when the flashlight caught their attention. He thought she was seeing things, until the black sheet raced over the Bronco.

Ray shivers, glad he does not have the flashlight now. He doesn't want to give the thing – it's standing in the same spot, fading and brightening, twisting back and forth – any reason to focus on him. He is exposed on the beach.

Where's Megan? She could be back in the tent by now. Does he really want to be out here alone with whatever that is? No.

Then, as he is about to return to the tent, and thinking of Megan, he realizes it's her, the thing down by the water. It's not silver at all, he sees now. It's Megan, waving a flashlight overhead, signaling him. He knows her shape, her hair, both of which he can see more clearly now with the flashlight, which she must be aiming at herself. He is already walking toward her, immensely relieved.

He walks faster, the sand tugging at his sandals, making his calf muscles work. She lowers the flashlight. Good. She knows he has seen her and is on his way. What brought her down here? He doesn't see anything else. No Leonard. No boat. She is in a windbreaker and her shorts from yesterday, the flashlight hanging at her side.

She must have gone for a walk. Needed a little space. No big deal.

He loses a sandal, stops, and toes around in the sand trying to slip it back on. He can't get the angle right, has to bend over to replace it with one hand. When he looks up again Megan's back is turned. She is facing the water, which is no longer rippled but perfectly smooth, the top of a gigantic onyx dinner table.

'Hey, what'd you find?' he says, ten paces away. 'I was worried about you.'

'Go for a swim,' she says in a dull voice, not turning to greet him. 'But couldn't without you.'

'Aw, that's sweet. You waited.'

Megan stares at the water, standing perfectly still, her hair down around her shoulders, shading her left ear and the side of her face. Something about her pose, the absolute stillness of her slightly slumped posture, halts him within arm's reach.

'Megan? You okay?'

She doesn't respond, but the pitch of her voice just a moment ago still isn't sitting right with him. It was too flat. Older. The outdoors, the lake, everything around them has fallen into absolute silence.

'Hey, what's wrong?'

Her shoulders lift, she almost turns, seems to want to ... but something won't let her, and her shoulders fall again. She is still staring at the water, the *black* black water inches

128

from her feet, and the surface has gone to a kind of darkness Ray has never seen, the blackness of deprivation chambers, total absence. The abyss.

He reaches forward and touches her shoulder through the fabric of her windbreaker. The thin nylon is wet, soaked. How did he not see this before? Her flesh beneath the cloth is cold, too full, her frame all wrong.

She turns, not Megan.

It is a woman he has not seen in thirty years. The mother who was pulled under in the storm. Her face is swollen white, her slashed cheeks cleansed of blood, revealing planes of bone. The emotion in her dark eyes under the limp strands of her wet hair is not anger or accusation. It is pain, pure pain, the deepest sadness Ray has ever witnessed.

She embraces him and he can't move, even after her cold body presses in, the rotten lake water of her tomb leeching into his clothes, taking him the way it took her. He has no emotion, there is no room for any other inside her shroud. She pours her grief into him with the abundance of time, all the time she has been waiting for someone to share it with her.

He lets her, knowing he never really had a choice, and the black water rises around their legs, over the beach, filling itself anew on her bottomless misery.

Brunch Is Served

Ray awakens gradually, warmed and then far too hot as the golden shaft of morning sun inches across the tent, over his sweat-soaked shirt, up the side of his face. He doesn't recognize the stand beside the bed at first, the shimmering fabric wall. Where he went to sleep. Oh, right. Long drive. Leonard with his gun and various mental illnesses. Megan's hips … the rest is a blur. Ray sits up, too fogged and derailed to realize this is the first time since childhood he managed to sleep past sunrise on a vacation.

Megan.

He stands too quickly, has to steady himself using the bamboo hamper as he attempts to push his sand-crusted feet into his sandals. Gotta find her. She could have been missing for hours. The leather footbeds are wet, cool. Darker than usual. Water marks across the bamboo floor. Water from …

Ray withdraws his foot and steps away from his sandals. He begins to shiver, pulling at his T-shirt. It's not sweaty. It's soaked, his shorts too, as if he fell into a swimming pool with all his clothes on.

– her swollen white face, her slashed cheeks cleansed of blood, revealing planes of bone. The emotion in her dark eyes under the limp strands of –

Ray peels his shirt overhead, kicks off his shorts, wadding the wet mass into a ball before throwing it out the front of the tent. It's on him, the lake water, he can smell it. He turns in a panic, wanting to run to the shower, but there is no shower, they are camping. The only way to bathe out here is in the lake.

Ray hurries outside and takes two bottles of water from the cooler, upending one over the top of his head, wiping his chest and arms and legs as it pours down, then douses himself with the other.

Back in the tent, he throws on a dry shirt and shorts, then plucks the lake-soaked set as well as the gritty sandals from the floor, carrying them out like a maid who's found a dead mouse in the pantry. He circles the camp site, looking for a good place to hide them so he won't have to explain them. By the time he reaches the brush at the back of the clearing, he decides that even if his father somehow managed to tow out a dual-load Samsung washing machine this year, he's done with these clothes. They have been soiled by ... whatever happened before dawn.

Ray lobs the clothes out into the wild grass, then flings the sandals boomerang-style as far away from camp as they will go. Another pair lost to this bitch sand. Like his old green Incredible Hulk flip-flops; now those were cool. He wonders what happened to them after that summer ... maybe they're still buried up on the point.

Megan.
He runs for camp.

It's not far enough to justify the exertion, but by the time Ray blunders into the center of Mercer Base Camp he is dizzy, heart banging, looking like a man who's spent the night in a sweat lodge. He rounds the last crop of bushes in front of the gleaming Airstream and all but slams into the extended picnic table before plowing to a halt.

An enormous breakfast buffet has been laid out on the red-checkered cloth, with steaming crocks of scrambled eggs, sausages and bacon, piles of pancakes, overflowing bowls of fruit, trays of muffins and bagels, chilled lox and two buckets of ice – one for the orange juice, another for the champagne.

The gathering of sunglasses and blank faces turn to him in unison, the conversation shutting off so abruptly, Ray is sure they were talking about him and are now wondering who invited him.

Warren is at the head of the table, wearing a green velour tracksuit with white stripes, the Florida retiree as a manager of hip-hop artists. Francine is in a wheelchair, mummified in a batik beach wrap whose bright colors only make her gray hair and pale skin seem more severe. Leonard is a bloodshot egg in his snug Coors beer shirt and safari hat. It is difficult to focus on Colette – her once radiant blonde hair gone to a dull shade of brown and cropped to her ears, a weathered flannel shirt of blue plaid far too loose over her bony frame – but mostly because she is holding a three- or four-year-old girl in her lap. Ray is so taken aback by the collective toll time has taken on everyone that a few more agonizing seconds pass before he is able to connect the pair of gold aviators and lips painted in umber to his missing traveler. Megan is wedged between the siblings, looking so relaxed she might have been a member of the family for years, veteran of half a dozen of these trips.

'Good morning?' Ray says.

Everyone murmurs some form of reply, then his father is springing up from his chair and moving around the table like a man of fifty, not seventy-six, his skin tanned nut-brown, his bald head glowing with vigor. He takes Ray by the shoulders, appraising his youngest offspring.

'Raymond. My boy. I'm very glad you were able to join us.'

Before Ray can respond, his father embraces him, the lean arms filled with simian ferocity. This morning's 'excursion' down to the black water, Megan's awful transformation into the drowned mother, is forgotten as quickly as that. Ray is overcome by his father's touch. He squeezes the old man in return, inhaling the familiar pepper and nautical rope cologne that has by now become a permanent natural scent.

'Hey, Dad. Been a long time. You look good.'

Warren steps back, chin jutting. He seems shorter, his power compacted. 'I *feel* good. Ready to sail to La Costa Brava. You look ... well, you've become a man. Gaspar tells me you've been through some turmoil back in Boulder but are still beating the market average. A well-deserved vacation, hmm? The *Big Lake*. Yes. Sit down, sit, *sit*! Can I get you a juice? Coffee?'

'The Kona blend is really something,' Colt says in her morning pharmaceutical drawl. 'Come say hi to your niece, Uncle Ray. She's been dying to meet you.'

On his way, Ray leans over his mother, standing between the wheels of her chair dug into the sand. He runs his hands gently up and down her arms and kisses her cheek.

'Morning, Mom. Some view, huh? I missed you.'

Francine Mercer nods slowly and half of her mouth attempts to smile. One tremulous hand rises to pat his own. She's had a stroke, or several of them, or has been invaded by Parkinson's, or is just about dead. Ray doesn't know which or what all, and isn't about to ask now.

'Can I get you anything?'

She hums a little something and pats his hand again.

'She already had her breakfast,' Warren says. 'Her appetite is formidable. Don't you worry about this young lady, Raymond. She'll outrun every John Deere in Nebraska.'

'Morning, sleepyhead.' Megan grins over her mimosa. 'I told them it was my fault we got lost and were up half the night getting settled.'

'Right. I guess you all met Megan,' Ray says, wondering what she told them about their relationship status, worried all over again how he is supposed to maintain the cover story, if he should even bother. 'I'm sorry I wasn't up earlier to introduce you.'

'She's a neat gal,' Warren says, topping off his Bloody Mary, gazing at her with a father-in-law's wolfish envy. 'Just delightful. I wish you'd told us you were engaged,

Raymond. We would have sent a gift. Your mother and I couldn't be happier and we insist on taking care of the wedding, lock, stock and smoking honeymoon.'

'Maybe this is the honeymoon,' Leonard adds. 'Wait, where's the ring? Or is this a shotgun deal like mine were?'

'Leonard,' Warren scolds.

'Nothing is set,' Megan says. 'Including the ring. But Ray found me the most fabulous sapphire and we are leaning toward next spring.'

Ray wants to burst out laughing, and yet he is oddly touched. Megan's swift integration into the clan is both disturbing and welcome. Some part of him actually wants to believe it is real, or could be, and who knows? Maybe it is real.

'Congratulations, Ray,' Colt says. 'I wish you far better luck than I had.'

Ray leans over his niece, pinching her cheek. 'I don't know. This one looks like pretty good luck to me. What's your name, cutie pie?'

'Sierra,' she says, turning shy. She is a towhead like Colt was, her blue eyes impossibly pure. 'I have a giraffe and Mommy is gonna catch me a toad.'

'I bet she will,' Ray says, swallowing a pang of disappointment to come. 'I'm your Uncle Ray. How old are you, Sierra?'

Sierra holds up three fingers and a bent thumb. 'Free and a half.'

'Big girl,' Ray says, immediately regretting his choice of compliment as Sierra shoves a wad of syrup-drenched French toast into her maw. 'So beautiful.' He looks at Colt, whose eyes are puffy, lined with crow's-feet, as if she spent the night crying. 'Well done, sister.'

'Well, I'll be a monkey's uncle,' Leonard says, 'I think we're having a family moment. I'd take a picture but my phone runs on a GSM chip through a carrier in Russia and I had to disable all the other applications for security reasons.'

Ray sits beside Megan and leans into her. 'Translation: my pre-paid phone has no camera and my credit score is four-ten.'

Megan elbows him in the ribs. 'Be nice.'

Everyone nibbles at breakfast and refills drinks while Ray piles a plate with French toast, eggs, eight pieces of bacon, some chunked fruit. He is ravenous, his last meal being the barbecue ribs almost twenty-four hours earlier.

Megan slides him a mimosa. 'Sorry I didn't wait.'

'Where were you?' Ray mouths around a strawberry.

'In the tent. Where were *you*?'

The strawberry lodges in his throat.

'I woke up around seven and you were gone,' she says, not terribly concerned. 'I figured you were already here, with your family, so I went for a walk.'

'You didn't see me on the beach?'

'I was in the trees, back through a meadow. Why? What happened on the beach?'

'Nothing. I'll tell you later.' He offers her a reassuring smile. She doesn't seem to buy it, so he kisses her on the cheek and looks down the table to his father. 'Did you do all this yourself, Pop? We would have been fine with Frosted Flakes, you know.'

'Colt helped,' Warren says. 'And Sierra made the French toast, didn't you, *liebchen*? Hmm? My little pastry chef, that one.'

Sierra's wide eyes do not leave Grandpa as her chubby little hand snatches another wedge of French toast from the plate.

'Anybody have any cigarettes?' Leonard asks the table. 'I left mine in the tent and I'm too gutted on sausage to walk back.'

'For God's sake, Leonard,' Colt says, pointing to the top of her daughter's skull.

'It's cool. I wasn't gonna offer her one until she hits the seventh grade.'

'All right then.' Warren clinks a fork against his cocktail glass.

Leonard shoots Ray a look of warning – here it comes.

Warren rises, surveying the table. 'Well, one needn't stand on formality with his own family.' He settles back into his chair but maintains the commanding posture of a chief executive before his most trusted veeps. 'I'm sure you're all wondering why we've agreed to gather here instead of in Miami or Boulder.'

'Oh, for God's sake. It's okay, Dad,' Leonard interrupts. 'Ray already knows you're dying.'

'Nice,' Colt says, glaring at him. 'Real nice.'

'This seems like family discussion,' Megan says, rising. 'Maybe I should—'

Warren snaps a finger and points at her. 'You are part of this family now, Megan. As such, this concerns you too. Please, stay.'

Megan sits.

'All I know is what Gaspar told me,' Ray says, but his words are lost among Colt and Leonard's bickering. Something about upsetting Mom, and what an insensitive prick Leonard always has to be.

Francine's eyes are closed. She is rocking back and forth in her wheelchair. Ray imagines a thought bubble over her head: *Please, God, take me away from these people, once and for all*.

'First off all, *I'm not dying*,' Warren says. 'Let's be clear about that now. My heart has never been stronger. No one here is dying. Not on my watch.'

All three Mercer children are silenced.

'I apologize for the subterfuge,' Warren continues, passing a hand over his scalp. 'But I knew that none of you would agree to this trip unless you understood it was an emergency of the last-chance sort, which I can assure you this is, albeit a controlled one. We have some—'

'Are you fuckin' shittin' me?' Leonard blurts, throwing his head back, barking at the sky. 'He lied about his own death? Jesus Christ with a rubber nut! It never stops!'

'Watch your mouth, you pig,' Colt snaps.

'Ubber-nut! Ubber-nut!' Sierra begins to sing.

'Be quiet!' Warren growls, slamming a hand on the table, making the silverware and Chinette paper plates jump. 'Something more important than my life is at stake here, Leonard. *All of you*. I arranged this trip to *help you*. Our family is unravelling. This used to be our second home, a place to reconnect, reflect and return home stronger than ever. The purpose hasn't changed, but we've waited too long. The lake, as you may have noticed, is dying. Our lake. We've neglected this land, this water, just as we've neglected one another.'

Ray is confused. Colt shakes her head, downcast. Leonard grins like a maniac, eyes locked on their mother as if reprimanding her for allowing this, for marrying this man and giving birth to the three of them.

'Now. Here's what I believe – there is no such thing as coincidence,' Warren says, softening his tone somewhat, now that he has their attention. 'Our problems are not accidental, and, though they differ individually, our fates have always been and will be intertwined.'

'All righty then.' Leonard rises from his lawn chair. 'I've had my fill of therapy. Thanks for the flapjacks, Pop. Hey, Ray, wanna go look for turtles and shoot the guns?'

'Sit down, Leonard,' Warren says.

'Why should I?'

Warren flicks a bagel crumb from the tablecloth. His voice turns menacingly low. 'Because you're hundreds of thousands of dollars in debt, wanted by the IRS, you've left three failed marriages in your wake, and you are on the verge of sliding back into addiction any day now, if you have not already done so. There are warrants for your arrest in Washington, Oregon and California. Certain high-ranking security men within Nevada gaming corporations have you in their sights. Need I continue?'

'That's such fuckin' hypocrisy. You don't know shit about my life!' Leonard is attempting to puff his chest over his belly. To Ray, he sounds like he is about to cry.

'I know more than I need or want to,' Warren says. 'I'm

139

offering you a way out of your messes, the whole lot of them. And that's a promise. But only if you *sit down and pay attention*. I'm still your father and I can still kick your ass and, if you doubt that, try me, you goddamned over-grown punk.'

'Fucking fascist,' Leonard mumbles. And sits.

Warren turns his steely gaze on Colt. 'Leonard is not alone in his mistakes and misfortunes. Colette, our dear daughter and sister. I am sorry that your senses have abandoned you the way your husband did. Gaspar mentioned something about an assault . . . his? Yours? A little of both, as I was given. Some chain of events that sent the two of you scurrying from the city with a trunk full of clothes. Well, you wanted to swim with the big fish, and who can blame you? You have Mercer blood in your veins. But it's time to get off the self-pity express and accept responsibility for your choices. Sierra needs you. We need you. And most of all, you need you.'

Colt begins to cry as Sierra attempts to burrow into the cup of her mother's shoulders.

Ray braces himself for the next round of machine-gunning, but to his surprise the patriarch draws a bead on his wife, patting her frail hand once before speaking of her as if she were not present at the table.

'Poor Mother, poor Francine, stuck with a mean old bastard like me. That's what you're thinking,' he tells them. 'Look how she suffers. And it's true, she has. Three strokes in the past five years. Early-onset Alzheimer's, though it's not so early anymore. Lupus. Your mother's ailments have attacked the body as well as her spirit. She

140

is a victim, you say. Well, perhaps. Perhaps we are all victims of time, and nature. But we're also victims of ourselves. Your mother traded health and sanity for snake oil long ago. She won't see the doctors. She won't take the medicine. She's spent a fortune on psychics, televangelists, fortune-tellers and all manner of predatory bullshitters I won't list here at the risk of wasting an entire morning. Irrationality has led her to throw hundreds of thousands of dollars down the toilet and the best years of our lives into a black hole of paranoid self-imprisonment.'

Francine's eyes are tight, her cheeks bunched high, and Ray suspects she is attempting to smile. Or cackle.

Warren plows on. 'God knows I've tried to help her, but even my most caring and precautionary measures have resulted in nothing more than hunger strikes, suicide attempts. What you see here is a shell of the mother you once knew. And it's her fault, as much as it is ours, most especially mine.'

'What is the point of all this cruelty?' Colt wails. 'Can't you leave her alone?'

'First we must atone,' Leonard tells his sister. 'Then we get cookies and wine.'

'Can you leave cancer alone?' Warren says. 'How about alcoholism, shopping addiction, financial ruin? Shall we leave these things alone too, Colette? When the devil points a gun at your children, your wife, all you cherish in this world, do you think it wise to get on your knees and kiss his feet? Sorry, daughter. But I won't accept that. Not me. Not my family. Not while I'm still breathing.'

141

'What about you?' Colt spits back. 'What have you done with your life, *Warren*?'

Warren smiles sadly. 'Isn't it obvious, dear? I've failed you. Failed all of you. And myself. Failed my employers and investors. The Mercer Corporation is liquidating as we speak. We expect to be in bankruptcy court by the end of the year. The restaurants, the flower chain, the real estate holdings. It's all going away.'

'What?' Leonard is suddenly captivated. 'How can that be?'

Warren opens his palms. 'Greed. Skirting legislation. Buying the wrong lobbyists. Living on the fumes of extended credit. You've read the news, Lennie. You know how these things work. Once the largest support beams begin to buckle, the entire structure comes down.'

'But—'Leonard begins.

'But there are more important things than money, a lesson I've forgotten over the last decade,' Warren continues. 'This is our chance to remember. To make amends with each other and ourselves. To peer once more into the darkness and tear down the big ugly curtain so that we may once again feel the light of the sun. You all know that which I speak of now.' He eyes each of them intently. 'It's time to rid ourselves of our demons. Think of this trip as a long overdue cleansing.'

Colt drains her mimosa, refills it and guzzles half of that one too.

'Once again,' Ray says. 'I have to admit I feel a bit left out. I'm sure I've let you down in some way too, Dad.'

'In what way might that be, Raymond?' Warren says.

Ray can feel the table turn on him. Their relish to see him get his own dose of the family medicine. 'At the least, I've been coasting. I have abused your trust. Taken advantage of my position. I contribute nothing, I'm sure Gaspar told you.'

'You've stayed out of jail and avoided siring any illegitimate offspring,' Warren says. 'Which puts you ahead of the curve.'

'Siring,' Leonard says, giggling.

'Your failure is more similar to my own,' Warren says. 'The sin of neglect. I'm more hurt by your abandonment of your family than the workload, frankly. Though to be honest, while you haven't done much wrong, you haven't done anything right, either. You are sleepwalking through life, avoiding challenges, afraid of risk and success and love, until now, I suppose. But your refusal to get in the game pains me.'

'I have goals,' Ray says. 'Plans. I just haven't chosen to share them with you. You never ask, anyway. I didn't think it mattered. That I really mattered.'

'Oh, pah,' Warren says. 'After the age of twenty-five, the children are supposed to be the ones who reach out. We never hear a word, Raymond. You don't find it important to speak with your mother? Write her an email?'

'I'm sorry,' Ray says. 'I should have tried harder to be there for you, Mom. Dad. All of you. I don't want to make excuses. I could have done better. But since you're being painfully honest here, I will be too. Every year since the last time we were here, I lost another piece of you. Each of you. You're talking about how things have gone south in the past ten years. I've been watching us drift apart since I was ten. Maybe that's what happens to a lot of families. Maybe it has nothing to do with what happened on our last trip. I really don't know why we turned out this way because no one ever felt I deserved to know the truth. And now ... Megan helped me realize something important in the car, on the way out here. Why I agreed to come, when every instinct was warning me not to. It wasn't because I heard you were dying, Dad. It was because I missed you. All of you. You are my family, but here's the problem. I hardly know you. I wish it were otherwise, but I really don't understand how you expect five days out here to make up for thirty years of secrets.'

Megan squeezes his arm, and Ray looks down in embarrassment.

Leonard clears his throat. 'And the Oscar for best performance in a supporting role goes to ... '

'Shut up, Leonard,' Colt says.

'It's true that you were not involved in the worst hours of the unfortunate events that unfolded here thirty summers ago,' the old man says. 'If you understood the truth, you would take that as a blessing. But I understand how unfair our silence has been to you. What I hope you will trust me on this morning is that, while you did not encounter the things the rest of us did, your life has been no less governed by our experience. Your family needs you now. Be a good son. Lend your brother and sister some support. Give us two or three more hours of your time, Raymond, after which you will understand so much of what we could not explain back then. If you no longer care

144

to be a part of our family vacation after we hash out a few details and complete one small errand, no one will try to stop you. I won't judge you. I will love you as much as I always have. Is that fair?'

Ray feels guilty all over again, as well as resentful about what now feels like a trap. He picks up a piece of pineapple, drops it back on his plate.

'Why doesn't somebody just tell me what *happened*? How about that? You were all missing for seven hours. You left me alone in the camper all night. You never told me what the hell you did with those people. Now this is my responsibility, that you're all a mess, your lives are ruined? I'm sorry, but I think it's a little late to pretend that I owe you – any of you – anything.'

Megan studies her mimosa. Colt and Leonard have turned stone-faced and pale. Francine appears to be sleeping, a thin line of saliva hanging from her chin and inching toward her chest.

Warren smiles ruefully. 'You were young. You chose to stay in the camper, and that was a bit of wisdom beyond your years. But understand, Leonard and Colette did what they had to do, in the moment, and they shouldn't be blamed for that. It was my choice to keep you out of it, and God knows they wanted to tell you, if only to unburden themselves. But I wouldn't allow it. We were trying to protect you.'

Ray is mildly placated by this admission.

'Well, I for one am deeply moved,' Leonard says, his sarcasm too tired to carry a bite. 'What is it you want us to do, Dad? Chop some firewood, build a survival shelter? Whatever the hell it is, I say we get on with it.'

145

'You're going to stay here at base camp with your rifle,' Warren tells Leonard, not missing a beat. 'To protect your mother and little Sierra. Colette, Raymond, and his fiancée Megan are coming with me on a short hike.'

Ray coughs. 'Why does Megan need to come? She's not a part of this mess.'

'We need four adults to carry out the mission,' Warren says, bending over. From under the table he produces a steel suitcase of the sort conspicuous drug dealers use. It requires both of his arms and a lot of back strength to set it on the table. 'Leonard is best prepared to stand guard here, which leaves us.'

Leonard licks his lips and points. 'What's in the *Miami Vice* lunchbox?'

'Restitution,' Warren says. 'For that which was taken thirty years ago.'

'Someone knows,' Colt whispers, teetering on panic. 'Someone else was there?'

They are all staring at the old man, praying for a punch-line.

'There was a witness,' Warren confirms. 'We're going to drop this at a place of his choosing, and pay our respects to the dead. And then, my dear children, we are going to enjoy our vacation.'

The Anchor

'Hey, Ray, wait up a sec,' Leonard calls to him, just as the elected foursome begin to make their way out of the clearing.

Ray walks back, not eager to get too close to his brother, who has the 30-06 slung over one shoulder and a beer going in the cupholder of his foldable canvas sentry chair in front of the Airstream. 'What now?'

Leonard leans in, close enough for Ray to smell his sweat. 'Be careful out there. The old man's not serious, you know. This is all head games to him. He's just trying to toughen us up. There was no witness. No ransom demand.'

'Then why do I need to be careful?'

Leonard tips his hat in salute to their father, who is waiting at the edge of the camp ground with Megan and Colt. 'Because it's Dad. He's crazy, Ray. Don't you know that by now? He never really left 'Nam. Mom's last wheel is about to come off, and now he's losing his company. He's scared, and *that's* why you need be careful.'

Ray is neither convinced nor relieved. 'That's Colt's

daughter in the camper, with Mom. Don't get bored and go start shooting beer cans or ... drink too much.'

'Little bro, more like my big bro now.' Leonard smiles. 'I love you, kid. You were always the best of us.'

Ray is so thrown by the rare display of sincerity, he thinks Leonard must be kidding. But no. There is an actual tear forming behind the yellow lenses of his sportsman's glasses. Still smiling and a little embarrassed, his big slob of a big brother looks so deeply sad and ready to fall to pieces, Ray is moved to take one of his hands, squeezing it between his own.

'I'm glad you're here, Len. Better days to come, huh?'

Leonard snorts, swallows. 'Maybe so.'

Warren whistles at the two of them.

'Giddy up.' Leonard slaps Ray on the ass. 'And keep your powder dry.'

Ray catches up with the others, and now one more thing among the many isn't sitting right with him. He looks back over his shoulder, knowing he should stay awhile, keep his big brother company. Leonard scratches his crotch, then waves him off, as if to say, *go on, get out of here.*

To Ray, it feels a little too much like *goodbye.*

Which is how, by eleven thirty in the morning on their first real day at the lake, Ray finds himself walking beside Megan, this mysterious new presence in his life, holding his hand and pointing at dead birds and beach debris as if they are on a romantic stroll on Cape Cod. Warren and Colt walk ahead of them, Ray's sister the one towing the heavy silver travel case on a shopping dolly leaving wheel tracks in the sand.

Warren has a small knapsack belted to his waist and uses a walking stick as the two of them keep a steady but unhurried pace up the beach. Their visibility extends so far in all directions, Ray doesn't think anyone could get very close without revealing themselves. But despite Warren's cavalier approach to this errand, and Leonard's suggestion it's just a game, the old man's idea of a midlife boot camp, Ray is on edge.

In the left side pocket of Ray's cargo shorts, the M1911 bounces against his thigh every few steps. It's no secret he carries it now. Warren asked him, in plain sight of the others, if he had brought 'my old pistol from the war' and Ray nodded guiltily, for Megan he supposed, but she didn't seem surprised. Why would she at this point? She's made her decision; what's one more gun thrown into the mix?

Megan looks cute and a little unsettling thrust into her new tactical role. She has a bandana tied around her fore-head, pushing her thick brown hair back. She wears her running shoes, nylon shorts, and Ray keeps reminding himself there are more important things to focus on than the outline of her black sports bra under her white T-shirt.

'You don't seem like you're dying of curiosity,' Megan says, after they've covered the first mile or so in silence.

'About?'

'Whatever this person demanded, and why.'

'Maybe I already have a pretty good idea.'

She waits. He can't think of a reason not to share his

suspicions. She's probably arrived at the same, and she deserves the chance to consider the worst.

'I figure someone got killed,' Ray says. 'Maybe several someones.'

Megan doesn't react with shock. She doesn't react at all.

'My dad said we were going to pay our respects to the dead,' Ray continues. 'The police never came, I can only assume. There was no ranger. Because something got out of control, and maybe one of them drowned, or my dad had to put one of them down in self-defense or just lost his temper. Either way, somebody's dead and it's not a Mercer.'

'Can you really imagine that?' she says. 'Your entire family taking part in . . .'

'Murder?' he finishes, gazing off to the great band of blue lake stretching to the horizon. Even in its shrinking capacity, Blundstone is something to behold. Ray realizes he hasn't had the chance to swim in it yet, and he promises himself he will, at least once, before this is all over. 'People never imagine someone they know killing someone, but people get killed all the time. Killed by people who were just . . . people.'

'Maybe it wasn't as cold-blooded as that,' Megan says.

'Cold-blooded enough it needed covering up.'

'Victims fail to report crimes too,' Megan says. 'Maybe they were scared.'

'Either way. There could be bodies out here,' Ray says. 'Buried in the sand. Maybe it was my family that buried them.'

Colt and Warren have been outpacing them, building a few minutes' lead.

'I need to tell you something,' Megan says. 'In case things get out of control. Or maybe just because it's time. Long overdue, actually.'

Ray doesn't like the sound of this. 'Okay.'

'There's another reason I agreed to come on this trip with you. Why I kept encouraging you to press on when we were lost, even after the warnings in the diner. Why I didn't take you up on all those offers to turn around and go home, after the weird things we saw on the beach. Your brother with the gun. And why I can't leave you out here now, no matter who's behind this payoff scheme.'

'I figured there must be a good one. I'm really not that charming.'

'Look at me.' Megan removes her sunglasses, taking his arm. He stops. She presses her palm to his chest, eyes vulnerable in a way he has not seen before.

'I surprised you in the tent last night,' she says. 'Yes?'

'Little bit,' he says.

Megan smiles. 'And before the tent, before this trip, taking everything you know and have sensed about me, did you ever think of me as the kind of girl who would give herself that way? To someone she barely knows?'

'Of course not.'

'Good. So, why would I let down my guard like that?'

Ray looks past her, up the beach to Colt and Warren, who continue to build a lead. Megan takes his chin and pulls him back.

'The answer isn't with them,' she says. 'It's here. Between you and me.'

Ray blushes. Can't think straight. Has to say something

or risk disappointing her. 'I think you like me. I believe that, but—'

'What I feel for you is a lot more than like,' Megan says. 'I've felt things for you since I first started working at the restaurant, and it's been growing in me, the way it has been inside of you. I know you felt it. I've seen it in the way you look at me, and even more in the way you pretend to avoid me. I waited for the right time to tell you, and there were reasons I had to wait. But when you asked me to sit down and told me about the trip, I realized this was how it was supposed to be. It's real. I don't know what's going to happen today, tomorrow, when we get home. But we are real. What I feel for you is real. You needed to know that regardless of what comes next, and *that's* why I gave myself to you last night. Do you understand?'

'Yes. Mostly . . .' Ray shifts from foot to foot. 'I feel the same way. But I'm missing something here. Something big.'

'I think we both are. But no matter what happens, you can't be afraid of me.'

'I'm not.'

'Don't ever be afraid of *us.*'

'Hey, foxtrot!' Ray's father shouts back to them, waving his walking stick. 'Come on, troops! Keep up, keep up!'

Ray waves and turns back to Megan. 'I—'

She cuts him off with a strong kiss, then leads him onward, up the beach.

'Raymond, you remember the anchor we used on the old catamaran?'

Funny thing, with almost no lag time Ray does remember it. To his child's eyes the anchor always looked like a giant Lego piece. 'The red one?'

Warren smiles proudly. 'That night after all the fuss died down, we went out a little ways past the cove and I dropped the anchor in what I estimated to be sixty or seventy feet of water. I guess I knew we'd have to come back someday. That anchor is our marker in the sand now.'

'What if someone found it already?' Colt asks. Ray's sister is sweating profusely, the work of dragging the loaded dolly up the beach wearing her down. Ray offered to take over for her half an hour earlier, but she refused, darting her eyes toward Dad as if to say, captain's orders.

'Entirely possible,' Warren says. 'But somehow I don't think so. The lake's never been this low. Whole state park's been closed for over two years. Even before that, the number of visitors had dwindled substantially.'

'Why is that?' Ray says. 'What's with all the signs? Danger! Keep out! Like this is a nuclear waste site now.'

Warren consults a digital compass of some sort. He glances at Ray, then at Megan, and leads them onward as he theorizes.

'Hard to get a boat in when the water is this low, for one. Then there were staffing problems, budget cuts, which meant more safety issues. Can't leave people out here un-policed, God forbid. But mostly I think it's something in the air, the water, the thing people sense even when they can't explain it. Have you felt it?'

Megan looks at Ray. He wiggles his eyebrows. Felt something? Last night they were *seeing* things.

'Death,' Warren says, more with resignation than drama. 'The lake is drying up. The wildlife is moving on. Last summer a couple of hikers found a two hundred pound channel catfish that had thrown itself up on the dam. Like some lake monster who'd survived for decades and finally had enough. The striped bass are gone, no one's caught one of those for years. Terrible shame. This used to be a source of pride for the entire state. Now it's a blight, and no one can do anything because the farmers need the water and nature isn't making enough of that these days. Sometimes I dream of snow, apocalyptic snowstorms covering the mountains to feed it once again.'

'Is that your anchor?' Megan says, pointing off toward three or four o'clock.

Warren raises the small pair of binoculars clipped to his belt. Glasses the beach. Lowers them. 'A red blanket, maybe a towel. We should have another couple hundred yards to go yet.'

'When did the messages start arriving?' Colt asks.

'About three years ago,' Warren says. 'In July, near the anniversary. First one didn't say much. Just "Hello, enjoying another summer at Blundstone, exclamation point". Scribbled on a postcard, like something from one of the old bait shops.'

Ray realizes he and Megan have missed part of the conversation. 'This person demanding the payoff, he sent messages?'

'Thirteen of them,' Warren says. 'One every few months. The last one arrived about two weeks ago. As if he knew we were planning the trip. Had inside intel.'

154

'What did they say?' Megan asks.

Warren looks back at her as if annoyed to be pushed into specifics. 'Earlier ones were hints. Cryptic comments about those nasty storms, safety tips, the need to be careful. Later, the messages turned ominous. "A family is a terrible thing to lose." Some were invitations to come back. "Don't stay away forever. We miss you! Why not make Lake Blundstone your next family vacation destination!" Coy threats, details proving they had been here and seen us go out on the boat. Finally, this silly demand.'

The messages are disturbing, Ray thinks, but not as disturbing as the fact that his father seems to be relishing this whole ordeal, the game it has become.

'Dad, what's in the case?' he asks once more.

'Something heavy,' Colt says, shifting the dolly from one hand to the other.

'How do we know we're not being set up?' Ray says. 'Ambushed?'

Warren shakes his head. 'He could have done that a long time ago. At home, late one night, anywhere. This is about a payoff, not violence.'

The mere suggestion of violence prompts them all to have another look around. They are a quarter of a mile from the bluffs, at least two full miles from the main point and the road leading in. The water is several hundred yards in the other direction, and it's nothing but beach for miles ahead and behind them. Unless someone is hiding under a trapdoor in the sand, there is little chance of being caught off-guard. But if they need to run for cover, it's going to be bad. Very bad.

'It's not money,' Ray says. 'That case weighs forty or fifty pounds.'

Warren eyes him keenly. 'That's right, Raymond. The case itself weighs eleven pounds. Inside are twenty thousand one-hundred-dollar bills, which weigh a gram each. There are four hundred and fifty-four grams to a pound, so we have forty-four pounds of currency and eleven pounds of luggage, for a total of—'

'You brought two million dollars out here?' Ray blurts.

Warren nods, using the binoculars again, sweeping in every direction. The others come to a halt, shaken by the news of their cargo.

'I thought you were broke,' Ray says.

Warren winks at him. 'The company is. But over the years, your mother remembered to bury a few coffee cans out in the backyard.'

'Hey,' Colt says, charging away from the group. 'I think I found it!'

The three of them catch up as Colt wrestles the object lodged in the ground, dug in below the looser top two or three inches of sand.

'Of course,' Warren says, kneeling beside his daughter. 'I should have known.'

The anchor's plastic shell has faded to a sun-bleached pink except for half of the dish-shaped bottom.

'It's been exposed for a while,' Colt says. 'You're lucky it's still here.'

'Or that we spotted it at all,' Warren adds.

Ray doesn't offer to help. He's too busy studying Megan, who watches the others in disbelief and mounting dread, as if expecting something more than an anchor to appear in the moist sand his father is digging out with his bare hands. Warren begins to rock the anchor back and forth, until it wrests free. He leans back, slapping the underside like the belly of a prize bass.

'Still here. Thirty years and not even cracked. Pretty good anchor.'

Ray notices the severed strand of rope knotted at the top of the stem, where a rusted steel eyelet protrudes. He imagines his father out on the boat, the rest of the family watching as he uses a pocketknife to cut the rope. Simple enough, but what were they marking with the anchor? What else did they dump overboard?

He can't help but study the ground, everything in a thirty-foot radius. But there is only sand. No skeletons with chains wrapped around their necks. Of course there wouldn't be any trace left. This was all covered by water, at least thirty feet of it, and maybe as much as fifty or sixty. Warren wouldn't have been able to bury the bodies, only sink them. What happens to bodies in water for thirty years? They turn to bloated flesh, fatty oil slicks, algae, bacteria, dust. The bones would last longer, probably decades, but if so, they would have been washed away, spread around by the currents, carried off by fish. But why mark the site of a crime at all?

Warren stands, dusting off his knees. 'Seems like it happened in another life, doesn't it, Colt? And now we're down to this one.'

Colt's mouth falls open in dismay, then anger. She glares at everyone, turns and stomps off toward the water.

'Colt, hey, hold up—' Ray calls after her.

Warren puts a hand on Ray's shoulder. 'Give her a minute.'

Ray slaps the hand away. 'What did you make her do? Mom and Leonard too? What was this Warren Mercer mission that wrecked their lives?'

Warren gazes around the beach. 'What became of those people? The other family. Isn't that your real question, Raymond? Did I ever tell you their names?'

Megan has become increasingly agitated, but at this last question of Warren's she flinches as if slapped.

'Megan? What's wrong?' Ray asks.

'Terrible tragedy,' Warren says, talking in Megan's direction without meeting her eyes. 'The thing is, even if the person who witnessed the events of that night was standing very close ... well, we all misinterpreted things, didn't we?'

Megan looks from Ray to Warren and back, tense, eyes wide and restless.

Ray turns to his father. 'You did it, didn't you? You killed them and sunk the bodies.'

Warren takes a step toward him. 'Your father and your mother and your siblings are cold-blooded killers. Do you believe that, Raymond?'

Was that a question or a statement? Ray doesn't know.

'I ... I didn't arrange this,' Megan says, quiet, stunned. 'The money. Those messages. That wasn't me.'

'Dad? Answer me,' Ray says. 'What did you do to them?'

Warren taps his index finger against the side of his nose,

then points the same finger at Megan. 'You're asking the right questions,' he says. 'Of the wrong person.'

Megan has begun to cry. 'Please, Ray, I swear on my family's lives. I don't know anything. I didn't send those messages!'

Warren bends over, heaves the steel suitcase up and drops it at Megan's feet.

She flinches again, releasing a small cry before covering her mouth.

'Who else could have been there that night?' Warren says.

'I only wanted to know what happened,' Megan says. 'To understand where they went. I promise, oh God, you have to believe me, Ray!'

'No, Raymond, you have to *trust* her,' Warren says. 'More than you trust your family. Are you prepared to do that?'

'I think I know—'

'Even though you've been *with* her for only four days?'

'How ...' *did you know*, Ray is about to ask, but he knows the answer, doesn't he? Gaspar. The family lawyer. His father's eyes in Boulder. Megan works for his father. They both do. Gaspar has a file on her, one that has nothing to do with her job performance.

Ray turns on Megan, stunned. Something he thought very valuable is dissolving before his eyes. She lied. Betrayed him. 'Why are you doing this to—' he begins, but something rustles within his left cargo pocket. A flash of arm withdrawing.

Ray turns to find his father holding the .45, releasing the safety, then stepping back two paces.

159

Warren tips the muzzle in Megan's direction.

Megan backs away, hands out. 'Stop! Please don't. I lied about my family, the car accident, okay? I admit that. But I wasn't lying about the rest! I *lost* them. They died when I was six years old. Think about what I'm saying, Ray! What we have in common. I *lost my family*. My father, my mother, my older brother ... the tent, the truck ...'

Ray's mind spins. This is why she started at the restaurant. To learn about his family? To blackmail them?

She saw what happened that night, the night of the storm.

She lost her entire family, and his family got away with it.

She pretended to care about him, and maybe she does, in some way. But whatever she feels, whatever they had, has been built on more lies.

'You're their daughter,' Ray says. 'I can understand ... but why didn't you tell me? Megan? You could have told me the truth.'

'I was scared! I didn't know if you were a part of it. I didn't send the messages – that was someone else! Think about it. If I wanted to blackmail your family, I could have done that any time in the past twenty years!'

'Calm down, Megan. Don't make it worse,' his father says, his voice hardening.

'You were never going to leave that money here,' Ray says, turning to his father. 'Were you? This was a bullshit errand to trap her.'

Colt keeps her distance, off near the shore, watching them as Warren bends over the case, unlatches it, and kicks the lid open. It's filled with sand. More sand.

160

'I suspected before you two left Colorado. I only wanted to confirm it.'

Liars, Ray thinks. All of them. 'You brought us all the way out here so you could get rid of the witness? Put her with her family?'

Warren ignores his son, steps toward Megan, the gun at his side. 'I need to know three things.'

'I'll leave,' Megan pleads. 'I won't tell anybody. I promise, okay?'

'One. What did you see?'

'Nothing!' she cries. Warren raises the gun, aiming at her. 'Just the fighting! In the waves, same as Ray. I was hiding. We were both scared!'

'Dad, stop—'

'You're holding out,' Warren tells her, and thumbs the hammer. 'What else?'

'You were trying to help them, I know that,' she stammers. 'I saw you attempting CPR, and then everybody was gone. I ran across the point. Francine was there. The storm was still out of control. She tried to help me, that's all I know!'

'TWO. Who did you tell? Who else knows about us?'

'Dad, calm down. This is insane—'

'Nobody!' Megan's entire body starts to shake. 'I promise. Please . . . please don't hurt me.'

'She told you everything,' Ray says, stepping toward his father.

Warren shoves him back. 'We can't trust her. She doesn't understand what we were up against. You don't know, Raymond. Get out of the goddamned way.'

161

'I heard gunshots,' Megan says. 'And when I got to the other side of the point, after Francine left me ...'

Warren's eyes grow with expectation. This is it. Everything he has been hoping to confirm. 'Say it!' he barks, charging at her with the gun. 'Say it!'

'They were gone!' Megan screams. 'My family was gone! I didn't tell anybody. I was six years old. I didn't understand ...' but she is crying too hard to continue.

Ray can't stand this anymore. Whatever Megan did or did not see, whatever she lied about, he's not about to let his father threaten her like this anymore. He has to get the gun away from his dad and get her out of here some-how.

He steps between them, his back to his father. 'You lied to me!' Then, under his breath, mouthing the words, '*Get ready to run.*'

She doesn't understand.

'Raymond—'

Ray turns on his father, seizes the wrist below the gun and slams his shoulders into Warren's chest. The two of them fall back, legs tangling, into the sand.

'Go!' Ray shouts.

'Goddamn it,' Warren hisses as the two of them wrestle over the weapon.

'Let go!' Ray shakes his father's arm, slamming it to the beach. The pistol falls in the sand. Ray jumps for it, and his father blocks him hard, sending him rolling past the gun. Ray scrambles to his feet, but Warren is already swip-ing the pistol up, rising.

Ray sees Colt running toward them, shouting, but Ray

162

can't understand her. Warren hesitates, distracted by Colt, long enough for Megan to make her break.

She dashes off, sprinting across the beach. She glances over her shoulder every few strides. There is no cover, nothing between her and the nearest trees except for a thousand feet of barren beach.

The old man's aim is steady, tracking her, his left hand supporting the grip, eyes drawing a straight line over the barrel, across the sand, to Megan.

'No!' Ray shouts, leaping to his feet. 'Don't you fucking do it!'

'Get back here!' Warren shouts.

Megan only runs faster. There's only one way, then. If he tries to knock the gun away again, his father will shoot.

Ray gives chase, running in front of the gun. His feet pound the sand and it becomes the nightmare, the one where you can never run fast enough, the air heavy as water, the sand too thick.

Ray is watching her hair swing across her back as the shot rings out.

Trust

Megan cuts toward the trees as the shot echoes across the basin. Ray cuts with her, looking back as Warren lowers the pistol, shaking his head, disappointed in his marksmanship, his son, or both.

Ray runs in parallel, keeping ten paces off her heels, giving her time to burn off the panic. She slips into a series of thickets and shrubs over a flat plane of firmer sand, then through a wider spread of deep weeds too ugly to be a meadow. He loses her, then spots her ducking and weaving along a trail. He calls to her, but she won't stop. A short minute later the path ends, rebuking her with a long row of mature cottonwoods along a barren hillside too tall for either of them to climb.

They are out of the basin, out of range and out of breath. The cottons cast wide patches of shade where she slows to a jog, but it is no cooler under their cover. They are winded, stomping along like the last two members of a search party.

Megan circles, her tears giving way to fuming anger and exhaustion. He raises his hands in surrender. She buckles, sitting in the sand, her face red and pouring sweat. A long, thick strand of spider web or insect silk clings to her neck. Ray backs into a tree and slides down, legs splayed out. The ground back here is gray, as if the fields have burned and ash has sifted into the sand.

'I always knew I was naive about relationships,' Ray says, pausing to swallow dryly. 'But I really missed the blinking red light on this one, huh?'

'Sorry about that.' She sounds more tired of apologizing than actually sorry.

'My dad just took a shot at you, so I can't blame you if you want to leave without explaining the rest. I understand why you came on this trip. The first time you saw the Bronco, you looked like you'd seen a ghost. But I don't know how you're going to get out of here *without* the Bronco. I have to go back and tell them something, or else we're both stuck.'

A look of weary resignation settles on her. 'The thing that drove me crazy for the past thirty years. I guess that's as good a place as any to start. It was always the question, who were these people, your family? Were they good or bad? Did they try to help my family, or hurt them? Because there were two very different sides to the whole episode, Ray, and another gap in the middle. That's why I never called the police. That's why I needed to get close to your family, to learn what I could before making any judgements or decisions.'

'Why now?' Ray says. 'After all this time, why this year?'

'It's just the way my life went. The story Aunt Vicky told me, it was always a boating accident. My family drowned in that storm, just like the story the waitress told us yesterday. My God, was that only yesterday? The police came out and searched for them, after a group of campers found me and called the police. A week had passed. They dragged the lake. Found our boat, but not the bodies. The lake was too big. End of search. That was it. That was the story.

'And I wanted to believe that, because the alternative was ... overwhelming. I couldn't talk, Ray. I was like that kid in the waitress's story, except I was even younger. I didn't have the ability to process it let alone speak of it, explain it. Not for years. My Aunt Vicky raised me in Colorado Springs, like I told you. Put me through college, where I met a boy. We got married young, and it wasn't a good marriage. He was too nice, tried too hard, like he was always trying to prove it would work. I was ... I made a bad spouse. He left after six years, and I started drinking, which had always been a problem but got worse. I lost my job in corporate communications. I drifted around the country, half out of my mind. Then one day I decided to look them up. The other family.

'I hired a private investigator. He found records of the permits through the Nebraska Game and Parks Commission. From the same year, the same month, same week. There weren't many families that stayed here during that window, and somehow I knew the name when I read it. The Mercers. Maybe I'd heard it on the trip, but even if I hadn't, everything else fit. The ages of the children. The camp site on Admiral's Point. After that it was easy to piece together, track things into the present. Your dad's businesses, all that success. Everything was online by then and I didn't need the private investigator for the rest.'

'So when were you going to tell me the truth? After the trip? After we were married?'

'A year ago, once I got a sense of you in the restaurant. But a couple months became six. Then there was a whole period where I decided not to. Maybe I wasn't supposed to until now. I mean, when you invited me, I thought, this is too good to be true. Now I can meet the family. See what they're like before I—'

'Now you know the answer to that. They're crazy, just like you.' His anger has begun to throb again. He is mad at himself, at his father, at her. 'You could have gotten yourself killed. Do you realize that?'

'I didn't know they were going to bring guns,' Megan says. 'They're your family. You weren't afraid, why would I be?'

'Because your family is dead.'

'But of what?' she says. 'I'm getting to that part, but you need to know where I'm coming from. Why I misled you.'

Ray rubs his eyes. 'Back up a bit. How did you find me? What led you to Boulder?'

'Your dad's profile on one of the company sites. It mentioned three children, your names. I couldn't find Leonard. Colette was in New York. I saw her on a fundraiser website. And then you, listed as a marketing guru with the restaurants. Boulder was a lot closer than New York, and somehow I just knew I needed to start with you.'

'Some guru,' Ray says.

'You were carrying the same kind of baggage as me, but I didn't know that right away. I followed you for a while, and I needed a job. My savings were running out. Finally I figured I might as well apply at Pescado. You were there all the time. They called me for an interview at the other restaurant, Cantina Rojo out on Baseline. But I said no, I was only interested in Pescado. I heard the tips were better. Oddly enough, something opened up a week later and they called me back.'

'And then you waited fifteen months to approach me,' Ray says.

'Technically, you approached me.'

'Come on, Megan.'

'You have to understand, all those years, your family were like people out of a myth, the most important thing that ever happened to me, and nothing about it seemed quite real. But suddenly there I am, working with you, seeing you in your booth every day, and I knew some part of me had always known about you. Did I ever seem familiar to you?'

'In the attraction sense,' he says. 'The way you integrate someone into your whole life, wishing them there all along.'

'That's sweet, but I'm not being romantic. I really felt we'd been there together. Don't you remember a little girl from the trip? I was blonde then. Small for my age.'

He blinks at her a few times. 'All those early trips my family took, they've sort of blended together. I was only three the first year, eight by the last one. They're all like a collage, but when I focus on one thing, I can figure out which trip it happened on. Except for the last one. The storm. The rest of the trip, the five days that came before ... it's like they no longer exist. I'm sorry.'

Megan nods, disappointed. 'Enough bad things happened on that trip, I thought maybe you were better off not knowing. You seemed sad, but not completely lost like me, and I didn't want to make it worse for you.'

'We both had ways of masking it,' he says. 'You were the grounded one, remember?'

Megan smiles. '*And* there was Pam. I sensed it was ending, the way you two acted toward each other. But I couldn't just punch a hole in your life. I was scared, too. Sometimes I thought I would die if I didn't talk to you about it. But other times, I was afraid to learn the other half of the story. In a lot of ways, finding out that your family killed my family might be less frightening than the alternative.'

Ray can only stare at her.

'But if I hadn't waited, I wouldn't have gotten to know you in the same way. We might have fallen ... you might have despised me, okay? And I don't blame you for despising me now.'

'I don't. I appreciate that you wanted to protect me too,' Ray says. 'But we are where we are, and you're still stalling, Megan. We have to share everything now, before someone really gets hurt. I will go to the police if someone doesn't start telling the truth. Tell me what you saw, don't leave anything out, and I promise not to interrupt.'

Megan takes a deep breath. 'Okay. But I don't think you're going to like it.'

'No, I probably won't. But it's time.'

She looks away, searching for a place to begin. And begins.

Black Water

Megan is terrified of leaving the tent. The storm is scary enough from inside – one of the side rooms has already collapsed, the rest of the canvas walls snapping as the metal poles creak and bend, sand and rain blowing through the screens – but outside would be worse. She can't believe her dad is actually talking about heading back out.

Her brother Shawn looks nervous and oddly excited. Mom looks tired, worrying about everything, arguing with her husband telling him they should have packed up and left yesterday, as if they could have known. Her dad keeps peeking out, looking around, saying he wants to make sure everything is tied down.

'Enough, Hugh,' Mom says. 'Stop trying to prove you've got it all under control.'

'Fine, but the cooler tipped over,' her dad says. 'Gonna be sand in the hot dogs tonight.'

Ever since the thunder and lightning started, Megan's thoughts have been blowing in circles, unable to latch onto anything. She lost her coloring book and her Dumbo floaty when they ran away from the beach, then Shawn yelled at her to help him throw the clothes and pots and pans in the back of the truck, then Mom yelled at them both. It is only now, at the mention of hot dogs, that Megan realizes she forgot something important. More important than her Dumbo floaty, more important than just about anything.

'Rusty is missing!' she screeches in the tent. 'We forgot Rusty!'

Her father backs into the tent, turning slowly, looking guilty beneath his rosy sunburn. They all look around the tent, as if the dog snuck in hours ago and has been curled up in the corner without anyone noticing. But he's not in here, obviously. Megan would have remembered unbuckling him from his bicycle, 'cause he can't lie down while he's wearing it.

Megan leaps up before the others can respond, slipping past her father, out into the wind and rain. Soon as she rounds the front of the tent, a cloud of sand stings her face and the wind shoves her back a step. She squints, screaming his name. 'Rusty! Rusty! Rusty, where are you?' Over and over, running half blind, and at some point the wind knocks her down.

Her mother is there to scoop her back up, pulling her back to the tent. Megan struggles to get away but Mom is too strong. Her dad and Shawn step out, calling for the dog, but they're not worried enough. Megan has a vision of Rusty being spun across the point, his legs not strong enough to fight the wind. She can picture him stuck in the trees, barking and whining, lost, alone. She starts to scream and cry in a pink fury.

Daddy and Shawn promise to go look for him, but she has to stay put. Mom stays in the tent with her, clenching her around the waist as they plop into a pile of sleeping bags. Pinned down, her dog lost in the storm, six-year-old Megan Overton knows this is the worst she has ever felt and ever will feel for the rest of her life. She wails, inconsolable.

The boys, as her mom calls them, are gone for over half an hour, and Mom begins to worry about them. Megan has cried herself into an incoherent state, not sleeping but curled up on her side, sucking her thumb. At some point her mom tells her to stay put, and damn it, I mean it, girl, or you will be in deep trouble. Megan doesn't respond. She no longer cares what they say. Her mom steps outside.

The storm seems weaker now, but it's not over yet. The tent leaks in places, the vinyl floor puddling, rain mixing with sand they have dragged in, making a goopy mess.

More time passes, could be ten minutes or an hour, Megan can't tell. She only knows it's been too long for all of them to be gone. Maybe they went really far to look for Rusty, but it feels strange that Mommy hasn't come back for her yet.

Megan decides to go look for him too. She remembers to put on her purple rubber clogs and, spotting her Minnie Mouse sunglasses next to their beach bag, decides those will be good protection against the blowing sand.

She steps out cautiously to find a dark gray sky pressing low overhead. The rain falls in fat lazy drops. The point looks empty, a bunch of other cars that were here earlier today are gone now. There is only one other camper, next to a big maroon truck with a boat trailer. She knows it belongs to the people with the yellow and red sailboat, the ones who did the crazy fireworks show last night out on the sand bar.

But the people are gone. Everyone's gone.

There is no sign of Rusty.

She walks faster, nearing the lone camper. All the shades are closed, so she can't see inside. She wishes her family had a camper like that. It looks safer.

Just as she is about to look away, a shadow fills in behind the frosted shade covering the camper door. Dark gray, shaped like a person. She can't tell how old, though, because the camper door is up three stairs and the dark sky only makes it look darker. She considers knocking on the door for help, but something about the way the shadow is just standing there … it's like someone is watching her, but it doesn't seem like a real person. She's scared the door is going to bang open at any moment. She looks back over her shoulder as she walks, and a few steps later the shadow grows heavier. The outline sharpens, as if the person were pressed right up against the window.

Definitely watching her. But also trying to hide.

Megan runs back toward their tent, and glances wearily over at the cliff. The way the grass thins out, then only the yellow flowers growing from the packed sand, then the jagged edge. It gives her another horrible vision – Rusty getting blown over the edge, tumbling down, hurting his back even worse.

She runs to the cliff, screaming his name, and barely remembers to stop before running past the yellow flowers, the ones Daddy told her never to cross because the sand was loose and it was too dangerous. She stops, but can't see good enough. She takes a couple more tiny steps. Looks down. The view takes her breath away.

The lake looks like an ocean, deep gray and white on top of the waves, crashing, roaring, furiously alive.

Her family are down on the beach, watching the huge waves smash their way in. Daddy is clapping and whistling at something out in the lake, just a little ways out but coming closer, a ring of something in the water that has turned it black. Shawn runs a few steps into the lake, then rushes back just as one of the big waves crumbles all around his legs. Her mom is yelling at Shawn, but it must not be too serious because he's still laughing.

Where's Rusty? Why aren't they looking for him?

What if he went in the lake?

No, they wouldn't laugh about that. They must have forgotten him already.

Farther out in the water, another family are swimming. Diving. The blonde girl Megan has seen in her green swimsuit is riding one of the waves, and everyone else is cheering her on. Then the dad, and the son. Now she understands. Shawn and Daddy want to do it too. They want go play in the big waves.

Megan is still sad and scared for her dog, but now her anger is like the water below. She wants to scream at them, drag them away, make them help her look for Rusty. He's already been gone so long, they can't waste any more time. She is tempted to jump, to get down faster, and even remembers Shawn saying he saw some kids cliff-jumping

175

down at another camp site. The sand was soft enough in some places, where there were hills, it was like jumping onto a big soft bed.

But when she looks down again, imagining herself doing it, there's no way. It looks twice as tall as their house back in Pueblo. Megan backs away and takes off running across the point. She will go the long way around. She will be out of breath by the time she reaches them, but what else can she do? If they won't come, she will look for Rusty herself.

She runs aimlessly, disoriented, and swerves back toward woods. The wind gusts in strange circles closer to the trees, almost like it's pushing her where it wants her to go. She looks back, and the tent seems way too far away. She calls out for Rusty again, and again, moving to the edge of the woods. It's so cloudy out, the woods look like night-time. The weeds inside are as tall as she is, and she knows there are probably thorns and sharp sticks in there. She could get lost like those kids in a movie she saw, lost and starving, hunted by bears …

But what about Rusty?

Staring at all the high weeds and thick branches growing together, she suddenly knows he's not in here. Even if the winds pushed him this way, he wouldn't be able to walk very far. His wheels would get stuck. This is the wrong way to go.

She continues on to the boat ramp, following the soft sand path beside the concrete, run-skipping down to the beach. She angles right and runs up the beach, clogs filling with sand, until she reaches the point that separates the cove from the rest of the lake. Out of breath, forced to walk fast.

It takes her another ten minutes or so to get close enough to realize her family are not on the beach any more, where they were supposed to be. They are out in the water, trying to ride the waves like the other family, except for her mom, who is standing in it only to her knees. Shawn and Daddy tumble through the waves, back into the shallow part, and when they get up again they look confused, dizzy.

She walks on hesitantly, instincts she could not explain warning her to stay away.

Mommy falls down, under the waves, and it looks like something pulled her feet out from under her. Megan starts to run again, but she's already close to hyperventilating and her legs are shaky. The sand feels like it's trying to suck her shoes off, her feet keep sinking.

A huge wave crashes to her left, only ten or fifteen feet away, and she yelps, hopping away from it as it froths and flattens, spreading across the wet sand. All along the edge of the water, where you can usually see the brown sand, the lake has turned deep black. But it's not all the water, only a thin layer below the top, and it looks different from any water Megan has ever seen. She follows it with her eyes as she trudges along, noticing some kind of pattern to it. She thinks of the letter S, a whole bunch of them together. It looks like the shadow of a huge black snake, lying flat on its side in the sand.

Another big wave rumbles over the shadow, reaching up the beach, soaking her clogs and splashing up to her knees. She screams, running toward the cliff, onto dry sand.

When she looks up again, toward her family, something

177

terrible has happened. She can't find them, but the other family is jumping around, fighting, throwing each other in the waves like wrestlers on TV. Or was that Shawn in the middle? Megan starts to shout for help, but no one turns. They can't hear her from inside the waves.

Where are her parents? Why is the other family attacking Shawnie?

Suddenly the fighting ends, and the other family are tromping around in a daze, the waves up to their waists, looking for something. Between two big waves, the water dips, sinking in like a trampoline with someone bouncing on it, and a big black blob bursts through the surface. Megan has no idea what it is, but it's not more water. Or a fish. It's almost as big as a car and shaped like a big rubber egg of some kind, squishing and bulging as it rolls over and sinks again.

The other family shout in panic, scared of the black thing that just swelled up between them. They run away from it, then circle back, trying to decide where to go, and Megan doesn't understand why they don't just get out of the water. She remembers the long black snake shape at the edge, and looks back to where she was walking a minute ago.

The black shape is no longer there. It moved. She can picture it slithering away, cutting through waves.

Went after them? After her family?

It might have gotten Rusty too.

No. Please, no. They will be in the tent! They have to be. She prays they saw it in time and ran away. It's not safe here, and her daddy is smart. Big and strong. He would have escaped, they all would have.

Megan turns and runs back toward the point. She trips, slamming into the sand, but gets back up and keeps going. The second time she falls, her right hand lands in wet sand and a wave breaks over her, drenching her entire right side. She screams and crawls away as fast as she can. She looks into the water and it's there again, the black ribbon, wide and smooth and squirming alongside her as smaller waves pass over it.

Megan runs to the end, around the point, and doesn't look back again until she reaches the path beside the boat ramp. The two teenagers from the other family running after her, a long ways off, and this scares her almost as much as the thing in the water. Because if they are scared, they saw it too, and it's real. Something terrible is happening.

She runs, everything warping into a blur of panic. The whole world dims, stuck between gray storm sky and premature nightfall.

Up on the point, a sand burr catches in one of her clogs. She stops to shake it out, panting so hard her tummy tightens up and she has to force herself not to upchuck. The wind howls again. Her feet are wet, and not just from the lake. She didn't notice until now, but the rain started up again, the wind too. The storm is back in full force.

Megan looks back toward the ramp, expecting the teenagers to be chasing her, but they aren't there now. Maybe the monster got them.

She decides to make one last sprint for the tent, but as soon as she turns and takes her first big step, she collides with a pair of wet sandy legs, her face pressing into a swimsuit as strong arms seize her own and shake her by the shoulders.

'What are you doing out here?' a woman shrieks in her face, so close and loud that Megan can barely see her at all. There is only a mouth, a face smeared with sand, wet black hair, the smell of coconut lotion mingling with sour breath, a combination Megan will forever associate with raw fear. 'Where are your parents? Dear God, what's happening?'

Megan starts to cry. 'I want my Mommy. I lost my dog. Daddy went swimming and I can't find any ...'

The woman rises to have a quick look around, then crouches again, still holding her shoulders but more gently now. She looks sad, her eyes are red and her nose is dripping. She's out of breath as if she's been running too. She rubs Megan's back and gives her a strong hug.

'Okay, it's okay. You poor thing. Where's your camper? Where is your family? Are they staying here? Do you know where your camper is?'

Megan knows the woman is trying to help, but she can't talk. Relief and fear and the lost feeling of being grabbed by a stranger, it's overwhelming. She can only point toward the tent as the sobs pour out.

'In that thing? That's all you have?'

The tent looks smaller now, another wall having collapsed. Two of the ropes used for the stakes are waving free and there's still a mess of gear around it.

'That's not – nothing is safe out here,' the woman says. 'You're coming with me.'

Megan resists, but the woman is stronger, dragging her back toward the boat ramp, asking more questions.

'Do you have a brother? An older brother about fourteen?'

Megan nods.

'Your parents ... your daddy is big? A big guy?'

'Uh-huh!'

'Oh my God.' The woman releases Megan and takes two steps back, staring at her oddly, her mouth open. Megan doesn't understand why, but for a moment she is certain the woman is afraid of her. 'Are you ... do you feel different? Are you hurt?'

Megan doesn't know the correct answer.

'Did you go in the water?'

'No!'

'Are you sure?'

'I want my mommy!'

The woman softens, taking her hand once more. 'I know. Come with me. I have to help my family. Something horrible is ...' But she doesn't finish.

When they reach the top of the boat ramp, the woman comes to a halt, screams, and turns Megan away. She looks back, down toward the beach, and screams again. Megan tries to pull away, but the woman won't let go. For the first time, Megan notices the scratches, thin slashes of red like cat's claws make, running from the cuffs of the white shirt down to her hands. One of her cheeks is scratched too.

'Listen to me,' the woman says, and immediately after a sharp boom rings out, which Megan thinks is more

181

thunder. But there is no flash of lightning. Another boom, followed by three or four more. The woman's face turns almost as pale as her wet white shirt. She looks down to the beach one last time, and covers her mouth.

'Get in the camper!' the woman shouts at Megan, louder than ever. All the kindness is gone. She looks enraged. 'RUN! Don't come out until I say so!'

Before Megan can respond, the woman shoves her and runs the other way, heading for the beach. Night is all around, it snuck in with the storm and now it's really dark out, the sky a deep purple pitted with growing spots of black. More loud bangs go off, and Megan knows whatever is causing them is not lightning.

She races off for her tent, but it looks like a broken down cardboard box. No longer their shelter, no longer a place to feel the warmth of her family and her dog sleeping beside her feet while the crickets chirp and the stars twinkle down through the screens. Just a big mess, like wet trash.

She runs to the camper but stops short, listening for more of the loud bangs. The camper is too strange, and she can't leave her family outside. The booms do not come back. She turns in confusion and heads back toward the beach. Maybe that woman will help her find her family.

Someone screams. Different from the woman.

It sounds almost like Shawn.

When she reaches the top of the boat ramp, Megan sees the others, down in the sand, beside their sailboat, its yellow pontoons barely visible in the night.

The family that is not her own are gathered around a big

pool of shining blackness on the sand. It looks thick and wet, streaked silver in places, like the black beyond the black between the stars. She moves closer, numbly fascinated by the black spot and the people, the only ones left out here.

The father holds a gun in one hand. Megan knows that was the sound of thunder. The boy holds some kind of sharp silver blade. The girl hugs the mother who seemed like she was going to help Megan, and their soft cries are intense, a private thing she cannot bring herself to interrupt.

A minute or two later, the family break apart and move down toward the water, where they take turns carrying something heavy. It reminds Megan of a giant sleeping bag, and it takes all four of them to carry it and swing it onto the sailboat. The mom and the girl climb aboard as the guys push it out. A small motor comes to life, chugging the boat out into the cove.

The black orb shimmers on the beach, then fades, becoming part of the night.

Far out in the water, someone begins to scream again. It goes on for a long time, fading across the cove and returning like a siren. It doesn't sound like any person Megan's ever heard.

She turns away and wanders off to look for her family. For something she can understand. She enters the woods, thinking only about her dog. Walking, sometimes crawling under low branches and thick bushes, searching very carefully. Behind every tree, into fields, behind hills made of sand and sharp grass. Sometimes the grass sways and rustles, coming alive with strange things that move but make no sound.

She is alone in a new dark world, and she doesn't emerge from it for a very long time.

Sabotage

'Six days. They assumed I was wandering around the lake and the woods the whole time, and that's probably true. I have no memory of it. Eating, sleeping, whatever I did, it's just blank space in the rest of my life. I don't even know if I existed during those long nights. How could I? I was here before, in my life with my family, and then I was somewhere else after, without my family. In between, the nights were endless. I lost my entire sense of time, the world, who I was, where I was, why there were even such things as day and night. Some part of me is still there, walking in the woods, alone. That little girl. She's out here, still. I think she always will be.'

The heat of the afternoon lingers around them in silence. He knows she is finished, there is nothing more for her to tell.

Ray watches her for a while. He feels sad for her, and stuck in something he thought he was prepared for but is not. Something inside him has changed, not only in mind but body too. His bones feel rearranged.

Megan pushes herself to her feet and walks away. He

knows she is headed back to camp, to confront his family. She will never leave the woods. Not until she has found the reason so much was taken away.

Ray stands, following her tracks in the ashen sand.

By the time Ray is within sight of Leonard's stolen tent, almost four hours have passed since their original foursome set out to find the anchor. The tent is no longer just a tent, or even the tent that belonged to 'that other family'. The Overtons.

Megan Overton? Had he really never asked for her last name, not in all of the past fifteen months? Obviously not, and there must be a reason for that too.

Her father's name was Gene, short for Eugene, but in one of those odd but affectionate twists of rhyme and tongue that occur between spouses his wife called him Hugh. He was a salesman for an industrial plumbing outfit in Cheyenne but worked out of Denver. His wife's name was Mary. She was the front-line receptionist at an elementary school, the kind who had been there for fifteen years and hoped to be there for thirty more. Loved the students, by Christmas each year knew all two hundred and eighty-six of them by name. Shawn was a math and science ace as well as an aspiring motocross racer, and the highlight of his short life was attending the Van Halen concert in Denver on his fifteenth birthday, a month before he was swallowed by the lake.

Now Hugh and Mary and Shawn are dead and gone forever and Ray still doesn't understand why, but he is staring at the coolers that once held their dinner and sodas, and there is Hugh's white Chevy truck, and the tent is still here—

'Have you seen Leonard?' Colt's voice comes from behind him, and Ray jumps. Didn't even hear her approaching. 'He wasn't at camp when Dad and I got back. He left Mom and Sierra alone.'

Ray turns, skin crawling. Colt is standing there in her same sweaty T-shirt, the dirty climbing shorts. She looks pale, thinner than this morning, and Ray has another pre-monition: his sister should not be here, and she definitely should not have brought her daughter along. This trip was a bad idea for adults. To bring a child into this mess exhibits a glaring lack of judgement. Fragile Colt and innocent Sierra – the two of them are not equipped to handle what's to come.

'What happened?' Ray says. 'Where's Dad?'

'In the camper with Mom and Sierra. They're fine. Everyone's fine. But no one knows where Leonard went.'

Ray's mind skips back to what transpired as they were leaving camp four hours earlier, as Leonard pulled him aside and warned him to be careful. Dad was crazy, thinks he's still in 'Nam, blah blah blah. But that isn't the dis-turbing part now. It's Leonard's sadness. Ray saw it then, didn't heed the warnings inside his subconscious, and now it seems terribly obvious.

'Little bro, more like my big bro now,' Leonard said. 'I love you, kid. You were always the best of us.'

Still smiling and a little embarrassed, his big slob of a big brother looked so deeply sad and ready to fall to pieces, Ray was moved to take one of his hands, grasping it between both of his own.

'I'm glad you're here, Len. Better days to come, huh?'
Leonard snorted, swallowed. 'Maybe so.'

'He didn't believe in better days to come,' Ray says.

'What?'

'He was saying goodbye. This morning. How bad off is he, Colt?'

She resists, then it comes out in a rush of guilt and relief. 'I told him not to come. I begged him to stay home and get some help. See a doctor. Ask for Dad's lawyer to step in, put him somewhere he could get treatment. Anything but this. He laughed, talked right past me. Working himself into a lather.'

'I know about the debt stuff. What else? How was he living before this?'

'Living?'

'His life,' Ray says. 'What was his life like the past few months?'

'He's become paranoid. He's basically homeless. He's been sleeping in that tent. Here. He's been at the lake for months, Ray. Hiding out. Waiting. He said he knew we were all coming back, it was just a matter of time. He told me that before Dad sent out the invite.'

'Jesus. What is his malfunction? Why is he like this?'

'Why do you think?' Colt nearly spits back.

'You know Leonard sent the messages, don't you? Not Megan. She's innocent here. Maybe the only one who is. Leonard was the one in debt, and he's the only one crazy enough to blackmail his own family.'

He expects an argument, but Colt only nods with the regret of the enabler.

'You knew,' Ray says. 'You knew what he was up to and you let Dad think it was Megan? How could you do that?'

Colt grows antsy, begins to pace. 'I suspected, but I wasn't sure. But so what if he did? Who is she, anyway? Dad said you just met her. Some waitress? He's *our brother*. And it's Dad's fault he turned out this way, why shouldn't he get some help? Who else is going to save him?'

'Leonard's forty-six years old,' Ray says. 'Dad can't save him. He can't fix any of us. Money can't do it. This trip might make us feel better for a few days, but we still have to go home and deal with real life. Do you get that, Colt?'

'Sorry we let you down, Ray,' she says with a sneer.

'You let yourself down. You can't blame the lake for all your problems. The parents. At some point, they're just your problems.'

'Easy for you to say. You don't know what we went through.'

'Megan lost her entire family when she was three years older than Sierra is now. Yet she's not an addict, a corrupt businessman, a thief and a fraud like Leonard, and she's not starving herself to death the way you appear to be. Why is that, Colette?'

Colt's nostrils flare with that angry breathing he recalls from elementary school, when some slight in the hallways after phys-ed class could render her capable of killing someone with a hairbrush.

'I don't know what Megan saw, and I'm sorry for her losses,' Colt says. 'But she wasn't on the beach during the real storm. She wasn't out there on the boat with us that

189

night. She doesn't know what we've had to live with. You don't know how lucky you've been, Ray.'

This is going sideways quickly. 'Look, we don't have time to argue. We need to tell Dad the truth. I'm surprised he hasn't figured this out by now.'

Colt scoffs. 'Where is your little friend anyway? Dad wasn't going to hurt her, you know. He would never do that. He just wanted to find out what she knew and what she was planning to do about it.'

'She's keeping her distance until I give her a signal, *if* I decide it's safe for her to come back. He could have shot her. Shot me.'

'It was a warning. He aimed it at the sky.' Colt sits down on one of the coolers.

'Is there anything to drink in that?' Ray asks.

Colt stands, checks. 'Just beer. No ice.'

He stomps into the tent, looking for a jug of water, but all he sees inside the steaming dark enclosure is a sleeping bag that looks as though it enjoyed its last washing in 1987, a pile of clothes, approximately seventy empty beer cans (sober for fourteen years!) and the rifle.

Leonard has left his gun here.

He was holding it three hours ago, kicked back in his lawn chair outside the Airstream. Which means he must have come back to his tent since then, decided he didn't need the weapon and then headed off to wherever he felt he needed to go. If he was scared, paranoid, or otherwise called away in distress, why leave the rifle? Doesn't make sense. But, then, Leonard never has.

Ray emerges from the tent, and the sight of the Bronco

reminds him – the cooler he and Megan brought should be in there, the last of their water and beer probably still cold.

'Be right back.'

'Bring me something,' she says.

He is six steps from the Bronco when he notices that the hood is unlatched.

'That wasn't like that,' he says, as much to himself as to his sister.

'What?'

Ray walks to the front of the Bronco, trying to summon an explanation. There isn't one. He finds the lever inside the front grill, but the hood has already been released. He raises it.

'What the FUCK! No, no, no!'

'What's wrong?' Colt hurries over and stands beside him, then flinches. 'Oh my God. Who did this?'

Ray glares at her.

She swallows. 'But why?'

'Because he's an asshole nutcase sociopath who should be behind bars. He wants us to suffer, Colette. Do you get it now? Our brother won't be happy until we are all down in the shit with him.'

'Did you do something to piss him off?'

'Other than foil his blackmail scheme, no, not really. But how would he know about that already?'

'Maybe this is about Dad. It's his truck, after all.'

'It's my truck,' Ray says. The sight of it vandalized hurts more than he would have guessed possible. 'Dad gave it to me for graduating high school.'

'But it's got Dad written all over it,' Colt says. 'That's

191

what Leonard sees when he looks at this truck. Dad. Childhood. The lake.' *And the untainted son*, Ray wants to add. Has Leonard always hated him? Or has his hatred grown over the years?

'You know, he pulled a gun on us. Aimed his rifle at our heads. Said he thought we were the bad guys chasing him for their money. But think about it, Colt. If he recognized this truck last night, then he knew it was family. Me. And he still pulled the gun.'

Colt can only blink at him in pained sympathy, most of it for Leonard, Ray knows.

He forces himself to have another gander at the severed wires, the gaping hole where the battery should be sitting. The apparent bucket of sand overflowing from the radiator, and more poured into the exposed cylinder heads. Jesus Lord, he removed the engine cover too. There were tools involved! This was not a frenzy. It was premeditated! Will cost thousands to repair. But never mind that. How are they going to get out of here? He and Megan can't leave on their own. Colt will have to give them a ride. She has the Audi . . .

'Oh shit,' Ray says, running to the white Chevy truck. 'Where's your car?'

'Back by the Airstream. Why?'

The Chevy's tires, all four, have been gashed. A puddle of green radiator fluid is still visible in the sand under the front bumper. Not that it would matter at this point, but any chance he left the keys in the ignition? Nope.

'When was the last time you checked it?'

'What for?' But the answer dawns on her as soon as she sees the Chevy's tires. 'Oh God. Oh no.'

Ray walks back to the tent. 'Dad's Land Cruiser too. We need to check everything.'

'All of us? Why would he do that?'

'He doesn't want any of us to leave, obviously. The next question is, what does he want us to do here?'

Colt hangs her head, covers her eyes. 'I think . . . maybe he wants to spend the rest of his life here? Three weeks ago he told me on the phone. 'It will be so beautiful, no one will ever want to go home.' I thought he was joking, and I never even considered he wanted us to stay with him. All of us.'

'Well, that's not happening. But it is pure delusion and pure Leonard,' Ray says. 'But what worries me? Where this looks like it's heading? What if it's not a delusion?'

'Not following you.'

'Say Leonard is still sane enough to know that the possibility of us staying here for a long time, as one big happy family, is ludicrous, okay? He has to know we would never agree to that. Or else why bother attacking the vehicles.'

'Okay . . .'

'But what if his definition of "the rest of our lives" isn't a long time at all? What if he thinks it's just three or four days? The way Dad planned it. The way Leonard's been preparing for it. And . . . you see?'

Colt gasps.

Ray slips back inside the tent. He picks up Leonard's rifle. He knocks over some beer cans (sober, my ass) and piles of clothing in search of any other weapons, shells, anything that merits a phone call to the principal's office. There, in the corner, peeking out from under a pair of filthy jeans. A leather sheath, thick metal handle with the compass at the end. It's almost funny, and then not.

'What are we going to do?' Colt calls from outside. 'Ray? What—'

He steps from the tent, weapons wrapped in a threadbare beach towel.

'Keep everyone safe in the trailer. Secure all the gear.' He pauses, opening the towel to show her the knife. 'Then we probably ought to find our brother, before he completes his transformation into John fucking Rambo.'

Awakening

Colt's Audi – which she claimed was actually her ex-husband Simon's Audi, the only thing he left her in the divorce, aside from their daughter and 'a bunch of bruises from the assault' – was hosed. Wires, timing belt, tires. Warren's Land Cruiser received the same tire treatment, plus a crowbar plunged into the ignition. They thought to at least try to start the engines on all four maimed vehicles, but no one could find the sets of keys. The only means of transport left at their disposal was the Old Testament kind – their own two feet.

Warren stood stoically, arms crossed as Ray explained his theories, Leonard's debts, his paranoia, the rifle encounter of last night, his obsession with the gear that belonged to Megan's family. Colt confirmed the rest, confessing to their father how Leonard had been staying here for weeks or months, unraveling, babbling about 'closing the loop' and 'making peace with their fates' as he first predicted and then prepared for the reunion trip.

'Which means you threatened the life of an innocent woman,' Ray finished, 'one I happen to care about a great deal. As of now, Megan is the only person I trust out here, and if you don't apologize to her the minute she comes back, we'll walk straight to the nearest police station and we will tell them *everything*. Are we clear?'

Warren puffed up his chest, looked his son in the eyes, and said, 'I was out of line. Please do whatever you need to do to bring Megan back so that I may apologize to her myself. I will tell her what I can about her family, as soon as we have finished locating the rest of ours.'

'No more games,' Ray said. 'No more guns, games, schemes ... only the truth. Is that too much to ask?'

'You'd be surprised.'

'What are we supposed to do now?' Colt asks for the tenth or twelfth time as they reconvene at the picnic table. Sierra is napping in the Airstream, while Francine rests on the larger bed, the air conditioning humming its lullaby to child and elder alike.

'We'll talk to your mother in a minute,' Warren says. 'She can't speak, but she communicates in other ways and is aware of more than we give her credit for. She might have seen something before she nodded off. Leonard might have said something or acted funny before ... this.'

Ray guzzles water, keeping an eye out for Megan. Unless she got lost she will have seen the signal by now – the Bronco. If it had not been moved, that meant it was safe for her to return to camp. Of course, it can't be moved now, she may see the damage and decide to keep her distance. He will have to go search for her soon, not least because Leonard could be out there right now, crashing around in the bush, and might run into her. It's possible that tracking down Megan has become Leonard's next priority.

'He had to have been working fast to do this,' Ray says. 'You and Colt were only gone for what, an hour and a half? This job ate some time. He couldn't have gotten very far, especially not on foot.'

'You can't see the beach from here,' Colt says. 'Which means Leonard wouldn't have seen our confrontation unless he followed us. '

Warren runs a hand over his mouth, looking sheepish.

'What is it?' Ray says.

Warren sighs. 'There were no messages. No attempts at blackmail. From Megan or Leonard or anyone else.'

Colt looks as surprised as Ray feels, though not as angry. 'What are you saying? If no one sent those messages ... you sent them. Jesus, Dad. What did I just say? No more games!'

Warren has his hands up in surrender. 'I started to tell you on the beach. We knew who she was. Gaspar informed me of her presence in the restaurant over a year ago. But we didn't know what she wanted, what she knew. I had to isolate her. Scare her. But that's all I was ever going to do, Raymond, believe me—'

'Believe you!' Ray shouts, jumping down from the table. 'All you've done is lie! You selfish bastard, did you ever consider—'

'We almost *died*, Raymond. Your mother, your sister, your brother. While you were tucked safe inside the camper, we were fighting for our lives, and we damn near

197

lost the battle. Have you ever thought of that? That maybe we were trying to protect ourselves? To save you too? My God, son, you have no clue what we were up against.'

'You're out of your mind,' Ray says, disgusted, turning away.

Colt chews on her thumb, pacing. 'The thing is, we still don't have an explanation for the cars. If Len wasn't upset about Megan and the whole blackmail thing, then what was it?'

'Think about your brother,' Warren says. 'Leonard might be unstable but he's not stupid. Also, he's grossly overweight, drinking all that beer, the amount of food he ate this morning. Does your brother strike either of you as a man in the frame of mind or body to go running around the beach playing spy, tracking us, doubling back to HQ for a riot of vandalism that would have taken whatever wind was left in his sails before he ran off again to hide? Do you see Leonard loping around the woods all night, stalking and taunting us for days? I did exactly that for two years in Vietnam, when I was twenty and built like a brick shithouse, and let me tell you, Leonard wouldn't have lasted eight hours over there in that jungle hell—'

The door to the Airstream opens with a bang, causing all of them to jump.

'Sierra—' Colt begins, turning for her daughter, and then yelps in surprise.

Everyone is paralyzed, except for the woman who actually should be paralyzed. The woman who is standing in the doorway, then planting her bare feet, one patient step after another down the three short steps. She stands firmly in the sand, gazing past them, across the green growth in the clearing and out toward the receded water they all feel but cannot see. Her voice has aged but is still strong and clear, the way Ray remembers it from his childhood.

'The lake has him,' Francine Mercer says, her eyes creasing above a beatific smile. 'It was waiting for us to come back, and now it has our first-born son. Aren't we so blessed?'

The Stranger

Francine leads them from the clearing without acknowledging their questions, making her slow trek to the beach on legs even her husband has not seen her use in more than four years. The urge to race ahead or berate her for more information is strong, but they are at her mercy. Warren tells them to shut up or stay at camp, let the woman follow her 'intuition'.

Now they walk respectfully behind her, Warren hewing near her right side and one pace back, Colt holding Sierra as she trudges alongside Ray. Even little Sierra, awakened from her nap, seems to understand something important is happening.

It's a miracle, Ray thinks. Or else the past four years were a ruse. Or else this weekend is one big practical joke, the psychological boot camp Leonard mentioned. How else is Ray supposed to accept his mother leading them down the beach like a prophet?

They are approximately halfway to the water when Ray notices movement off to their left. Megan is near the Bronco, observing them. Her posture is one of acute balance, the jack rabbit prepared to bolt at the coyote's first launch into action. He doesn't have it in him to shout right now, the prospect of which seems akin to shouting in church. He waves casually – come on back – and a few seconds later she begins to walk toward their strange little procession.

Colt glances at Megan and continues on as if her return is last week's news. Warren studies Ray's tired-looking girl-friend, this new addition to the family at whom he aimed a pistol only a few hours before, with a bit more interest. He gives her a kind of apologetic version of the elevator eyes, lips humbly pursed, and then offers a pointed nod: *I'm sorry, welcome back, please observe the silence.* Then he moves on, walking abreast of his wife, their eyes on the horizon.

Ray drops a few paces behind Colt as Megan joins him. 'Are you all right? Did you get some water?'

'I see your mother's health has improved since this morning.'

'I think she was faking it all along. Oh, and Leonard's missing.'

'I saw the damage to the Bronco.'

'He went berserk. All the vehicles are completely dicked,' Ray says. 'Then my mom stepped out of the trailer and announced that the lake took him.'

Megan tenses, looking more alarmed by this develop-ment than Ray can bring himself to feel. He reminds himself that she has had first-hand experiences out here with disappearances. The situation is more real for her.

'You don't have to play along,' Ray says, unsure whether

he is making light of it all to comfort her or himself. 'You can wait back at our tent. I'm not walking all over the place with them, just down to the water. I'll be back soon.'

Megan frowns at the prospect. 'What did your dad say about me?'

'He knows it wasn't you. Colt too. My dad made it all up, the part about the blackmail, the money, the postcards. It was all a charade to—'

'I get it,' Megan says. 'I figured that out two hours ago.'

'How—'

'Because I know something everyone else seems to keep forgetting,' she says. 'There was no one else there that night. The storm chased the other campers away, and the rest of us who stayed were too busy trying to survive, or too busy dying, to document a crime.'

Ray doesn't know what to say to that.

'We should help them look,' she says, leading him on.

The entire bay opens before them as they crest the last rise on the beach and the view slopes gradually down another hundred yards. Despite the constant faint breeze moving over the water, tugging the green-brown surface of the shallows into crystalline folds, the heat is nearly unbearable. The peak afternoon sun hammers at their backs, their necks, and Ray can feel the first tight sting of its burn on his nose.

'We can leave any time,' he tells her. 'We don't owe them anything.'

She doesn't respond, and he wonders what it is, this thing in people, that allows some to move on from family altogether in adulthood, casting off the implied duties and ritual get-togethers, while others spend their entire lives shackled to blood clan? He supposes it is character, but also something deeper and more mysterious than quaint notions of being a good son or a bad daughter. People, even the best children, simply aren't that selfless.

Years ago, when Ray was fresh out of college, Uncle Gaspar took him to one of their check-in lunches, during which he invited Ray to accompany him on a routine visit with his mother. Ray didn't want to go, but something in the lawyer's eyes made it difficult to say no. Ray had heard stories of Gaspar's mother from Warren, back in his teen years, probably after some minor spat Ray had endured with his own mother.

Warren had told him, in a world-weary manner, that Gaspar's mother had been abusing him his entire life. The Hungarian woman suffered through the Second World War in ways Warren did not care to detail, and, though she was never diagnosed, she displayed all the common symptoms of severe bi-polar disorder. During her episodes, which usually came late at night and for no discernable reason, she would beat Gaspar with a broom handle, with her cast-iron skillet, cut him with her fingernails. She was a short woman, stout and furious, with no husband to tamp the flames of her fury.

She broke Gaspar's arm when he was seven. Broke his nose twice during his early puberty. Broke three of his ribs when he was a junior in high school. The physical beatings were the least painful expressions of her cruelty. Far worse were the insults, the inability to commend him for achiev-ing honors in his class, making varsity squad in three

203

sports, including as a state champion shot-put. She was bitter and withheld her love, Warren said, as though it were gold teeth and Gaspar was the little Nazi who would steal them on sight and give them to the first girl who opened her legs for him.

None of these horrifying anecdotes and Freudian asides was responsible, ten years later, for Ray agreeing to accompany Gaspar Riko, who was then in his late fifties, to the assisted living facility in south Boulder that day after lunch. In fact, Ray had forgotten all about the woman's history of abuse until he observed the way her son behaved around her.

Gaspar's withered crone of a mother was in the grip of Alzheimer's, an almost perversely ironic disease to befall a woman who had been an emotional black hole for so much of her life. Perversely unjust for Gaspar, not the woman, who could no longer recall battering her son until he fled home and enlisted in the Army – and therefore could never apologize to him, or even suffer privately for her sins.

It was a small facility, more of a boutique hotel and spa than a nursing home. The cost, Ray understood later, must have been tens of thousands per year. On their way over, Gaspar had stopped at a Mercer Florists branch to buy her a bouquet of fresh flowers, two dozen white roses, her favorite, and in the trunk of his Mercedes was a soda crate he asked Ray to carry in. The box contained all kinds of special ointments, salves, perfumes, lotions, allergy medicines, gossip magazines, herbal teas, as well as a 24-count box of Reeses' Peanut Butter Cup 2-paks. Her favorite treat.

Inside her sunny, modern art deco room, Gaspar's mother accepted the attentions of her son without rebuke or insult, but she never thanked him either. Never acknowledged his kind remarks, the kiss on the cheek, the dusting and picking up after her, stocking her refrigerator with the candy, arranging the flowers, and his hour-long tour pushing her around the block and up to the nearby park, at Veely Pond, where he stood beside her on the small wooden bridge and talked to her about the ducks quacking and shitting below. She loves the ducks, he told Ray later, though Ray had not once, in the entire three-hour visit, seen the old woman smile at the ducks or anything else that filtered through her bifocals and hearing aids.

Gaspar performed the same routine three times per week, and sometimes on Sundays, as well as on all major holidays and her birthday, most of which she could no longer observe on a mental or paper calendar.

It was not a visit, Ray realized. It was a second job.

'Goodbye, sweet Lydia,' Gaspar sang in farewell, nudging Ray to the door. The music in his voice was neither forced nor laced with sarcasm. 'All the boys love you, especially your son.'

Riding home in Gaspar's yellow vintage Mercedes, Ray sat in stunned silence for a mile or two, until he could stand it no more.

'Why do you do so much?' he asked. 'Dad told me what she was like. How do you find the energy for all that?'

The lawyer seemed briefly embarrassed that Ray found his doting excessive, and then a strange darkness passed over his features. Gaspar's face slackened, his eyes seemed to withdraw in their sockets, and for the first time in memory Ray sensed a dangerous, calculating coldness lurking somewhere inside his father's old friend.

Then the brooding malice vanished with a sad smile. Uncle Gaspar tilted his head as if in apology and said simply, 'It's what one does.'

Ray hadn't thought about that day in many years, but he never forgot the words, and they come back to him now, walking down the beach, following his insane parents on their way to find his insane brother.

There could be no question that Gaspar was *behaving* as a good son. But that wasn't what troubled Ray, and troubles him now. The question is, was it real? Chosen? If his mother's psychological and physical abuses were not enough to break him, is it not reasonable to suggest that Gaspar and all children like him are damaged hostages? Where does that leave Leonard, Colt, me? Why are we still here, in this surreal nightmare with each other?

'It's what one does,' Ray says.

Megan looks at him, waiting for an explanation.

'Never mind.'

Sierra watches them over her mother's shoulder and Ray thinks of smiling and waving to the girl but doesn't. How strange that I don't know her, the little girl. I would like to. Someday.

They cannot have been strolling for more than twenty minutes, but Ray feels as though they have been walking all afternoon. Even though he is wearing his battered Paul Smith sneakers with their little rainbow stripes, the soles of his feet are hot. The sand must be scorching his mother's bare feet, but if so, she shows no sign of discomfort.

Ten or twenty paces ahead, Warren's hand hovers at Francine's back, but Ray can't tell if his palm is actually touching her or if he's simply cupping air, preparing to catch her if she falls. Neither, he is suddenly certain. Dad's afraid. He wants to touch her but he's been wary of her for years, and now he is afraid to disturb her, afraid he might awaken something else.

Then, a short minute or two later, she does fall, slowly and of her own volition. Francine kneels less than ten steps from the water, extending her arms in what would be, in the context of a health club or studio, a yoga pose. Ray can see the soles of her feet, callous-cracked and coated with sand. She is praying, he realizes.

Ray's father moves beyond her, stepping into the lake.

Megan releases Ray's hand. 'You should go on,' she says, and he resents her letting go, urging him forward.

Off to their right, a strangled cry issues from Colette. She twists away and runs from their parents, heading up the water line with Sierra stuck to her chest. She watches the water, then darts away, turning back to camp.

'I won't do it again!' Colt shrieks. 'It's not real!'

No one calls to her or chases her down. Colt carries Sierra over that last rise, and Ray wonders if she will wait for them or simply keep walking until she finds the highway and another ride home.

Ray looks to his father for some explanation. Warren removes his sunglasses and studies something in the water, then looks back at Ray with a stark openness no child ever wants to see in his father's eyes. It is fear but only a little, mixed with unfathomable sadness.

Sixty or seventy feet beyond Warren, something bobs near the surface, a solid black shape, its turning motion releasing a burst of white wash.

Warren rushes after it, the lake rising up the nylon bottoms of his fly-weight pants as he dives after it and begins to swim.

Ray is only vaguely aware of the cool water enveloping his own ankles and then rising over his shins as he follows hesitantly, not understanding what the old man is up to but beginning to worry he has become possessed, lured by some spectre light or black creature of the sort they glimpsed last night, the one that surfaced at the end of Megan's recollection.

Warren pulls up, treading water. He looks back, shouting, 'Hurry! We have to hurry!'

Ray does not see the black spot, but the surface ripples off to his father's left, and then smoothes itself into an oval depression as if something is about to rise up. Warren strokes out a little farther, draws a deep breath, and dives. He is under for only a few seconds, and when he bursts through again he seems to be dragging something heavy behind him. He strokes with one arm until his feet catch bottom. He stands, water draining, sticking his shirt to his chest, towing the bulging black thing behind him like a boy with his inner tube. His face is a mask of agony.

Ray rushes out, taking his father by the arm, holding up

while trying not to look at the rubbery misshapen thing behind them. After a few more steps, Warren pushes Ray aside and muscles the slick mass onto the wet beach.

Francine rises again, hands folded at her chest, her expression blank. Beside her, Megan screams, covers her mouth and backs away from the water. From them.

From this thing.

The orb is almost eight feet long, thicker than two bodies, and some kind of dense weight inside the filmy shell seems to continue propelling it even after Warren lets go. In daylight, the outer skin shimmers, silver in certain round sides, coal-black everywhere else. It makes Ray think of membranes, jellyfish, tar balls like the kind that wash up after an oil spill.

'What is it?' Ray hears himself whispering. 'Dad? What is that thing? Dad? No, don't touch it!'

His father has removed something from his pocket and dives over the swollen slug. His torso lands on its center and the sides all around bulge out. Warren slashes down, puncturing the membrane with what looks like a pocket knife. Black fluid fans out in a wide fine spray, coloring the sand like ink. A metallic odor like burned wires and stale lake water fills the air and Ray turns away, gagging. He looks for Megan through watering eyes but can't find her.

'Oh God!' Warren cries. 'Please! Not yet, not like this!'

Ray turns to find his father on his knees in the sand, the black sac deflated and tearing apart like tissue and sticking to his arms, other pieces dissolving into the beach. For a moment, Ray is sure the black stuff is hurting his father, pulling him down, and he runs a few steps before sliding in the muck and falling. He lands on his side, rolls over in a panic, and stops.

Warren holds up the pale slippery corpse as if offering it to Ray, begging him to look, to help. He is gasping in a deep and horrible rhythm, suffocating on the clean Nebraska air.

'Do you see?' Warren sobs. 'Do you see now what it does?'

The stranger in his father's arms is slender, not yet a man. He has no stubble to make a beard and his crew cut is from another era. His belly is hairless, the legs loose and dragging over the sand like the tentacles of a washed-up squid. Ray hates the boy; whoever he is, he is not worth such anguish.

Ray reaches for his father, to stop him, shake him away from this mess, and the cold body presses against his thighs. He doesn't want to see the face but he can't bear to look at his father's any longer, and so he does.

The recognition comes gradually, as if he were gazing down through the pages and years of a family photo album, up at gap-toothed Sears portraits lining the bedroom hall. Ray grew up in this house. He has seen this boy's face. In those years he was always trying to keep up with it, chasing it through bedsheet forts and treehouses filled with baseball cards and switchblades, across playgrounds where the boy was always three steps ahead of him, tricking him with stolen lighter fluid that turned his hands flaming blue, leading him into the cellar on Friday night to catch the ghost, daring him to stand in front of the apple tree and hold perfectly still as the bowstring was drawn, promise I will never hurt you, and in a blink the arrow flew true.

Ray understands now. The lake has folded him back thirty years, asking him to forgive all that went wrong and take his brother home.

Digging

By the time sunset electrifies the sky over Blundstone Lake, Ray feels the day has been both the longest he has ever known and that its end, inevitable nightfall, has come too soon.

He knows the things they have done since finding Leonard in the water (if that teen Leonard-ish thing could by any sane standard be considered his brother) are real, he has the calloused hands and sore back to prove so. But the past three hours exist now in his mind like jump-cut scenes from a poorly spliced Super 8 home movie, footage belonging to some other family, something from a hoax.

The sort of stunt Leonard would have appreciated, if he were around to see it. But he's gone now. At least, Ray is pretty sure his brother is still missing.

The alternative is unacceptable.

Megan helps Francine make her way back to camp. Colt and Sierra have not returned, and Ray feels like the last line of defense against his father's insanity. He is still in some form of shock, oscillating between terror and numbness, Warren's bizarre logic wearing him down.

'We can't leave him down here, away from the family. Not where anyone could find him. In some tent on the beach. Middle of the afternoon.'

'I wish you'd stop talking about it like that,' Ray says. 'Calling it "him".'

'The heat,' Warren says. 'Not to mention, how would we explain this to an outsider? We have enough problems as it is. I'm saying, get him out of sight, figure the rest out later.'

Ray can't stop seeing the bloated Leonard of last night, naked in the dark. At least *that* Leonard had been warm, alive, with a nice lead on his tan this summer. This kid version was white as a striped bass and cold, too cold, as if they'd found him in a mountain river instead of a lake almost as warm as a swimming pool.

'Is this what Mom expected?' Ray says. 'You've all seen this before?'

Warren rests his hands on his knees, breathing deeply. 'Last time was different. Worse, in some ways. We can discuss that later. Right now we have to act. There's no telling where this goes. What comes next. I'm asking you to help me get him in the ground, for now. It's the right thing – the only thing to do, no matter what he is or isn't.'

'For now?' Ray repeats.

'We have a responsibility here. Raymond, please.'

They stop at the Overton tent, making a shroud of two sleeping bags. Ray worries that his seventy-six-year-old father will not be up to the task of carrying the body

213

another hundred or more yards up the beach, into the clearing. But Warren's grief seems to have been replaced by the steel-spined determination of a soldier who's been trained never to leave a man behind.

Ray hefts the thicker, now padded end over his shoulder while Warren supports the legs. One horrible reality of the thing is also a relief: the boy is thin, not all that difficult to walk under, couldn't have weighed more than a hundred and forty pounds. Old Leonard would have crushed them both, blown out one of his father's knees.

The hard edges of the ribs pressing into Ray's neck and shoulder muscles make him think of the winter they were skiing in Vail when Leonard fell over in the lift line. Ray had been standing there watching the other skiers shuffle over the red line as the chair scooped them up. Leonard was joking around and trying to poke Ray in the balls with his ski pole, until Ray caught the pole and shoved back. Leonard lost his balance and fell through the rope partition, landing sideways on the packed, icy snow.

What seemed only an embarrassing nuisance in front of the other skiers had broken Leonard's collarbone, a fact confirmed by two resort medics only after the boys had ridden to the top of the mountain and skied back down a black diamond run without incident, whereupon Leonard complained of 'some soreness' and Ray saw a disturbing lump through his sweater. Had Leonard been fifteen that year? Fourteen?

The memory is enough to bring Ray to the edge of . . . well, not tears, but the idea of crying. If any of them start crying now, they might never stop, hysteria will pass

214

through them all like a contagion, and they can't afford that. Ray does not want to break down in front of his father, but the uglier truth is that he doesn't have to fight back the tears at all. It's simply impossible to accept that this boy is Leonard.

By the time they reach the clearing where the trailer is parked, fatigue and the gravity of the predicament have forced them into a businesslike shorthand.

'Here?'

'Sierra. The women.'

'Right. Near my tent?'

'How's the sand back there?'

'It's sand.'

'Good enough.'

A spot slightly behind the dome tent Ray and Megan share seems to present itself. Not too close, in the deepest patch of shade they are likely to find.

'Under the two cottonwoods?'

'Back out a few paces. The roots.'

'Take a break first?'

'Just get him there.'

The sound of the polyester bag dropping to the lake bed is dull but fast in its slide through the arms. Ray turns away while his father refolds the top to cover a patch of exposed hair, shorn and brown and damp over the pale young ear. Even though Ray had been cradling the limp, still wet body just a short while ago, the sight of that ear almost makes him vomit. How his father is doing this, what the old man is making of it, is beyond Ray's ability to guess.

'The shovel is in the right side storage . . .' Warren says,

215

panting, '... compartment, closest to the rear wheelhouse. Should be unlocked.'

'This is temporary, right?' Ray says. 'Just until we can call someone, get the proper help out here.'

Warren looks at his blue Timex. 'We don't need to make it too deep. Just enough to get under the heat, minimize decomposition. As a precaution.'

'Precaution?'

Warren braces Ray with a look of frank annoyance. 'I'm saying, he may not decompose. He may not be here at all come tomorrow morning. There's no telling.'

'Where's he gonna go?'

'Go get the shovel.'

Ray is relieved none of the women come out to confront him as he rummages through the tool bags and gear stashed in the Airstream's storage compartment. Glad, too, not to hear their crying, if any of them are. They probably don't want to see or hear anymore of this until someone arrives to take them home.

The question of how, exactly, they are going to get out of here floats through Ray's mind again. Does anyone even know they are here? Uncle Gaspar is the only one he knows of. Ray considers calling the lawyer now, while his father is waiting, but are the phones even working? What would he say?

The question of which of the two remaining male Mercers will do the digging is answered easily enough. Warren, always the more prepared, has brought two shovels. One full-size, along with a shorter spade designed for edging, turning a few weeds, but a welcome addition nonetheless.

The sand is firm on the surface, dry for the next eight inches, then moist and loamy, with more of that black peppering Ray keeps seeing on certain stretches of beach and in the woods. It only darkens and softens as they carve out the remainder of the three- by seven-foot trench. Smells like fresh bog mud, sweet and rotting and frothing with microscopic life.

'Hey, Dad, what time is it?' Ray says between breaths, wondering if the old man will remember their little routine from the past.

Warren grunts, planting his shovel in the grave. 'What do you care? You got some place you need to be?' He carves out another pile, heaves it aside.

Ray grimaces and continues digging.

Water seeps into the pit as they slop out the last two inches. Even though the nearest edge of the cove is at least half a mile away, a subterranean layer of the lake has managed to hang onto this land, the furthest perimeter of its old self, when Blundstone had been at her mightiest. We are below the lake of Leonard's childhood, Ray thinks, and digging deeper into the past.

Ray's mind wanders for a while and very suddenly, it seems, they are rolling the package in, shoveling sand over the faded blue skin of the bag. Tamping the loose piles into a smooth plane, kicking leaves to restore a natural patina over the glaring fact of the grave, and finally a few words of prayer, his father wiping away a tear from his dirt-streaked cheek as he utters words of remembrance Ray cannot follow.

Every moment of the burial is swallowed by something

wise inside him, devoured by memory worms the moment they turn and walk away. They stand near the tent once more, backs to the twin cottonwoods, pouring beer into themselves as fast as their sore throats will allow it.

The sky has changed. Everything has changed.

'Maybe we should call Gaspar,' Ray says absently.

'Absolutely not.'

'Who else? I thought he was your fixer.'

'Gaspar hasn't fixed anything for a long time,' his father says. 'This is family business, no one else's. Put the man out of your mind.'

Ray doesn't recall the orders his father gives him after that, only knows he is wandering through the brush and over combs of dry black grass, collecting armloads of driftwood and kindling, some of which remind him of fingers and arms, splintering gray ribs, the litter of the dead.

Campfire

It is the fire which brings them back together. The ancient light and its wild heat emanating from the circle of stones allows them to take comfort in tribe without forcing them to peer too closely at one another. The flickering flames and the nightscape beyond give each camper a transitional mask, human and animal coexisting until the two can be reconciled or one stakes its claim over the other.

Ray is dirty, sore, numb and scared out of his mind. The growing blaze and the large tumbler of gin and tonic in his hand are helping, but not nearly enough.

Megan is next to return, in clean clothes, her hair wet from a makeshift shower back at the tent. Hands planted defiantly on her hips, she surveys the camp site, the fire, Ray. Asks, 'Where's your dad?'

'In the camper,' Ray says.

'Go get him. Now, Ray. I can't take it anymore. I deserve to know.'

'That was my brother,' he says. 'My father's first-born. You and I have the same needs now. My dad will be out soon. Will you sit with me? Please?'

Megan takes the cup from him, drinks deeply. She sits in the chair beside him.

Colt emerges from the trailer, alone, and Ray assumes Sierra is sleeping by now, perhaps tranquilized. What must a free-and-a-half-year-old girl make of this day? Colt looks cried out. She proceeds to the picnic table, where she pours herself six inches of Mount Gay rum on the rocks, adds half a lime and then takes a chair across from them. She stares into the flames, drinking. Her eyes widen to their limits and stick that way. She is and is not here, Ray knows.

'How's Mom?' he asks. When his sister doesn't answer, he says, 'Colt? Tell me about Mom.'

Colt blinks. 'Sleeping. She can't move her legs now. Won't talk anymore. I had to lift her into the bunk.'

Warren pushes the trailer door open and descends with a platter of grilled cheese sandwiches cut in half, a bag of potato chips and a stack of napkins pinched between his fingers. Grilled cheese was always the traditional dinner for the first night of the trips. The rule was they could have as many as they wanted. One year Ray bested Leonard, 6–5, and Warren said, 'That's it! You two animals ate all the bread for the entire trip!' Leonard tried to call it a technical forfeit, but Ray knew he was relieved.

'I know no one probably feels like it,' Warren says. 'But we're not getting out of here tonight and we have to eat.'

'I'll have one,' Colt says without hesitation. Warren bends with the platter and she takes three halves, setting them on her thigh.

'We need to talk,' Megan says to him.

'We will,' Warren says. 'But dinner first. I insist.'

Megan takes two halves and a napkin.

The cheese is white with little green squares of chili peppers inside, oozing from the seared golden brown bread. Ray's stomach produces a sound closer to moaning than growling.

'There's a reason people bring food to a funeral,' his father says, hovering over him. 'Food is life, never more than when we are in the midst of its opposite.'

Ray is sure he will not be able to hold them down, but he takes two halves anyway.

Warren sits, chomping into his own as he passes the bag of chips around the fire, and they dig in, cramming Ruffles into their faces before the strings of cheese have time to cool on their chins. Ray's stomach feels cavernous, his tongue scorched with salt. The platter makes its rounds until it is empty. Ray refills their drinks, thinking that his father got it only half right. Food might be life, but we eat and drink to keep our minds off death. This is a distraction, the vending machine in the hospital.

Warren leans two more logs over the growing bed of orange coals and then stands for a moment, one heel on the rock, the sole of his hiking boot turning shiny, almost liquid, before he steps back and tamps his foot in the sand. It's a test of sorts, one Ray has seen the old man put to himself on trips past. Control, at the edge. Their father opens the necessary next phase of the adventure in a soothing tone, speaking to all of them while peering only into the fire.

'I know you are all as desperate to know what happened

to Leonard as Megan is to understand what happened to her family. There are similarities between the things that took place here thirty years ago and what happened to Leonard today. It's time she and Ray heard everything we know. But that doesn't mean I can explain it all, or that I know exactly how to proceed.'

Warren pours himself a cup of scotch at the table, then returns to sit beside Colt.

'I offer my word, if I had the first inkling that Leonard or any of us were in danger, I would never have planned this trip. I admit now, I made a horrible mistake bringing us here. I will do what I can to get us home. Before I can do that, however, we need to clear the air and move forward with equal knowledge.'

Ray would like to inquire as to why they are not all running blindly for the fields right now, walking all night back to town if that's what it takes. How any of them could think it was safe to return.

Megan beats him to it. 'You knew it took my family. You knew what it was capable of. Who do you think you are, risking our lives again?'

Warren answers her gently, but his eyes are as cold as Ray has ever seen them. 'I'm the one who survived. We are all survivors. The question is, did we ever really escape? That is the matter at hand.'

Megan simmers, and Ray knows she won't hold her tongue for long.

'We owe each other a fair chance to choose our own courses of action here,' Warren continues. 'As of now, no one here owes anyone anything. You are adults, free to leave or stay as you see fit. You are free to go home, contact the police, whatever you feel is best. I believe we need to confront our enemy here, not run, but I could be wrong. I have been before. If any of you wish to leave now, there will be no hard feelings or repercussions from me or anyone else, is that agreed?'

They all nod, pretending to consider these reasonable options. But Ray knows the very thought of explaining this situation to an outsider must seem as ridiculous to them as it does to him.

'It's not like we have a way out, anyway,' Colt says. 'The cars are ruined.'

'There's always a way out,' Warren says. 'Someone has to go for help, to get another vehicle. We will not, by Christ, be stranded here. Either Ray or I will go, on foot if we have to – after we debrief.'

'About Leonard,' Ray says. 'Isn't that the big decision? What to do with Leonard, if that's really Leonard.'

'You think it's not?' Colt says. 'Who else could it be?'

'That kid is sixteen years old at most,' Ray says. 'And, yes, he looks exactly like our brother did, a long time ago. But there's one small problem. We saw Leonard this morning, if you all remember. He was forty-six, overweight with graying beard, and most of all alive. So I'm not sure what kind of trick the lake pulled, or someone pulled, but it is some kind of trick, all right? Because that thing Dad and I put in the ground to keep cool? That's not my brother. It can't be.'

'But what if it is?' Colt says. 'What if we leave him and he …'

'Comes back?' Ray says. 'Is that what we're talking about here?'

'Calm down, you two,' Warren says.

'I am calm,' Ray says. 'I'm asking you, Dad. If you think that's possible, I want to hear you say it. Is that boy going to wake up? Is the lake going to spit out the old version of him when the moon is full again? How will it work? Is that poss—'

'Nothing is impossible,' Warren says.

'Leonard knew it was going to end,' Colt says. 'We all did. Here, there, home, on the other side of the world. It was always going to culminate this summer.'

'What was going to end?' Megan asks.

Colt begins to answer, but Warren stays her with a raised palm.

'I promise that once you hear this,' Warren says to Megan, 'you will wish you hadn't. And I promise it will be the truth, as I understood it. Is this what you really want, Megan? Raymond? To know the terrible truth?'

'I've been waiting thirty years,' Megan says.

Ray wraps an arm around her. 'We both have.'

Warren studies the young couple for a moment, then begins, leading them back into the storm. The one they were so fortunate to have missed the first time.

Cocoons

After most of the gear and the sailboat have been secured, the storm has been expending its energy across the lake for more than an hour, and whatever danger it poses no longer seems imminent. Leonard and Colt are with Warren down on the beach, shoving lawn chairs under the trampoline, securing the life jackets with bungee cords. Francine returns to let them know that Ray has been stowed safely inside the camper. The four remaining Mercers head back toward camp, and Colt is the one to suggest they follow the beach around the point, using the cliffs as windbreak.

They are tired from running around in a panic, so they walk beside the cliff, watching sand devils wheel overhead, which in turn draws their attention to the sky. They have not really paused to look at it since all hell broke loose, and now it halts them in awe.

The storm clouds hang down like wine grapes, draining sheets of glittering rain across the lake. Streaks of purple and silver crack the darker gray plane stretching to the far end, the expanding creases of sunlight etching in like gold marbling. The lightning has moved beyond the dam, the thunder receding. Warren estimates the wind has come down from eighty or ninety knots to a relatively sane forty. They reach the point and round the corner, the view shifting from the swells funneling into the cove to the real stuff, the waves that have been building for four miles across the lake and ten or more down her length.

The water is a magnificent gray-blue, almost metallic, and, despite all the surface activity, Warren remembers how the lake floor under it all is so smooth, soft, free of rocks and reefs as in the oceans. And shallow, the slope so gradual they have all been wading out hundreds of feet before their toes can no longer touch bottom.

'We could surf that,' Warren says, not sure if anyone hears him. In truth he isn't really thinking of the kids or Francine right then. He only knows he wants to dive into that chaos, feel its force and try to catch one of those waves. He'd done a little surfing in Vietnam, so he knew the basic timing. When to turn, when to paddle, and how to stretch his body out. He wades out, ignoring his wife's protests, and catches the first one he tries, scissoring off the steep face and swimming with it until he feels his weight lift off. The wave carries him most of the way in, and he can't stop laughing, even when the wave decides to give him a spin-cycle into the beach. The sand doesn't hurt, it's like crashing in warm snow, into a bowl of thick soup.

Leonard doesn't need to be invited. He tromps out and spears through two smaller waves before catching the third. Colt edges out up to her waist, and even Francine looks more excited than afraid. They surf for less than an hour, and Warren feels like he is ten years old again. To a man who's been through war and raised children, that's not a feeling that comes around too often. He doesn't want to let it go.

Megan's people make their way down the beach, watching, curious and cautious. Warren and Leonard encourage them, promising them it's safe. The husband goes first, then the son. The wife loses her footing, but no one thinks much of it.

It seems to happen in a matter of seconds, the change that comes over them.

One minute they are all surfing, chasing new sets. The next, Warren looks up to see Megan's father punching his wife in the mouth. He is swimming for them when the husband starts to strangle her, the kid cheering his father on, and Warren knows they have a real problem. The man is big and the kid has a screw loose, is on drugs, maybe all of them are, he thinks. He can hear Francine screaming behind the roar and crash of the waves. Warren is confused, then scared, then just madder than hell these fucking idiots are screwing up such a rare day.

The fighting breaks out. A mess in the waves, bodies slamming into one another.

At some point Francine is screaming about everyone drowning, the three of them are all face down, the waves rolling them closer to the beach, and the only people Warren really cares about are standing. Scared, crying, but standing. The whole thing seems like a set-up, an ambush. Vile, poisoned people looking for trouble from the start.

He is in a sort of combat mode. Eliminate the threat. Account for your troops. Administer help to our guys first. Worry about the enemy fallen and take hostages later.

The labor of dragging them up onto the beach takes its toll. They are soaking wet, with sand stuck in their eyes and mouths and ears. The hell of it is, the lake seems to keep reaching after them, the waves surging over new dry sand every time they think they are in the clear. The Mercers groan and heave in a tug of war, until the three bodies are clear, on dry sand at the bottom slope of the cliff.

Warren goes through the paces of CPR but gets no response. He can't find a pulse in any of them and none is breathing. Not enough time seems to have passed. He can't understand why they are so lost. It's as if the waves have filled them solid and slammed the door, and nothing is coming back out.

Warren tells Leonard and Colt to go back around the point, try to find another party, send someone for help. Barring that, Leonard needs to drive the Bronco back down. Francine stays with her husband, and they take turns on the three of them with no success. They are exhausted at this point, dizzy, in danger of passing out. Francine pulls Warren off the kid and they sit back on the beach, trying to recover their wind.

The minutes feel like hours. They begin to worry about their children, who have not come back. As much as they want to help these poor people, they fear it's too late, and they can't risk losing track of their own. They head back toward the point.

Colt is on her way back, waving and hollering, but they can't understand her. Leonard, they later discover, is back at his tent looking for the key to his cycle so he can race on down to the store and call the police. Warren tells Francine to go on with the kids, get everyone in the Bronco and come back down to help him get the bodies out of here.

He walks back to Megan's family, but halfway there he knows something is wrong. Something is different. They'd left three drowned bodies on the beach, but that isn't what Warren sees now, halting about a hundred paces away while his mind works to find a reference for the scene, a logical explanation.

The bodies are gone.

In the spot where Megan's mother, father and brother had been left unconscious, dying or already dead, there are now three black blobs. Imperfect orbs, like long eggs or swollen body bags. Someone has thrown a tarp on the bodies, Warren thinks, but he knows immediately this isn't the case. The skin is too organic, membranous. He knows it is a natural phenomenon, like insect cocoons. Freakish but a product of nature nonetheless. He remembers oil spilled from a Navy ship in Thailand, the tar balls floating in the sea and washing up on the beaches for weeks after. These are similar but larger, longer . . .

And they are stirring.

Warren has been walking closer and closer in hypnotic fascination, but now he stops. The cocoons are arranged in a loose triangle, head to toe, though he has yet to consider exactly why the smoke-colored surfaces of them are expanding and shrinking like balloons, like lungs. He

229

wants to believe they are some kind of freshwater squid, jellyfish, a trio of nests containing thousands of smaller eggs laid by some prehistoric ancestor of the channel catfish ... anything but hosts to the three bodies he left here.

The sacs burst open as if slashed from inside, deflating as thick black fluid spills over the sand and the bodies crawl out.

They are the people the Mercers tried to save from drowning, and they are not those people any longer. They are not really people at all. The bodies have turned pearl-white inside the layers of black and gray sludge that sloughs off as they struggle to find their footing. They appear naked in the way of newborns, or in the way of the unborn. All the requisite human aspects – eyes, fingers, ears, nose, teeth, genitalia – have been remade or sealed over with rigid white skin that seems fused to new bone structure. The basic shape has not changed all that much. Two legs, two arms, a torso, a head. But everything else, everything crucial to mobility, has somehow been streamlined. They seem unfinished, larval, even now remaking the bodies inside.

They crawl around on all fours, blindly searching for something. Less than a minute later Warren knows they have sensed him and decided he is of interest. He backs away, unable to take his eyes off them, still coming to grips with their reality. Other than being repulsed and generally shocked, he is not yet experiencing real terror.

This is a mistake.

At first it is only a slow progression down the beach, one

230

that later will make him think of a very wide open field with three dogs off in the distance. The dogs are blind, clumsy and slow, but they are also rabid, their mouths dripping white and black mucus by the bucket. You fear that if one bites you, you will die, or become something monstrous like them. You turn to run, and you are faster than them, but they can smell you. They are patient, moving a little faster with each new step, coming together in a formation, tracking you.

They are learning, rapidly.

The dogs are not dogs at all, but adult human-sized children made of wet black mucus and bright white bones. The heads are bald, the faces flattened save for one feature, a single black orifice at center, gaping and closing repeatedly as if starved for breath, or food.

They aim their flat faces at him, their spines arching, heads lowering, and then begin to scramble on all fours in a clumsy but increasingly stable rhythm.

At last, Warren turns and runs.

His wife waves from the tip of the point, screaming for him to hurry. He catches up with her and together they run down the other beach, back into the cove. He shouts for her to get up to higher ground, back to the camper, to stay with Raymond while he finds Colt and Leonard. The things are loping after him, swerving and colliding with one another, but finding their way nonetheless.

Warren wants to fetch the guns from inside the tool box inside the Bronco, but he can't leave the beach until he has Colt and Leonard. The two teenagers are waiting at the end of the cove, beside the beached catamaran,

231

and Francine shouts at them before breaking away, running up the boat ramp. Colt and Leonard are pointing beyond their father, and he looks back.

Three black-hole mouths bob and snap as they crab along on all fours, moving at a clip at least three times their original speed. The membrane layers shed in long strips, leaving a trail of dead jellyfish stuff in the sand.

'Get into the woods!' Warren screams. 'All the way back to the road and wait for your mom and me back there! If we're not there in twenty minutes, follow the road and go for help. Now, run!'

They all look back once more to see the gray and white creatures bounding along, their bones knifing through layers of slug-flesh, then Colt and Leonard dash off for the trees. They know the trails, the short cuts. Warren believes they will be okay so long as he can fend these things off. But with what weapons?

He runs to the boat and turns the gear bag upside down. There is rope, the anchor chain, the anchor itself lodged in the ground, and not much else. A few wrenches and tools for repairing the sail or tightening a cleat.

Warren uses the sailing knife to cut the anchor rope and hauls it into a coil along with the chain. The anchor is too damn heavy to swing quickly, but it's better than nothing. The knife is too small, but he has no intention of getting that close to the things. The only other possibility is a rubber mallet, the one they use for hammering in the tent stakes. He has no idea how it wound up in the boat kit, but later will remember using it to pound a strip of loosened rubber trim around one of the pontoons before the epoxy could harden.

232

Before attempting to challenge the three of them, Warren tries to get out of sight, on the slim chance they are not actually hunting but simply running in blind panic. If they head for the trail leading behind the cove, where Leonard and Colt went, he will chase them down and bait them to protect the kids. If they pass the other way, perhaps they might all escape this mess without a confrontation.

Warren is no fool, but he is in denial.

He makes it hardly twenty steps with the anchor, chain and other tools in his arms, running toward the first line of trees beyond the boat, when the bone-slugs change course and close in around him. He brings up the chain, using a six- or eight-foot lead to swing the anchor overhead, hard and fast as he can, helicoptering the twenty-five pound satellite before they can strike. The motion seems to confuse them, slow them for a few steps, and then they crouch, scurrying in low to the sand.

It is beside the point their skins are almost solid black now and he can no longer see the mouths and white bone beneath. He aims for the heads, bringing the chain down in a final sweep. The anchor bounces off the sand and jumps up into one creature's side, smacking it with enough force to break half a dozen of a man's ribs. The thing topples sideways and rebounds from the beach. The other two are already arcing to his left, circling, learning on the fly.

No time to get the anchor chain winging again. The second one hits him from behind like a bull, butting his legs out from under his upper weight, and the third crashes down on him from the right. Their limbs slip and slide over his skin, the flesh hard but still sloughing the last of the membrane. The rest is black, and frighteningly strong. Something pulls his leg, sending pain through his hip socket, and another weight slams down on his chest. The bodies slide, then clamp down. A concentrated sucking sensation pulls at his navel and Warren feels as though his organs are about to be siphoned out of his body. He looks down to see one of the mouths attached to his belly like a giant leech and he begins to scream.

He punches down, the sailing knife in his left hand. The little blade stabs into the thing's back, over and over, with no effect. The skin punctures like leather hide, pouring black fluid, and the knife slips from his grip as they continue to swarm over him.

Warren knows he is going to die soon.

He swings wildly with his fists, teeth gnashing, kicking and prepared to bite.

A shot rings out, then another, loud enough to hurt his ears and leave them ringing. Something wet opens overhead and black fluid drains over his waist in a cold splash. Another shot, and then they are scrambling off, shoving his chest and face into the sand as they leap away.

Warren sits up to discover Leonard screaming and wildly firing the pistol, and it's probably a miracle he hasn't put a bullet into his father yet. Behind him, Colette attempts to chamber a round into the rifle and Warren regrets waiting another summer to teach her how. One of the creatures jack-knifes into a squat before launching itself at her, driving into her as the other two split to each side of Leonard.

Colt screams and goes down, losing the rifle as they drag her away.

Warren scrambles to his feet and picks up the 30-06. and works the bolt, which has been clogged with sand. He throws it home and marches after the things trying to devour his daughter. He shoots the first in the back, then at the base of the neck up through the top of the head. The second one begs off. Warren shoots the wounded one again, aiming for the heart or whatever vital organs lurk behind the soft shell. Its center carapace explodes and the rest falls still.

The other two collide with Leonard and he loses the pistol. His arm is thrown out, the small axe they used for picking kindling off the dead trees spinning across the sand. Warren shoots one in the head and it leaps away, shrieking like a dying rabbit. It falls flat and lurches belly down across the darkening beach.

Warren locates the pistol and fires into the last fighter, catching it in the leg, then once more in the shoulder area, and then the pistol clicks empty. The last of them has rebounded again and comes at father and daughter in a broken gallop. Warren trips over Leonard, spins away, finds the fallen axe in the sand and rises up just in time to split its head open. Black viscous fluid spurts straight up and Warren walks into it as if it were a lawn sprinkler, hacking the thing from chest to face to neck until the axe blade lodges in the sand. The beach has become a black and silver deck of slaughtered membrane. He slips and staggers through it, looking for something else to kill.

Colt's crying sobers him somewhat. He carefully reloads

the .45 with the extra clip Leonard brought down, and methodically makes a final round, shooting each of the three monsters in the head three times.

All clear. Dead. Done.

He pockets his sidearm and tends to his children.

They walk back to Leonard's tent to fetch the gas can he used for his motorbike. The plan is to burn the creatures.

The Mercers are battered, scratched and wandering in a spirit world of post-combat adrenaline wash. But they are together, alive. The storm devoured the afternoon, and now dusk has come. They linger at the tent, recovering their strength, drinking water, ears twitching, still on guard.

The gas can is all but empty. Not nearly enough to ignite the wet mess on the sand. They may have to bury the remains, but Warren doesn't trust this second choice. He would prefer to siphon some gas from the Bronco and turn them to ash.

They return with two flashlights, the guns, Leonard's pocket knife and the small axe. They aren't expecting more trouble but they are not going anywhere unprepared at this point.

When they get close to the boat, Warren notices Francine standing at the bottom of the boat ramp. She is staring at them like she doesn't know who they are, can't trust her eyes. When she hears their voices, she runs to her children and hugs them, crying, checking them for injuries.

Warren walks to the massacre beside the boat. He puts

236

the flashlight on them, and everything he understands about the world goes to pieces.

They are slaughtered, scattered, broken, bled out. There is no risk of another attack.

But the dead are no longer as they had been, the larval creatures born out of that black and gray membrane. The shells have disintegrated, and everything else has dried up or been absorbed. Warren runs the flashlight up and down the beach but can find no trace of the alien biology.

What remains are people. Human beings.

A mother, a father and their son.

Megan's family.

The Mercer family are brought out of the insanity that has gripped them for the past two hours, only to be dropped into a different kind of nightmare. They are forced to confront the possibility that the cocoons and the creatures birthed from them had all been features in a mass hallucination. Had Megan's family become infected, changed and then reverted to their human state in death? Or had Warren and his family been made psychotic and violent by something in the water?

Francine takes it the worst, perhaps because she had not been hunted in the same way and forced to kill. She can't believe those things loping down the beach were the people now dead before her. The children defend their father and themselves, but soon they are all arguing, hysterical.

'It's too late!' Warren shouts, his voice booming across the cove. 'What's done is done, and now we have to solve the problem at hand. That is all, and it is everything.'

There is no time for a philosophical debate or some kind of amateur search for traces of the inhuman inside the human corpses. The bodies have already been more than autopsied, and it's completely dark now.

'We acted in self-defense,' Warren says. 'We know that. But, come morning, the police or park rangers or any other campers who happen by – anyone we could possibly call – will not see it this way. No one will believe our explanations. We have no evidence beyond this mess. These people. But whatever it was, it was evil. It was fight or die. We almost lost each other out here. I'm not about to put our fates in the hands of the law or anyone else. We decide what to do tonight. We do it. And it's over.'

Their silence is their agreement. Even Francine, still crying, nods her approval. 'I want to take our children home,' she says. 'That's all that matters now.'

Graves are not an option. Buried things have a way of turning up at a later date, Warren knows. The lake or something in it had done this, sent these people into a frenzy and changed the rules. The lake will have to take them back.

He wants to finish the job alone, but Francine and the children won't allow him to separate the family. He needs their help, anyway. Warren has no idea whether the dead will stay dead, or become something else. But even if the remains of three dead bodies are all they have to reckon with, there is still real work to be done. They are exhausted, but together might find the strength to get through the terrible night.

They wrap the three bodies in two of the sleeping bags

and it takes all four of them to lift the burden onto the Aqua Cat's trampoline. The little catamaran isn't designed to hold more than four adults, but Warren knows she will accept the weight. The storm is well over now. The lake is utterly calm. They won't have far to go, and they will be half the weight on the return trip. He attaches the trolling motor and the foursome walk the boat out and lower the prop as the children climb aboard.

The Aqua Cat sputters out through the cove and the motor sounds loud enough to wake the residents four miles away, on the opposite shore. Warren cannot imagine what he will say if they are met by another vessel or a ranger upon return. Fortunately, there hadn't been many campers on the point to begin with and the storm has chased away what was left of them.

They chug beyond the cove and Warren hopes to make another mile before sinking them, at a depth of seventy or eighty feet. He is counting on the anchor and chain to keep them down long enough to decompose. If something of them washes up days or weeks later, the Mercers will be home, rested, in frame enough of mind to have concocted a reasonable story, should the authorities bother to trace them through the park permit. The storm can be blamed for most of it, except of course for the chain and anchor. And the nature of the wounds. But if the bodies do turn up, that would mean they had come free of the gear and the connection to another family will be difficult to make.

The hour has grown late and very dark, more so because Warren will not allow them to use the spotlight, which could draw attention. Staring at their tired faces in the dark, seeing the sublimated terror in his children's eyes and their shaking hands, Warren knows he must choose a location soon and get back to land. There is still the matter of checking the rest of the beach for evidence, then packing up all of their camping gear to drive out before sunrise.

'This is far enough,' Francine says. 'I can't stand being out here another minute.'

Warren shuts off the motor and they drift. The lake is as still as they've ever seen it, black as a starless sky and so quiet he is sure their voices are carrying back to land, to strangers who are watching, listening, growing suspicious. Leonard helps bind the sleeping bags with rope, then the chain, and Warren cinches the anchor at the center of the bundle. Colt and Francine scoot to the bow while father and son drag the mass to the stern, heaving and shoving with their legs until the tipping point arrives.

The shroud disappears into the black water as swiftly as a round stone. Colt covers her mouth but can't keep the wounded animal sounds from escaping between her fingers. They watch the ripples spread until the surface is smooth once more. Warren knows he needs to start the motor and head back immediately, but the gravity of what they have done, under his leadership, won't allow him to move. His mind races with possible additional precautions, anything they can do to cover their tracks. He has to think it through, the before and after, because once they return to dry land and sweep the beach and head home, there will be no coming back.

The light comes first, from below the boat, from something far down in the deep. At first it is like a round lamp,

240

glowing softly, then expanding into a ball as it rises toward the surface. It is faint purple, with streaks of white or silver, illuminating the water in a volume whose diameter reaches one hundred, then two hundred feet. The first detail to emerge from its center is the nautical rope, snaking its way back up to the surface. The rope has been severed from the chain, the end frayed as if chewed off. Warren snags it in one hand and frantically begins to reel it in while his family members lean over to peer down into the surreal light.

'What is it?' Colt asks. 'Daddy?'

'Start the engine,' his wife says. 'Oh God, please help us. Start the boat!'

Warren gapes at the shredded rope. The chain stayed down, and with it the bundle of bodies. There is no sign of the double-bagged coffin down below.

The lake brightens, turning sharp white with spirals of blue like a marble or an eye, the streaks of light spinning as the boat drifts. It is dizzying, as if the lake is turning around them, the earth rotating while they are stuck.

'Hold on!' Warren barks, scrambling to get the motor started.

Some kind of music carries over the water and Colt shrieks, clinging to Leonard, who gazes into the light mutely, hypnotized. Francine looks so pale in the white glow that her husband fears she is about to faint, to topple over into the lake. No, the music is not carrying across the lake. It is emanating from *inside* the lake. A foreign music of murmuring voices and long, deep tones. Wordless, without rhythm, keening one moment and droning like a foghorn the next.

Warren's hand is on the starter cord when the lake falls out from under them, cratering into a bowl that causes the catamaran and her passengers to fall, dropping through an immensity of distance and time where such terms no longer hold any meaning. Their screams are drowned out by the chorus of ancient lowing, and still they fall. Eventually, something catches them, suspending them in a starlit void.

Where it shows them things the human mind was never meant to see.

Multitudes

The campfire has burned down to a bed of orange coals, and no one bothers to rebuild it. Ray is still sitting close to Megan but he can't see her face as well as he could an hour ago. At some point during the story, his arm fell asleep around her shoulders and she seemed relieved when he pulled away. She's been sitting in stony silence since hearing of her family members considered dead, the moment Warren gave up trying to resuscitate them. She has yet to interrupt him or accuse them the way Ray expected her to. Maybe it's because of the things they have seen on this trip. Only one day in, and they have come to expect the unreal.

'It happened so fast,' Colt says, tucking her knees under her chin, curling up in her lawn chair like the frightened girl she was that night and, Ray understands, has been in one form or another ever since. 'I was falling under my own screams. Everyone was screaming.'

'The falling only lasted a short while,' Warren adds, returning to the fire pit, stretching his back and sipping at his newly refilled cup of scotch. 'Something caught us, but in another way it was like we never moved.'

'What happened?' Ray prompts. 'What made you scream?'

'I thought the boat turtled,' his dad answers. 'But there was no wind, only that light, and then the lake was being swallowed by something ... deeper. We were upside down in a blink, then falling, then slowing to a rest, in some kind of free-floating stasis. But not on the water, not in the water, but deep under *something like water*, looking up at the sky and still able to breathe. You could see the stars, more than I saw in the Indian Ocean. Maybe all of the stars.' Warren pauses. 'I was screaming because I thought I was dying.'

'Yes,' Colt says. 'We had no idea where we were. There was no "we". I felt so alone, lost, falling like in one of those dreams. Something powerful had taken me away.'

'But what was it?' Megan asks. She sounds at once broken-hearted and close to running out of patience.

'That's the problem,' Warren says. 'I can only tell you what it wasn't. It wasn't water. It wasn't air. Wasn't the lake. It wasn't here or out there or underground or in the sky. I'm not sure it was a place at all. I might have been another state, one very different from Nebraska. Time seemed to bend. Every thought seemed to weigh a ton and take forever to crawl through, to absorb. That was the agony. Like psychological torture.'

'I don't understand,' Ray says.

His father eyes him carefully, saddened by a memory. 'Remember when I used to go away on business for a week? Your mother said it was like a month for her. It hurt her. And when you were just a little boy, how a few hours

244

of waiting seemed like days? The last hot week of school before summer ... the days I counted in the war, praying to make it out alive. It was like those things, but much worse. Time *dragged*. For lifetimes.'

'That's just it,' Colt says. 'What it showed us. Lifetimes, huge complex structures. Our lives. So many of them. And you could see and feel every one.'

'Same for Leonard, your mother,' Warren says. 'Many lives, then each with a glimpse of a pivotal moment that would come in the future, about thirty years as it turned out.'

'Mine was a betrayal,' Colt says. 'Simon. Which I won't detail now, because the details aren't important, but the meaning is. Leonard saw himself living on the beach here, on the run from what he called "the worst three men in Idaho", because he owed them money. Mom saw herself in a wheelchair, stuck in the sand here, waiting for the thing in the lake to give her her legs back. See? They were like triggers, and they all came true, more or less.'

'You had some visions,' Megan interjects. 'But frankly I care less about what you saw than what caused it. You must have some idea, after all this time. Right? First the lake turns my family into monsters, then it shows you the future? I must be missing something here because this sounds fucking ridiculous.'

'How can you say that?' Colt responds. 'Haven't you been listening? We went through hell—'

'She wants to know what took her family,' Warren says. 'What made us do it, and where they went. Isn't that right, Megan?'

245

Megan glares at the two of them, and Ray can feel her rage as he felt the fire before it burned out.

'Anyone in your position would,' Warren continues. 'But I'm sorry. I don't have an answer for you. That's part of why we came back, to understand it and to stop it.'

'Stop it from doing what?' Ray says.

'Making the things it showed us come true,' Colt says.

'Then I guess you better hurry,' Megan snaps. 'What did you see, Warren? Besides all the beautiful stars.'

Ray knows his father's strategies for dealing with confrontation, and sees him employing them now with Megan. The angrier she becomes, the calmer he will pretend to be, in order to diffuse her. He crunches up an ice cube as he answers.

'I was back in the war for a little while, napping just outside of a village, under a cool canopy of brush. I woke up and it was night, all of my soldiers were gone. The Viets were gone. A bunch of little chickens and a few oxen milling around in the dirt. I got to my feet and looked past the thatch huts. Saw the three of them, Colt and Len and Mom, standing on a plank bridge that crossed the rice paddy. I got up and walked to them, and as I got closer the rice paddy became the lake. Is it time to go home? I asked them. But they didn't answer. We stood there together, not speaking, under a sky filled with many moons. Some red, others white, orange, yellow, a sky no telescope has ever captured from here. Then time began to reel me in again, and we were back in the Big Lake.'

'That's how we came to describe it later, at home,' Colt

246

says. 'We always said the Big Lake, but that was just a catchall for the thing that held all the versions.'

'Versions of what?' Megan asks.

'We didn't have any idea at first,' Warren says. 'In the moment it was chaos, insanity, multiple personality disorder. Like they say about your entire life flashing before your eyes, during a near-death experience. Except this was the inverse. We didn't see the lives we had lived up to that point. We saw our many possible lives, many possible versions of what was to come. Dozens, then hundreds, then thousands, too many lifetimes to count. Like watching ten thousand movies across a single giant screen, in which you are the star of every feature. Different ages. Friends. Classes. Jobs. Big changes and small ones. Injuries, sickness, loss. Your mother and I were divorced in this one, had another child in that one.'

'I was pregnant at age seventeen in one,' Colt says. 'A drug addict in another. I chewed through fashions, careers, men, spending years with total strangers, friends I would later meet in the most innocuous of circumstances. Simon was there, and Sierra, but not always in the same lifetime. I worked as a concert promoter once. A pediatrician somewhere else. I broke my ankle stepping out of a cab in Detroit, running late for a blind date. I saw the same man in another life and he was staring at a photo of me, crying. I never knew why. Once, I wrote a book on female athletes. I had three cats, and then dogs, and I loved them all, knew all their names, their lives, even the veterinarian appointments. Everything was in flux, but I was always me.'

'Leonard saw this too?' Ray says. 'Mom?'

'All of us,' Colt says. 'We could spend all night giving you examples. Too many lives to digest, all mine, all there for the taking. Or living. You were in them too, Ray.'

'Don't,' he says. 'Don't talk about me in this, because I don't want to know.'

'They were our futures *then*,' his father says, as if trying to console him, 'but not now.'

'They were all true,' Colt says. 'I believe that. This is only one of the millions, and they are all real. We just can't be in more than one at a time. No, we can. We are. We're just not aware of it, I think. We can't be, or we would never be able to function. We'd be reduced to stammering idiots.'

Warren focuses on Megan, who looks truly miserable. 'Of course we understand how this sounds now, far-fetched and metaphysical compared to the very real fact of your loss. Your immeasurable loss.'

Megan is crying. Staring into her lap, fists clenched, shoulders bunched up. 'Finish it,' she says. 'Get it over with.'

Warren sits down. 'After what seemed an eternity, it ended suddenly. We were left swimming in the lake. The light show was over, the boat was upright. We were wet and terrified, gasping and clawing our way back onto the trampoline. When we were all accounted for, I started the motor and pointed us back to shore. We were physically and mentally shucked clean, unable to speak. We tied the boat up and staggered up to the camper, which is when Ray got his first look at us in seven or eight hours. We tried

248

to sleep but couldn't. I knew we had only a few hours till dawn, but I no longer feared running into a ranger or the police. I was scared of the water. What it might do if we stayed another day. I could almost feel it pulling inside me, wanting us to stay, and in some corner of my imagination we did just that. Stayed another day, a week, all summer. Prisoners to it. That's true in one sense, and it might be true in a more literal sense. Another lifetime where we never left at all. This became home, the last of them.

'I had to get us away. Off the beach first, then down the road. Step by step. I told myself we could at least make it to a motel, the next town, and piece by piece we got free of it. We drove all morning and shut ourselves in the house for the rest of the summer.

'The main concern was, still is, that all those paths we glimpsed reached their own end, hitting a solid wall in time. We all saw the end of every possibility. That *end-time* was this summer. Why show us so many possibilities with that one common trait? Was it not reasonable to assume that all were possible but ultimately finite? The implications have shaped the lives we have led. My drive in business. Leonard's risk-taking and addictions. Your mother's quest for quack cures. As if we were hoping to outrun the inevitable. After decades of failing to find any helpful answers, we had no choice but to conclude that, however we conducted our lives, this summer was to be the end of . . . all possibilities.'

'I don't understand,' Megan whispers, and Ray's arms crawl with gooseflesh.

'What I said this morning over brunch, the purpose for

249

our trip – I thought I was *saving* our lives. I thought if only we could somehow atone for the part we played ... for covering it up ... somehow find peace with ourselves. Open the door once more, find the meaning behind it all. But that was before the cars. The phones. Leonard. Nothing is working, you see? I no longer believe it is by our own free will we are seated here tonight. We have no way out but our own two feet, and we will try. But I am certain ... the lake, yes, the *lake* will do everything in its power to keep us here.'

Ray's tongue feels thick, his brain revolving inside his skull. The old man is joking. Telling Boy Scout ghost stories around the campfire to give them a thrill before packing everyone off to sleep. Trying to teach his family to stop wasting their lives. Any moment now, good old fat middle-aged Leonard is going to spring out of the trees with a skin of antlers on his head and yell *boo*!

'We're not going home?' Ray says, pleading with his father to answer the only way a father ever should answer his children. 'You think we're going to die here?'

Warren's eyes are pooled with regret, the way his mother's were earlier that day. Ray understands that his mother knows, too. She has been trying to make her peace with it, and living with such knowledge has ruined her.

'I'm sorry,' Warren says. 'It's only a matter of time.'

Splitting the Herd

They fall into arguing and shouting immediately, and as a result no one hears Sierra until it's too late.

Colt is busy ranting about Leonard. Megan accuses Warren of harboring suicidal tendencies and a power complex. Warren defends himself with a convoluted series of apologies and disclaimers. They're half drunk and acting like a bunch of disorderly airplane passengers, and Ray knows if they don't pull it together and form some kind of serious plan to get out of here, more bad things are going to happen.

'He's not GOD!' Ray finally shouts.

To his surprise, they all shut up. Cheeks tear-stained, eyes bloodshot from smoke and liquor, they turn on him, awaiting his command, a glimmer of hope. He just reminded them Warren is not in charge, and in doing so nominated himself for the remainder of the campaign.

'Whatever the hell you all think you saw that night,' Ray says, 'none of it matters. We need to find a way out. Our fates are not decided. Someone tells me I'm going to die here, there, anywhere, anytime – I don't care who it is –

Dad, God, a team of doctors at my bedside in the hospital, showing me MRIs of the tumors – fuck that, and fuck them. *I* decide. And I didn't come all the way out here to commit suicide by surrendering to crackpot ideas about fate and time and the magical mystery thing in the lake. I love you all, but I have to say, I'm shocked at, no, I am sickened by ...'

Ray pauses for breath, and in the silence they finally hear her. The little girl's cries inside the Airstream shift into something more than post-nap crankiness. She is actively screaming.

'Who is that?' Warren says.

Megan is staring at the trailer, eyes wide, as if the door is going to open again, this time disgorging something far worse than Grandma Mercer. A little Blundstone version of the Loch Ness Monster perhaps.

'Sierra!' Colt yells, stumbling to the door.

It's going to be locked, Ray thinks, but a second later Colt is throwing the door open, stepping up into the cabin. Talking over the child's wailing.

'Honey? Sierra, what's wrong? Calm down, baby. Calm ...'

Sierra's crying becomes a series of whoops and relieved mewling. Warren heads after them, taking the first two steps and disappearing into the silver shell.

'She what?' his father says. Then, 'Francine? Franny!'

More mumbling, then Colt says, 'She doesn't know. You're scaring her!'

'You said she couldn't walk!' Warren yells.

'She walked today!'

252

Ray steps up into the trailer, entering the fray. Even in the dark, with only a small overhead light to give him a snapshot of the trailer's interior, he is struck by this recent feat of travel engineering his father has managed. Warren has outfitted, stocked and jerry-rigged every single inch of available wall and counter space with food, equipment, tools, household utensils, flashlights, spare batteries, knives, nets, shelves, pouches and pockets, radio equipment, condiments, hoses, solar panels, compasses, digital weather meters – there are blinking lights and watches and more knives and fishing rods velcroed to the ceiling, for God's sake. It is as though NASA was tasked with cramming a hardware store, sporting goods store, and twenty or so items from every aisle in the supermarket into a single eight- by sixteen-foot space, and succeeded.

This isn't preparation, Ray has time to think, before he notices the window and its missing screen. This is hoarding, OCD, and survivalist paranoia gone haywire all rolled into one. My father's last stand against the death he perceives to be headed his way, and ours.

'Your mother's gone,' Warren says, eyes glassing up. 'She was just . . .'

The window over the dining table and bench seat is a hole, the dark brown cliff nearly abutting the backside of the trailer now unobstructed and within arm's reach. The blinds have been torn down. The twisted frame of the window screen is dangling by the last two inches of its rubber gasket. Ray is finding it difficult in the extreme to imagine his mother's hips wiggling through the tight space, which seems barely wide enough for Sierra to slide through.

'That wasn't Mom,' Ray says.

'FRANNY!' Warren bellows, shoving his way past Ray and out of the trailer. 'Oh God, not my wife! Franny!'

'She didn't see anything?' Ray asks Colt, who is backed into the rear foldout bed with her daughter standing between her legs.

Sierra is sucking her thumb, staring up at Uncle Ray like he is going to send her to a time out.

'She just woke up,' Colt says. Her hands are white with tension on her daughter's shoulders. 'She said "the lake take Fa-Fa away".'

Ray blinks at his sister several times. Fa-Fa? That's what you get when you combine Francine and Grandma, he supposes. He walks a couple steps and crouches in front of his niece, working up a big smile, hoping she doesn't smell the pint of gin rolling around in his stomach.

'Hey, baby. Remember your Uncle Ray?'

Sierra nods but continues sucking her thumb as if working to take the rest of her hand with it.

'You saw the lake? What did it look like? Can you tell me?'

Sierra doesn't respond.

'It's okay, sweetie. You can tell me. I'm gonna find Fa-Fa, I promise. But it would help to know what it looked like.' He turns and points up at the window. 'Did you see it come through there?'

Sierra allows a tiny nod.

Ray keeps the smile going. 'That's kinda funny, isn't it? A whole lake coming through that little window. Wow, huh?'

The thumb comes out with the pop of a wine cork. 'Not the real lake, you dummy.'

Ray makes a funny-crazy face, sticks his tongue out. 'That's Uncle Ray. He has caramel corn for brains, and sometimes, when he's had too many bowls of Rice Krispies, he forgets how to tie his shoes.'

Sierra isn't laughing, but there is light in her eyes. Her chest is puffed up as if holding her breath with delight.

'Of course it wasn't the real lake,' he says, slapping himself on the forehead. 'Hey, owie, that hurt.'

Sierra chuckles. 'You hit yourself.'

'Yep, I'm a real donkey butt.' Then, quickly, before the mood can shift once more, Ray says, 'Now tell Uncle Ray what the little lake in the window looked like, pretty please with caramel corn on top?' He slaps his head once more for effect.

Sierra rushes into his arms and whispers. 'White light. Like the magic wand.'

'Really?' Ray whispers back. 'That sounds kinda neat.'

'It was neat, until it got Fa-Fa,' Sierra says, pulling away, her smile vanishing. 'Then I didn't like it. I hated it.'

'Okay, baby, don't worry. I'll make sure it doesn't come back.' Ray stands, looks Colt in the eyes. 'Magic wand?'

'It's my favorite movie,' Sierra adds.

'Favorite movie?' he asks the two of them.

Sierra's thumb has gone back into her mouth.

He nods at Colt: *well?*

'I don't know. She has all the DVDs. Probably one of the animated ones.'

Still smiling, Ray says, 'Come on, Mom, you can do better than that.'

'Not right now, Uncle,' Colt snaps. 'My mind's a little preoccupied lately. Jesus.'

'All right. How about lately? Something in the car on the way out here?'

'Tinker Bell!' Sierra exclaims.

'Peter Pan, that's it,' her mother adds.

Peter Pan. Tinker Bell. Magic wand. Okay, didn't Tinker Bell's wand shoot magic light or dust or something? Don't they all? Ray can't remember much about Peter Pan, it was never one of his favorites, but here we go.

'What does Tinker Bell's magic wand do?'

Colt rolls her hand impatiently. 'Brings them to life. Makes them fly, is that right, honey?'

Sierra nods.

Ray can't bring himself to ask his niece if some kind of fairy appeared, threw a little magic gold dust into the camper, and Fa-Fa flew out the window. The broken screen would indicate something less than a magical departure, not quite Peter and Wendy and that little one with his teddy bear lifting off in a happy string. But in the end, does it matter? Ray's Mom is gone. Sierra saw something take her.

'Honey? Was anybody with the magic wand? Someone like Tinker Bell? Or Peter Pan? Any person?'

'Nu-uh.'

'Just the magic light? Gold or white light?'

Sierra nods repeatedly.

'Well, this had been very helpful,' he tells Colt. 'Thank you, Sierra.'

Ray is out the door and on his way to help find Fa-Fa, but already another worrisome question has presented itself in his mind. Why would the girl equate white light from a magic wand with the lake? Only one reason Ray can figure – Megan's white people. Down by the lake, in the lake, last night or this morning, it doesn't really matter.

What matters is, Sierra has seen them before.

Ray and Megan catch up with Warren less than halfway through the clearing, sitting in the sand, shoes off, rubbing his left foot and pulling his toes toward his kneecap as if trying to relieve a nasty cramp.

'Dad, what happened?' Ray asks. When Warren doesn't answer. 'You come barreling out here without a flashlight? You want to get lost, or worse?'

'She may have been missing for hours,' Warren says, defensive and chastened. And Ray doesn't like that, because it's quite a drop from the man out on the beach today, the swashbuckling pirate in search of his anchor.

'You're staying back at the trailer with Colt and Sierra. They need you,' Ray says, empowered now that his dad is down with a bum wheel. 'Megan and I can move faster. I have your old spotlight in the Bronco. We can cover a lot of beach with that'

'Twenty minutes she's been gone, at least,' Warren says, shoving himself to his feet, wincing as his weight settles on the left foot. His legs seem too thin, bandy, the shins brittle. 'Maybe an hour. She could be anywhere.'

For the first time, Ray sees age in his father, and it's not the ankle injury. His skin looks too dry. His hands shake.

The eyes in their sad pouches are darting about, looking for something solid to hold on to. The old man is actually an old man now, he thinks, panged with regret over the years wasted.

'Easy, easy,' Ray says, reaching to steady him.

'I can walk,' Warren growls.

'You should wrap that in some ice,' Megan says. 'Elevate it.'

'Thank you, dear,' Warren says. 'I was a medic in Vietnam.'

'You never told me that,' Ray says.

'Well, my unit spent enough time with the medics. Usually getting sewn up. And then one day the medic assigned to our platoon got his guts blown out, so for the next thirty-four days we had to take turns. Believe me, I picked up a few things.'

'Wait!' Colt says, materializing from the bushes with Sierra in her arms. 'You can't leave us here.'

'We're not,' Ray says. 'Dad's coming back with you.'

'What happened to your leg?'

Warren opens his mouth in protest, but something about the sight of Sierra in Colt's arms gives him pause. 'Okay, here's the deal. Megan can stay with us in the trailer. Colt, you go with your brother.'

'What?' Ray sees no logic in this.

'It's the safest way.'

To say that Megan looks uneasy about the prospect of staying behind, locked in the trailer with the man who less than an hour ago proclaimed they were all going to die here, would be an understatement.

'Think about it,' Warren says. 'You two are the only ones who weren't a part of that night. You were there, but you didn't go in the water. You didn't see the things we did. Come into contact, if that's even the right word.'

'What's the difference?' Ray says. 'Why split us up?'

'He's not splitting you up,' Colt says, understanding now. 'He's splitting us up. Making sure there's at least one untainted adult in each party. Right, Dad? You think I'm weak and can't be trusted.'

'We can't trust ourselves,' Warren says.

'I'm not leaving my daughter!'

'You think it's ... *in you*?' Ray says, thinking of bacteria, bird flu.

'I don't know,' his dad says. 'But we're losing people here. We have to assume the worst. Colette, honey, please consider the situation. Balancing our two parties might be the safest thing for your daughter.'

'And now Mom,' Colt says. 'Suddenly she can walk? I mean, how's that work?'

Ray knows it would better to minimize the chances of another one of them going off the deep end, but he doesn't want Megan out of his sight for even a little while.

Warren addresses her directly. 'Megan, you have a vote here.'

'I think your dad might be onto something,' she tells Ray. 'Just – let's not turn this into an all-night adventure, no offense to anyone.'

'It's okay, we deserve it,' Warren says.

Sierra has begun to cry. Colt looks miserable, torn between their logic and her stronger maternal instincts.

259

'All right, whoever's going, we gotta go now,' Ray says. 'We'll give it an hour, two at the most. If we haven't found Mom in, say, ninety minutes, I'm sorry but . . . Colt, yes or no? Time to roll.'

Colt allows a tearful nod.

'Thank you,' Warren says, then reaches for his granddaughter. 'Come here, *liebchen*, you're staying with Pop-Pop for a little while.'

Sierra begins to howl, and Ray is sure this is going to turn into yet another scene. But, to her credit, Colt offers Sierra up. Warren hop-steps to retrieve his granddaughter and then nearly buckles from the weight. Megan rushes over to help.

'It's all right, honey, be strong for Mommy. I'll be back soon, I promise.' Colt kisses her daughter on the forehead. 'Be brave for Fa-Fa. I love you so much.'

Sierra is still reaching for her when Colt wheels on Megan, eyes ablaze. 'She's all I have. Got it?'

Megan swallows, nodding. 'I won't take my eyes off her. You just keep your brother in line, and come back soon.'

Colt glares at them once more, then walks away, wiping her eyes.

Ray hugs Megan as Sierra continues to bawl. 'I owe you one.'

Megan shoves her flashlight in his pocket. 'Don't screw around out there, Ray. She needs her mother, and I need you. Got it?'

'We're leaving before sunrise,' he says, giving her a heroic wink that feels stupid and dishonest.

But Megan is already turning away, dipping under Warren's arm for support. Sierra thrashes one more time, then falls limp, making them drag her. The threesome hobble off toward the trailer.

Colt and Ray run for the Bronco.

Ray doesn't have the keys to power the rear window down and thus can't open the tailgate, so he has to climb through the cabin, over the bench seat, to reach their bag of gear. The spotlight is sitting on top of a thick brown bag. He snatches it up and turns to grab some water from the cooler, but something about the bag pulls his gaze back. It's got lettering on it. Faded logos. This wasn't the bag Megan brought.

He triggers the spotlight. It's a Louis Vuitton. Worn, well-traveled. Familiar, but definitely not Megan's. Whose, then?

Mom's.

He remembers it now. Warren bought her a whole set years ago, around the time Ray was still in high school and they were planning to travel to Europe. The family businesses were growing exponentially by then. Mom was in her nouveau-riche phase. Upgrading the house, furniture, jewellery collection, and all her brands into the bargain.

Ray's back has gone cold. He draws the gold zipper. Shines the light down into the bag. He draws his hands through brittle fibers of human hair –

No. Ray blinks. Not hair. Wires. Black, blue, and some yellow, a nest of rubber-coated wires and black plastic pieces. He drags a handful up. The distributor cap to one of the trucks comes out in a tangled mess.

'Oh, Mom, no . . .'

Was Leonard trying to stop her? Or was it the two of them? Maybe once he had been lured away by the tar people or whatever else got him, Francine seized the opportunity. She knew we wouldn't be back for a while. Sierra was napping in the trailer. She was alone. How many other chances would present themselves?

'Come on, Ray!' Colt calls to him. 'Time's wasting!'

Ray drops the tangle, hefts the bag and backtracks out of the Bronco.

'What now?' she says, seeing his face.

Ray drops the bag in the sand. 'Recognize this?'

'Mom's bag.'

'What's it doing in my Bronco, filled with car parts?'

Colt gapes at him.

'Maybe it doesn't matter now who did it,' he says. 'Maybe they both lost control of themselves.'

'But she obviously wasn't hiding it. She knew someone would find it.'

'Dementia?' Ray says. 'You know how some old people get. Like children again. In her state, she could have thought she was being very clever.'

'But what if wasn't her or Leonard? What if we find her and something else has control over her? How do we know it's really Mom? How do we know if it's safe to bring her back?'

Ray has no answer. They turn and look up the beach. He triggers the spotlight, cutting great swaths through the darkness. Ahead. Behind them. Toward the water. All along the hills and cliffs. The cold whiteness makes everything inside its cone look barren, alien, dead.

'Which way first?' he says.

'Toward the entrance. Where the boat ramp is, and the road.'

'You think she's trying to escape? Hitch a ride back to Miami?'

'I'm sure she's not. But it might be a good idea to remind ourselves where the exit is, before it's too late.'

They head off, jogging at first, then walking as fast as they can without sacrificing any blind spots. They call out for her. Sometimes they yell Mom, sometimes Francine, and sometimes Franny, the way her husband talks to her.

Other times, especially after the first hour, they don't call out anything at all, as if the idea of finding her has become more frightening than simply letting go.

The Cliff

Ray doesn't like wearing a watch, hasn't since high school, but he wishes he had one now. He can almost hear his father admonishing him for the lapse. A prepared soldier never goes out into the bush without a timepiece, a compass and a knife, and dry matches, and and and . . .

The M1911. The .45 caliber they do not have because they were in such a hurry to leave and Mom's bag full of auto parts threw them into another tailspin, they didn't even bother to look for it. Warren had it last. What did he do with it?

Ray makes a mental note to get the gun back from his father as soon as they return. Round up all the weapons the way he started to, and . . . keep them for himself. To be safe. To keep everyone safe.

'Colt?'

'What?'

She is walking some thirty feet to his right, closer to the cliff, or the hills resulting from cliffs eroding over the years. When they first set out, they kept close, a tight unit, beaming in opposite directions as they marched in near lockstep. But as they have grown tired, they've lost some of the urgency, the fear of losing one another. Plus, they need to cover as much ground as possible. As soon as possible. Before they run out of time, and other things.

Ray can feel the hope evaporating from his sister as clearly as his own sweat. He doesn't have much confidence they will find their mother tonight, but he can't bring himself to call it off or turn back. The woman who brought him into the world and fed him from her breast and cleaned blood and broken glass out of his hair after Leonard played 'airplane' with his baby brother on the way to bed and wound up crashing Ray's skull into the bedroom mirror; the woman who argued with Ray's elementary school teacher and refused to let him be held back to repeat fourth grade because she knew he was smart, if prone to day-dreaming; the woman who never once doubted him, even when he lied to her – that woman is out here all alone, missing, lost, probably terrified out of what is left of her mind. And whatever has come of her, she is his mother and Ray intends to find her.

'Ray?' Colette calls.
  'What?'
  'You said my name.'
  'I did?'
  'Like five minutes ago. And I said what?'
  She did?
  'What did I want?'
  'I have no idea.' Colette's flashlight beam sweeps up the cliff face, over the vertically gouged runnels of dark brown

265

sand, over the occasional yellow flower dangling from a long, fuzzy green stem, and then back, until it hits him the eyes, making him flinch. 'What time is it, Ray?'

'Oh, yeah. That's what I meant.'

They spent some time closer to the lake, worrying she could be in the water; but, without discussing it, they quickly retreated back up the beach. Ray caught a glimpse of his sister's face when the two of them were down there staring at the blackness, and he knew she was barely maintaining her composure. It wasn't so much the sight of the black water, what little they could see, that disturbed them. It was the idea of the *rest of it*, the acres and miles and millions of gallons they could not see. The half-empty lake was still a very large body of water, vast and deep and deceptively dormant, hiding its secrets from them, especially at night. Standing before it half an hour earlier, Ray was reduced to a child standing atop the high-dive, the one they never had at the local YMCA pool, because this one was filled with black water and there were no children below, laughing and telling him *jump, you can do it!*

'I left my phone back in the trailer,' Colt says.

'Phones don't work out here.'

'But the clock on it.'

'Oh, right.' Ray tries to picture his cell phone now, and can't. But he does remember his father reminding him not to bother asking what time it was, not on vacation, trying to teach Ray that the whole point of vacation is to stop watching the clock. Did he understand that then? When he was six or seven or –

'So, how long, do you think?' Colt says.

'What?'

But she doesn't answer for a while, and so he must ask her.

'Have we been out here?'

The growing delays between their replies to one another confirm what he suspected. If she has to think about it, her internal clock has gone as wonky as his own. Are they merely tired, or is the lake actively trying to disorient them?

'An hour?' he says, knowing it's been at least that. Maybe two. Or three. My God, if it's three a.m. we need to get back. Even if we make a bee-line, it will take us two hours to reach the clearing. And that's assuming we don't get lost.

'About an hour and a half,' Colt says with more confidence than he feels.

'We passed the boat ramp at least an hour ago,' he says.

'She could have gone the other way from camp.'

'We placed our bet. At least we know how to get home.'

Colt doesn't answer, and a few seconds later he realizes her flashlight beam has stopped moving. He's gotten so used to the peripheral visual of it, the way they've been bobbing and wagging along like tethered miners, the sudden encroachment of darkness feels like he just ran into a wall.

Ray stops, turns. Colt's beam is aimed directly at the ground before her feet.

'What is it?' he says, backtracking.

'Hmmm.'

Ray walks faster. They finished the two pints of water some time ago. His mouth is dry and his head aches, the gin from earlier really making itself known as yet another bad idea. He trains the stronger light on the sand in front of her light.

'Are those footprints?' Colt says.

At first Ray can only make out the usual wavy dips and depressions, then a pattern. The heels, the thinner middle from the arches, the wider areas from the toes. He follows, walking beside them, and they are not quite consistent enough to form a clear trail. But there are too many of them to be a coincidence, or anything other than human. Last time Ray saw his mother, she was walking barefoot. He remembers worrying that her soles were burning on the hot sand.

'How tall is Mom?' he says.

'About five seven. An inch shorter than me, at least before she started to stoop.'

'Let me see your feet.'

'You think they're my prints?'

'The size,' Ray says. 'If Mom's only an inch shorter, you guys must wear close to the same size.'

'I'm an eight, eight and half. Mom was a nine. She had three kids.'

'What?'

'Pregnancy.'

'What the hell are you talking about?' The trail seems to have faded out.

'You never heard that? Pregnancy makes your feet bigger. It's the weight, spreading the bones, swelling

268

everything up. Mom always warned me, and then one day it was true. I couldn't fit into my favorite heels anymore.'

'Huh. How about that,' Ray says.

'Fucks up your body, man. Lot more than your feet, believe me. You should see my—'

'Okay, that's enough, thanks, sister.'

'Oh, grow up.'

But Ray is no longer distracted by the marvels of pregnancy and its effects on the human body. He has found a new trail of prints, same source but branching away from the other line. This series is headed directly toward the edge of the basin, where the sand slopes down and forms what looks like the beginning of a small hill.

'There's more,' he says. 'But if they keep going this way, we'll never find her.'

Colt catches up to him. 'Why not?'

''Cause there's nothing out there but fields, prairie grass, trees. We'll never be able to follow footprints.'

Colt shines her light ahead, to the low berm of sand, higher, over a few sparse patches of weeds, and then higher still.

'Uhm, Ray?'

He sees it, following her softer yellow light with the intense white beam of the spot. The hill is not a hill at all. It's a pile, the fallout from the cliff itself. The pile of clods and thick sand rises for ten or twelve feet in elevation, then runs into a nearly vertical face, cleaved and darker brown, like cardboard insulation.

Colt's light drops back down as she gives up the possibility.

Ray is curious to see how high it goes. He traces the contours and ridges of the cliff, noting those few yellow flowers that seem to sprout here and there. They look like dandelions or daisies, if the stems of such things grew to human lengths. Higher, and higher, until he has to crane his neck painfully and finds himself backing up several steps to take in the wider view. It's vast, spanning at least a hundred feet in either direction, rising at least thirty and perhaps forty vertical feet.

'Damn,' he says. 'I didn't think there were any of these left. All the cliffs around the point are pretty much broken down, washed out. This is old-school.'

He looks back at Colt. She is standing with her arms held tightly at her sides. Shivering. The night has cooled, he just didn't realize it until now. A light breeze has picked up, the first wind he has noticed all night. She wants to go back. Sierra needs her.

Ray takes one final look up the cliff face, sweeping the spotlight over the grass-topped ridge, fifty feet or so to his right, admiring its resilience, a little further to the right, and –

There's a woman up there.

Her.

His mother is standing on the precipice, staring into the spotlight. Through the light, it seems, right into his eyes. Time bends around them, holding them in a long moment, and Ray sees everything about her. How her hair is no longer gray but rich black, her papery wrinkled skin now glowing with suntan. How her posture is firm, upright, and she is not dressed in the kind of elderly beach

270

wrap get-up she wore all day, but in her other clothes, the old clothes, her one-piece blue Speedo under the white Oxford dress shirt that started as Warren's but became her lounging shirt, her bare legs and, though he cannot see them from down here, her bare feet, just as she was that day she nearly dislocated his shoulder hauling him off the beach.

Colt sees it too. Sees Mother. Who is not a memory or a hallucination. Ray knows this because his sister is screaming.

And then he is shouting at her, and his voice sounds very meek. 'Mom! Mom! Stop! Mommy, don't!' Thinking she is about to jump, though she doesn't.

There is no need.

Without sound or warning, the entire cliff face, a section at least six feet thick and twenty feet wide and forty feet high, cleaves from the earth behind it. Francine goes down as if in a chute, arms wheeling, legs kicking, the billowing white dress shirt flapping like wings.

The ground does not rumble, there are no clouds of dust. There is no more aftershock than a sleeping boy feels when a stack of folded laundry lands at the foot of his bed, the way his mother sometimes coyly roused him on those lazy summer mornings. The smell of fresh blue jeans, her delicate humming of contentment pausing to deliver a ghostly kiss on his cheek, and in a shaft of morning light she'd be gone.

Bathing

The fallen shelf spares them by no more than twelve teasing steps of beach, and they attack the mound, legs spread, bent over and shoveling with both hands, frantic as dogs trained in war.

Here. No, there. Deeper, but what if she's right behind them, only a few inches below the top layer? They jump, dig, change positions, and dig some more.

Minutes speed by, far too many, and they haven't covered even a tenth of the mass. What's worse, they could be walking on her, packing the sand over her even as they fall to their knees and slug their way past her. The only hope is that she secured a pocket of air, shielding a few more minutes of oxygen in some miraculous angle of limbs or cupped palms as the darkness filled in. The work becomes mentally agonizing before the pain registers in his back and shoulders, and worsens as the cramps turn his hands into trembling claws.

Colt sounds like a locomotive barreling down its tracks, determined to blow its engine and shred its gears. Her breathing has become a constant heaving, and if it doesn't end soon he will have to carry his sister back to camp, or leave her while he runs for help. Sweat streams into his eyes, from his nose like blood, and they burrow from one spot to the next, abandoning one den for another.

Until Colt's fingers snag in the clogged hair.

'Here!' she screams, her voice unrecognizable.

Ray scurries over the hillock and together, scraping around the shoulders and hips and one arm bent behind her back, they work in a final frenzy to free her from the warm avalanche. Colt excavates and Ray reaches under his mother's armpits to drag her backward, up, and then down the berm to the flat beach.

Francine is mummified in dark brown sand. Even free of its tomb, her body seems to have doubled its mass. Her mouth and eye sockets are packed with layers of it, still moist. Ray plunges his fingers into her mouth, slinging clods of it from within her cheeks, scooping it from her throat. Her esophagus bulges, her chest has hardened. Ray knows before he begins that her lungs must be sandbags by now. His mother's lips are warm, gritty. He chips a tooth trying to force his air into her.

At some point they roll her onto her stomach, as if a miracle might yet prevail and the change of position will allow her to regurgitate the earth. Colt lifts at the hips and Ray clears a path under her face, bracing her chin with his legs. She slips, her head rolling to one side in a loose swing. He feels along the base of her skull, to the lump below it. Her neck is broken, so much of her must be. Then she is only cooling in the night, this mysterious woman who was his mother, and he wishes for all the missed opportunities to return, or even one, the most meaningless of them, that he might prove his love for her.

'Stop,' he tells his sister, who is still massaging their mother's back, trying to roll the sand out, bully the life back in. Colt begins to pound between the shoulders, and their laboring over the broken vessel seems obscene. 'She's gone, Colt. Stop. Stop!'

Colt does, resting her hands flat, the body the only thing keeping her from collapsing onto it.

'The weight,' he says. 'Tons of this shit. On her. Inside her. Nothing we could have done. Even if we'd found her in the first thirty seconds.'

This is not consolation he is trying to offer. He felt this coming the moment he saw her standing up there on the precipice of time. Made young again, to remind him. As if she were telling him, *Don't forget me, Ray. Don't forget how I was, before the darkness and the bitter years had their way with me. I was beautiful, wasn't I? I was really something . . .*

She isn't like that now. Young, pretty, strong. She is only dead, then not even the *she* he once knew. Mother. Mom. mom. mmmm. Flesh, bone, hair, water. Her conviction has departed, and now she isn't anything he can hold.

Colt glares at him in the dark, cheeks smeared with sand. It is all over them, up to their elbows, necks, in their ears and grinding between their molars. His sister looks half dead herself, panting her way into mute surrender. She looks past him, following some riddle over the beach, to the water. Colt rises, lurching her way down the broken column, to the lake that had once been a river and, flow-

ing, carved their mother's death from the valley before she
and her children were born.

Ray sits on the packed damp rim where the night's
thinnest waves ripple and spread like sheets of molten
black glass. The water is soothing on his toes. He longs to
plunge his entire being into its dark depths, washing himself and swimming in Blundstone for the first time in thirty
years.

Colt stands in it knee-deep, sixty or seventy paces out.
She is naked, her lean legs and taut backside pale in the
moonless night. Ray does not try to stop her. The vacant
look in her eyes as she cast aside her sand-packed bra and
choked out the last of her sobs – he understood she
needed to swim. Needs the change of atmosphere, escaping the lethal element that has taken their mother by
springing into its opposite.

Colt moves in deeper, the lake seems to be lowering her
on an escalator, until her oddly wide hips sink below the
surface, where she becomes an arrow, diving out to greet
whatever waits for her, and to wash it off.

He feels it clinging to him all over, the sand. But he is
not ready to swim. Not so soon after Leonard.

He watches Colt, grinding his teeth as she sinks all the
way in.

He walks up the beach as she dresses, and when he
returns something he cannot identify has been rinsed from
her mind as well, leaving only a cold resolve.

'I've been thinking,' she says. 'We've been gone most of

the night. We don't know what could have happened to the others. They don't know about Mom. So, what difference does it make, when we get back?'

'You don't want to tell them?'

Colt shakes her head. 'I mean we don't go back now. What if we go for help first? Tonight. Before it's too late.'

Ray thinks of the promise he made to Megan. 'What about Sierra?'

'Mom was standing up there like she knew. Like something told her this spot was going to cave in. And then something in her agreed with that. Wanted it.'

'That wasn't Mom,' Ray says. 'Not the real Mom.'

'Exactly. Which is why the real Colt needs to be strong and track down some real help for her real daughter. Being away from Sierra for another few hours is the tougher choice, which means it's probably the right one in the long run.'

'Well, we have to head that way anyway,' he says. 'If we haven't collapsed by the time we reach the boat ramp, we'll follow the road out to the highway. By then the sun will be up. We can flag someone down, maybe. If not, we'll have walked another eight or ten miles for nothing. We'll have to come all the way back or walk the next forty miles into town.'

'I guess we better get started then.'

'And if something happens while we're gone . . .'

'We'll never forgive ourselves,' Colt says. 'But that's a point I reached a long time ago.'

Ray flicks his flashlight on but the bulb is very dim. The batteries are almost finished. 'You can't blame yourself for Mom. Or Leonard.'

Colt bends to tie her shoe. 'You misunderstand me. I blame myself for not leaving Simon before things got really bad. For bringing my daughter on this trip. For not trusting that little voice in my head that warned me it's too late. That since we left here thirty years ago, it's always been too late.'

She rises, and together they march on.

Gatekeeper

'I need to ask you something about New York,' Ray says, anywhere from ninety minutes to three hours later, as the sky begins to trade black for navy blue. They are above the boat ramp, on the dirt road and a good mile past the old well, where they paused for much needed hydration. Finding the road was a milestone, but they were too tired to celebrate. Their conversation has dwindled to a few brief remarks now and then. Is that a turtle? No. How are your legs holding up? No answer. He says things, no longer expecting her to respond, but this time she does.

'Ask away.' Her slender body moves in a stiff, hitching rhythm.

'When Dad was giving us that speech at brunch, going down his list of failures, he slipped in some comment about the, uh ...'

'The assault. You want to know about the assault.'

'Yeah, that.'

'What mess did poor little Colette wind up in this time?' she says. 'When will she ever learn?'

'That wasn't my assumption. Nobody ever told me, that's all.'

Colt laughs. 'It was my husband. How about that?'

'Simon?'

'There was only one. He hit me. Several times over several months.'

'Piece of shit,' Ray says, with no real enthusiasm. 'This was before or after Sierra came into the picture?'

'About a year ago. I had come to despise him. Some part of me wanted him to hit me, I think. So that I would have a clear reason for leaving, and taking his daughter away. I know that sounds sick, and it was. I was not well. But he was worse.'

'What was behind all this? What was the problem?'

'Hard to remember. For the first few years, we had a great life. Money, jobs, social events. Simon was a rising star in the bank, managing risk for their international real estate portfolio. Mexico and South Korea were his specialties. I was on the boards of two charities, after I sold the TV channel. We had Sierra. Everything was ... well, things are never perfect, but we were working hard to be a part of the exciting things. The restaurants. The theater. Underground art. Actors and filmmakers. All these amazing *things* ... in the greatest city in the world. And the world went round and round, and then one night he raped me.'

'Simon ...'

'Raped. Me. You're the first person I've told. Everyone else, I said it was fighting, verbal abuse, slapping.'

Ray is shaken. It takes him a minute to ask, 'Why me?'

279

'You're my brother. And maybe it's time.'

'Not even Len?'

'Only would have made him crazier,' she says. 'Anyway. We were going to a lot of dinners, functions, gallery openings. Neither of us drank a lot, or did drugs. I was just coming out of the pregnancy, birth and staying home, that whole two-year phase, and I threw myself into things as if I'd missed every party and important event in the city. I was still post-partum. Wasn't aware of it at the time, but I was. Suddenly I started drinking a lot, it was like someone flipped a switch. I was nineteen again. We hadn't had sex in a while. A long while. I hadn't even noticed, but Simon did. He was always harping on me. Making these snide remarks. I know he resented Sierra, too. Like she was the reason. But she wasn't. Or not the main one. It was me. I didn't want him to touch me. I couldn't stand the thought. Maybe it was hormones. Maybe I never really loved him. I don't know. All I know is, it changed, we changed. It was gone. I couldn't have him touching me anymore. He joked about hiring a nanny to take care of us. Help us *all* out. The way he said it, you knew he meant something vile.

'The third or fourth time he made his little joke, I told him to go right ahead. Hire the youngest, prettiest, freshest little twat he could find. Said I would pay for it. Said I would rather he stuck his pathetic little banker dick inside someone who worked in our home than in me ever again. Sorry, I know you don't want to hear this.'

Ray doesn't. But he understands that his sister needs to tell it. 'No, it's fine. We are in therapy now. This is a safe place.'

Colt laughs. 'All this time, I thought Leonard was most like Dad. So intense. But you're the real hardass of the family.'

'Right,' Ray says.

'I'm serious. You haven't cried once on this trip. Despite everything that's happened. Not over Len. Not after Mom. You're made of steel, Raymond Mercer.'

Ray realizes she is right. Not about the steel. But that he didn't cry over Leonard, or Mom. What's wrong with him? Something that can't be pinned on being away from them for a decade, that's for sure.

'I must seem pretty cold to you.'

'I didn't mean it that way,' Colt says. She seems more awake now. Walking straighter. 'We need you like this. I need you.'

'You do?'

'Someone has to be strong, and it's not me,' she says. 'Dad is trying, but you can see it slipping out of his grasp. He's old, Ray. Tired. I'm not sure I believe him about his heart condition.'

'You think he's sick?'

'I think he's scared. He thinks he can save us, but he's convinced he wasn't meant to leave here. Once he finds out what happened to Mom . . .'

The road is beginning to bend. Ray knows they must be nearing the highway. Another mile, two at most. The eastern horizon is pinkening in beautiful relief. Ray was beginning to doubt he would ever see another sunrise.

Colt doesn't seem to notice the coming dawn. 'He didn't blow up at me or anything, when I said he should go

281

find someone else. He just got real quiet, and stayed like that for a few weeks. I don't know if I thought he had taken my offer to heart or what. I think I was hoping it would all go away.

'About a month later, we went to a party these friends of ours held in this ridiculous five-story brownstone on the Upper West Side. It was supposed to be a classy affair, some benefit fundraiser for a youth program these three couples were launching. Two hundred people showed up. The place turned into a scene. Everyone was doing coke, breaking these pinatas, screwing in the bathroom. I got very drunk. Embarrassed Simon in front of several of his clients, though I knew he wanted to be doing what the rest of them were doing. Turning into animals. Fucking some girl in the coat closet. I remember eating sushi with a fork, chasing it down with endless champagne. I'm sure I was off my ass. I don't remember leaving, or being asked to leave, but that's what Simon said on the way home, in the cab where I was busy throwing up.

'Simon had to drag me past the doorman, haul me out of the elevator. Our place was two stories and I had to crawl up the stairs to check on Sierra. She was sleeping and I didn't want to wake her, so I tiptoed to the bathroom. I shut the door and locked it. I am very clear about that. Locking myself in there. You see? I was afraid of him. I wasn't thinking about it, I'd never even considered it. But some part of me must have sensed he was capable of it. I locked the door and slumped down on the cold tile floor in my cocktail dress and fell asleep. Well, passed out.

I wasn't as drunk by then but I wanted him to think I was.'

Colt is crying again, Ray sees. Her voice begins to crack.

'And when I woke up, he was still there. The door ... the door wasn't even broken. He'd picked the lock. Like a burglar. That's how intent he was.'

'You don't have to go through this again,' Ray says. Bad enough they are walking all night. Mom. She has to endure this too.

'I do, though. I do. I never told anybody this part, not even my psychiatrist. I always said he was just slapping me around.'

Colt draws a deep breath and wipes her eyes. Ray wants to offer her a break, get her to sit down on the side of the road, but she is moving faster now. It's fueling her along. Maybe stopping wouldn't help her at this point. The sky is veined with gold, the few clouds turning silver. Goddamn it, where's the highway?

Then he sees it, a few hundred yards ahead and off to the right, in the grass. Not the road, but the shack. The little pointed top of the ranger station. They are very close now. He's about to point it out to her when Colt resumes her confession.

'My wrists were tied around the toilet base. I was on my stomach and my dress was torn up. I couldn't breathe very well because my underwear was in my mouth. I thought someone had broken into our home and that Simon was hurt. He must be dead, lying back there in the hall or down in the kitchen. I tried to look back, see his face, the man who was doing this to me. Killing me. That it was

283

rape only crossed my mind later, near the end. I only knew then I was being cut in half. Divided. And I was right about that. Because after that night, part of me went on living our lives, what was left of them, taking Sierra to day care and shopping at D'Agostino's and Saks and eating lunch with my girlfriends because I had to show them nothing was wrong, and the other part of me was busy doing something else. Not dying. But not living. The other girl, she was preparing to get away, transferring funds without leaving a trail. Covering her tracks. Because I saw it all, what I would do, and how it would be so easy once I did it and left the city.

'He cried afterward. Falling on me in a heap while my blood pooled on the floor. He took the wad out of my mouth and he kissed me and cried and said he was sorry. I'd figured it out before then, of course. The sounds he made. I'd never heard them before, and yet I recognized them. It was Simon, the beast version. The animal inside my husband. He untied me, taking the scarf with him. I never saw that again and I used to imagine him stuffing it down the garbage chute out in the hall. He waited in the bedroom while I showered. He was drinking a glass of scotch there in his black socks and his T-shirt and shorts. Some of the blood was still on him, and I told him so. He looked embarrassed and said, 'Oh, thanks', and got up to shower. I checked on Sierra again and she was sleeping. I thought I had been screaming the whole time, but I must not have been. Probably that was best, to keep her away. I went to bed and Simon slept somewhere else in the house that night. He tried to come back a few nights later, to the bed with me, and I said no. Quietly. That was all it took. No. Because he'd gotten what he wanted. And he'd shown me his ugliest self, and there was nothing left to do after that.'

She adds nothing more to it. Simultaneously, Ray wishes he had met this Simon, so that he could put a face to the monster, and he is glad that he never did, because he doesn't want it to be any more real than it already is.

'Colette,' Ray says. 'Colette. What are we going to do with Colette?'

'It's okay. I'm okay. I made it out. That life is over now.'

'Is it?'

'Gone forever,' she says. 'I sold everything. Even the apartment. Sierra and I have the car, some clothes, and our bank accounts. The rest is history.'

'I wish I had known. I would have come to New York.'

'I know. But I had to do the hard part on my own.'

'So. What happens after this? Where will the two of you start over?'

Colt looks at him strangely, blinking as if the question had never occurred to her. She looks away, drawing deep breaths, and then offers him a false smile, trying to put on her normal face again. All for his benefit, he can tell.

Ray is about to invite her to come back to Boulder, to stay with him and Megan, until she figures out the next move, or to make a new, permanent home close to her brother, when he notices the dust. They are only a couple minutes from the ranger station and there is a cloud rolling over the weeds, drifting from the bend in the road. He can hear the engine now, very faint but growing louder, coming closer.

'See that?'

'Whuh?' Colt is lost in thought, moving slowly again.

'Someone's coming. Our ride is almost here. We're going home.'

Colt raises her weary head and squints into the morning sun. 'Oh, that's nice. Our lucky day.'

Ray crosses the road and takes her arm. He hugs her tightly, holding her tangled hair as he kisses her cheek.

'I love you, Coco. More than I ever said.'

'I know.' She is rigid in his embrace. Too thin, her arms and back like stretched cables. He wonders if life will ever let her be soft again. 'I love you, Ray.'

When they release one another and turn into the sun, the truck has already come clear of the bend, not going fast but rumbling at a steady clip. Its single headlight blinks three times before shutting off. The windshield is grey in the dawn, shading the driver.

Ray begins to wave his tired arms overhead.

Colt just stands there, disbelieving or no longer able to care.

The truck slows. It's green, faded almost yellow, the color of key lime pie, and when it swerves just a little, sliding on the loose dirt, he catches a glimpse of the brown badge on its door. His eyes dart to the tiny wooden shack off in the weeds, a silver-orange glare of sunlight catching on the dusty window, obscuring that which hangs inside.

The driver downshifts and edges onto the shoulder. Colt is bent over, hands on her knees, mumbling a thank you to whoever has answered their prayers. Before Ray can find the words to express the trepidation that has crept into his belly and is now firing undiluted primal terror through his nerve-endings, it's too late.

The bad ranger is here.

Dust

'Run,' Ray tells his sister, before the truck comes to a halt. 'Go, now.'

She only stares at him in tired confusion. They have walked all night and buried their mother along the way. Plus a therapy session starring Simon.

'Something's wrong. I can't explain it right now, but you need to get away from here, Colt. Go, go!'

'Run?' she says. 'You think I can ... we need help. I ...'

The truck's engine turns off. The tracked up dust swirls and spirals low across the road, into the wild grass. The engine ticks and creaks. The nearest trees and bushes, the only places to hide, are several hundred feet across the field.

'He's bad,' Ray says in a low voice. The figure behind the windshield is visible now, and seems very small, as if a child has stolen the truck. 'I don't have the gun. I can stall him while you get a head start. Please, turn around, leave!'

She turns her back to the truck and looks at Ray with her sad blue eyes. 'Why are you doing this? This is our only chance. Please, Ray, don't make me run.'

'You have to,' Ray growls, waving at the truck, making a shoo-fly motion. Go away, go away, we don't need your help. 'There's something wrong with him. Always has been. Goddamn, you, Colt, listen to me—'

The truck door opens with a squeal of metal. Colt turns to have a look. Ray steps around her and stands between the truck and his sister, one hand behind him warning her to stay put.

A pair of worn-down moccasins settle on the gravel. Dirty white denim cuffs. A hand on the door, pulling himself up and out of the cab. The driver is as short as an elementary school child, four feet nine at most, but he is not a child. He is eighty years old if he is a day, and ninety is within the realm. He is not dressed like a ranger or any other kind of official. His grease-stained chambray shirt is half tucked and a plain red baseball cap rests on his narrow head. He looks like a man who spent more of his working years selling popcorn at a carnival than enforcing the law. He smiles at them cautiously, squinting one eye, even though the sun is behind him.

'Morn-*eeng*,' the fella says, his voice not nearly old enough for the body. 'How you folks farin' to-day?'

'Fine, thanks,' Ray says, studying the pockets and small hands for any sign of a gun or knife. But the old guy isn't holding anything.

'Didn't know anyone was campin' out here. Or maybe you having you-selves an early hike?'

'Our cars broke down,' Colt blurts, stepping out from behind Ray.

'Wait—' Ray begins.

289

'We need a ride, mister. We're in bad shape, stuck like you wouldn't believe.'

The little man tilts his chin up and pushes the bill of his hat back with two stubby fingers, sizing her up. 'That so?'

'Are you the ranger?' Ray says, unable to help himself.

The old man leans back as if stretching, then lightly stamps one foot. He glances back at the truck, the open door, the faded brown badge. He coughs once.

'Truck belonged to my brother. I's a metal fabricator for forty-three years, retired now.'

'Do you have a phone?' Ray is not ready to get in a truck with this seemingly harmless old coot, but they are desperate for some kind of help. Borrowing a phone would seem a good compromise.

'A phone?'

'A cell phone.' Ray reminds himself to smile, speak naturally. For reasons he can't pinpoint, revealing the level of panic and depth of their problems seems like a bad idea. 'Or maybe you could send someone back for us. We need to get in touch with a towing company.'

'The lake's closed to visitors,' the old man says, amiably enough. 'Ain't even worth fishin' anymore. You'd sooner pull a flounder outta here than a walleye.'

'Jesus Christ, we're stranded,' Colt says. 'Our family is stuck here. We lost—'

'Colt, stop,' Ray says.

'You're lost?' the old man says, looking from Ray to Colt, as if he's not sure who's in charge.

'We're not lost,' Ray says. 'Our phones aren't working. Our car battery went dead. All we need is one phone call.'

Colt tugs on his sleeve before addressing the man directly. 'For God's sake, Ray, ask him for a ride. Please, sir. My mother needs a hospital.'

Hospital? Was that intentional or is she slipping?

The old man passes the cuff of his shirt under his nose. 'You can use my phone, sure enough.' He walks back to the truck, in no hurry. Or too old to hurry. He leans into the cab and rummages between the seats.

'What's your problem?' Colt says under her breath.

'This was too convenient, him showing up out of the blue. What's he doing out here? Retired but not fishing?'

'What choice do we have?'

The old man comes forward, a thick black cell phone in his left hand. The phone is at least five years out of date. Looks more like a walkie-talkie than a smartphone.

'Reception out here ain't worth a sow's ear,' he says. 'Had to go back to my old Qualcomm. Made in America. Transistors in them new Chinaman phones don't cut the mustard.' When he is close enough for Ray to shake his hand, he offers up the phone. 'Help y'self.'

Ray hesitates, but what else is there to do? He takes the phone, very much doubting it was made in America and that it will work any better than their phones did as soon as they arrived.

The man lowers his arm and pats his hand over his white jeans. Not really white, though. They used to be blue, Ray notices, but have been washed a thousand times, or never, merely bleached by the sun. And then – who's he supposed to call?

'What's the nearest repair shop?' he asks. 'Anybody who can send a wrecker.'

The old man nods. 'Nine-one-one.'

'Emergency,' Ray says. How does the old man know they've had one?

'No towing company's gonna come out here. I don't know the number for the local police station. But give dispatch a call and they'll send someone for you.'

An obvious and logical solution, but something about the way the old man said nine-one-one is not sitting right with Ray. He holds the phone, feeling the old man's low eyes press into him.

'Ray, come on!' Colt says. 'What's the hang-up?'

'No, no! Don't hang up,' the old man says, using his red cap to scratch his nearly bald head. 'If you get through to mission control, do what you gotta do quick or else you might lose all contact. Air waves out here is slippery.'

Ray frowns at the phone. The outdated gray screen shows 87 per cent battery life and four bars of reception. He punches 9-1-1 and TALK. He puts the phone to his ear and absently wipes his hand on his shirt. The phone is not ringing. There is a single click, then more flatline.

The old man looks away, off toward the lake.

Colt watches Ray with prayers in her eyes.

The phone still isn't ringing. Ray pulls it away from his ear and looks at the screen. It shows the same things as before, plus the word CONNECTING ...

Alongside the phone, Ray's thumb is black, as if he just pressed it to an ink pad. He opens the rest of his fingers and sees they are smudged in the same way. He looks down at his shirt, where he absently wiped his hand a moment ago, and sees more black ink. Grease? But when he switches the phone from his right hand to the left and rubs his fingers together, the black stuff feels grainy, silty like fine sand, or ash. The phone seems to hover ten feet away, as if Ray's arm has grown four times its normal length.

'Ray?' Colt's voice is remote, thick.

He turns, but she is not by his side. He turns the other way, and she is there, hands clasped at the waist of her denim shorts in nervous anticipation. Her face is contorted, almost scowling. Her hair seems to glow with sun, the thin strands dancing as if charged with static. Ray's right ear and cheek are tingling, not unlike the sensation that follows a Novocaine shot at the dentist's. His fingertips are tingling as well.

'My hanths,' he says. 'Some-fing . . . –un! R-run!'

'What's wrong?' Colt says, walking toward him.

The old man shifts his gaze from the lake and returns. His left hand is out again, palm up, as if to say, hand me that stupid phone, I'll show you how to do it. Two very long steps later he is staring into his own hand with the fascination of a child who has found his first ladybug. The soft brown moccasins make *shush-shush-shush* sounds on the road and to Ray's tingling ears they sound like rattlesnakes.

'Col-ut, un, oh God, rrrruuuuuhhhhh,' Ray tries to scream but produces less than a whisper. His legs feel stuffed with feathers, and the fields and the truck and the sky are turning, wheeling around him.

The old man steps to her, raising his open hand, and blows.

Black silt blooms, and a terribly drawn out moment later Colt recoils, gasping in surprise, *inhaling deep*. She slips from Ray's field of view, coughing violently.

The old man turns to Ray in a blurred ballet. His hand is still up, the palm open, and Ray has time to see the small thumb, bent in a perfect, knuckleless arc, curled back on itself as if it is nothing but nail and bone, the pink flesh hardened to a little chapped horn. The thumb-horn lengthens, becomes the focus of everything, and something pointy grazes Ray's cheek. The scratch is like the cold burn of dry ice. Then the old man retreats with his phone, the thumb encircling it like a worm.

Ray feels weightless, even after his ass lands on the road and his teeth crack together. The sky is wide open blue and shimmering. Ray tries to sit up but can't, can't move, can't feel anything, can't talk, can hardly breathe.

The truck door creaks open once more.

Ray half rolls, half falls to his side, his numb ear and cheek pressing into the gravel. Moving on a tilting plane, Colt staggers across the grass, swerving and stumbling forward, and she seems acres away, though even in his poisoned state Ray knows she is only a dozen steps off the road.

The old man walks after her patiently, something new in his hand, not the phone.

It is thin and silver, gleaming in the sun.

Ray's vision turns fuzzy, blurred as if by tears, then hazy red. He is blind with his eyes open. There is only pink-red light. His numb face. The smell of the dust and crushed gravel. And the warbling siren sounds of his sister's screams.

He tries to sit up and maybe he succeeds, but he no longer knows whether his body is responding to his commands. The numbness has spread to his neck, arms, into his chest. He wonders if his heart is slowing or if it has already stopped.

Before he loses consciousness, Ray registers the quiet fallen around them. His sister is not screaming anymore.

The Shovel

Colette stands in the driveway, wearing her favorite outfit of this summer – pink terry shorts, a blue military tank top, her red suede Kangaroos with pink laces. Her blonde hair is held back in a tail by a poofy rainbow scrunch, the one she sometimes wears as a bracelet. She is dribbling their red, white and blue basketball, and then holding it before her chest. Concentrating, waving the ball aloft. It rolls over the summer morning and descends through the net with a pleasing snap.

'*Yes*,' she whispers to herself before turning to look at him.

Ray is standing at the mouth of the garage, just inside the open door, banished, forbidden to cross the line into the driveway. The Bronco is parked behind Colt, the camper hitched to it. The camper's door is open, a small stepladder before it. Ray can't see inside. It is all shadow, another door, this one black. But he can hear Dad banging around in there, cursing, stowing the last of the gear. It is almost ten in the morning. They were supposed to be on the road an hour ago, but Mom's not ready. She's still in the house, fussing with her clothes, double-checking the grocery bags. Ray was hovering, offering to help, but she told him to go play outside, he was driving her nuts. It is as if they all despise him now.

'Don't look at me,' Colt says. 'It wasn't my decision.'

Ray can feel his lips trembling but he doesn't want to cry. If he starts now, his father will come out of the camper and yell at both of them.

Leonard is missing. Ray hasn't seen him all morning, and they won't tell him where his big brother is. If he even came home last night.

'Do you wanna play horse?' Colt says, trotting to retrieve the basketball from the gravel strip along the driveway.

'I wanna come with you,' Ray says. 'You can't leave me here by myself.'

'It's only a week. It's not like I wanna go either.'

She twirls away and delivers a layup. The ball thuds off the backboard and circles the rim once ... and slips off. No score.

'I can't stay here alone. I'm too young.'

'You hate the lake anyway,' she says, catching the ball on its third bounce.

'No, I don't!'

She dribbles idly, walking toward him. 'I left you some Girl Scout cookies in the freezer.'

The thought of eating the cookies alone in the house while they are playing on the beach does it. Can't hold back any longer. The tears flow.

Inside the camper, something bangs loudly. As if a tool-box just fell off the top bunk and spilled on the floor. 'Sonofabitch,' his father growls.

Colt dribbles faster, passing the ball from ground to hand to ground and between her legs with amazing skill. She is staring at him as she dribbles, approaching him with a playful snarl. She is tall for an eleven-year-old. She could pass for thirteen, Mom says, usually with a frown.

Wham wham wham goes the basketball.

She is sweating along her upper lip and near her hair. Her face is flushed, her cheeks glowing.

'You're safer here,' she says, snatching the ball with both hands. She stuffs it into his belly. Ray clutches it, unable to look up at her. 'Bad things always happen out there, you know. If I were you, I'd count my lucky charms.'

Ray sniffs. 'Don't go. Please.'

'Have to.'

'No.'

'Yep.'

'What am I supposed to do without you?'

Colt pries the rainbow band from her hair. 'I'll bring you a turtle, how about? You can keep him under your bed.'

Ray stifles another sob.

'You have to be the strong one now,' she says. She leans in to kiss him on the cheek and her breath smells like orange gum. 'Time to wake up.'

'What?'

'You heard me.' She snatches the ball, walking back on her heels. Staring at him in angry desperation. She mouths the words this time.

WAKE UP.

Inside the camper, a cabinet door slams.

'Colette!' Dad shouts. 'Hurry up, chicken legs. We're gettin' on the road!'

'Colt, don't go in there,' Rays says.

Colette looks to the camper, then at Ray. 'Sorry, buddy. Time's up.'

'Don't, please ...'

'Wake up. Wake up, Ray.' It becomes a song. 'Wake up, little Raymond, wake up. Wake up. Come on, Ray, time to wake up ...'

He can still hear her words as she throws the ball out into the street and skips across the driveway, up into the camper. Into the darkness.

The camper door slams behind her.

No one touched it.

The Bronco's engine starts. The brake lights glow, then fade. The Bronco eases from the driveway, and he knows they are in there, Mom and Leonard were hiding, and now they have Colt too, and his father is in the camper and someone else is driving. Someone else is taking them back to Blundstone Lake this year and Ray is alone, his corduroy shorts are turning hot and wet as the urine soaks through, and his family are locked in the camper with it, the thing driving them off to Nebraska, gaining speed up the cul de sac. And he can hear her voice, long after the loaded mobile home has disappeared around the corner.

Wake up wake up wake up wake up wake ...

Flesh-red-pink, a wall of it. Then a crack of brightness, white as a star.

A slit of blue.

Blackness again.

A rumbling vibration under him, whistling wind above. The clank of metal on metal. Brighter, darker, brighter. Light again, pain in his eyeballs, stabbing his brain. His head throbs. His tongue is leather, tingling.

Wake up.

He does.

Colt is staring at him, eyes wide, bloodshot. They are on their sides, as if facing each other in bed. But the bed is hard, bouncing under them, its wall behind her a short metal ledge rusted and faded to the color of key lime pie.

Colt's hair is streaked with red. Her face is wet, dirty, with flecks of red. Snot trails from her nose like a winter cold. She closes her eyes, nodding off, and then they snap open again.

'Wake up,' she says, softly.

The groaning noises increase, then shift into a smoother droning hum. The wind pushes her hair around. The ride is rough. They bounce, slide, and sometimes swerve. It's like a sleigh ride in summer.

He remembers walking with her. Talking about Simon. Ray can't picture him but the name conjures a nebbish man in a suit, square glasses framing beady eyes. The one who hurt her. Did this to them. Is driving the truck? What did Simon do this time?

Colt's eyes water and roll inside their sockets.

He looks down, past her sweating chest inside the V of her ruined shirt. There are blotches of blood everywhere. The shirt is torn, the blood around the holes darker, thicker. Spreading as he watches, soaking her shorts,

300

filling the metal grooves they lie upon and sliding like rain in a gutter.

'Colt!'

She hears him this time. 'Didn't finish,' she says, groggy but just loud enough.

'What?'

She swallows, forcing herself to stay awake. 'Therapy.'

He can't remember, has no idea what she's talking about.

'S'okay now,' she says in a hopeful rush. 'Made him pay. I got him, so doe ... don't think I'm weak.'

Ray struggles to sit up but his arms are numb. His face is still tingling. He wants to kill Simon. I have to kill him, he thinks. And I will.

'Got him,' she says again, almost smiling.

'Who's driving?'

'S-S-S-simon. Before we left. Five ... days ago,' she manages. 'For what he ... did.'

Then he sees it in her eyes, which are cold and satisfied and deadly. She killed him. Killed her husband for hurting her that way. This is what she wanted to tell him all along. She needed to confess.

'Good girl.' Ray struggles to sit up and his legs respond. He pushes an elbow against the hard bed of the truck.

'Wait—' Her eyes widen in alarm.

He hesitates. Doesn't have the strength yet anyway but wants to try. He has to hurry. Looks down again. She's bleeding like a dressed deer.

'Shovel,' she says, eyes darting down.

Ray cranes his neck. Sees a wooden handle in the truck

301

bed, between her ankles. Other tools near the tailgate. A tangle of rope. A white bucket. The truck bounces again and it all clarifies. They are in the ranger's truck, moving down the beach. The wind flows over them and Ray can feel the sand beneath the tires, giving way, allowing them to slide.

Sand. Black powder. The silty kind he saw in the cove with Megan, like ash. Something bad in the lake. The old man's hand. The cloud of black powder. Black water. Megan's family. Goat-horn thumb. Fucking demon shit.

'Hold on,' he says.

Colt closes her eyes and shudders. 'S-s-sorry.'

'It's okay.'

'G-g-g-oing to hell. Like Len.'

'No. Don't think that. Never.'

'P-p-p-romise.'

'I promise. Stay with me, Colt.' Ray's heart is thrumming. He has a mission now. Time is everything. He rolls onto his back. His legs are not as numb. Only his right arm and hand, but those are waking up too. He can move. He will force himself to stand, before this fucker arrives at whatever graveyard he has in mind.

'Sierra,' she says, eyes lowering with sleep.

'Colt! Stay with me!'

Her eyes open, much slower than before. 'Take ... good care your daughter.'

She's letting go. No. 'Colt. She needs you! Stay here for Sierra!'

She doesn't open her eyes this time. Her cheeks appear to sink in, her jaw shifts to one side, lips parting.

302

Numbness or not, it has to be now.

Ray sits up with a grunt and his head swims with motion. The lake is flying by on one side, the flat plane of beach on the other. The truck is going at least forty miles per hour and it feels like a hundred. If Simon looks in the rear-view ...

Clawing at his sister for leverage, Ray pulls himself forward, clenching her blood-soaked shorts, her hips, twisting and turning on his side. Almost. The wooden handle is there, below her knees. He grabs her thigh and heaves, until he is sideways in the truck bed. If this weight hurts her, all this clawing and bouncing, she gives no sign.

He reaches, fingers curling over the wooden handle. There.

Slips.

He plows forward, fingers scraping the handle – got it.

He looks back, up at her. Her eyes are closed. The truck bounces over another sand ridge and her head knocks against the bed. She doesn't seem to notice.

'Colt,' he hisses. 'Colt, wake up!' Loud as he can without shouting. 'Colette!'

She doesn't move.

She's going to die here. Maybe already did.

Motherfucker.

Ray pulls the shovel up, hand over hand, until he has the metal base in his left hand. His right grips the handle at the middle but he can't feel it. Squeeze, he orders, willing his arms and fingers to do what they were made to do.

Hold. Fight. Kill.

Ray slams his knuckles into the truck bed once, twice,

a third time, the pain welcome, bringing his hands back to life. He pushes himself up. Sways, gets his knees under him, inching along until he is facing the cab of the truck. Through its dusty window, the back of a small head. Red cap. A target.

You ready, Simon?

Ray looks down at Colt. One of her teeth is streaked with blood. Her face is so pale. We got him, honey. Hold on.

The truck's engine peaks, then quiets. They are almost coasting but still moving fast. The wind makes his eyes water.

The rear-view mirror. A small wrinkled hand on it, adjusting.

Their eyes lock into each other's, and the truck swerves right. Ray lurches to the left, pushing off the sidewall with his good hand. He balances, inches forward on his knees, planting his weight as best he can.

He raises the shovel.

The truck swerves left and the force sends him to his weak side. He throws the shovel blade out, over Colt's chest, aiming for the sidewall to stop him from vaulting out. The metal blade screams against the faded green wall, slips, sticks to the floor. Ray levers himself upright, resetting his grip.

Last chance. Won't be that lucky again.

The truck speeds up, engine roaring. Ahead, a thick green bush rushes toward them and goes under the front end. The truck bounces hard, Ray's knees leave the bed and come down with twin bolts of reverberating pain. His anger soars, he is shouting incoherently.

Ray spins the handle like a baton and drives the shaft forward with all he's got, slamming the blade through the rear window. The shovel meets no resistance, or none he can detect, as if the man were made of air and the shovel has taken flight, passing through the cab and windshield right on over the hood.

The truck swerves suicidally to the left, the tires dig and shudder against the beach and a wall of sand rises up, curling over his head. Shards of glass tumble past, nicking his face and ears. The truck bed bucks like a rodeo bull and Ray becomes weightless, soaring. A glimpse of sand, whistling sky, sand, sky, brown-green water, and sky once more.

He comes down on his shoulder and hips in less than three inches of water and rolls six or seven times, catching lake and wet sand across the face like shotgun pellets. Closes his eyes as the sand bar pounds him, slamming his knees and back and the back of his head before sucking him face down into the muck.

He can't breathe. All the air has been stolen from him in the roll. His diaphragm hurts more than any other part of his body. He raises his mouth from the water and crawls, mouth opening and closing in silent, worthless pleas for oxygen. His brain is stuck and his body animates itself, crabbing forward, limbs twitching with their own expectations of survival, leading him one way and then another like a dog whose tail has been chopped off. His hands slip in the wet sand and he falls forward, collapsing onto his chest. The jolt feels like a crowbar behind his heart and something as heavy and hard as a manhole cover pops free.

Ray sucks air, groaning monstrously and flopping onto his back, breathing, breathing, breathing as his vision darkens and then gradually comes back into focus. He feels the lake's reluctance, squeezing, pulling at his lungs. But not now, not yet. He is trembling all over but still breathing, and that is enough.

He pushes himself to his knees, swaying, and looks across the beach. His head pounds magnificently. His vision blurs and sharpens as if his eyes have not stopped shaking. Another hundred feet or more across the sand, the truck is upside down, the tail raised, white smoke funneling from the front end.

There is no sign of Colette or the driver. What was he going to do? Dig a hole with his shovel and bury us? Where was he going? We could be miles away from camp, Ray realizes. No idea how long I was unconscious, how long he was driving. Could be on the other side of the lake.

The truck. Start there. The battered green hunk looks like a toy some kid got bored with and tossed aside in his sandbox. Ray gets his feet under him and the chorus of pain throughout his body reminds him he is lucky to be alive. The lake saved him for another day. He limps off toward the wreckage.

Someone has to confirm what he already knows.

Survivor

No matter how he imagines the scenario, Ray can't reconcile how he wound up in the water while the rest of the mess found its way most of a city block further down the beach. The steaming, twisted, roof-flattened truck indicates several barrel rolls prior to slamming down in its final destructive path. The laws of physics – the same ones that keep children and their parents glued to the walls of a spinning amusement park ride – may have helped the truck hold her fast to its tumbling steel bed for the long five or six seconds that followed Ray's splashdown.

It's possible, he has to admit. Just as it is possible she's not dead yet, the impact shocked her awake, and adrenaline-wired nerves allowed her to crawl away, delirious with notions of escape.

But he hopes not. He hopes it's already too late. He hopes she died before he took the shovel in hand and with it made his gamble.

Of course it does not matter now.

Colette Mercer, mother of Sierra, slayer of Simon, is dead. That is the word he puts to it in his mind now, standing over her broken form. Not at rest, or at peace (though, truth be told, she does look more peaceful than he could have imagined, the way her arm lies over her belly, her chin tilted up, her eyes closed to the sun, her expression neither mangled nor frozen in a final portrait of distress).

Leonard is dead. Mom is dead. And now Colette is dead with them.

Gone. Forever.

Warren and Megan and Sierra probably aren't doing so hot either.

But Ray is here. Ray is a survivor! And that seems almost funny now, as if the lake is saving him for something special. Tailoring his vacation to suit his place in the fam—

Pay attention! some voice thunders down, or wells up from inside him. Sounds like Warren, or Gaspar, or some evil hybrid of the two veterans. Ray stops, realizes he has been walking in circles, staggering a groove into the sand, losing his grip on the day, his place in it. He's not crying, no no. Only breathing raggedly, rubbing the sand from the stinging patches of road burn (beach burn?) along his arms and knees. *See, Colt? You were right. I'm the hard one. I shed no tears for any of you. I can't. I don't have it in me anymore. I am here because I am here.*

It's what one does.

But he has to do something else now. Can't leave her like this. The thought of picking her up and carrying her back to camp is ludicrous. Ray is not sure he has the strength to walk another hundred yards, let alone carry her. Where is camp? The sun is higher, but not at its zenith. It's still morning. He believes he is still on the north side of the lake, the same side they are camped on, but he can't be sure.

He turns, mouth opening, on the verge of asking Colt what she thinks they should do. And then he sees his sister again.

Colette. Her face sallow, a little blood on her lower lip. Her hair knotted. Her clothes are dirty, and soaked through with blood. The sand alongside her torso is dark with it, sucking her dry, it seems. The stab wounds are thin but deep.

Why her first? Why not me? Was he saving me? Maybe it was because she ran away. He lost control, needed to subdue her and in the process wound up sticking the blade in too deep. Like Simon. He tried to subdue her, and failed. Colt made him pay for his violence. Ray knew Simon was dead, poisoned in his sleep, shot in an alley in the city, thrown in front of a subway train, but dead somewhere. And for what? So that she could flee the past, her awful life, and spend a relaxing weekend with her family, catching up on old times? Was this her destiny, the way the lake wanted it? Last night around the campfire, his family members sounded insane. Today . . .

Behind him, the cry of a rusted hinge.

Ray turns and studies the overturned ranger truck. The passenger door is open. Was it before? He can't remember. Was it . . . no. The driver is probably not alive, let alone in any kind of condition to crawl from the truck. Eighty years old, at least, small and brittle as a baby bird. No way.

But.

309

Did Ray actually hit him with the shovel? Was aiming for the back of his skull, the neck as a second option. The window went with a beautiful explosion, but maybe only startled him, he saw it coming, ducked, and then swerved, lost control. The shovel felt thrown, not planted, passing through the cab like a sword in one of those magic tricks, missing the lady in the box altogether.

It is the ranger station all over again. He has to go look, because he has to know. But this wasn't a dummy, some prank or warning about the bad ranger bogeyman. This was *the* bad ranger, a sick man, a hunter. If not the tall man I remember from childhood, his brother, his cousin, some other sick fuck from the same bloodline.

Those thumbs. Genetic connection. Or mutation.

De-evolution.

Ray hobbles away from his sister, relieved to have something to distract him from the reality of her death and the decision of what to do with her. He shuffles along, the numbness from the man's poison dust gone now, replaced by pain, whole-body pain. He is too broken to experience much fear. The little old man will be dead. Or injured badly enough to no longer pose a threat. If the latter, Ray intends to kill him. Finish him without mercy or deliberation. He is too tired for the prolonged theatrics vengeance would demand.

He walks a little faster, moving wide of the open passenger door. He takes a final survey of the beach, but there is no one out here and no place to hide. The bastard is either inside the cab of the truck, under the truck bed, or vanished like the steam that is no longer hissing from the ruptured radiator. In the morning heat there is the smell of gasoline fumes and something burned, like melted rubber or charred upholstery, but Ray sees no sign of fire. He forces himself to stay alert. Takes half a dozen deep breaths and bends to one knee to peer into the cab.

The driver is out of his seat, torso draped over the dash, fastened to the steering wheel. Legs bunched above his upper body, suspended like an astronaut. His face is turned away, and Ray wonders if, when he gets to the other side, he will be able to see the tip of the shovel blade protruding from the man's mouth. It's buried that deep, the wooden handle extending from the back of the man's head, through the smashed back of the cab where the window used to be, like a roasting skewer.

Ray walks around the front end. A weathered red baseball cap sits in the sand. The driver's door is ajar. Ray attempts to open it, but portions of the cab's frame are bent around it, the top edge lodged in beach. The window was either rolled down or blew out in the crash, and in any case, kneeling again, Ray can see the ranger's face just fine from here.

The nose and upper teeth have popped free, the rest of the mouth and jaw a smear of bone and yellow tissue and blood. Much of the side and back of the skull are split open, a hand-sized patch of glistening brain visible between the purple, mouth-shaped wound. The lower eye is shut, the brow dented inward, while the other eye is aimed out the window as if checking the side mirror for traffic.

The eye is bulging, the lid leaking fluid that is closer to oil than blood. The viscous substance is either deep, deep red or black, and layers of it have spilled and begun to dry

311

to form small waves on what is left of the man's forehead, over the bald pate. Ray is not a doctor or a forensic specialist, but he is pretty sure blood doesn't leak or dry this way. Or turn black as it leaves the body.

Ray doubts that his first and only strike with the shovel could have wrought such damage. He must have punctured the skull enough to lodge the shovel into the head, and then the careening truck and the indifferent beach did the rest. The way the old man has been thrown forward into the dash, combined with the velocity of the speed into a suddenly halted object.

It is with only a small measure of nausea that Ray realizes he needs the shovel. True, he could dig the hole with his hands. The sand is soft enough, and in some way that would seem a more appropriate form of burial. But he doesn't have time or physical stamina on his side, and the shovel is his best, perhaps only means of sending Colette off with dignity.

Ray is gathering his courage to reach in and withdraw the shovel when the top layer of sludge slips from the ranger's eye like a fallen pirate patch, onto the truck's roof liner. The bulging but otherwise undamaged eyeball lurking behind it nerve-twitches to one side, then up, pinning him with its awful gaze.

Ray can't leap but takes two quick steps back, all his aches and pains flushed away in a literal blink as his adrenal glands prove they're not empty. He can almost see the man moving, the arms flying into action, shoving its carcass off the steering wheel and then dragging itself from the wreck like a startled crab.

312

But none of that happens. The body is still stuck. Not breathing.

Ray steps closer, bending again, in hopes he was mistaken about the eye, but no. It's still twitching, this way then that, locking on some new detail for a couple seconds before moving on to another. What does it see? What else is there to see? Sand. But it's not interested in sand. It's looking for Ray, the man who did this to him.

'Jesus! Fuck no! Stop!' he shouts at the grotesque dead man. Except he's not really talking to the man now. Only to the eye, whatever unholy life gleams within its elderly nerves. 'Stop! Stop!' he screams.

Ray can't bear looking at it. And he doesn't dare turn his back on it. Part of the mystery is here, in the glaring eyeball. The blackness. It's not blood, not real blood. It's from the lake. Something vile and unnatural is in this man, this ranger, this eighty-five year old lunatic who blew black powder into their faces and – how about this! – found the strength to load them into his truck.

This is ugly business, Gaspar, my dear old guidance counselor. Did you and the old man ever see one of these back in the day? When you were blitzed on Coors and that cheap seventies weed, dancing on the sand bar after the kids went to sleep? You two ever see this shit in 'Nam, big guy? Ever see this black goo leaking out of the Cong's eyes, before or after you two hardasses celebrated another ambush with that pure China white? Cause this is something from another level, a nasty –

'Die! Die!' Ray shouts in idiotic repulsion. 'Fucking die!'

The eye blinks, lid and all. Blinks once quickly, and

313

then again very slowly, as if trying to communicate. Impart a final message. Morse code for help or some whacko-hypno shit trying to lull him into mounting a rescue before it slashes him with a knife or one of those demon claws.

Blink-blink————blink——blink-blink————BLINK!

And that is all Ray can handle this morning. He has reached the end of many things, not least of all his patience.

Ray backs along the side of the truck, ducks under the overturned bed and reaches in to grab the shovel handle. He has to lie down on his side in order to brace himself and get a good grip, at which point he channels his anger and yanks hard. The shovel comes away easily, and maybe that is a relief to the Bad Ranger but it is not to Ray.

Hop-stepping back to the window, Ray rears back, teeth bared, and this time the truck isn't moving. The worst has already happened. They crashed, and Colt is dead, and so the target becomes unmissable.

Especially given that Ray has more than one chance to get it right.

Quite a bit more, as it turns out.

A while later, he would not be able to say how much, Ray stands navel-deep in the lake. He is sun-scorched and steaming, the lake shockingly, beautifully cold around his aching lower back, tightening his crotch, soothing his shivering rage.

He winds up three times, fist tight around the old man's wadded chambray work shirt, and on the fourth lets go.

The wind opens the shirt like a sail but the severed and crumbled head continues its flight, neck tendons and the stub of spine flashing white in rotation. Just as rocks never seem to do when hurled over a large body of water, the ranger-head does not travel as far as he had hoped, and splashes down with about as much fanfare as their old red anchor used to make.

Ray sways, toes sinking into the peanut butter-soft sand, and allows the water to rise over his nipples, his neck, up to his nostrils. He stops there, sitting with his crocodile eyes level to the surface, waiting for the lake to bring his temperature down.

In the glove box is a small box of Diamond matches, under a pile of AAA roadmaps and a canister of electrical fuses. Ray uses the State of Nebraska 1966 trifold to make another kind of fuse, stuffing it into the fill tube. He has no idea if there is enough left in the tank to do the job, but it's worth a try.

He counts his steps as he retreats, one hand shielding his face, and when he reaches eighty-one the truck bed lifts, a beautiful *whump* flourishes over the beach and a mighty bang follows. The truck bed spins away from the cab before all the other parts and the rest of the ranger inside are consumed in a rolling ball of flame, and this is the most fun Ray has had since their third trip to Blundstone, when his father taught him how to throw ladyfingers at the plastic infantrymen they'd set into the sand cliff face, playing war.

*

315

When the joyous pyrotechnics smoulder down to a mere boiling funnel of black smoke, Ray returns to his sister in repose, the washed shovel in hand. Steps away from her body he is greeted by yet another, but entirely new, sort of awful.

Colt is covered in sand. Not buried. She is supine on the beach, as he left her, only now there is no portion of her exposed to the sun. Her clothes are covered, her entire form veiled in a skin of fine beige sand, a color that nearly matches her hair, before the sand got that too.

Ray screams for the tenth or twelfth time today and falls down at her side, frantically dusting her off. The sand isn't moving except when he brushes at it, yet he can't shake the feeling it has a mind of its own. The fucking sand is alive. Swallowing her. It is an obscenity and one he cannot escape, for the beach is all around them, miles of it, billions of tons and layers, and how deep does it go? Where does it end? Right now it is something other than sand. It is a cancer of the earth. The cells are eating her. No matter how carefully he plucks the grains from her lashes or how hard he blows air across her lips, he cannot get rid of it. He cannot make her clean.

It is sand and, out here at Blundstone, there is always more.

He concentrates on cleaning her face, leaning in so close he can see it in the pores of her nose, between her brows, the dry cracks in her chapped lips. The sand is lodged deep, and it's too late, the sand is caked on his hands, under his nails, stuck in the whorls of his fingerprints, so that every effort he makes, for every grain he brushes from the groove of her ear or age line in her neck, he only adds another to take its place.

He plows his hands under her back and thighs, rising, stealing his sister away from this ungodly sand. He hurries across the beach, losing one sneaker, tripping, nearly dumping her to the right, wobbling the two of them forward in six desperate steps that leave him breathless and on the verge of becoming a failed pallbearer. But he finds his balance and goes forth in shorter, cautious steps.

'I got you, baby girl, I got everything,' he says, smiling down at – he sees her face clearly and stops. Ray lowers her to the ground and sits back, releasing her.

'Oooooooh, no. No, baby . . . I'm sorry . . .'

She is not the woman who bled to death in the truck bed, whispering beside him. She is not the woman who sat in the morning sun less than twenty-four hours ago, holding her daughter in her lap while they argued like spoiled children over brunch. She is not the post-partum-depressed mother playing at high society in New York, suffering the greatest of brutalities at the hands of the man who vowed to love and protect her above all others.

She is only his sister, Colt. Eleven or twelve and coppered by the sun, her blonde hair radiant even when wet, her green one-piece swimsuit still damp from her swim. She is the way he always preferred to remember her, diving into the magic they discovered that fateful day, as he watched and envied her from the safety of the camper bunk. Laughing and splashing and cavorting in the waves, as if she knew there was nothing to fear. As if she had seen the future in a bolt of lightning, and understood that no

317

matter how the dark clouds teemed, how wickedly the wind raced across the lake, the real storm would never catch her.

But where?
   There is nowhere else. This is the world now.
   No place for her but here.
   With Mom.

He buries his smaller, lovelier, time-capsule-preserved big sister close to the water, using his hands to dig and then later fill the hole. He marks the grave with the last thing he can do without, all he can find, his worn-out Paul Smith sneakers. Their weathered rainbow stripes are as much of a nod to flowers as the day will allow.

The sun takes its throne in the afternoon sky. The sand is a griddle and he sticks close to the lake, dunking himself every mile or two, and then walks on until his clothes have dried out and swims again. He makes his way up the beach on blistering bare feet, a pair of fresh legs, and a second wind he never expected to find so late in the game.
   This might be the right direction, but he has no way of knowing. The lake is a shrinking orb, distorted and sprouting new tentacles in a desperate battle to hang on. But in the end it is only a lake, not a sea. A drunken circle that will lead him home, eventually.
   He walks, and the sun burns, and he takes what he deserves.
   He is tempted to look back now and then; on those

occasions he hears her voice calling after him, her young voice begging him to come back and play a game of horse before it's time to go. But he does not indulge her. She had her chance and left him in the driveway. He increases his pace with each of her lonely appeals to his sympathy, hurrying toward the last of his family, hoping for a little more time with them before succumbing to that nameless thing that awaits them all.

Mimicry

Nearing a sand point that seems familiar, with its grassy median and a base populated by real trees, Ray strays from the beach and cuts through the field, which should be faster than walking all the way out to this point – not theirs – and back down the other side of the narrow finger. The sandy ground fills in with sharp grasses and dry weeds that tickle at his shins. A few hundred yards later he enters a low woods, the shade and cooler sand such a relief he nearly moans in gratitude.

He is forced to move slower in the foliage, avoiding brambles and deadfall debris that snag at his arms and clothes. He winds around patches of black mud, sheets of dead yellow leaves that taunt him with the prospect of sleep. He ducks under thick webbings of white silk, hammocks of gunk that might be insect habitat or tree fungus or something else he doesn't care to dwell on *(but now that I already am dwelling on it maybe it was the stuff that cocooned Megan's family and turned them into crabs and maybe I'm next, so keep ducking and try not to touch it).* The woods are fragrant with swamp rot and bitter shrubs that make him sneeze.

Subtle movement on the ground.

Ray pauses.

A few feet ahead and off to his right. Something small and brown and not much bigger than a rope of licorice inches forward, its sinuous movements the only thing setting off its beige spots from the rest of the leaves and ashen sand. The wildlife and insects have been such a non-factor on this trip, he has forgotten what it's like to stumble upon another creature in situ. He stops, scanning the area, missing the living portion of it several times before the pattern slides a few feet more, revealing itself. A welcome thrill runs up Ray's spine.

It's a snake, and not a dangerous one. A medium-sized Western Hognose, so named for its upturned snout, which looks remarkably like the bill of a duck or platypus, giving the reptile an exotic but cute aspect. Leonard and Ray used to catch terrestrial garter snakes out here, as well as bullsnakes, but the hognose were less common. For this reason, and because of their docility, they were always Ray's favorite find. He must have handled a dozen of them over the course of those five trips and never once was bitten.

Ray moves in slowly, stepping around it, avoiding sticks and leaves. He takes another step, and crouches, the hognose within arm's reach. He longs to pick it up, carry it with him back to camp like a good luck charm, but he hesitates. The hognose feeds on smaller amphibians and fish that can be easily ingested without the dramatic strangling or venom so many other snakes rely on. Its preferred meals are toads, and though he and Leonard and Colt used to catch those by the bucketful, the trusting creatures lining the beach at night like an audience, Ray hasn't seen a single toad on this trip. Which makes this encounter a weirdly affirming sign. Where there is predator there must be prey. Ray has no intention of removing the optimistic little guy from his blighted habitat.

He leans down for a closer view, setting one hand in the sand to keep his balance. The hognose reacts, twisting its neck and pushing its snout into the sand, digging back and forth as if trying to burrow under.

'Easy, fella,' Ray says, knowing the snake can't hear him. They don't have ears. 'No one's gonna hurt you.'

A shiver spirals through the hognose's muscled length and the tail curls into a question mark as the snake rolls onto its back. Its jaw, no wider than the pad of Ray's index finger, clicks open. The thin black tongue waves out, flickers once and is still. The snake is apparently dead.

It's a convincing act, Ray knows. Leonard showed him this years ago. Some snakes hiss and strike to ward off threats, or simply flee. Others, like the bullsnake, vibrate their tails in the loose cover to mimic the rattlesnake. The hognose plays dead. In a bit of theatrics – the open mouth, lolling tongue – the creature literally goes belly up. The species' abdominal scales happen to be a starkly contrasting mosaic of black and yellow tiles, a detail Leonard never explained but which Ray thinks now must have something to do with the black and yellow of death, rot, decomposition, poison. The belly is the hognose's last-ditch effort to throw up a warning sign.

Go ahead, do what you want with me, the little hognose

seems to be saying with this ruse. *You can't hurt me because I'm already dead. And why would you want me for a meal? I've spoiled in the sun. Eat me if you must, but you probably won't feel too good later. You might even suffer, dying the slow, inside-out death of a poisoning.*

Ray hooks a finger through the curled loop of tail, draping its limp form over his left palm. The snake clings to its own illusion a few seconds more, then reluctantly rolls over and begins to slither through Ray's fingers, tongue flicking, inspecting the giant that has called his bluff.

'See? I told you I wasn't going to hurt you.'

The snake flares the looser skin of its neck, but otherwise seems resigned to whatever fate Ray has in store for it. He wonders what it must be like, this simple existence. Reptiles don't have the higher brain functions, no real emotions. They know only the positive and negative of primitive drivers: hunger and thirst versus satiation, cold versus warm, dark versus light, shelter from exposure, movement or stillness, danger and the much rarer peace.

No one to help him forage or keep a home, pass the long nights in waiting for another dose of sun. He is surrounded by nature but perfectly isolated. Alone, without the curse of loneliness.

Bask, eat, grow, breed, rest, die.

Survival.

'It's not so bad,' Ray says. 'What do you think? Mind if I stay a while?'

The snake's tongue comes forth in a slow lash, wagging over the hair on his wrist. The tiny gold rings around its black pupils shift robotically and then freeze. The snake slithers higher, balancing on his arm, no more afraid of him than of a tree branch.

'Fuck 'em, right? Let 'em come for us.'

Ray sets the snake down in a divot of sand. He runs the pad of his thumb over its dorsal scales, feeling the tiny hard spine inside. Tickled or simply wanting to take advantage of the pardon before it can be rescinded, the hognose transits away in a blur, crossing a blanket of yellow leaves and then vanishing under a blackened comb of grass.

Ray listens to the quiet scrapes and scuffle of its locomotion until the woods fall silent, then rises and continues through the growth, looking for toads, hoping to spot at least one, even a dead one, to prove the little hognose has a fighting chance. If not for years to come, then at least one more meal.

He never does, though. The toads must have packed it in years ago. Loaded up the toad campers and toad SUVs, tossed all their toad beer cans in the weeds and taken one final pee in the sand before hopping off to a better, kinder place.

The trees thin. The grass breaks up. Ray is out in the sun once more. He is severely dehydrated, and his appetite has passed beyond hunger into a kind of euphoric hyper-arousal. He has not slept for more than seven of the past fifty hours. He no longer remembers what the point of the trip was, why any of them are here, or what he was hoping to take home when it is all over.

He's thirsty, that's all.

Very thirsty.

Airstream

Half asleep and staring at the sand moving below his feet, Ray comes upon the old green tent, nearly tripping over one of the staked ropes. The sudden presence of it, along with the knowledge that base camp is so close, renders his arrival a seemingly magical turn of events. He had forgotten he was looking for camp at all, but thank goodness someone dropped it here to remind him.

He yanks the Bronco door open and roots around in the cooler, coming up with the last of the water bottles. He guzzles the entire warm contents, hiccups once, and the liter of water spouts back into the air and is taken by the sand.

He tries again, this time with a hot can of pale ale, forcing himself to sip as he walks into the clearing. By the time the picnic table is in view, Ray feels drunk and lobs the remaining half of the beer into a bush. He finds a cooler under the trailer, digs out a new liter of shockingly cold water and plops down in a lawn chair. The beer seems to have calmed his roiling belly somewhat, and the sips of water stay down.

'Megan,' Ray tries to shout. 'Megan? Dad? Hey!'

No one answers.

Heaving himself up, Ray shuffles to the trailer. Inside, the darkness is so deep – after hours of sun but no sunglasses – Ray can't see past his groping hands.

'Sierra? Honey?'

No one answers.

Because they're already dead.

'I can't do that,' he says to the empty trailer. 'Not now.'

Pupils expanding, he opens the refrigerator and grabs the nearest container. It's heavy, filled with cubed cantaloupe. He sits on the bench seat and begins to stuff his sore mouth with cold sweet blocks of melon, chewing each piece once before swallowing. He can feel the chunks in his belly like ice cubes lobbed into a plastic cup.

He knows he should check the dome tent where he and Megan spent last night

… or was that two nights ago? Feels like they have been here a month, all summer … no more walking … the Leonard-thing is buried back there, where the sand is turning black. His hands shake almost violently from low-blood sugar. Hurry, hurry.

He bites his fingertip, hard, to keep from passing out.

Think.

He needs to get up, go look for them, find help, escape this barren beach and get away from this evil body of water forever, all of those and in whatever order is fastest – but right now he can barely chew food and string together a coherent thought. So, eat as much as possible without

326

throwing up. Drink another liter of water. Wait for the dizzyness to fade. Because until we have taken care of the machine, the machine will not take care of us. Or the free-and-a-half-year old.

Ray rummages in the icebox again. Zippered pouch of deli meat. About a pound and a half of it. Something from the gourmet side of the ham family? It is spicy and sweet on his tongue. He folds half a dozen slices into a ball and stuffs them into his mouth, chewing, swallowing. He takes another bottle of water from the fridge, fumbles the cap off and the bottle slips from his shaking hands. He bends for it, raises it, chugs more, and his head swims. He stood up too fast, his vision blurs. The trailer turns spotty black, spinning. No, no, wait—

Ray faints.

The world was black, then gray. His father was telling him about the curvature of the earth, reminding him to look across the surface of the lake as they drove in across the dam. The lake had turned to slate, flat as a table. For a moment there, Ray was sure he could see to the end.

'Ray?' Megan says. 'Are you awake? Are you hurt?'

Ray sits up, blinking, trying to remember where he is. Megan is staring at him with controlled concern. Sierra stands behind her, watching him as if he might bite. 'No, yeah, I'm good. We're good.'

Megan sits on the bed beside him, clutching the girl. 'I told you he'd come back, honey. See? Uncle Ray's all right. Aren't you?'

'Absolutely,' he says, for Sierra's benefit, though in another way it is true. He no longer feels hammered with sun fever and his headache is gone.

Then he remembers where he is, what has happened.

Remembers the dead.

'Where's Mommy?' Sierra asks. 'When's Mommy coming back?'

Ray swallows hard and looks to Megan, whose expression carries the same question but far less optimism about the answer.

'Mommy went with Fa-Fa, sweetie,' Ray tells his niece, which is terribly true. 'They had to go home a little early. But it's okay. Mommy said for me to tell you she loves you very much, and we'll be with her soon. We're all going home real soon.'

Sierra collapses in such a mess of broken-hearted tears, Ray can't help but wonder if she knows the real truth. And maybe she does. Maybe she senses the greater truth behind all of this, the way Ray himself has begun to, since leaving his shoes for a headstone. That growing sense that none of them are getting out of here alive.

Megan reads their obituaries in his eyes. The way he stares at his niece, no longer smiling. She leans into him and whispers. 'I'm sorry. So very sorry.'

'Where's my dad?' Ray whispers back.

'Up on the point,' Megan says, no longer whispering. Apparently this is common knowledge, suitable for all ages. 'He wanted to go look for you two, but I made him promise to stay within running distance. We compromised. He's keeping a lookout.'

'For me?'

'And for help,' Megan says. 'Or, uhm, anything else that might happen along.'

'He shouldn't be alone. It's almost dark again.'

'He took Leonard's rifle.'

The rifle. Guns. What Ray wouldn't trade now to have had the pistol out on the road this morning. That he forgot to take it when they set out to find Francine now seems an oversight akin to a priest forgetting to take his crucifix into an exorcism.

And yet, in another flash of retroactive premonition, Ray doubts the gun would have saved Colt. Even if he'd shot the ranger on arrival, something else would have gotten her. Or him instead. The lake is time, or maybe the sand is time, and this is one big hourglass they are trapped in. But whatever it is, time has all the power here. And you can't change time. Isn't that what his father said? What his mother knew? Time moves in one direction. Defeats all efforts to slow it down. Always wins.

'Ray? When did you get back?' Megan nudges him back to attention.

'I don't know. I think I fainted. Where were you two?'

'In the tent, our tent. Napping.'

He looks around the trailer, puzzled. 'This is safer than any tent.'

'I don't know about that,' Megan says, biting her lip.

'No white light in the tent,' Sierra adds with a sniff.

Megan moves to the door, bending a little to peer through the window.

We have to get out of here. Now. It's going to kill us all.

But he can't say such things out loud. Not in front of Sierra. Scaring her to death isn't going to solve anything. He needs to stay calm but get them moving. Now.

'So, what's the plan, Sierra?' he says, attempting to cheer her up. 'Should we go get Grandpa and blow this giant bathtub? Hop on the road and—'

'Be quiet,' Megan says. She is still staring out the window, then pressing her ear to the glass. 'Both of you, hush a minute.'

Sierra pouts, crawling across the floor to sit closer to Ray. He tousles her hair, watching Megan. For the love of God, what now? Sierra digs into one of the travel bags. She comes up with a doll, the plastic kind, and it's not wearing any clothes but there is sand in its hair. Little beige granules on its legs and arms. He wonders if Sierra was playing with it on the beach earlier and if it was her idea to bury it, or if something . . . inspired her.

Ray looks away from the doll to find Megan staring at him, her face a mask of alarm.

'What is it?'

'There's a woman nosing around the camp ground with a flashlight,' Megan whispers. 'I thought I heard someone on our way here, walking behind the trees. There's something not right about her . . . I could swear I've seen her before.'

'Some-ting not right 'bout her,' Sierra mocks. 'I seened her before.'

They both look at her, wondering where that came from, or was she just trying to be a part of the conversation? No. The girl looks worried again, though not scared,

330

not exactly. There is a stillness to her, an adult kind of weariness.

'What, sweetie?' Megan says, crouching beside Sierra. 'What about her?'

'I dint like her,' Sierra says matter-of-factly. 'She try scare Mommy away.'

'When was this?' Megan begins to stroke Sierra's hair. 'When did you and your Mommy see her?'

'At the store.' As if this were obvious, where else?

'What store?' Ray says. 'At the lake? On the way to the lake, or before that?'

Sierra nods. 'At the milkshakes. Mommy had chocolate and I ate strawberry.'

Store. Milkshakes.

'The truck stop,' Ray says, staring at Megan, his trepidation already turning to fury. He did not trust the woman's eyes in the diner, and after all that has happened since, even the memory of her raises his hackles. 'The waitress. Andie. The one we pissed off.'

'She tried to warn us,' Megan says. 'She told us to stay away.'

'Warned us at first,' he says. 'But after I cracked the joke about her moral outrage, remember that? "You know what, young man? You go right on ahead. Go on out to that lake and see what comes of it." Like she knew we would come. I think you need to trust your earlier instincts.'

'Maybe,' Megan says. 'But what if it's just some innocent camper? Our only chance for a ride home? We need help, Ray. We need a whole lot of help.'

Ray almost spits out the truth, but stops himself for

Sierra. How can he make her understand? 'Okay, look. We tried that earlier. The ride. The helpful ranger. He wasn't very nice. He tried to sell us a park permit and we refused and the fines turned out to be *extremely* expensive.' Ray casts his eyes to Sierra and back to Megan as if to add, *That's where Mommy went. Get it?*

Megan's eyes widen and she covers her mouth.

'The ranger is missing,' he adds. 'She could be looking for him. We can't trust anybody now. This woman outside, not a coincidence.'

Sierra keeps flapping the doll's head against her thigh, bored, agitated by their whispering inattention, and probably still angry that they let her mother leave without her. She opens her knees and begins to whack the Barbie's head against the trailer's solid wood floor. In any other situation, the sound would be innocuous. Now, in the contained silence, it seems to carry like a jack-hammer.

Megan seizes the doll and presses her other hand over Sierra's mouth.

Outside, a tree limb or something like it snaps with a sharp crack. A flashlight beam streaks across the window behind Ray's head. The orange cone pierces the interior, flattens on the wall and dances up to the ceiling, quivers, blinks out.

Ray wants to believe the woman found something else to shine her light on, has given up and moved on. But he knows better. The doll gave them away.

Can't get up and lock the door, not now. Can't fumble around for a weapon.

Can't risk even the slightest sound.

They sit on the floor, eyes darting, holding their breath.

Click.

The trailer door opens, and a few seconds later the light is on them.

Offering

Megan is closest to the door, and Ray would have to leap over Sierra and knock Megan out of the way to beat her to the front line of defense. To his surprise, Megan springs to her feet first, facing the bulky figure groping at the wall and wagging her flashlight around the galley.

'Hey! Excuse you!' Megan barks. 'What do you think you're doing?'

The woman rears back. 'Oh, jeez, you scared the heck out of me. I'm sorry. I didn't mean to—'

'You walked into someone else's camper uninvited. Where's the "didn't mean to" in that?'

'Calm down, now, honey,' Andie the waitress says. Ray can't see her face but he remembers her pear shape and the country twang. It's the coarse voice of a middle-aged woman still trying to sound like a diner flirt long after the necessary hormones have abandoned her. 'I saw them trucks vandalized and no one around, I got to worrying something happened to you all.'

'Get that light out of my face,' Megan says. 'And step outside, please. I'll be with you in a moment.'

Andie makes a *hmmppff* sound, pokes the beam down at Sierra, then clicks it off. 'That girl looks scared. Where's the rest of your party?'

'I'm asking you to step outside, and this is the last time I'm asking,' Megan says. 'Anything you care to discuss will happen out there, not here.'

'There goes your city manners for ya,' Andie grumbles, twisting and fussing to get turned around and back down the steps, drawing out her exit as long as possible. 'Only trying to help.'

Megan tromps over and slams the door.

'Wow,' Ray says. 'Nice work.'

Megan returns, exhaling. 'I think I can talk to her, now that some ground rules have been established.'

'No, no way,' Ray says. 'You stay with Sierra. I'll handle it.'

'But what if she's not part of it? How do we know?'

'I'll find a way. But we can't afford to be wrong again.'

Megan looks uneasy. 'Are you sure?'

'Any chance my dad's pistol is in here?'

'He wanted me to take it but I'd only end up hurting myself. Not sure where he left it. Sorry.'

'Okay. Lock the door behind me. Don't come out until I say it's safe. I don't care what kind of trouble you see or hear. If you don't hear me say *it's safe*, you don't open this door. Got it?'

Megan nods. 'But what does she want, Ray? Even if you're right?'

Ray scans the walls and shelves of his father's rolling Army surplus store, searching for a weapon that won't announce itself. Lots of tools, none large. Various nets holding utensils, pots and pans. He settles on a sleek bamboo fishing rod braced to the ceiling in a foam-rubber clip. The rod is light, thin, at least seven feet long, with a fly reel and no line. Something about its cork grip feels right in his hands, and they're out of time. It'll have to do.

Ray looks down at Sierra, reminding himself of the promise he made to Colt.

Your daughter now. Take care of her.

'I don't care what she wants. She can't have it. Be back in a minute.'

'Be careful,' Megan says.

Ray shuts the door and steps back into the sand.

Their visitor is sitting in one of the lawn chairs on the other side of the fire pit, facing the mouth of the clearing as if admiring a passing parade of geese. An old square-block flashlight is at her feet. The inverted lantern casts a murky yellow glow wide enough for Ray to see her peddle-pusher acid-washed jeans, and the University of Nebraska sweatshirt, the usual big red swapped out for blue with a sparkly pink NU logo and the adjacent breast cancer-awareness ribbon. It's Andie, all right. The same sourpuss hiding behind her jowly customer service mask, decked out for a night-time walk on the beach.

'I am so sorry about that,' she says, waving a hand at him. 'Hope you don't mind if I rest my pups a minute before turning back. It's not an easy hike down here for any cousin, but for a woman my age it's a double tax.'

'What can we do for you, Andie?' Ray says, idly casting

336

the rod toward the lake. It feels like a sword in his hand, which pleases him.

'Wasn't sure y'all recognized me, but I'm glad you did,' Andie says. 'That your girl in the camper? I didn't meet her when you stopped on your way in.'

'Those are indeed my girls.' He smiles wide, baring his teeth, and flicks the rod a few more times. 'So, what brings you out? On foot, no less.'

'Friend of the family went missing. Old partner set out around five this morn, shoulda been back by seven but whuzn't. His kids are worried. Maybe you seen him? Drives an old Game and Parks vehicle. I been by half a dozen camp grounds already and you're the only folks out here.'

'Huh,' Ray says. 'You call the police? I'm sure they could help.'

'That a no? You ain't seen him?'

Until this moment, Andie has been avoiding eye contact. Now she studies him with her brows bunched, mouth set in a pucker.

'Since we set up camp two days ago, we haven't seen another living soul,' Ray says in a lazy drawl. 'You weren't kidding. This lake is closed. She's drying up, and taking all the fun along with her.'

The big woman raises one foot to her knee, removes her sneaker and taps out the sand. 'I see. Where'd the rest of your party get off to, anyway?'

'What party would that be?'

'Said you was meeting family. There's two abandoned vehicles down there on the beach, two more here.'

Ray considers where this is going, why she is sitting down,

337

putting on the tired act like she would be content to wait all night. Maybe more of her people are on the way. Which means she knows something happened to her ranger partner, the two of them were tied together in whatever evil shit is going down out here, and the only end to this meeting is more violence. Giving the ranger the benefit of the doubt, letting Colt's hope prevail over his own instincts, sealed her fate. They can't afford to chew the cud with this cow tonight, not unless he wants to get Megan and Sierra killed too.

Time to shut this situation down.

'Oh, you know how it is. Bad things happen at the lake,' he says, still smiling, wagging the fly rod at waist level as he walks around the pit, his back turned to her. 'You warned us, but did we listen?'

'Oh? Had some trouble, had ya?'

Ray flicks the rod and turns, fencing forward until he is standing fewer than six feet from her kneecaps. He lowers the tip of the fly rod to her neck.

Andie stares up at him as if he has lost his mind.

And maybe he has. Because if he gets this wrong, he will never forgive himself.

'They're all dead,' Ray says, summoning his best impression of a hit man who isn't actually scared shitless. 'My party. Your ranger partner. I cut his head off with a shovel and burned his corpse in that old truck. Now empty your pockets before I whip one of your eyeballs out and eat it, you evil bitch.'

Andie emits a cry of shock, then sits there gaping at him. Ray can see the fury struggling to get out from behind her watery eyes.

338

'I'm going to count to three,' he says, raising the fly rod over her head. 'One.' He lowers it to her neck again, tickling her. 'Two . . .'

Andie blinks, and Ray lashes the fiberglass switch down as savagely as he can, cutting across the brow of her left eye, the bridge of her nose and the right cheek. The woman howls and covers her face, rocking forward and back, keening like a banshee. When she removes her hands, Ray sees a beautiful diagonal stripe of raised flesh, not yet bleeding but might be soon.

'Empty your fucking pockets.'

Shaking, the woman lifts her hips and wedges her hands into her tight jeans, turning the rabbit ears out. A few coins, a lighter and a mashed pack of Pyramid cigarettes fall in the sand. What is it with these locals and their Pyramids? The girl at the convenience store shared the same brand loyalty. Maybe she was Andie's daughter. Maybe they will have to kill her on the way home.

Andie raises her hands in surrender, breathing hard, eyes wide.

'Back pockets too.'

'There's nothin' in there. I left my wallet in the car up on the boat ramp.'

Ray lashes the woman across the face as before, and again with a backhanded stroke that snaps blood from her nose. She jerks back in the lawn chair, shrieking, arms over her face, and Ray dances to one side, swiping down across her thighs, whipping her three or four times before the lawn chair gives out and Andie topples backward into the sand.

It would be helpful to see the blood, he realizes. Red for human. Black for whatever the ones like the ranger have become.

'Empty your fucking pockets!' he screams, whipping the rod across her back. Now that she is on the ground, he has more room to wind up. He strikes her six or seven times across the back and neck before she stops trying to get up and flops on her belly, legs kicking behind her like a toddler throwing a tantrum.

'Please, stop, oh help me, God!' she screams. 'I'm sorry, mister, please!'

'Do it myself,' Ray says. Planting one foot in the small of her back, he reaches down and digs a hand into one pocket, then the other, but they're empty. A wet spot has appeared at the lowest middle of her butt. He's whipped the piss out of her. The realization almost makes him feel bad, until he remembers Colt, the holes in her shirt, her thin body draining in the truck. This woman is connected to the man who pushed a steel blade into Colette Mercer. She might only be human, not cursed the way the ranger was, but she is kin to evil.

'Roll over,' he tells her. 'With your hands out in front of you.'

Andie grunts and rolls to her back, raising her arms. Her face is red, swollen, her tears mixed with blood and patches of sand stuck to her cheeks and one side of her mouth. The blood is dark, but in the dim light he can't tell if it's purple or black. She looks genuinely scared and this makes him happy.

'Don't move. If you move, I will take one of those rocks

from the fire pit and smash your head flat. Do you believe me?'

Andie nods quickly.

Ray backs up to fetch the lantern, keeping his eyes on her as he bends. He carries it back in his left hand, the fly rod still cocked in his right. He shines the light into her eyes, wanting to disorient her further as he peers at the blood on her face. It's not black, but very dark. Too dark, he thinks. He aims the light at her hands, checking the thumbs. They are plump but otherwise appear to be normal.

But what about under her sweatshirt? She could have anything stashed in there.

Andie notices the drift of his eyes, and smiles.

'What the fuck are you smiling at?'

'I know what you're thinking.'

Give her nothing. Don't play her game, whatever it is.

'You want to lift up my shirt and have a peek at my tiddies,' Andie says. 'Because you think I might be hidin' a weapon between 'em, and because you're a pervert, like all the other mens who can't get enough. Well, go on, then, if you really want to know.'

She smiles wider as blood drips from her nose over her lips, down her chin.

Ray feels sick, for all kinds of reasons. 'Your ranger stabbed my sister to death. We both know you're rotten. All I want is the truth. Why she had to die. Why you're here now. I don't want to kill you, but I will. I absolutely will.'

'Coward,' she says. 'I'll help ya.'

341

Andie reaches under her sweatshirt with her right hand.

'Stop!' he shouts, raising the fly rod. 'Not another inch!'

'Easy, young buck.' Using her left, Andie taps a finger on the breast cancer ribbon pinned to her sweatshirt as her right continues to wiggle higher under her shirt. 'You wanted to understand what you're up against out here. I aim to show you.'

Ray steps back two paces, the lantern held out, waiting for the first sign of trouble. He glances at the fire pit, fixing on a medium-sized rock, in case he needs to brain her quickly. A wooden handle is sticking out from the pit, just like the handle on the shovel he used on the ranger. Did he bring it back with him? No. Must be one of the shovels they used to bury Leonard. Maybe Dad threw it in the fire last night.

'Diagnosed stage four,' Andie says.

Ray whirls, focusing on her again as her breasts flatten, her hand withdraws and she drops two flesh-toned plastic inserts in the sand at her feet. For a moment he is so wound up, expecting another trick, he has no idea what he's looking at. Then he looks at her now-flat chest again, and it dawns on him. They are fakes, what they used to call falsies.

'You're ... cancer?' he says.

'Not no more. Doctors and hospitals said nothing could cure me. I made my sacrifices, but those don't account for much. Seven hundred or more people have died in Blundstone's waters and on her beaches over the last half-century, must be thousands over the ages. What have you sacrificed? What do you know about suffering?'

Ray is too overwhelmed to answer.

'Nothing, that's what. But you're about to learn.' She starts to sit up.

He charges at her with the fly rod again. 'Down! Stay down!'

Andie chuckles, hands raised. She lies back, resting her head in the sand. 'Yes, sir.'

He can't go on like this, torturing her. And he can't let her go. Someone will be coming for her soon. So, the only options are to kill her and flee, or tie her up and flee.

But there are other things he needs to know first.

'Tell me about the lake,' he says. 'Everything you know. If you do that, I'll tie you up and leave you some water and we'll be gone. If you don't, I'll set you on fire the way I did your daddy or whoever that piece of shit was.'

'No one knows how it started. Some people say it's old, that it's been here before the dam, when this was just a river. Before the cities and towns. Before man. An *ancient* that managed to hold on, the last of her kind. But there's another theory that she isn't so old. That she came after we built that dam, fiddling with nature and upsetting the balance like we always do. Maybe those of us with family goin' back a long ways, we're carrying the rituals over into modern times in order to restore balance, payback for human sin. Blood-letting. Drownings. Littering, contaminating the water with our chemicals and trash. Violence against our neighbors, our own kin. We created a big pool to hold our sickness, and then we helped it grow.'

She seems more relaxed now, and Ray senses she is almost enjoying the chance to share it with someone new.

'Tell me about the black stuff in the water. The sand. The ranger's blood. How it gets inside them, why it changes them.'

'Nature's funny like that,' Andie says. 'He was my granddaddy, by the way. Our eldest ranger. Hunnert and twenty-three years old, passed his eye exam at the driver's license bureau last fall.'

Ray presses the tip of the rod to her lips again. *What is it?*

'You're young,' Andie says, smirking as she pushes the rod away. 'You still believe in answers, tidy little explanations for every mystery in this life. You ain't gonna find that out here, but I'll tell you another true story like I told you in the diner. Maybe you're smart enough to take what you need from it, but I doubt it.'

'Make it fast.'

'One night a few years ago I couldn't sleep, clicked my way into this show on the TV. About these tigers over on the coast of India. The big cats, striped ones like you see at the zoo. But these were unique, a single colony that lived in some of the densest jungle along a coastal river. Most of the big cats don't go out of their way to hunt man. They might defend their turf you come near their cubs, but otherwise they'd just as soon eat something that doesn't walk on two legs. But this particular clan, they had a real nasty way of ruining someone's day. What they did was, they hid in the trees along on this riverbank, waiting for the villagers to paddle by in their canoes. Just as silent as you please, and oh so patient. One of these canoes came sliding by with a couple of people in it, the tiger would leap from the bank. They had footage of this. Them tigers stand eight, ten feet when stretched out, and you better believe they can launch themselves halfway across the river. Villagers thought they was being smart by sticking to the middle, but it was like when your house cat makes a leap from the couch to the windowsill. Picture that, but with an animal weighs sixteen hunnert pounds and got teeth like bullhorns. Hungry, but not just that. They was mad, angrier than hell, the scientist man on the show said. Vicious for vicious' sake. Do you know why?'

'Because the villagers were trespassing in the tigers' territory,' Ray says.

'That's what I thought,' Andie says. 'But those villagers were doing everything they knew how to give the cats a wide berth, and they still made catnip of 'em. No, see, the scientists got in there doing all their studies the way they do, taking soil and water samples, putting the tiger poop under a microscope, the whole bit. Eventually they cut one of them tigers open, studied her organs, her brains, the blood. Do you know what they found?'

'Human flesh.'

'Well, sure, in the stomach. But in the liver and kidneys? They found a whole lot of salt build-up. Sea salt. Salt from the ocean waters that pushed up into this neck of the river, turning it unusually brackish, kind of water animals usually know better than to sip at. But this jungle was an inferno, and these particular cats didn't have anywhere else to drink. Big cats need a lot of hydration, like our crops, and so it was the salt water or death. Salt got into their brains. Made them ten times more aggressive than the same species a hundred miles inland. Those villagers are primitive peoples, thought they were dealing with demon tigers, bad spirits, like maybe they'd angered the gods. But it was just too much sea salt in the water table. Simple as that.'

'There's no salt in Blundstone,' Ray says. 'But there's some kind of imbalance, is what you're saying. Poison in the water.'

'Who said poison? I'm talking about *nature*, young man. You think you know her, but you don't. We can call it spirits or demons or climate change or the hundred year flood, but, in the end, it always comes down to nature being nature. The lake is just a means to concentrate what we bring in, what's lived here for thousands of years. These things are nature, part of us, and they combine with other nature. We call it invasive species, but nature doesn't know invasive. She thrives on it. On us, because we too are invasive. Your family experienced visions, and it changed them. Other survivors claim to have seen God, leviathans in the deep, sunsets that lasted four days, anything you can dream up. But it's all *mind*. Mind is nature. A tiger brain full of salt.' Andie looks up, elbows digging into the sand. 'Can I get up now?'

Ray nods, awed not so much by the depth of her lunacy as by the conversational, unforced conviction with which she describes it.

'You and your family actually do this. You take people and kill them and dump them in the lake.'

Andie sniffs and looks around the camp ground, at the trailer, the Audi, all the gear and technology. 'Our people

346

own half of this county and most of the next one,' she says. 'What's your family got? What does your father do now? Did he make his fortune before or after you discovered our little paradise?'

The fly rod quivers in Ray's right hand. His father was a vice-president at a humble little regional bank the first few years they camped here. After the storm, he built a fortune in ten years, with hardly a false step.

'My family never sacrificed anyone.'

'Didn't they? Who was it disappeared here, on this very point, when you were just a boy? Whose family was that?' Andie turns her gaze on the Airstream. 'Your girly knows. It was in her eyes before she ordered her milkshake. You can always tell, the ones who've been touched and lived to tell.'

'You're out of your fucking mind.'

'I'm a tiger,' Andie says. 'You're the one's decided to bring your canoe.'

'That's what you came for tonight,' Ray says. 'To take one of us.'

'Your people are dying. She might give you a few more years, the way she done us. But only if you make your offering, and this time you better mean it, Raymond. It can't be an accident like the others. It has to be *true*.'

Ray is relieved. Now he can do what he should have done twenty minutes ago. With the rod or a rock or with his bare hands if he has to.

'Go on, whip me some more,' Andie says, reading the decision in his eyes. 'You can do anything you want to ol' Andie and you can make it last all night. I don't mind, you

347

see. Because I've already been through hell, and that little girl that belonged to your sister? She's already gone.'

The meaning of this takes a moment to sink in. Ray's spine stiffens and his heart folds over on itself before springing into panic mode. He drops the fly rod but keeps the lantern, aiming it at the Airstream's door. It's closed, and he would have heard it open. There's no way anyone could have . . .

The window.

The way his mom slipped out, when they were all sitting around the fire. While Andie the sociopathic waitress has been regaling him with her theories on Mother Nature gone haywire, someone (or some*thing*) could have come through the window on the other side of the trailer.

Ray runs to the door and yanks the knob – it's locked.

'Megan! Open the door! Megan! Open the door—' then he remembers that he told her not to, no matter what.

Behind him, Andie laughs.

'It's safe!' he shouts. 'Megan! Say something! Are you all right?'

Footsteps inside. Something like a cabinet door slams.

'Megan! Talk to me!'

'I'm here!' comes the muffled reply.

'Are you all right? Is Sierra with you?'

'She's in the bathroom. What's going on?'

'Is she safe?'

'What?'

'IS SHE SAFE?'

'Yes! We're fine. What's happening? Ray?'

This doesn't make sense. Then it does. She tricked

him, but not with her long story. Only the end. The last thirty seconds nothing more than a head-fake.

Oh, shit.

Ray turns, swinging the lantern to where he left the Cornhusker on the ground. She's not there. He swings it right, peering under the picnic table and across the fire pit. The wooden shovel handle he saw earlier jerks sideways, sliding into the dark.

She planted it. Her weapon was sitting there all along.

He swings the lantern, can't find her. A bulky shadow scrambles across the ground, coming at him. His light catches a flash of pink and blue, the sparkly letters way too close and rising up, and then her screaming moon face pokes out of the night.

Andie shrieks, her eyes wide and black as the lake itself. A concentrated weight slams into his left thigh, then slips past, grazing his other knee as her arms swing wide and a brilliant hot pain ripples through his leg, followed by a warm drench that runs down his left knee, slopping his feet.

Andie stumbles back, rears up and resets the wooden handle in both hands, the way a batter chokes up on a baseball bat.

Ray's left leg buckles and the lantern tumbles to the ground, throwing a flash of light over his thigh. The bottom front of his shorts and the flesh behind it have been gashed to the bone. His flesh is wide open and his blood is flooding out of him.

He throws both hands over the wound as if trying to pack the blood back in, and the woman shrieks again. No, not a shovel at all. A blade flashes through the lantern's beam on its way down. Ray doesn't have the name for it. He only knows it's curved, like the tool the farmers used before machines, the kind for cutting wheat.

'Help!' he screams, raising one arm, which takes a nasty slice below the elbow but saves his neck. More of his blood leaps through the night as the force of the blow knocks him sideways to the ground.

'Help me! Somebody! Oh God no no NO!'

Andie roars into another swing, her long rusted sickle coming for his head.

Cold White Light

Ray falls flat, ducking the blade as the trailer door opens with a bang.

Someone steps on Ray's back, smashing him to the sand, and then the weight is off, away. He writhes in agony, his only thought to get out of its path, away from that swinging blade, before she cuts him into pieces that can't be put back together. He tries to stand but his coordination has gone spastic, as if the woman cut all the strings he never knew he needed to get through the day. One of his palms flattens on something sharp, feels like glass, and he screams again, fearing the blade.

No, it's a rock, he's falling over a circle of them, the smell of ash and coal in his mouth. Campfire leftovers. If they had made a new one tonight, he would be rolling in flames now and it feels the same. He is enveloped in a fire of pain. He lurches forth, scraping his hips, and flops sideways, trying to see her, afraid to stop moving, the blade will find him. Everything is odd shapes and shadows. Bushes, a chair, more sand, and he keeps digging along with his elbows and toes.

351

Behind him, another murderous scream erupts, this one higher than the woman's. The crash of an overturned cooler, followed by the sounds of two bodies grunting and snapping at each other's throats. A choking sound. Feminine rage, animal fury. Another collision, weight slamming into a car door.

Only now does Ray grasp why the woman is no longer attacking him. Megan has taken the fight to her, and in so doing saved his life. He forgets all notions of escape and shoves himself up, the hardest push-up he's ever done in his life, and somehow gets his right knee into the sand. His other leg is dragging behind him in an invisible trap, the pain so intense he can perfectly visualize a shark or an alligator with its jaws clamped around his thigh, tugging, thrashing, refusing to let go.

The fighting behind him continues. Flesh slapping flesh, ragged breathing.

More shrieking.

He reaches for a lawn chair and turns it over, falling to his knee. Another stripe of hot pain sings through his arm and ... 'Ah-ah-ah-aaahhhh!' – he lets out a long cry, bargaining with the pain. His body is ordering him to stop, but he can't stop now. If Andie gets past Megan, Sierra will have no one left to protect her.

Dad! Where's my dad? Andie must have gotten him before she came down. Found him up on the point, where he was supposed to be playing lookout.

A spot of white light races across the ground in front of Ray, a sharp cone, different from the yellow light of the lantern he took from her. The light shoots off into the clearing, racing along like a little flying saucer, lights up a shrub, then comes racing back, scanning the camp site. The disc catches the side of his face. It stops on his left eye, sending a blue solar flare into his skull.

Ray closes his eyes, ducks, rolls, afraid it's her, she's found him again. He is on his back, using his elbows to crab away from her. The light chases him, moving down his chest, his legs, showing him more of his blood, sand and blood clumped together and smeared over his legs like war paint.

The light retreats, and Ray expects the next swing of the blade at any moment, but it doesn't come. The light dances over the picnic table, to the hind end of Colt's blue Audi, and from this distance Ray can see the actual beam of it, the long tube of white light. The beam is coming down at a sharp angle, from somewhere high above the clearing. Helicopter spotlight? No engine sound.

The light glides over the Audi and finds them. The women are locked in some kind of death grip, clutching each other as they stand pressed against the side of Colt's SUV. They are no longer shrieking and screaming. Andie's thick arms are wrapped around Megan's waist, one of Megan's hands locked around the woman's throat, trying to squeeze, claw, puncture. Her head is tucked low, butting Andie's chest. Their legs are locked, pushing the bodies together at a lopsided apex. Andie is trying to crush Megan before Megan can strangle her.

'Out!' a strong but distant voice echoes down. 'Get out of the way!'

It sounds close but not level, coming from above the camp ground.

'Megan, let go!' the voice booms. 'Get out of the way! Ray! Get her out of there!'

It's his father, Ray realizes, following the long beam up, up, at an angle that narrows to meet the top of the cliff. The brown vertical face they parked so close to.

Everything falls into order, then. Ray understands what his father wants, and why. Warren has the spotlight. He's standing fifty or sixty feet above them, with Leonard's rifle. He can take the woman out, but only if Megan gets free of her first.

The possibility is enough to shake Ray into moving again. He shoves himself to his feet and limps forward, hopping on his good leg, trying to find the clear route through the mess of chairs and overturned picnic table and fire pit.

At least twenty hop-steps away, the spotlight tracks the two women as they slide along the blue sheet metal, the light trying to hold on Andie's face, blind her, disrupt her. Andie's head shakes from side to side, up and down, a vampire evading the burn. No, not the light. She's trying to get away from Megan's fingers, which are searching and probing, trying to sink into the woman's eyes.

'Megan, let go!' Warren hollers again, as if it were so simple. Andie has her in the ugliest bear hug Ray has ever seen. Megan is bent against the grip, bowing the wrong way. Another few minutes of this and her spine will snap.

Ray is halfway there, only six or eight good hops away. The light darts over, hitting him in the face again.

'No! Raymond, get back!' Warren shouts. 'Stay out!'

Ray tries to shout back. 'She's stuck!' but his voice is shredded. 'I have to help her! Don't shoot!'

'Back!' his father shouts, the spotlight jumping back to the women. The light rises from their hips to the rear passenger window beside their heads.

The dark pane of glass instantly transforms into a white frosted sheet, and a fraction of a second later the rifle report arrives, spraying glass pebbles into the car.

The two stuck bodies lurch away from the small explosion and the spotlight follows. But it's not really the light tracking them, Ray understands now. The light *is* the gun. Warren attached it. Where the light goes, so goes the next bullet.

'Wait! Stop!' Ray yells, doubting his father can hear him. He hobbles a few more steps, looking around for something to bludgeon the woman with, anything will do. Can't see anything in the dark. A lawn chair? Not heavy enough. A rock from the fire pit would work, but that's behind him now. Maybe three steps back. He twists, hobbling sideways, and a second shot rings out.

Ray flinches and looks back as the white spot moves over Andie's head. Missed, but close. Does his dad know he's running out of time? Another two steps and they will be slipping behind the SUV, the rear hatch preventing a decent shot.

Andie screeches, lifting Megan up and turning her around, then slams the smaller body against the car, throwing her weight into it. She's trying to put Megan in the next bullet's path.

Ray leans down to find a rock. The pain is too much and

he falls again, clawing at the sand. Left, right, far left – there. He drags it closer. It's heavy, too big to hold in one hand. He sets his other hand on it, using it as a focal point for his next push-up. Right knee up, he wobbles, raising himself on one trembling leg.

The light is on Andie's back. A shot rings out. She jerks forward and a dark blot opens in her shirt. The woman groans like a bull and Megan slips through Andie's arms.

'Megan!' he rasps, holding the rock out, terrified the bullet went through Andie, into Megan's chest.

Before he can call out again, the spotlight settles on Andie's lower back. She is leaning into the Audi as if Megan is still there, but Ray can't see her, not even a shadow. The shot takes Andie low, just left of the spine. She arches back, screaming, and falls to her hands and knees. Another shot cracks like a whip and her arms shoot forward, her face plowing into the sand.

Ray drops the rock.

Pop. Pop. Pop.

Andie's body rises, flattens. One knee digs in, an arm reaches out. She's still trying to stand up. She either has the strength of a horse or she's just plain fucking nut—

Pop. Pop. Pop. Pop. Pop. Pop.

A string of shots, followed by a series of seemingly endless echoes. There is a brief pause, and then it resumes, each sounding louder than the next.

POP. POP. POP. POP …

The body is still jerking under spits of red mist as Ray feels the sting of blasted sand hitting him in the face. He falls backward, the dark face of the cliff giving way to the big tent above, a black screen filled with thousands of tiny stars. He can almost imagine himself among them, light years from the sun.

He feels no pain now, only the relentless cold, and that isn't so bad.

There are worse things than being cold.

The Medic

The warmth returns in the form of aromas. The charred bitterness of strong coffee. The burned fat of bacon frying in a pan. The astringent bite of medicine. Clean bed-sheets, soft against his bare skin. He smiles inside, lips too dry to give up the real thing. It's over. They have been rescued. He will never have to feel the sand or look at the lake again. He grinds his teeth and runs his dry tongue over them, working his jaw loose. A single piece of grit catches in his molars.

His eyes spring open in alarm. The room is bright, the ceiling hazy. The pain threatens to spike once more, but it ebbs quickly, leaving him loose, weak, his hunger stirring on the wafts of breakfast cooking close by.

He dozes a few minutes more, only to be jolted back by the clanging of pans, a whisk or fork beating rapidly. He tries to sit up and it's not so bad, but he can't get past his elbows. He turns his head on a stiff neck.

His father is standing in the galley, Sierra on a foot-stool beside him, the two of them working a series of skillets, dishes, spice bottles. Beyond them, under the table, Megan's bare feet dangle over the dining-seat cushion.

'Hey,' Ray whispers. Then louder, 'Hey. Dad.'

Warren looks over. 'Don't get up. I need to check those dressings first.'

Ray stares at him dumbly.

'Hold this,' Warren tells Sierra, handing her a silicone spatula. 'And don't touch the pans. Hot hot, remember?'

Sierra nods and Warren pats her on the butt on his way to Ray, looming over him with his serious face and a peek at his blue Timex watch. He rests the back of his hand on Ray's brow, checking for fever. He reaches up to a bracket mounted behind the bathroom's rear paneling, pumps three squirts of hand sanitizer into his palm, then rubs his hands over each other and shakes them dry.

'Lie back.'

Ray feels the sheet lift off, then the warmth of his father's hands moving up his shin, his knee, gently squeezing his thigh. 'Feel that?'

'Yes.'

'Hurt?'

'Yes.'

'All of it, or only here?' Warren squeezes harder, near Ray's groin, and Ray winces, air blowing through his clenched teeth.

'Now all over,' Ray hisses.

'Okay. Not bad. You didn't pass out this time.'

Ray looks down. His father is removing a thick gauze bandage from his thigh, bordered with medical tape. Underneath is a yellow horror, his flesh stained or rotting, a jagged ten-inch line sewn with what appears to be green fishing line.

'Minimal seeping,' Warren says. 'That's good. Don't mind the color. That's just the Betadine.'

Warren turns to an open tackle box at the foot of the bunk. There are forceps in there, gleaming silver scissors, bricks of bandage, ice packs, heat packs and a bunch of other medical equipment. No fishing lures or rubber worms. Warren rips open a fresh pack of something resembling a small diaper and squeezes clear ointment from a fat tube into it, decorating it like a cake. He drapes the bandage over Ray's thigh, then begins tearing strands from a roll of medical tape. A few seconds later the job is done.

Or not: 'Turn on your right side. We need to do the arm.'

It is only then that Ray sees the plastic line running from his forearm up to the curtain rod, where a bag of saline hangs. Another bag, one he can't read, must be antibiotics. The cut on his forearm is not as bad, but shares the same green suturing.

'Why do you have all this?'

'Once you've seen the things I've seen, you learn not to travel without a good first-aid kit.' Warren lifts him up and administers a B-12 shot into his son's butt cheek.

Megan sighs heavily and her feet withdraw as she sits up. 'Hi, Ray.' She sounds tired, nothing more or less.

'Hey you,' he says. 'Nice to hear your voice.'

She doesn't reply. Ray sits up and his father adds another pillow behind his back, then gestures at his tackle box.

'Got ampules of morphine in there, Raymond. You can

360

probably still feel its effects. Helped get you through what could have been a much worse night.'

'Yeah' is all Ray can think to say.

Warren smiles coyly. 'Know what I used to seal those lacerations in the leg and your arm?'

'Fishing line.'

'No, that's the real thing. Hospital sutures, heavy gauge, the stuff they bring out in terrorist bombings. I'm talking about below that, to close the flesh below the skin. Because, let me tell you, those went deep. Woman used a goddamned grain scythe on you, Raymond. You don't fuck around with a cut like that, excuse my language, ladies. So I scrubbed you out with surgical sponges, tweezers to get the sand out, though probably not all of it. You're gonna take some of that sand home with you, I imagine. But then, we always do, don't we? After I had the wound as clean as I could get it, I gave you a nice dose of what we used to call the ol' Saigon Super Juice.'

Ray's appetite has abandoned him. He sets the bacon on the plate and leans back. 'Yeah, what's that?'

'Superglue. Just like you buy in a hardware store. I kid you not. Once the Army figured that out, the way it can lock up a sheet of skin tight as bunk cot, and the body dissolves it over a week or two? They airlifted pallets of it incountry. We carried tubes of glue the size of Crest toothpaste through the jungle. Can you believe that?'

'Dad?'

'Yeah?'

'When can we go home?'

Warren wipes a hand over his mouth, nodding, and to

Ray he looks almost disappointed. 'Soon. Very soon. But you and I have something to discuss first.'

'What's the plan? I can't walk like this, can I? Megan, can you?'

'I'm fine, Ray,' Megan says, in the same flat tone.

'She got off easy, a couple of fractured ribs. Two broken nails from the lady's cheek. She'll be fine.' Warren pats his shoulder. 'Finish your breakfast now. You're going to need it.'

Later, after a few more hours of rest, Warren removes the IV lines. He helps Ray out of the trailer, one arm around his waist as his son slings another arm over his father's shoulders. Megan wears an Ace bandage around her cracked ribs, between a purple bikini Ray hadn't seen until an hour ago, and he wishes he could be alone with her, back in the tent, kissing her bruises and tasting the sweat from her navel. Wishes they were still free enough to be together that way, and wonders if they ever will be again.

Ray is shocked by the sight of last night's disaster zone. He is not sure what he expected, maybe that his father would have made a cursory effort to tidy up, for Sierra's sake if no one else's. But everything is as it had ended, and daylight reveals the depth of the madness in which they now exist.

The Audi is riddled with bullet holes, at least ten shots in addition to those Ray recalled. Broken glass in the sand, shattered beer bottles, overturned coolers, food stores left to spoil, punctured fruit and soda cans spilled everywhere.

The picnic table rests on its side, its tablecloth streaked with blood. The stone circle of the fire pit is kicked open, the ashes scattered

Andie's prone form is as it had been put down in the turkey shoot, the massacre that unfolded in the clearing. Ray knows the body is not bloating already, but it seems so, her girth rising in a hump and pocked with red holes and trails of dried black crust. Half her head is blown off, as well as most of one foot. A scoop of her ass dug out like a carton of ice cream, the ones you see through the window in the parlor freezer. Maybe coyotes did that. Or the raccoons. But more likely his father's rain of bullets.

Ray looks from the gore to Megan and finally to Sierra. Colt's daughter stares at the body expressing no signs of fear, sadness, confusion or even disgust. Nor has she retreated into catatonia. From her quiet inspection, one might guess she is looking at a mangy dog sleeping in the shade, nothing more. Megan's quiet distance and their collective acceptance frightens Ray more than Andie or the ranger ever did.

Megan and Sierra head off for the beach, leaving father and son to walk together, and it takes a while.

'What's the plan?' Ray asks again.

'Good day for sailing,' his father answers.

Ray focuses on walking. A yellow craft comes into view, beached and waiting, its sleek pontoons angling up from the packed damp shore. The red- and yellow-striped sail lies in an accordion pile over the boom. Their boat, the one and same, from thirty years ago. The Aqua Cat.

Ray doesn't bother asking where it had been hidden for

the past three days. Probably in the trees, or under a camouflage tarp. His father has prepared for every eventuality, as if he knew this day would come.

Two lawn chairs are set out beside the boat, a cooler between them, filled with ice and bottles of a brand of beer Ray has never seen, some lager Warren had grown fond of in Florida. The label has no name, only a toucan sitting on a palm frond, its giant orange bill standing out below two dark eyes. Neither man remembered to bring sunglasses, and Ray wishes his father had some now, so he wouldn't have to see the old man's eyes. They have turned a deep brown, with only a little white showing around the corners, lifeless as the toucan on the beer bottle.

Megan and Sierra are a quarter of a mile away, strolling the beach hand in hand like figures on a postcard.

All of this preparation – the breakfast, the chairs, the cooler, sending the girls away, and most of all the Aqua Cat, preserved and sailed through time by his father's attachment to the past, to the lake itself – is part of an upcoming ceremony, Ray understands now. His father has a plan for their exit, probably their last and only hope. Ray knows, too, that Megan is in on it. Warren must have talked to her about it last night, or this morning, and whatever he said must have earned her loyalty, otherwise she wouldn't be so calm. Calm and distant.

Warren drinks, pushing his bony feet into the sand. Mom and Colt seem to have been forgotten already. Ray realizes he still hasn't told his father how they died, and the old man hasn't asked. Tempting to assume Megan told him, except Ray never had time to tell her, couldn't do it in front of Sierra. And things spiralled out of control so fast after he woke up yesterday afternoon, it's not possible any of them know the truth.

Ray can't stand it anymore.

'Mom was on the cliff,' he says, taking another deep gulp of beer. 'Last night. The night before, I mean. The wall came down. She was buried. Colt and I tried, but it was too late.'

Warren nods, gazing out at the rippling blue water. 'I'm sorry, Raymond. Sorry you lost your mother. She loved you always.'

Ray wishes he could cry, but knows he won't. Can't, won't.

'Colette was murdered by the ranger,' he says, 'or someone related to the woman. She was poisoned, and then stabbed ... she died in the back of the truck. Right after she told me Sierra was my daughter now. She knew it was coming, before the ranger got out of his truck, I think. She confessed things to me on the road. I buried her in the beach, about seven miles from here, I guess. I don't know.'

'They all knew,' Warren says, emptying his beer, then flipping the cooler lid to open another. 'As soon as we arrived, and maybe before that. They knew, and they tried to beat it, but there is only one way to escape it and we were too late for that. That's my fault. I told you we saw everything, the rest of our lives. And we didn't know it would culminate here, but I should never have tried to bargain with it. We should never have come back. That we did, that I organized this, is on me. All of this is on me. I failed my family, and for that I can only regret every second until I am gone.'

'That is so much bullshit,' Ray says, his anger as worn out as the rest of him. 'You're all insane. I wish you could admit that, once, if only to me.'

'Maybe so,' Warren says, stealing a glance at him. 'But in the end, does it matter? We are here, we are stuck, and you have to get out. We have to get you three home. Better we focus on that.'

'The three of us, or the four?'

'Megan heard everything that woman said last night,' Warren says. 'When you had her pinned to the ground with my fly rod. The trailers windows were open. She related it all to me this morning. And, you know, I saw it in Megan's eyes before she finished describing it, how much she understood. We are in agreement on this, Megan and I. Sierra, too, in her instinctive way.'

'You want to go out on the water,' Ray says. 'To do what?'

Warren drinks, wipes his lips. 'To break free from the storm. Get out from under the cloud of evil that has been hanging over us ever since that night, first blessing us with fortune, then turning on us over the years, as if we had done what it wanted, but not enough to last. Like the woman said. You have to feed it, or it feeds on you.'

'Dad . . .'

'This time we'll get it right.'

'Dad . . . stop.'

'All along I've been arguing that the lake changed Megan's family, made an abomination of them. That it

366

tricked us, compelling us to put them in the water. Out there,' Warren tilts his bottle toward the lake. 'But the real trick was letting us escape, thinking we could resume our lives. We know better now. It's time to finish what we started. This time the real thing. Not an accidental encounter, not a mercy. A true offering. The last one.'

Ray is afraid to turn his gaze from the lake.

'Look at me, son.'

Ray does. His father's eyes are ancient, black as night. The deep brown of his retirement tan has been drained away, replaced by a pallor mapped with the veins crossing his skull. War and loss and the murder of innocents have left salt in the tiger's brain.

Ray does not realize he is backing away from his father until his lawn chair topples over. He lands in the sand and his father leaps up to stand over him, lips spreading, teeth stained yellow.

'Stay away!' Ray cries. 'Don't touch me!'

Warren looks furious for another moment, then confused. He backs off, hands up. 'I'm sorry. I wasn't going to – I thought you were injured. Please, Raymond . . . this isn't about you. My God. No. Never.'

Ray uses the pontoon to pull himself to his feet. The pain in his leg awakens once more and he pounds his fist against the boat, a flood of anger surging along with the pain.

His father steps forward to help.

'Just give me a minute!'

'Okay.' Warren retreats to his lawn chair and hangs his

head. 'I can't blame you for thinking your father's become a monster. I have.'

Ray hops back, twists around and lowers himself. He is out of breath. The wind is picking up, sharpening the ripples in the bay, the water turning dark green as the first rows of clouds begin to march in, breaking up the sun.

'I'm sorry,' he says. 'My nerves are shot. And you're talking about . . .'

'The only way out.' Warren turns to him slowly. 'Not you. Me. I'm the one. Today. You will put me in the place where I was happiest, before all of this. It will be difficult, maybe the hardest thing, and that's why it will count. Together we make a sacrifice, so that you and your family can go home.'

Ray looks over his father, up the beach. The girls are returning. Megan waves tiredly. Sierra hops along like a toad. And it is while watching them, his girls, that the last link in the chain tethering Raymond Mercer to the world that makes sense – a world where families grow old together and spend Thanksgiving in a mountain lodge with football games on TV and roast turkey on the table, where laughter and silly old resentments and arguments break out with no real consequences, a world where grandmothers and grandfathers go quietly into assisted living and chemotherapy and Hospice, and one last birthday cake with eighty-six candles on top is wheeled into a darkened room filled with friends and three generations who all help blow the candles out – this last slips through his hands and is lost into the mud of his soul.

'Yes,' Ray says to his father. 'I will.'

Aqua Cat

Ray sits on the trampoline the way he did as a boy, letting his father do the heavy work of shoving the boat out. His leg wound is too fragile, his arm too weak. Warren lifts the aluminum spar at the stern, a rope clenched between his teeth, and for a moment Ray is sure he will not be able to free them from the wet bank. But with a final growl, tendons snapping taut in his neck, Warren summons the strength of a man half his age and the pontoons rise. The lake carries the bow and the craft severs from land. Warren leaps on deck, his face neither white nor tan but dark red, a dangerous pulse visible in his throat.

The red and yellow billows, crackling into full sail, and the wind rocks them to port as the waves beat against the hulls. Overhead, the sky thickens with puffs of white and silver, another line of black clouds piling up at the north end. They cut through uniform rows of waves, the murky brown from the shallows giving way to the expanding blue that is already turning gray.

Ray looks back to the beach and the remains of Leonard's tent, the Bronco, taking in his first real view of the cove from anywhere but inside it. Sierra stands at the edge of the water, her brown hair a tattered flag. Beside her, Megan watches with one hand at her brow. Ray waves but she doesn't return this one. She must know what lies ahead.

Warren inhales the wind as the waves grow taller and throw spray over the pontoons, drumming the canvas. The lake has turned a stone gray, black where the shadows overlap, and Ray begins to notice patterns under the surface. Long, circling blobs that slide like eels, their ends opening like tunnels before swallowing themselves.

Ray looks away. Five or six miles to their left is the dam, a low ridge of rocks spanning another mile or so, the last patch of blue sky shrinking as the gray dome slides east. To his right lies the rest of Blundstone, something like twenty-five miles of it, though Ray knows by now it could be much less than that. For the first time, he can see the end, from gray lake to green land. There is a limit after all. If the human eye is capable of detecting the curvature of the earth, it's not here, not on this flat plane of ugly chop, and Ray feels cheated.

Another wave smacks the starboard hull and a crater opens under the swell. Ray leans away as the Aqua Cat dips violently. Just a few feet beneath the receding foam, a bloated white corpse rolls over, sexless and hollow-eyed, one arm reaching out as the pontoon passes by.

Ray recoils, dragging himself to the other side, and Warren yells for him to duck. The boom swings overhead and the sail ripples in confusion until his father sets another rope. The boat jostles Ray onto one elbow and he hangs forward, watching the lake rush between the pontoons. At a depth of no more than six feet there is a logging river running within the lake, crowded not with trees but bodies. The drowned, the lost. Twenty, thirty, dozens, dead hair swirling, their skin whiter than marble. The mouths gape below the black eye sockets as they drift and collide with one another. Others, closer to the surface, claw blindly for what they sense passing overhead. Cold blue fingers. Missing limbs. Men. Women. Children. Deformed variations of each, then only blackness. Then a mass grave as another slew of twisted forms daisy-chained together drift in the current, until a tar-worm of liquid nothingness rises ahead and devours them in a loop and descends back into the leaking abyss.

Ray shoves himself back from the edge and closes his eyes, a scream locked in his chest. His father remains oblivious, captaining them through his final nightmare.

The tip of the point retreats. Rain comes in a series of walls.

Lightning crashes and more waves assault them, washing over the little craft as it slows. Warren shouts for Ray to duck, releasing one rope, and the boom swings overhead. The sail ripples in confusion, beset by wind on either side, and then collapses. The Cat drifts in a rocking, seasick circle as Warren drags the rubberized canvas bag onto his lap. He begins to withdraw a heavy length of chain, then rope, and finally the anchor. The red anchor of old, not the bleached pink shell they found the other day. He sets the coil in a pile beside him, the anchor at its center.

Ray stares at the new red anchor, knowing it cannot be the same one, but terrified of the possibility.

'Time,' his father growls, wiping another broken wave from his eyes. 'One life! My life!'

Thunder returns the old man's challenge with a chorus that rumbles through Ray's skull. The clouds are black, the lake obscenely so, all the light in between compressing into a surreal borderland that is neither day nor night but something more awful than total darkness.

'What time is it, Raymond?' his father barks.

Ray braces himself, arms spread wide, his wet hands slipping along the aluminium frame holding them inches above the chaos and death below.

He starts to speak but chokes on lake water, rain: impossible to tell the difference. He spits overboard and finds his voice. 'What do you care? You got some place you need to be?'

The old man lunges forward, crawling until he latches onto Ray's shoulder with one hand, the other squeezing behind his neck. Silver nodes of water stand on his brow, his eyelashes, and their foreheads touch.

'Whatever time it is,' his father says, in a calm and heavy voice that walls out the storm, 'must be the right time. Whenever it comes. I tried to understand that in the war, and here, so long ago. But I never fully understood it until this weekend. And it's not the right time because God says so, or because men frame it in such a way they may take false comfort in the promise of Heaven. It doesn't work that way. Not for me, and I hope not for you.

'We choose our lives. Accept what we are given. We

fight for more, and in the end we go with grace. There is beauty in that, regardless of duration. One good year in a marriage. One perfect sixty minutes on a football field. One night saving your best friend's life in a sweltering jungle as the fire rains down. The morning spent watching your son being born. A week at a lake in Nebraska, with the only people who matter.

'We are real. Our days are real. And that's enough because a day can mean everything, Raymond. If we understand that all of it is a precious gift. One big vacation.'

A massive tree of lightning forks over the cover and his father releases him. The black water lifts the stern and drops them as another waves pitches over the bow, the lake's hunger bursting up in mindless turbulence.

'Put the sail up!' Ray shouts. 'Not here. Not like this. Let's go home!'

'This is my real home,' Warren calls back, coiling his rope. 'This place. It's always been here, on the Big Lake.'

Warren reaches into the anchor bag once more and comes back with his sidearm, the M1911 he carried through South East Asia. He lobs it to his son, who finds himself reaching out to catch it.

His father taps the center of his chest with two fingers. 'One shot and we'll both be free.'

Ray raises the gun, aiming at his father's chest. His hand shakes, steadies. His finger curls around the trigger. His jaw tightens. He stops breathing.

His father bares his teeth.

Ray squeezes, squeezes, and releases the trigger. 'No! NO!'

He lowers the pistol.

Warren is furious. 'We're out of time! Everyone's going to die here if you don't make your sacrifice. This has to be it. Now! Now, goddamn it, NOW!'

Ray throws the pistol overboard.

His father seizes him by the collar, shaking him, spittle flying. 'How can you deny me? How dare you!'

'You're my father,' Ray says. 'You made me. And I say fuck the lake.'

Warren releases his son in disgust, choking back a sob. He swallows it down, nods to himself.

'Good boy,' he says with a rueful laugh. 'My son. My gift.'

Ray shudders, guilt-stricken, lost.

His father leans over and kisses him on the cheek. 'I love you, kid.'

Before Ray can respond, Warren spins on his knees, digs a camping knife from the bag, flicks the blade open and slices through the rope. He hauls the anchor from the stacked chain, heaving it up to his chest. His mouth opens, but the words are drowned out by an electric hum. The smell of burned copper hangs inside the rain, and a colossal flash transforms the sky and lake and all else bright white. Too many fingers of lightning to count dance across the lake in a symphony of explosions.

'Please forgive me,' his father says, hugging the anchor to his chest. He rocks back, down between the pontoons, and is swallowed by the lake.

The coil of severed rope and twelve feet of steel chain sings in a quickening trail across the canvas, chasing the anchor. Ray throws himself forward, diving after it. He snags the last foot of rope in his wet right hand as his momentum and the sinking weight carry him headfirst into the waves, down into the churning silence.

Into darkness absolute.

The Eye

Raymond wakes inside a soft womb, the pale blue dawn creeping over the red skin of Leonard's tent, the two-man Coleman his brother let him sleep in last night. The morning air is laced with the scents of woods and field flowers and sage weed. His young body slides within the cool soft fabric of his sleeping bag. He rises with the knowledge he is in the kingdom, it is theirs. The heart of summer, where thoughts of school and homework and his father's business and chores and the boredom of life back home are not allowed, not here, not today.

The day awaits him like another life, infinite.

The tent door fills with the mouth of a huge catfish, whiskers and brown-gray hide, a stinking beady-eyed monster that flops into his lap.

'Boo!' Leonard shouts, falling in with his catch, breaking into peals of laughter.

Riding on the back of the little Honda, Raymond holds his big brother around the waist. They burn the sand trails, weaving through trees and over fields of sharp grass and yellow flowers, the morning sun chasing them as they startle a jack rabbit from cover. The two-cycle engine screams as Leonard winds him into terror and ecstasy, the ground blurring into a tunnel with the rabbit at its center.

It is better than *Star Wars*.

Between additions to his sand castle, Raymond munches on a frozen Zero bar, the white chocolate making his teeth ache. He watches his parents in their lawn chairs, drinking cocktails, laughing under the shade of their umbrella. Francine is young and beautiful, his father a strong wolf. He leans in to kiss her from time to time, and she whispers in his ear.

Raymond abandons his moat and wanders into the lake. The water is pure, the sand rigid under his toes. He swims on his back, kicking himself out a hundred yards, two hundred, safe in the cove.

He looks back to see his father leading his mother up the trail to the top of the point. Raymond knows where they are going, why. Into the camper, while the kids are at play. He is embarrassed for himself, happy for them.

As the sunset throws pink and purple bands across the horizon, the family gathers around the fire pit atop the point. Colt sits Indian-style in a deep canvas chair, wearing a thick hooded sweatshirt that cups her surf-roughened hair. Leonard is hunched over a log, using a pocket knife to carve its branches into spears. Raymond reclines on the wicker longue, mesmerized by the fire and the scent of his favorite meal coming from the barbecue.

Dad uses the tongs to worry over the five baseball-cut filet mignon that have been marinating in his special Blundstone-only concoction since they left home, a glass of scotch on the grill's warm fender. Mom is inside, plattering the boiled corn on the cob, tater-tots and blackened hearts of romaine. They debate using the picnic table, but their current arrangements around the fire win out. They saw into their steaks and occasionally look up to watch the giant orange fireball descend below the horizon, finishing their marshmallow s'mores in the dark.

Warren, feeling his buzz, enchants them with stories. He is a master storyteller, taking them through some of the strange encounters he had in Vietnam, though never the combat stories, or the ones labeled R&R. He tells them about a suburban husband who lost a hand to his lawn mower, another about an employee who got caught stealing money from the bank. The last is a tale they've heard before but never seem to tire of, the one about Dad and Uncle Gaspar's cross-country road trip after the war, the policeman who chased them for almost three hundred miles across Montana and wound up drinking beer with them all night, all three of them landing in jail.

Around ten, when they should be exhausted but no one is, Leonard suggests they do the fireworks. It's a perfect night for it, with no wind, he insists. The sand bar is calling us.

'You know that's our tradition for the last night, Len,' Dad tells him. 'We still have two nights to go.'

378

'I think we should go for it,' Colt says. 'It just feels right tonight.'

'Yes!' Raymond piles on. 'At least let us do some fountains and sparklers. We can save the rest for the last night.'

'All or none,' Warren says. 'You know how it goes. Once we start, we can't stop. But I really think we should wait. Waiting makes it better, right?'

A round of *boos* and *aawww-nnaaaahhhs* ensues.

Dad looks to Mom. Francine shrugs. 'This is your thing. I don't trust any of it. Someone's going to lose an eye one of these years.'

'Not on my watch,' Warren says.

Sensing that the final verdict still hangs in the balance, the kids lean forward expectantly. Warren reads the unification in their eyes, and his eyes turn serious as he peers at each of his children over the flames.

'Well, what's so special about today? I want to hear it, from each of you. Leonard goes first.'

'You're on.' Leonard sets down his Dr Pepper and stretches his arms. 'So, this morning I'm out fishing in my tube, past the cove. Four trips now, I still haven't landed a striper. Plenty of walleye, perch, some big catfish. But never the striped bass. I spent last month reading up on the tackle, the best bait. Brought out the shad this year. I figured, this year or bust. Well, three hours went by, no striper. I reeled everything in and started changing out my lure, and I don't know what it was, but something came over me. I just kind of felt like sitting for a while. I set my rod down. The wind died. Everything was so quiet, I could have heard a minnow jump a mile away. Then, maybe twenty feet off, I see this silver-white patch in the water go cruising by. I didn't move a muscle. A few seconds later, to my left, I see it again. This pale flash. Maybe thirty inches. I couldn't move. I thought he was gone, and then the water behind my legs sort of *churned*. He passed right in front of me a couple seconds later, an inch from the surface, and I saw him. Huge striper, at least four feet long, probably thirty pounds, maybe forty. Circling and circling, one eye on me, six or seven times before he got bored and left. And I can tell you, I am absolutely sure, he knew I'd laid my rod down. He let me see him, because he knew. It was the most perfect thing that ever happened to me, no joke.'

They keep quiet for a spell, imagining Leonard's great fish.

Warren nods in appreciation. 'Not bad. Not too shabby at all, Leonard. Onward with ... Colette?'

'Mine wasn't as exciting as *Jaws* here,' she says. 'But I had the best day. I was sitting under the umbrella, reading my book. I don't know where the rest of you were, but the beach was completely empty. I was alone. Usually when I read, if the story's good, I'm completely transported away, like, into the story, you know? But today wasn't like that. I was really into my book. Hard not to, cause it's a classic. *Gone With the Wind*. I could see that world like I was living in it, and I was also here, totally aware of the lake and the beach and the sky. My feet in the sand. It was almost like time-traveling, like I was two people, two places, balancing them both inside me. And for a few minutes, it wasn't *like* time travel. It was real. I could step from one time and

380

place into the next at will. I was traveling through time and I lived more than this one life, which I love, but I loved the other one too in different ways, and the whole thing made me happy. So happy. That's all.'

Francine is staring at her daughter with some kind of understanding the boys can't quite get a hold of. She blows a kiss to Colt and whispers something Raymond can't hear, but he doesn't mind.

'Raymond, my man,' his dad says. 'Got yourself some tough competition here. What was so great about your day?'

'Everything,' Raymond says. 'But I know, I know. Have to pick one. So, okay, I walked a long ways up the beach, past the point and the next two camp grounds. I didn't find any toads, but all the sudden I see this girl.'

'Ooohh,' Leonard coos. 'Ray's got a girlfriend!'

'Shut up, Len,' Raymond says. 'It wasn't like that. She was younger, and I thought it was weird how she was out there all alone. Playing by herself. Well, she wasn't totally alone. She had this dog with her, and he was crippled or had a busted leg or something, because he was in a little wheelchair made for dogs. Anyway, there wasn't any danger I could see, but I had this feeling she and that dog were far from home. Camp, I mean. She kept picking stuff up, looking for fossils or stones to chuck, I guess. About the fourth time she bends down, she comes up with something special. I couldn't tell what it was. Then she did something strange. She stared at me like she knew me, or was noticing something different about me. She waved, and I waved, but ... something else. There was this white light around her, different from the sun. Kind of mysterious. And for a second ... like, what if she was an angel? Like a real girl, but an angel somehow too? Then she set the thing back down in the sand, leaving it for me. And she ran off, back to her camp site or wherever. When she was gone ...'

He digs into his jeans pocket, holding it up above the fire for them to see.

'It's like a crystal or something. Looks dark now. But in the sun, you can see right through it. It's got spiral shape like a seashell, except there aren't any seashells at the lake, right? I've never found one. Never. Not even a crabshell or a crawdad.'

He passes the object to Leonard, who rolls it between his fingers and smiles before passing it on to Colt. The little oddity makes its rounds almost too quickly, as if they don't trust it. Raymond pockets it again as he finishes.

'I don't know if I should take it home or leave it here, on the beach. That girl might want it back, whoever she is.'

'Angel, huh?' Mom says. 'I think that's lovely, Raymond. You should keep it. She probably wants you to remember her.'

He hopes they can't see him blushing in the firelight.

'Welcome to your first crush,' Leonard says, and the rest of them crack up.

'What about it, Dad?' Colt says. 'I'd say we're doing pretty good so far. Give us your best, Captain.'

Warren knocks back the last of his scotch, offering them a wiggle of the eyebrows and a devilish grin.

382

'Your mother and I had a nice swim in the cove after lunch. Then we treated ourselves to the famous Blundstone foot massages, and that is always something. When I was in the war, what the jungle does inside your boots ... I tell you, I spend all year looking forward to digging my feet into this sand. But that wasn't the best part of my day.' He pauses, glancing at Francine, who is frowning in concern. 'Best part of my day was when I took your mother here up into the camper and we had ourselves a little—'

'Warren, that's enough,' Mom says.

Warren chuckles. 'Well, it sure beat the hell out of Len's fish, Colt's romance novel and the pirate treasure from Raymond's little girlfriend.' He leans into his wife and plants a big one on her cheek. 'I love you, woman. I sure do. My Franny girl.'

Mom waves a hand over her bosom theatrically. 'Okay, get back, get back. For Pete's sake, you.'

'Your turn, darlin',' Warren tells her. 'Saved the best for last.'

Francine leans forward, running a finger around the rim of her wine glass, rosy and alive and feeling more than she is used to.

'This,' his mother says. 'Now. This moment. With all of you. My precious children. My crazy husband. I would not trade this for all the world.'

Leonard looks down at his feet, bashful. Colt gazes into the fire, stunned. Raymond feels content. Now everyone will say goodnight, off to bed, that was the end. And that will be all right.

Warren rises without a word, stepping up into the camper. He returns with two triple-layered, extra-large paper shopping bags overflowing with fireworks, a bundle of punk igniters sticking out of his clenched fist.

'Tomorrow night could be windy,' he says. 'Shall we?'

They hop up, cheering, and make their way down to the beach.

Out on the sand bar, in the deeper darkness approaching midnight, they stand back from the arsenal arrayed. Fountains, roman candles, flat spinners, helicopters, scores of Black Cat bottle rockets, small bricks of jumping jacks and regular old firecrackers, snakes and smoke bombs – it's all been laid out in stages.

Before them, the lake is a smooth black mirror.

Each Mercer holds a punk stick, even Francine, who is scared of so much black powder in the presence of her offspring. Leonard is wearing a bandana, as if he's been in the bush too long. Colt is hunched over, a runner waiting for the starter shot.

'Ready?' Ray says. 'Can we go? Is it time?'

'Almost.' Warren is either sublimely playing the part of fire marshal and platoon leader, or actually so lost in character he's discovered a new self. 'Gather with me. Closer. Down here.'

They form a circle at the middle of the sand bar, crouching with their father. They can't see his face, but the whites of his eyes reveal a contagious intensity. Ray feels the gooseflesh of delicious anticipation running over his arms, up his neck.

Warren flicks the lighter at their center, illuminating their faces in a singular jack-o-lantern glow. Their shoulders touch. The night gathers, holding its breath.

'For our family,' Warren says. 'For our love. For today and ever after.'

They stay that way, huddled in close formation, savoring the moment that is their perfection.

And then it's time.

The rockets transform the black mirror into a universe of stars and comets, blue and orange, green and purple, with flashes of white-hot booms that leave trailing galaxies of smoke. The beach takes the thrusting fire and sparks of liftoff, sending the missiles off without fault or complaint, and the lake douses a rainfall of embers. Geysers of red and green make Christmas trees in June, while elves of pink and blue flutter and dance across the sand twenty-four at a go. A battery of rockets travel two hundred feet above the lake to blow rainbows against the darkness. They ride the night, the fireworks their bulwark against it, claiming it as their own. They take turns running forth to the tip of the point to set off another cannon, hurrying back to stand in alliance, heads back, mouths open, eyes reflecting the bombast of their celebration.

Just when they think it is over, Warren retrieves his surprise encore.

Mom holds the flashlight as he unsheathes his Excalibur from a tubular gun case. The homemade rocket has been constructed of tapered balsa doweling, around which five spear-tipped display torches have been bound with electrical tape, a tail delay consisting of five illegal cherry bombs, and a single ten-ounce aspirin bottle packed with black powder snugged inside the cone. The fuse is six feet long and thick as a pencil. The flaming surface of its launch sears the sand with a tentacled bomb shadow that seems wickedly alive. Then it is aloft, hurling into the sky, higher and higher until the orange flame of its booster fades into the dark.

They wait, and wait, and the sinking feeling sets in. All that work, ending in a dud. They stand in reluctant acknowledgement, slowly coming back into their bodies, trying to make peace with the dismal end to an otherwise perfect celebration.

The tangles of lightning come first, spearing out in all directions, until each tip mushrooms into a white flash that joins one to another into the ultimate circle, devouring the night in great bites, eclipsing itself in escalating stages of shattering white. The bombs go off in rapid succession, casting the five of them and the entire cove inside a star. Raymond feels the beach rumble beneath his feet, up in his teeth, through his soul.

It is as though God has taken their family portrait, capturing them at the summit of their true vacation. So that they will never forget, even after tomorrow comes.

And with it the storm.

Ray stands near the end of the sand point until the stars reappear. Until the flash-echoes of the grand finale dim behind his eyes. Trails of white smoke from the black powder circle and diffuse on a gentle breeze. The cove falls silent. No one speaks for what feels like a very long time, and Ray wonders if Colt and Leonard are afraid too, the way he is. The stillness becomes a vacancy and he turns around, surveying the beach in both directions.

The cliffs loom, the boat is anchored where they left it this afternoon, but Ray's family are gone. They returned to the camper without him? He can almost imagine it, Colt yawning, murmuring goodnight and walking to her tent. Leonard not far behind, maybe detouring through the woods to smoke one of his secret cigarettes. Mom and Dad watching Ray out on the point all alone, arm in arm, wanting to give him some time to digest the magic. But would his parents really leave him alone, without even whispering goodnight?

Ray walks uneasily across the sand bar, cutting through a tide pool to reach the main beach faster. The tide pools are usually hot as bath water from the long day of intense sun, but now they are cool, almost chilling. They are only a few inches deep, but Ray can't even make out the pale sand in this one. His legs are visible only down to the ankles, where the water is so black it provides the illusion that his feet have been cut off. He scurries out of the tide pool and glances back, across the cove, then the other way, and the water in all directions is the same, a solid shining black table. Even though he has come to know this cove and her beaches as well as their backyard in Boulder, and has never found a reason to fear it, he longs for a flashlight.

Anxious but not wanting to give into irrational panic, he trots over dry beach and trips on something that rattles dryly. He stops, turns back. It's the three-ply grocery sack his father used to carry the fireworks. Must have left it here. Strange. Dad is usually stern with them about anything resembling littering. A good camper always leaves the camp ground in better shape than he found it, he has reminded them countless times.

Ray picks up the sack, struck by a bit of ingenuity. There might be something left in the bag, a lighter or more punk sticks, any light would be welcome comfort for the rest of the walk up to the camper. He kneels, rooting around in the bag, and comes up with a pair of medium-sized sparklers. Perfect ... so long as there's something to light them with. He runs his fingers around the bottom of the bag, and there it is. A lighter.

Ray turns away from the paper sack, back against the breeze. He flicks the lighter and uses the light to align the tips of the sparklers, then holds the flame to them until they crackle to life. The hissing orange spray seems pathetic compared to everything else they just set off, but the corona around them is almost as good as a lantern. He can see a good ten feet in all directions now, and wanders up the beach with the sparklers held at arm's length the way he has seen people in castles do in the movies.

He walks faster, knowing the little rods will burn down in only a minute or two. No problem. He just has to find the cutaway path in the cliff before then, the one that leads up to the point only a few car lengths from the camper. The breeze comes at him head-on, pushing the sulfurous blue smoke from his torch into his eyes. He bunches them closed and makes the mistake of inhaling, drawing more of the smoke into his nostrils, down his throat. The bitter stink is overwhelming, and he whirls away, gagging, dropping the sparklers in the process. His eyes burn, his tongue feels coated with chemicals. He coughs, spits, rubs his eyes with the arm of his sweat-shirt.

Hurry! The sparklers are going to burn out in the sand!

He searches through watery eyes, picks one up by the wire stem, and turns for the other. His foot finds it for him. The searing burn comes a second or two after the thorn prick of the steel point registers in the middle of his bare sole. He cries out, leaping away, his weight shoving the fiz-zling ember into the sand, killing it.

'Aw, crap, no!'

He considers trying to relight it, but there's not enough time. By then the one in his hand will be toasted too. It's already halfway spent. He leaves the sack behind and rushes on, jogging despite the raw burn under his foot, aiming the sparkler to his right, trying to locate the path in the cliff. But it's all vertical wall, rough-edged, the hard-ened and much darker sand he remembers from a spot way past their camp site.

Has he gone too far, past it already? Seems impossible, but he doesn't recognise this section. He runs faster, loses confidence, doubles back.

The sparkler has burned down to its last three inches. It's okay, he tells himself, you can't be lost here, but he runs faster anyway. Back to where he started? Yes. That's the smart thing to do. Find the sand bar, he knows the way from there. Take the other beach, to the boat ramp or Leonard's tent. Easy.

Ray holds the sparkler up above his head, squinting as

he runs. Only an inch left, the twinkling fire already shrinking, dying. He can't see more than a few steps ahead, but something stands out against the long stretch of beach ... those dark outlines ... are those people? It looks like three or four people clustered around something.

Ray shakes his little magic wand. 'No, no, wait!'

But the sparkler fizzles out, a final curl of smoke threading off toward the lake. Dark again. Even harder to see through it now, his eyes slow to compensate for the loss of light. Ray tosses the metal stick aside, squinting ahead.

The people are there, standing side by side. He can't tell if they are facing him or have their back to him, but he can count them. Four. Mom, Dad, Leonard, Colt.

'Hey! You guys!' Ray calls. 'I'm down here!'

They shift slightly, but do not holler back.

Relief propels him on, jogging, grinning at what an idiot he turned into there for a few minutes. The foursome solidify as he approaches, their varying heights distinguishable. Man, woman. Leonard's thin form. Even the girls' longer hair.

'I'm okay,' Ray calls, some fifty feet away. 'I thought you all left!'

He's breathing hard, sweating, but there's no need to panic now. He slows to a fast walk, even the burn under his foot a minor complaint.

The four of them cluster again, as if huddling in conversation, and then crouch. It reminds Ray of the way they all gathered before starting the fireworks, for his father's toast. But why now? Are they going to set off one more? Was there anything left in the bag? He doesn't see a light, no flame, not even the tiny orange tip of a burning punk.

He is within conversation distance.

'Hey, what are you guys doing? Didn't you hear me?'

They do not stand to greet him, but one, maybe Colt, turns to face him. He can't make out her features but knows her shape. The way her hair falls. She waves for him to join them, and then another of them turns, Len or Dad, gesturing urgently at the ground like they found something amazing.

'A toad?' Ray says, without his usual excitement.

He stops. Something here is off, and not only how they won't answer him. Aren't talking with each other. Something is different about them, the outline of their bodies, their clothes. They look bulkier, darker, as if they are all dressed in baggy pajamas.

The last two look up from their kneeling position, and for a moment Ray catches the pale shape of his mother's face in between the others. She smiles, opening her arms to him while the others continue to peer down at the little spot of beach.

Ray takes two or three more steps, trying to make out what they are so fixated on, but it's impossible. The beach is darker than the night around them, dark like a hole.

It *is* a hole. He can see the edges now. It's not very wide, only a foot or so, but longer, a clean black plank about as long as . . .

His family aren't moving anymore.

They are staring at him, all four, and he shouldn't be

able to see their eyes but he can. They are vacant, black like the hole, set close together in their pale faces.

Not pajamas. The rest of the black on them. Not clothes at all.

Black, thick ... some sort of rotten *wetness*.

Ray backs off, and they rise.

He turns and runs, but only makes it a few strides before something cold and wet snags his ankle. He slams face first into the sand, breath pounded out of his chest. He kicks and reaches for something to hold onto as more hands tighten around his legs, dragging him back. Sand piles around his chin, into his mouth. He tries to scream but can't breathe.

He flails in full-blown terror as they roll him over, two at his legs, two more scurrying on each side to grab his arms. He is raised from the beach, gasping, thrashing, and they carry him to it. He knows what the hole is for.

His shoulders bounce against the edges, spilling sand over his face, into his mouth, and then he slips through, falling four or five feet before landing with another thud. He screams.

'Help! Please don't! I'm sorry! What did I do? Mom! Mom! Please!'

Four black faces loom over him, the black gruel of their skin dripping coldly, running off in streams, squishing behind his back, between his legs. Some horrible change has come over them, but that obvious truth hardly matters because he knows *they are still his family*. Ray recognizes the shape of his father's skull inside the black gunk, then Leonard's chest, his collarbones, his insane grin. They moan like animals in some kind of terrible pain, but between these sounds is a wet hissing, pneumonia breathing. Hunger.

Colt reaches down with one impossibly long arm and her cold slimy fingers poke into his mouth, his ears. Ray throws his head from side to side, spitting, choking, tasting something he has never tasted before. It makes him think of oil and metal and rotten lemons.

Sand falls around him, mixing with the thick mucus, a heavy clod of it sticking to his belly, and Ray understands they are trying to bury him. His family hate him and they want to kill him. The magnitude of it shatters what was left of his coherence. There is no more thinking, only raw screaming, raving terror and a sadness that feels like a spike has been driven into his heart. The weight of the sand grows heavier. He can no longer move his legs.

One arm slips free, he throws himself forward, but his brother dives in, smacking his head through a puddle of black fluid, to the sand bottom, hard enough to make him see yellow sparks. The wet sand seals around him like a blanket of steel.

Ray tries to scream again, and it fills his mouth. He swallows involuntarily. One of his eyes stops working, half the world turns black. He knows the eye is stuck open, he can feel the cold black gel on his bare eyeball.

The last thing he sees from the other eye is Leonard's hungry face – two holes where his eyes used to be and deeper, set inside swollen black lips, his brother's teeth.

They are white, small and sharp as pins, and there are hundreds of them.

Soon after the sucking and cutting begins on his neck, a coldness trickles down his throat, into his lungs and belly.

Ray's chest hardens, his heart stops.

He drowns.

A bolt of pain thunders inside his chest. His heart pounds once, stops for a small eternity that is nothing but pain, and pounds again.

A blast of light reaches down through his eyelids, shuts off.

A woman's voice, garbled, screaming his name. She sounds like she is underwater.

Another blast of light, golden yellow, then orange. He blinks, and a blue sky springs open above him like an umbrella.

Something slams into his chest again, forcing him to cough. He feels like he is coughing, over and over, but the only sound is the woman.

'Ray! Raymond Mercer! Come back! Ray! Come back! Can you hear me?'

His body heavy, cold, wet all over.

Her face flashes over him, descends, blocks the sky. Warm soft mouth, stuck to his own. His face swells, water shoots into his sinuses.

He coughs again, the force of it throwing his mouth open as a stream of water jettisons forth.

The woman jumps off, shoves him to his side, and begins to pound her fists over his back. The water rushes out like something alive.

The woman starts to cry, shaking him, saying his name over and over.

He realizes he is lying on a red and yellow tarp, a stiff and soaking wet sheet of some kind. He rolls onto his belly, barking, spewing more water and then filling himself with new air.

'Go slow,' she says. 'Let it come. Easy. There, good, count the breaths.'

His father's sail. From the Aqua Cat.

Lake. Storm. Dad. Gun. Bodies. Anchor. Black lake. Bottomless.

'Yes!' The woman pulls him upright, hugging him, kissing his cheeks, his mouth, his blurry eyes. 'Thank God, I thought it was too late. I had to leave Sierra ... swam out ...' more crying, 'but she was with us, she's here, we're alive, you're alive, Ray! I saw the sail in the cove. Red and yellow. The colors showed me! You got stuck in it, you were sinking. But without it, I was sure you were ... Talk to me, baby, please say something, say something so I know you're okay.'

Dad. Screaming, de-rigging the sail, using the knife to cut the ropes.

Her hair is wet, cheeks smeared with sand, her eyes bloodshot and naked with relief.

'Say something,' she says. 'Anything. I need to hear your voice!'

'M ...m ... my dad's gone,' he says. 'I tried ...'

She takes his face in her hands and kisses him on the mouth, then drops her head on his shoulder and squeezes him.

'All dead,' he says, unable to hold it back any longer. 'I'm sorry, Dad. I let them die. I'm so sorry. So sorry ... I'm so ...'

The sobs that have been building for the entire trip, for thirty years, tumble out of him in waves. Sharp crashing waves that bear him up, ushering him across the lake, over the beach that became their graves, to the road out.

All the way home.

Sisters

A new home, in a warehouse loft above the storefront, in an historic building at the far north end of Broadway, back in Boulder. Close to the mountains, in a once sketchy neighborhood now rejuvenated by coffee shops, a wood-fired pizza bistro and artsy entrepreneurs of the sort Ray still can't believe he and Megan have become.

He had been outnumbered two to one, so Sisters it was. No apostrophe, no Lounge, only the original concept re-envisioned for girls. More of a boutique than an old-school shop. Not too high-end, aspirational yet playful. They would offer hairstyling, manicures, pedis, an all-organic cosmetics 'laboratory' where girls could not only try on new looks but learn how to make their own base applica-tions, eyeliners, personalized lotion formulas, soaps and fragrances. Megan felt it was a progressive take on the girly things that never go out of style, empowering in some way Ray had yet to grasp. To him it all seemed cloyingly princessed-up.

'Princessed-up?' Megan had responded. 'Maybe you need to lighten up.'

Their living quarters above required remodeling, new fixtures, and little touches like bedroom and bathroom walls, toilets and plumbing, a kitchen. The exposed walls were crumbling and drafty, forcing them to sheet-rock over the historic brick and mortar. They painted the three iron girders running the length of the apartment a sky blue. Winter persisted until late March, and the cool spring was still seeping up through the old maple floorboards. New wool carpeting helped, a little. Summer would find them again, they reminded each other. It always does.

The entire endeavour – business and home under one roof – had kicked off as a survival tactic, the only thing keeping them from falling apart during those first few months back in the world – and probably would remain one for years to come. Soldiers return home to family, civilian life. But how do you leave war behind when your family, what's left of them, were in the war with you? They needed a long distraction, something to build and look at so they would not see the lake in their dreams, and in daylight, when the normal world felt alien and a swirl of cream in a cup of coffee could send you careening into flashbacks of your father drowning.

Well, life goes on.

It's what one does.

Everything is coming to fruition, or is expected to, within the next two weeks. Coinciding with the grand opening of Sisters, Gaspar expects to finalize the legal documents granting Raymond Mercer and Megan Mercer permanent adoption rights to Sierra Mercer. The wedding had been quick and dry, three months after their return, in the private chambers of a judge with whom Gaspar was friendly. The vows lacked all poetry and were exchanged hastily, the two of them eager to get through the adoption process before the courts or other outside parties decided to dig into the family records, attempt to track down Sierra's missing father.

'How did you do it?' Ray asked the lawyer one night last fall, over a steak dinner at one of Boulder's finest restaurants, not a Mercer gastro, for those had been liquidated along with everything else. 'There has to be more to it than this.'

Swirling his cognac, the Hungarian measured his words. 'As I stated last summer, your father knew his time was near and put his affairs in order. He made certain no one could trace him or Francine to the lake. Leonard was off the grid, had been for years. Colt had her own arrangement with him, the details of which he never shared with me, only to say that she needed a quick exit from New York and that Simon would not be relocating with her and her daughter. Excuse me, your daughter.'

'Did you ever find Simon?' Ray asked.

Gaspar's eyes cut at Ray in cold warning. 'London was all anyone could tell me. I wouldn't lose sleep if I were you. Men like Simon have a way of ... surrendering their parental rights, permanently.'

Ray wondered then if Colt had really been the one to do it, or if she had only given the order. Like Warren, Uncle Gaspar had been a soldier in his youth, and his wealth, accumulated through his own firm and as primary counsel for Mercer Corp., could buy a lot of things, including silence everlasting.

Environmental clean-up, for instance. Ground crews to dispose of the unfortunate wreckage left in the sands below Admiral's Point. Political influence, for another, to shut down any possibility of investigation by local police, fire departments, the state's Game and Parks Commission. Hush money. Another real estate deal. For all Ray knew, Gaspar and the last shingle of Warren's estate now owned a few miles of property on one side of Blundstone Lake.

All of this was speculation on Ray's part, and he has been trying to stay focused on the launch instead. But as the date of their grand opening nears, Ray can't help feeling like everything they have built is a house of cards. Or a castle of sand. All it will take is one wave of suspicion to wash it all away. The judgement to follow might result in criminal proceedings or something worse. A psychological dismantling, his or Megan's or Sierra's, from which there will be no recovery.

Ray loves Megan and knows that she loves him. But their soul-searching conversations tapered off within weeks of their return – along with their physical intimacies – and he longs for anything but the insensate fog swallowing a little more of their hearts each day.

If only he could stop catching Megan looking at him so strangely, in those moments she thinks his attention is elsewhere. What he sees in her questioning eyes the moment before she averts them is usually a mirror of his own troubled stew. The questions he asks himself late at night, when sleep refuses to come.

Who is this person I've decided to build a life with? How can we possibly have escaped? What awful bargain have we struck, and with what dark forces, in order to walk away from so much wickedness and loss, as if that weekend never really happened and we are two ordinary people, the kind you see in a TV commercial for new and improved *clinically white* teeth-whitening strips?

There is beauty in the way fate has chosen them, he allows, spitting them out of the nightmare in an almost perfect troika. Two lonely singles, their families gone, old enough to see the door to parenthood closing but young enough to raise a new life between them – plus a little daughter, inherited. How neat.

We became a family on the deaths of two others.

Megan is a devoted mother, doing all the right things – the reading, the feeding and bathing, and even the discipline, reminding Sierra that the loss of a loved one does not constitute a license to get everything you wanted every day for the rest of your life. But does she love Sierra? Really love her – if not as deeply and instinctually as her birth mother had, then at least deep enough that she can't imagine being without?

Ray has never *seen* anything unhealthy or cold pass between Megan and Sierra, but he's felt it. The cold seeping into the living room after dinner, while Sierra colors in her books or makes another bead necklace, and Megan always congratulates her, thanks for the gift, putting on the necklace no matter how mismatched and lopsidedly it has been cobbled together. A lingering chill after bedtime, lurking behind the walls, as if Colt is watching over them. Francine. Warren or Leonard or the woman Ray whipped with the fly rod ...

'*She might give you a few more years, the way she done us. But only if you make your offering, and this time you better mean it, Raymond. It can't be an accident like the others. It has to be true.*'

Leonard, Mom, Colt, Dad. They paid their dues. The lake took them, and sent us home. But we cheated. We never made our true offering.

Any of them could be here now, in the halls and bedrooms late at night, at dawn. There had been no funerals or memorial services, never would be, not in this lifetime. Gaspar had seen to that too.

Ray and Megan had not protested, which was another form of consent.

It is a warm Tuesday in May, the hour creeping toward four o'clock. Megan has finished the last panel in her mural, this one a playful but almost hallucinatory caricature of Sierra's favorite animated heroine, Tinker Bell, she of the fairie wings and the magic wand that showers the neighboring garden mural not with stars or pixie dust but 'butterflies'. Oversized white and red moths with cold black eyes, or so it appears on those mornings when Ray is hungover. A not uncommon occurrence, now that things have stabilized and he can't find a reason *not* to unwind with a few cold ones, or six, or fourteen, usually uncapping the first toucan about the time Sierra tromps in from day care, demanding cookies and calling him Uncle-Daddy, which he should view as a healthy transitional moniker but instead gives him the creeps.

Like the nail polish. Last week he caught Sierra painting the tips of her little fingers black. When he confronted

Megan about it, she didn't understand why he was so rattled. Little girls go through phases, she told him, they want to try all the colors. What's the big deal?

It could be a coping mechanism, or a sign of something worse. But the big deal wasn't really the nail polish. It was Megan's inability (or unwillingness) to take it seriously. Rather than start another fight (like the one they had after Megan dyed her hair black last winter), Ray had let the matter drop.

Now he is working at the back of the retail space, in the playroom that will double as a waiting room, stapling the last of the shingling to the area's centerpiece: a doll house large enough for the little girls to climb into and decorate, making up the beds, serving tea to friends real and imaginary.

Between the bleats and hissing of the air compressor powering the staple gun, he hears voices up front, and realizes Megan is not on the phone with another contractor or delivery service. Someone is here unscheduled. Inside their unfinished home. The intrusion sends a spike of paranoia through him. He sets the staple gun down and sneaks toward the front parlor to see what's afoot.

A woman in a camel-hair coat, professional office attire beneath, is nosing around with her daughter, who looks to be ten or eleven and wears a plaid skirt and matching beret. Ray goes no further than the end of the dessert bar, pretending to inspect an electrical outlet.

'Sorry for the inconvenience,' Megan says, offering the woman a brochure containing a rate card for the basics as well as exclusives. Sisters aims to reap extra profits hosting private parties after normal business hours or by appointment. 'Here, take my card. Show it to anyone when you come back and we'll give you twenty per cent off your first visit.'

'How sweet of you.' The woman beams, moved to seize Ray's wife by the arm. 'I am *so* thrilled, I can't even tell you. It's beautiful what you're doing. Something so positive for our little women and for the community. I've already told every mother I know and a few that aren't there yet but might want to start trying just so they can be a part of this, the … *Sisterhood*!'

'Oh, wow, thank you so much,' Megan says, nailing the role of the down-to-earth-yet-chic entrepreneur. She has a new wardrobe to go with her cropped black hair, and sometimes Ray can barely see his waitress under all the make-up. 'We hope to see lots of you and … I'm sorry, what's your daughter's name again?'

The woman ushers her rather sullen looking child forward. 'This is Colette. And I'm Rachel.'

Ray flinches as if he'd stuck his finger in the outlet, knocking over a pickle bucket filled with paint brushes and scrapers, setting off a racket that causes the three of them to turn on him in dismay.

'Sorry!' he says too loudly, waving like a creep. 'Just the clumsy husband back here. Thanks for stopping by. I'll just get this out of the way …' At which point he throws the tools into the bucket and hurries to the family-friendly restroom and slams the door. He is sweating, shaking, on the verge of throwing up across the fold-out diaper-changing station.

I didn't hear that. Not a chance in hell. Coincidences happen, but come on. Colette isn't a common name. Someone – or some-thing – is sending me a message.

Ray moves to the sink, where he cups cold water over his face, closing his eyes, trying not to think of Colt, the lake, the dead.

Somewhere in Nebraska the clouds are rolling in. The storm is coming. Coming back for all of us, because I never made my true offering.

Ray turns the faucet off and pulls two paper towels from the dispenser, blotting his eyes and chin. He breathes deeply and squares himself in the mirror.

Megan is standing behind him, in the bathroom, staring at him. Her eyes are solid black. Like her hair, and Sierra's nails.

Ray cries out, whirling and staggering into the corner. He catches one leg on the toilet and falls back against the handicap rail, throwing a hand out to keep her away.

'For God's sake, Ray,' Megan says, taking one step toward him, then retreating. 'What happened?'

Her eyes are no longer black. She looks the same as she did a few minutes ago, except for the scarlet flush in her cheeks. She's not worried about him. She's angry.

'I'm sorry,' he says. 'I thought . . . I got turned around.'

'By?'

'That girl, her name.'

Megan throws up her hands. 'Her name? What are you talking about *now*?'

'Are you telling me you didn't you hear it?'

'My hearing's fine. What did *you* hear?'

405

He swallows. All of the unanswered questions piling up in his mind. The morning Megan revived him on the sail. The long walk to the road. The black Mercedes that happened to be cruising down the highway only three miles after they reached it.

'Gaspar,' he says, 'I still don't understand.'

'Gaspar . . .?'

'How did he know?' Ray says. 'When to come? How to find us? Why that morning? Haven't you ever asked yourself that?'

'Jesus, Ray. We've been over this a dozen times. Your father sent—'

'An SOS with the nautical radio in the trailer,' he finishes. 'Right. I *know* that's what Gaspar said. But you know as well as I do the radios and cell phones were useless out there, not to mention my father was *beyond* the point of asking for help. The lake had him in its grip from the first morning, and you agreed with me about that too. How can you just ignore that?'

Megan pinches the bridge of her nose. 'You know what, Ray? I don't have time for this anymore. Gaspar got us the hell away from that place and that's *all* I care about. I'm buried here, doing everything I can to help us move on, but you don't seem too interested in that these days. I don't know what kind of help you need at this point, but you're not helping anyone. Not me, not Sierra, and definitely not yourself.'

'I'm sorry,' he says. Why is he always sorry these days? 'You're right. It doesn't matter.' He shuffles toward her, offering a hug.

Megan puts up a hand. 'Stop being sorry. Stop living in the past. That's what you can do if you're so sorry. The vacation's over. This is real life, so get on board with it or stay out of my way.'

She stomps off before he can add anything else. He stands in the bathroom, listening to her heels click-clocking up the stairs.

Ray stays down in the shop, pretending to work, as he helps himself to a couple of toucan beers. He tells himself this is what Megan wants, for him to keep his head down and prepare for the grand opening. But he knows this isn't the real reason he avoids sharing the evening with his two girls.

The real reason is that he is afraid of them. The way he was afraid to get in the black Mercedes with Gaspar on the highway that day, afraid to find the real reason they were allowed to escape.

Because it never let us go, and we are already on our way back.

Glitch

Megan left the front door unlocked. She did not *forget* to lock it. He is certain of that the moment Gaspar Riko's shadow spills across the floor. Megan might have called him after the little meltdown in the bathroom, asked him to come over and give Ray another pep talk. Then again, she might not have needed to.

The old Hungarian with his bushy eyebrows and droopy ears is no longer serving as Warren Mercer's eyes in Boulder, but he must be someone's eyes. Gaspar has been watching over the three of them like a hawk since they returned, involving himself in their business and personal affairs at every turn. He has probably sensed the cold tension in the new family, whether Megan reached out or not. Ray himself has been expecting this visit in one form or another, a small but growing part of him wanting to get it over with, and now here it is. The shadow on the floor, the shadow over their lives.

Gaspar lets himself in, strolling through the front parlor, past the styling stations, taking in the murals and most recent finishes with avuncular pride. He wears another of his new black suits, under a long black trench coat, its lapels blotted with raindrops. He finds Ray holding a sheet of sandpaper in one hand, the beer in another, standing behind the dessert bar with his shoulders slumped, as if Sisters were not opening in three days but is closing. Closed.

Ray suddenly knows it is over. All of it.

'You've come a long way, young man,' Gaspar says. 'I'm impressed. Any last minute hang-ups, problems with your permits?'

Ray watches the man and says nothing.

Gaspar nods as if Ray answered anyway. 'Where are the girls?'

'Why?'

'I was thinking the three of you might like to step out for some dinner, my treat.'

'Megan has a headache. Sierra had a long day at school.'

'Is she having problems adjusting?' Gaspar idles in the middle of the room, talking to the walls.

'Which she?'

'Either. Or you, for that matter.'

'We're fine, Gaspar. Just very busy.'

'Hm. You don't look fine, Raymond.'

'It's almost eleven and I'm almost drunk, so what can I do for you?'

Gaspar pulls the collar of his white dress shirt as if finding the room ten degrees too warm. But he does not remove his coat.

'It seems there've been a few snags in the adoption proceedings. I'm confident we can overcome them, but these things don't solve themselves.'

409

'Oh?' Ray is alarmed but not surprised. 'Did Simon pop out of the woodwork?'

'I think we both know that's never going to happen.' Gaspar grins briefly. 'I'm afraid the issue stems from something a little closer to home. How are things between you and Megan, by the way? Marriage-wise?'

'Solid. Committed. And who's asking?'

'Social services,' Gaspar says. 'In a manner of speaking. And me. I care about my grand-niece a great deal.'

Ray places his hands on the bar and strikes his best bouncer's pose. 'Look, Gaspar. We're working hard to build a new life. We're doing all the right things, for Sierra and ourselves. If there's a problem, why don't you let me sit down with these people? Better yet, bring them here. Show them what we're building. I'm not afraid of social services.'

Gaspar makes a *tsk-tsk-tsk* through his crooked yellow teeth. 'We can't go down that road. Too many questions. Think of this meeting as the next best thing. You allay my concerns, I'll handle theirs.'

'Sorry, but I think I'm done worrying about everyone else's concerns. I'm grateful for your help, we all are. But that was family business. This is new business. And it needs to be our own.'

'I understand,' the counselor says. 'There is a time to grieve and a time to move on. But I must ask, speaking of business old and new, how do you think this is possible? Who do you think rescued you from that sinkhole and has been rescuing you in one way or another every day since?'

'Once again, you have our thanks for the ride home,'

Ray says. 'And for looking after my father's estate, without which there would be no Sisters.'

'Your father's estate, as you call it, is me. He liquidated everything to my offices.'

'I see. And when did—'

'Years ago, Raymond. Many years ago.'

Ray is stunned but only for a moment, until he sees the next level of the darkness in his uncle. 'You took it. You drained it all. Dried it all up, like the lake. My father didn't give you anything.'

'I am hurt you would ever entertain such notions,' Gaspar says. 'He saved my life in that mess of a war, gave me my first real major client – himself, the Mercer Corporation. I would never, on your mother's soul, take anything from Warren Mercer that was not given freely.'

Ray is almost tempted to believe this. 'He didn't think I was capable of managing my own future? You're holding the purse strings for the rest of our lives?'

Gaspar helps himself to one of the barstools. 'Warren was a brilliant salesman, a deal-maker. But he made some very costly mistakes over the years. Some of them before we first stumbled upon Blundstone, before you were born. We both knew there was something magical out there, something that could be used to make our futures. But he was afraid of it. I was the first one to crawl into the tunnel. Same as in the war. Your father always preferred to let someone else do his dirty work, and I obliged. I let him have a peek, explained the potential windfalls, but he refused to listen. Said I was still banged up from Vietnam, not right in the head. But I kept his desk spotless, and we

411

were a good team, until the last decade. It was terribly painful for me to watch them unravel, like watching my own family suffer, but my hands were tied. He refused my help, until I was the only lender left in town. I told him what needed to be done, explained the risks. I was a fool for believing he'd finally come around. He made his final gamble last summer, tried to bargain with it long after the negotiations had ended and it was time to sign the papers. Well, we all know how that turned out.'

'Gaspar hasn't fixed anything for a long time,' his father said that afternoon, right after they had finished burying Leonard. 'This is family business, no one else's. Put the man out of your mind.'

'You hated him because he was better than you,' Ray says. 'You crossed a line and he didn't trust you anymore. Now that he's gone, you need another Mercer to sink your hooks into. You're still trying to win.'

Gaspar's face reddens. 'The Mercer *estate* has several outstanding *debts*. Certain clients who need to be fed on a regular basis. When they get hungry, they have a way of becoming mean little tigers in the jungle. If we neglect to feed them soon, none of this will sustain. We will all lose. Everything will come down, and I do mean *everything*. That is what your father never understood, and in failing to do so, passed the burden onto you. The timing is actually quite convenient. Summer is almost here again, Raymond, and it appears to me that you and the girls could use another vacation.'

'You can't possibly be suggesting—'

'I'm suggesting there's been a little *glitch*,' Gaspar

412

interrupts. 'The loophole your father left in the contract. The one that's been keeping you awake at night, pushing Megan to the other side of the bed. You want to move on with your lives, find peace, feel love again. I want to stay in business. As it turns out, the solution to what we both want sits on the same stretch of beach. A good lawyer never leaves a loophole in the contract, and that is why I am here, to protect all of us.'

'I'll consider it,' Ray lies. 'But only if you tell me what's really behind this. Who do you work for now? You're talking like a lawyer, but I want to hear you say the name.'

'Who do I work for!' Gaspar leaps from his barstool as if the football game has reached an exciting overtime. 'That's good! Yes! How about, the man upstairs? The man downstairs? The man with a clock for a face? There's really only one man, Raymond. I work for him. Your father worked for him. You work for him. Everyone works for him. He has many names, but I like to think of him as another father. I call him Father Time.'

Gaspar turns and scurries over to the doll house and peeks inside the windows, hopping from one to another as if searching for a lost child. He stands, whirling back to the bar. His eyes are dilated to impossible proportions and, for the few brief seconds Ray is able to look into them, the black pools inside them seem to be swirling.

'What gives him such power – you will love this, Raymond. It's brilliant, the corner he has on the market. Everyone, and I do mean everyone, wants more of it. More time. More time with loved ones. More time with friends. More time to think deep thoughts. More time to eat and drink and frolic and take pictures of the fleeting moments. More time to create a spreadsheet. More time to eat the drive-thru cheeseburgers, more time to fatten in the cubicle, more time to sit in the den watching the ball game telling your wife nothing's wrong. More time to shop in the stores, more time to click the blood-filled news links, more time to look at all the naughties on the devices, more time to steal and wage war and short the stocks and take the drugs and cheat on the taxes and fuck the little children in the ass and dig the tunnels in the earth to fill with more brown bodies. And that's all right, that's the way of the world. The world spins. Time marches on. We play our part and we always could use a little more. Time. More can always be arranged. That's why I'm here, Raymond. To help you buy more, as much as you want.'

Ray is in the presence of evil. That is all he understands. Evil has invaded his home and soon one of them must die.

'What would you do with more, Raymond? Hm? Would you like to live to be a hundred and twenty-eight? Two hundred eleven? Run some marathons? See the world? Make four hundred million dollars? Meet the celebrities and go to the parties and experience it all? All of it, the rest, not your boring life, but the good stuff only the healthy happy pretty people get to do? Or is it simpler for you? Perhaps you only want to see your family again. Eat brunch. Swim. Tell them how sorry you are, this year will be different, you promise. Maybe you can go back in time and save Colette and Leonard, pull your mother back from the cliff, tell your father not to give his middle finger to the storm and try to turn partly-cloudy with a chance of thundershowers into an amusement park, because the water isn't safe. Or better yet, stay *home*, stay away, don't take that vacation. Vacations can be dangerous, and some-one might get hurt! Stay inside, be a hermit, home-school your children so they don't get shot in the halls, make them wear helmets when they ride their first bicycle and do not ever let them pedal past the end of the driveway! Is that what you want? To keep them safe? Because that can be arranged too. You can go back to the Big Lake. It was an annual tradition, it can be one again. Every summer, not for a week, but for a month, all summer, *ENDLESS SUMMER*!'

'Are you done yet? I need to check on Sierra,' Ray says, thinking of his father's M1911. If he hadn't thrown it in the lake, Gaspar would be dead by now.

The lawyer sighs. 'It's what one does. My mother understood that, wicked old bitch that she was. My, how I miss her. But no matter. I'll see her in August. So . . .'

And speaking of the girls, why hasn't Megan come down yet? She must have heard them arguing, Gaspar's ranting. Something's wrong. Megan's hair. Sierra's nails. They brought something of the lake home with them. It's in them now, the way it was in Andie and her ranger grand-daddy. The way it's in Gaspar.

Which means, Ray thinks, it must be in me too.

'I guess all I need to do is pick one,' Ray says. 'Which one would you recommend? Young and innocent is best? Or the one who's dearest to me?'

Gaspar scowls. 'Don't be flip. He was our last ranger and a cherished member of the community. And his granddaughter? You all but water-boarded her before your father gunned her down. There's a balance to these things, kiddo, and now your family are suffering. What, you think they just *passed away*? You tell yourself they are at peace? Didn't you learn anything in the sandbox? It's not over. Your family are waiting for you. You know that. They will always be there, suffering in the heat, and you know that too. Suffering the way Megan's family suffered. They'll all be suffering until you go back and do what you were supposed to do the last time around. Don't you want to put an end to their suffering?'

'Get the fuck out of my house, old man.'

Gaspar yawns, looks at his watch. 'Very well. I've offered my advice. You have your priorities. My last duty is to inform you that tonight has been our final meeting. Once I leave, you will never see me again. Say the word, and I will book your vacation, your future will be secure, your family will suffer no more. Say the other word, and I will leave you and your *new* family to manage your own affairs as you see fit. You will no longer have to answer to old Uncle Gaspar, only to time, like the rest of the civilians. What's it going to be, nephew?'

The answer is easy, but therein lies the problem. Ray knows that going back to the lake will only beget more suffering. His father tried that last summer, and the lake won, because the lake always wins. He does not trust Gaspar, but where does the alternative lead?

'What time is it, Dad?'

'What do you care? You got some place you need to be?'

Ray wishes his father were here to help. Then, in a way,

416

he is. It's not magic, only a memory. The last time they went through the routine together, out on the Aqua Cat.

'Whatever time it is,' his father says, in a calm and heavy voice that walls out the storm, 'must be the right time. Whenever it comes. I tried to understand that in the war, and here, so long ago. But I never fully understood it until this weekend. And it's not the right time because God says so, or because men frame it in such a way they may take false comfort in the promise of Heaven. It doesn't work that way. Not for me, and I hope not for you.

'We choose our lives. Accept what we are given. We fight for more, and in the end we go with grace. There is beauty in that, regardless of duration. One good year in a marriage. One perfect sixty minutes on a football field. One night saving your best friend's life in a sweltering jungle as the fire rains down. The morning spent watching your son being born. A week at a lake in Nebraska, with the only people who matter.

'We are real. Our days are real. And that's enough because a day can mean everything, Raymond. If we understand that all of it is a precious gift. One big vacation.'

'We're not going back,' Ray says, wiping his last tear from the corner of his eye. 'We had what we were supposed to have, and it was enough. It was ours. No one can take that away. My father knew what he was doing, and so do I.'

The lawyer regards him with sad puppy eyes. 'Believe it or not, I loved your father like a brother, and I respect what he was able to make in this life. He loved his family above all else. You're all that's left of his family now, and I only wanted to help you provide for them, the way your father provided for you.'

Ray looks down at Gaspar's coat pockets. 'You never took your hands out, Gaspar. Not once all night. What's the matter? Nails a little dirty?'

The lawyer seethes for a moment, then smiles. 'I'll tell you one last thing about time, kiddo. Last summer, that fateful trip thirty years ago, what happened to Megan's family, to yours. It really doesn't matter which life you choose. Not in the long run.'

'Yeah? Why's that?'

'Because there is no long run. No short run. No tomorrow, no today. Your old man called them spokes on a wheel, ten thousand million trillion movie screens projecting at the same time, the many paths unknown. They're all meaningless, because there is no such thing as time. Time is an idea, a silly system created by humans to count meaning into their mediocrity. Our deaths are nothing more than a failure of imagination and a lack of courage. Once you accept that, you really can do anything you want, and there is no more pain. Only fun. Lots and lots and lots and lots and lots and lots and lots and lots and ...'

Gaspar's voice is still stuck in the needle groove as the front door closes behind him and his shadow lurches past the windows.

Ray stands behind the bar another minute before walking up to lock the front door. Gaspar is gone. They are on their own now. Ray can feel it. They are free. He knows that may change some day. Next year, next month, tomorrow. The money from his father's estate might disappear. Simon might come back, asking for his daughter. Sierra might grow up to be an addict, or a Wimbledon champion. Megan could have an affair with a bicycle courier, or be diagnosed with breast cancer like Andie.

But whatever happens, it will be theirs. Life, with all the triumphs and tragedies, risks and hopes and fears, everything everyone else must contend with on a daily basis. That's the deal. And it may not always be fair, but it's true.

'Daddy?' Sierra's voice calls to him from the back stairs.

'What is it, sweetie?' Ray can't bring himself to look away from the windows, the density of darkness pressing itself against their home.

'There's something wrong with Mommy,' the girl says, and starts to giggle.

Sand

Sierra is not at the stairs when he turns, and the giggle is already fading inward, like the ringing that comes around bedtime. It has no source. It is only the sound of the ear drum adjusting its dials, clearing out the day's accumulation of obnoxious sounds in preparation for a good night's sleep.

Ray walks to the stairs and begins to climb, one hand on the sidewall, his feet heavy with dread but still moving, delivering him up through the main floor of the apartment. The loft's single hall runs ahead to Sierra's bedroom and the full bathroom, and behind him to the master bedroom, and then on to the open kitchen and living room. The hall light is on.

Normally he would go to Sierra's room first, to check on her before turning in, but when he looks at his watch, a blue Timex with a nylon band he cannot remember buying, and learns that somehow it has gotten around to twenty after one, he doesn't want to disturb her. He is turning for the master instead when he notices a light coming from under Sierra's bedroom door, and this gives him pause. Megan must have forgotten to shut it off.

Ray decides to poke his head in and shut the light off, give her a quick peck on the forehead goodnight. Then he will return to Megan and apologize and tell her they are free. He's made his peace and is ready to move on. She will know he means it this time. She will see it in his eyes.

The new carpet feels too firm, even through his shoes, but at least it's warmer now. The long chilly spring is behind them, and summer will be here soon.

Sierra's door is open, just a crack. He presses the back of his hand to it and nudges it wider, stepping into her room. The bedside lamp is on, its shade casting a warm orange cone over her bed. Sierra is facing the wall, her pink comforter riding up past her shoulder, making a little tent over her head.

Ray pads to her bedside, reaching for the lamp. What stops him from turning the switch or finding it with his fingers at all is the strange way Sierra's chestnut-brown hair looks blonde on her pillow. Not light brown or dirty blonde, but actually blonde. It reminds him of Colt's hair, the way it looked when she was about Sierra's …

Ray lowers his hand and takes two steps back. His chest is tight and he realizes he has been holding his breath since he reached the top of the stairs. He exhales now, mouth gone arid, and a tickle presents itself in his throat. Swallowing three or four times doesn't help it go down. He gags involuntarily, the tiny speck freeing itself on a bit of saliva, catching in his teeth. Ray wipes his mouth, and what remains stuck to his second finger is the same color as Sierra's hair.

A grain of sand.

The hump of pink comforter shifts and Sierra rolls over, sitting up. It was not a trick of the light.

'Uhhhnnn . . .' Ray manages, before losing his voice and the ability to move.

Her hair is blonde, but it's not Colt or Sierra, this thing in the bed. It isn't anyone but a doll without a face. There are no eyes, no mouth, no nose. No such indications or shapes that there used to be. There is only a flat ovoid of flesh stretching from hairline to chin, and ear to ear, if these could be called ears. The two slightly elongated nodes are sealed over, smooth as halved pears. It is blind, deaf, mute and no one knows what else. Ray knows one thing, though. He knows that *it* knows he is here.

He feels certain he is screaming but there is only ear-ringing silence. Underwater silence. He commands himself to run, look away, fall down, but his body won't respond.

The girlish thing in Sierra's bed makes no attempt to reach for him. Her arms hang at her sides, where her ribs are showing like white bones through the cellophane of skin. Somehow it is worse this way than if she were leaping at him or screaming. It wants something of him, of whomever it senses standing by the bed. He can feel its longing like a hunger of his own, but not for food, not for blood. Maybe only for comfort, for love, and that he cannot give.

Not to this faceless thing under Colt's girlhood hair.

Thinking of his sister for the last of many times today, a bit of sympathy combined with insanity swells up inside him and he finds his voice. It sounds older, like his father's

422

used to, when his father was Ray's age and Ray was this thing's age.

'I'm sorry. I can't help you. Go back to sleep now.'

The doll does not react, not then, and not as he begins to step away, his father's voice somehow breaking the paralysis in his legs. Ray backtracks the same way he came in, never taking his eyes from the empty flesh that used, or someday hopes, to be a face.

The room feels as long and wide as an airport terminal, the time spent evacuating it measurable in hours not seconds, but eventually he is in the hall, inching the door back to its original position. He leaves a small gap of light, the prospect of shutting it all the way seeming a cruelty undeserved.

It is still sitting upright, watching him in her own way. Silently pleading for him to stay. Ray turns his back on it and walks down the hall, to discover what has become of Mommy.

The carpeting is still too firm. Passing under the central hall light, he notices that the fibers – a soft gray tone the decorator referred to as gunmetal but which has a pleasing violet hue in daylight – are clogged.

Ray bends, running his fingers over the carpet, and grains of sand spring loose. There is more, he knows, and he doesn't want to inspect the rest of the hall to find out how much.

The master bedroom door is latched firmly, leaving only a thin blade of light across the gray carpet. Ray opens the door and finds himself there, back in the restaurant,

Pescado Rojo, one of several his father once owned. He is standing beside his old booth in the corner, the afternoon hot, the open-air patio sprinklers misting patrons while desert music plays from the stereo system built into the walls. It is just like that day three days before the trip, when he still had time to say no.

It is like that day, but it is not that day.

Time has had its way, moving in the opposite direction.

As always, he feels her before he sees her, and he pretends to be busy at work, staring at meaningless to-do lists and his laptop, nervously waiting for her to come and say hello, ask him if he would like another Modelo or if he had dinner yet, and will it be the lobster mole enchiladas again, for real, doesn't he ever want to try something new?

But he can't avoid her forever, he is always dying inside with the desire to see her, because he loves her, even though he knows nothing about her, except that she is a waitress who, using nothing more than a smile, gives him enough kindness to get through his lonely days.

Her tanned bare ankles and the smooth calves above a pair of bright yellow flats are the first things he sees, and the jolt that normally causes him to look down, until his blush of desire has cooled, this time causes him to look up.

Where her tanned bare ankles and the smooth calves above her worn down, no longer bright yellow flats sway in the air. There must be a draft in the room, an open window, some other reason for the fractional motion, the twist that turns her one way and then another in almost imperceptible increments. It is not because this was recent. No. He is sure of that.

424

Ray's favorite waitress, the only girl he ever loved, has been up here for hours. She is gone now, no longer a part of this, no longer with him, no longer holding on inside this shell. He looks up, higher, over her small black apron, where she always kept two pens and her order pad, above her pretty peasant blouse and the pale shoulders it revealed, and higher still to the historic brick building's interior steel girder, an architectural irrelevancy they decided not to panel over for the sake of character and instead painted sky-blue.

Her features are all there, but the faded white nautical rope coiled around her neck has turned them a deep swollen purple, soon to be black, and there is nothing he can say to this one. She wouldn't hear him, his Megan, and, besides, Ray has no comfort left to give. She waited for him, always. And he made her wait too long.

He turns away and leaves her in her chosen state, the way she wanted him to see her at the end, because he refused to buy them more time. He refused to make a true offering, and so she sacrificed herself, and there can be no more time because this is the end, her end, their end, his own.

He leaves the door open as he returns to the hall and finds his way back down the stairs, never noticing, through all the hours he stood inside it with her, that their bedroom floor was covered in sand.

Inches of it, enough to fill his shoes.

Then there is only one door left, set in the exact middle of the two massive store windows. The pink stencil lettering that once read Sisters is gone, or smothered by such blackness it is no longer visible. No more than are the street, the sidewalk, the cars and bikes and café tables and lampposts, the portrait of his new neighborhood that barely had time to form an impression on him, let alone become a solid enough place to build a future upon and one day call home.

Ray does not fear this door, the one that leads into the blackness pressing itself to the glass with the howling fury of gale-force winds. He knows now what awaits him on the other side, and he is ready to become a part of it, even if there is nothing but a void, a fathomless pit, a cold universe where the nearest warmth is forever out of reach, light years and lifetimes away.

Because Raymond Mercer has outlasted all his people, and helped send them to their graves. He has no fear left inside him, no more love to give.

He has become ancient, with but one thing left to do.

He opens the door, and steps through.

Down . . .

Ñí Brásge

... into the sand, and the moment his sandals reach the ground, the howling wind tears the camper doorknob from Raymond Mercer's small hand, throwing sand at his eyes. The storm has been raging for hours, hours he has been trapped inside, scared and wondering when his family would return.

Hours that felt like a lifetime.

He hurries through the camp site, and the wind swings up a lawn chair, sailing it at him with a gust that nearly blinds him just before the aluminium frame pinwheels into his forehead, drawing blood.

Raymond cries out, covers his eyes with one arm and presses on. He ducks low to the ground and dashes around the overturned picnic table, only to trip on Leonard's Honda. The wind knocked the dirt bike down, leaving the kickstand up like a spike. He falls over the front end, gashing his knee on the kickstand, smelling spilled gas. He rolls sideways, crying out again, hating the wind, hating the big invisible bully.

He sits up and rubs his knee, and the sight of his own

blood makes him want to run back to the camper. But he's already out, he has to try and locate them, make sure they are okay.

He gets to his feet and runs the last twenty steps, to the place with the best view. The wind assails him, shoving at his back, as if it wants to throw him over the edge. Standing atop the cliff, he sees them. His mother and father, Colt and Leonard. And a little further down the beach, another family, the ones who've been camping in their big green tent. The parents are heavy, their teen son thin, and beside them the little blonde girl Ray saw on the beach yesterday with her dog. Yesterday? Or was it this morning? His sense of time is all mixed up, stretched and folded around itself like one of the crashing waves below.

But she's there. Her dog seems to be the only one missing.

All of them, both families, are standing in the moist sand where the waves break down and surge over their ankles. They are staring at the lake, mesmerized by the incredible rows of water, broken waves as tall as his father and as wide as a school bus. The raging lake is deep gray like the sky, except down there, closest to everyone, where it is turning black. The blackness spreads in an expanding circle, half of which lies under the waves with unnatural stillness. The other half, he decides, must be hidden in the sand.

Raymond's father shouts to the others, excited, pointing at the waves as he hop-steps out a little further. He laughs, head thrown back, mouth open to catch the rain. He hollers like a cowboy and comically beats his chest. Raymond can't hear their voices over the wind and the waves, but he understands what's about to happen. His father is in a rare mood and, now that the gear has been secured, he wants them to dive in. Swim the waves, embrace the danger and get a little crazy on the second to last day of their vacation.

But do they see the black shelf, the darker thing spreading out from the beach? Raymond doesn't think so. He knows from his time spent playing down on the beach that you can't really see the lines in the lake, where the soft brown becomes green and then the deeper blue. Also, if they were seeing what he is seeing now, they wouldn't be considering diving in. They would be running away as fast as they can.

Raymond has no idea what the blackness is, or why this moment feels so important, but he is overcome by a terrible premonition: if his family dives into that water, the black thing will find them. It will do something bad to them, or to the other family. Someone will get hurt, or drown.

The little blonde girl yells at her parents, and at first Ray thinks maybe she understands. She is smarter than they are, she sees the black thing too. But that's not it; she is simply crying. Stomping her feet, looking up and down the beach, shouting for something. She is looking for her dog, the missing dog with his wheels. He must have gotten lost in the storm.

Her brother comes to her side and takes her hand and leads her to the water. Something in the girl seems to give up. She does not call for her dog again, only holds onto her brother while he drags her out near their parents.

'Stop!' Raymond yells down. 'Stop! Stay out of the water! It's not safe!'

No one turns to look up, and he knows they can't hear him. It's at least a thirty-foot drop, the water line is another hundred feet from the cliff, and the storm is too loud. He tries again anyway, screaming as loud as he can. Over and over, until his throat hurts. Still no reaction.

They are transfixed, backs turned to him, wading in. Tiptoeing, then taking a couple bold steps, sometimes hopping back again, laughing. Raymond's father is in up to his knees, the others to their shins and everyone is gaining confidence.

Raymond no longer believes the wind and crashing waves are the reasons they can't hear him. They're not that far out. It's the lake. The lake has captivated them somehow.

He has to go down. It's the only way to stop them.

To save them.

But he doesn't have time to run to the boat ramp, or even to the cutaway path his mother led him up just a few hours ago. Every second counts now. The fastest route down is the scariest one.

The drop is sheer for at least twenty-five feet, the last five or eight a grade of steeply sloping sand. But it's not the same white powdery stuff as down on the actual beach. This sand is dark brown, chunky, with clods that looks like rocks. Some are small as pebbles, others like deformed bowling balls. If the clods break apart easily, he will probably be all right. They will help absorb the shock. But if they're hard, if he lands on the wrong one, or at a bad angle . . . he may never see his ninth birthday.

Raymond looks out one more time. His father is in up to his waist, waving them on. Leonard paddles on his back, Colt is up to her knees, and Mom and the other family are not far behind.

The black sheet spreads below the frothing waves, waiting.

Ray can't wait anymore.

He pushes off with his right foot, and the wind seems to welcome him, pushing at his back again, sending him farther out than he meant to go. He throws his arms forward as if to push off a wall but there are no walls up here, only his mind filling with images of his body breaking into pieces, and then he simply drops.

He screams all the way down. Not in hopes they will hear him. Only because he is certain he just made a fatal mistake. His legs kick involuntarily. His hands flap in circles. The lake rushes up to greet him, the waves flashing before him as if close enough to touch. Raymond's stomach contracts into a hard ball as it floats up into his throat.

The impact feels as if he has jumped out of a tree into a pit of gravel, jarring his teeth with a crack that cuts the side of his tongue open. He tastes blood as he loses the ability to breathe. His spine compresses down upon itself and springs him somersaulting over jagged clods, sand bursting in his eyes, his mouth, until he flops uselessly to a halt.

He can't hear or see anything. His heart feels as though it is beating inside his skull, through his jaw. He has no idea whether the gray field in front of his eyes is the lake or the sky, and he cannot draw a breath. His lungs are being clamped between two massive steel walls. Raymond tries to

431

sit up, falls to his side. He can't see the lake. It must be behind him, stealing his family away. All he can see is a wall of dark brown sand. He reaches for it, reaching for anything, begging to get his air back. Something in his throat clicks like a door latch, again, three times. But still he cannot breathe.

And then the big brown wall is leaning over him, shaking the ground under his back, and Raymond closes his eyes to hide from it. The weight is gentle and perfect, enveloping him in a blink, snugging his entire body inside of a very dark glove.

Muffled voices. Faint screaming. Total darkness.

Pressure above his arm. Something poking into his leg. A flash of brightness, the taste of sand in his open mouth. Dry, full. He tries to breathe, swallows more sand. Coughs fractionally, continues to suffocate. The weight on his chest eases, the voices grow louder. People are shrieking, grunting, and one of his ears takes a rough scrape that opens another door. Blink of gray-brown light. Another scrape, this one cranking the volume back into the world.

'I found him!' his father shouts. 'Here! Here!'

Sand carves away from him by what feels like ten different brooms, some of them sharp. His left leg jerks up, pain in his ankle, as another set of hands grips his right arm. Fingers probe his throat, his hip, one eye.

'Get back!' his father yells.

'Raymond! Baby, say something!' his mother cries.

All at once, Ray is borne up from the sand, layers of it sloughing off him as he rises into pure air, aloft in his father's arms.

Everyone rushes by in a merry-go-round, wiping at him, shaking him, hands over his eyes, fingers in his mouth. He recoils, coughing, and starts to cry.

He can breathe again. He can see.

Over his father's shoulder, through a screen of tears, the lake continues to rage. The beach jogs beneath them, splashing, and his father dunks him clean.

'Spit it out!' his father yells. 'Spit! Spit! Good, good . . . good boy.'

An hour or so later, they are all in the camper. All nine of them, packed in side by side, watching the storm wear itself out. The floor is a mess of sand and wet towels, the seats wet from their suits, the smell of lake water thick in the cabin. His father is quiet, solemn. His mother can't stop sobbing and hugging him, kissing his cheeks and asking if he's sure he's all right. Raymond's ankle hurts, his tongue is swollen and his neck is stiff, but otherwise he's fine. Mostly he feels worn out and incredibly relieved to see them all together, safe.

Raymond watches the blonde girl, who is no longer crying or talking about her dog but still looks sad. Rusty is still missing, she said two or three times, but no one seemed to hear her. They were too busy fussing over him.

Mrs Overton hands out cups of Hawaiian Punch. Colt pretends to read her book in the corner seat. Leonard is up in the bunk, watching the lake like Raymond was earlier. Dad and Mr Overton lean over the dining table every few minutes, faces close to the window, mumbling things to each other.

'Ever seen anything like that, Warren?'

'Hell no. Not even the monsoons churned up such darkness.'

'What is it, though?' Mr Overton asks. 'If you were a scientist, how would you try to explain that?'

'It's not soil,' Warren says. 'Not water. Not a reflection. Sky's almost blue now.'

'I can't get over it,' Mr Overton says. 'We were ten steps from swimming in that shit – excuse me, ladies and kids. But damned if I don't feel like somebody just removed my blindfold and informed me I was walking on the ledge of a skyscraper.'

'Oh my goodness,' Mrs Overton says, peeking through the small window above the galley sink. 'Is that a tent? Somebody's orange dome tent, rolling across the middle of the lake?'

'Yes, ma'am,' Warren adds. 'I've spotted two more boats since that white Hobie. Both of them turtled.'

'Any people?' their teen son asks. Raymond heard them call him Shawn.

'No,' Warren answers. 'But that doesn't mean they drowned.'

Mr Overton shakes his head. 'If not, they're in for a helluva swim.'

'The ranger's here,' Leonard announces from the bunk. 'I can see the front end of his truck, but he isn't getting out.'

'He'll wait a while,' Warren says. 'Probably come check on us once the wind loses another twenty knots.'

Mr Overton, who can barely fit between the dinner

434

table and seat cushions, turns to Raymond and blinks several times. He looks to his daughter, his son, then back to Raymond. He swallows hard.

'I don't know what that is down in the water,' he says. 'And I'm not sure I want to know. But I think you were right, Raymond. It's part of why we couldn't hear you. We weren't ourselves. For a minute there, I'm not sure I knew where I was.'

'We were all so confused,' Raymond's mother says. 'I don't trust this place. We never should have parked so close to . . . ' She pauses, her tears welling up again. 'That cliff almost took *my son*.'

'I'm all right, Mom,' he says for the tenth or twentieth time. 'We're safe now.'

'Damn lucky,' Mr Overton says. 'I hate to say it, but I believe it was ready to crumble, and maybe him jumping is what triggered it. If that wall hadn't come down, we might never have snapped out of it. We might still be down there, in that bad business.'

For the first time since washing the sand off him, Raymond's father looks him in the eyes. They all stare at him that way, wide-eyed, a little scared of him. He knows it is because the sand buried him, they thought he was dead. They're glad he's not, but he can't help feeling like he did something wrong.

Warren walks to him, crouching as the others continue to stare. Raymond looks past his father, to the little girl, Megan. Her father strokes her hair.

'When can we go look for Rusty?' she asks, her eyes never leaving Raymond's. He must be scaring her too.

435

'Soon, baby. I promise. But we have to be sure it's safe. We had enough danger for one day. Rusty will be all right. He's low to the ground and he's got his wheels for balance.'

Raymond knows what she is thinking, because he thought it too. What if Rusty got buried in another falling bank of cliff sand?

'Raymond, look at me,' his father says, taking his chin in his warm hand. He looks frighteningly serious. 'Were you scared to jump?'

Raymond nods.

'I bet you were.' His father thumbs the band aid at his forehead, where the lawn chair cut him. 'All that wind. Chaos. Stuff flying around. I'd have been scared to jump too. I'm very sorry I put you in that position. It's my fault. I don't know what I was thinking, trying to get everyone to go swimming in that. I guess I got mad the storm was ruining the end of our trip. Especially after yesterday, which was about as perfect as they come, wasn't it?'

Raymond smiles, nodding.

'You liked those fireworks your dad made, huh?' Mrs Overton says. 'We did too. We watched the whole show.'

'Actually, we thought you were all crazier'n hell,' Mr Overton says. 'But we loved every minute of it. Megan's never seen anything like that, but she'll probably never forget it.'

'I should have put my family first,' his father says, staring into his eyes. 'Your safety, everyone else's safety first. But that's not what I did. Turns out, that's what *you* did, Raymond. You risked your life for your family, and a family of complete strangers.'

'But we're not strangers anymore,' Mrs Overton says. 'God bless.'

'That's right. We made some new friends,' Warren says. He places his palm over Ray's chest, patting his heart. 'That was an incredibly brave thing you did, son. Something only the best soldiers do, in the heat of battle. You know what we call that? When someone is willing to give up his own life for the good of others?'

Raymond blushes, and can't help but look down, away from all of the eyes. He doesn't feel brave. He doesn't feel like a hero.

'We call that the ultimate sacrifice,' his father says.

Everyone applauds, even the little girl who lost her dog. Ray feels hers the most.

'And don't you *ever* do anything like that ever again, you little shit,' Francine adds, which earns a round of laughter.

The wind dies down, the sun returns to the point. The camper grows unbearably hot, everyone feels cramped inside. Not to mention hungry, the adults in need of a stiff drink. Warren insists the Overtons stay for dinner. Leonard and Shawn crack jokes together, and sometimes Raymond notices Shawn sneaking glances at Colt. Everyone files out, joking and marveling at the mess the storm made of the camp ground.

Francine begins preparing the vegetables and chicken breasts while Warren and Mr Overton amble over to tell the ranger everyone is safe and accounted for. The ranger is a tall old man in cowboy boots, with a thick mustache, and he inspects the fallen cliff with whistle of disbelief.

For a brief moment, hearing of the rescue, he cuts his steel-blue eyes at Raymond and shakes his head very slowly. Raymond supposes there is a little sympathy in there somewhere, but he senses another itch in the man, something displeased and wishing to mete out a dose of punishment. He looks away as Warren talks on, hitching his big chapped ranch hands into his belt loops and agrees to keep an eye out for the missing dog.

Leonard, Shawn and Colette walk the point with trash bags, collecting the clothes and chairs and other equipment that has been scattered around. Mrs Overton and her husband head back to their tent to make sure it's still staked to the ground, promising to return with a bottle of wine and some homemade cherry pie for dessert. Raymond realizes he hasn't seen Megan for at least fifteen minutes, and he walks around the camper in search of her.

She stands at the end of the point, wrapped in a thick blue towel, alone, with the cove on her left, the rest of the lake to the right. Scanning the beaches, the woods, and even the water, Raymond supposes. This is the best available lookout.

He approaches quietly and stands beside her. She glances up at him with a blank expression, then returns to her watch.

'No luck yet, huh?' he says, knowing how dumb it sounds.

'I'm not giving up,' she says. She sounds older than five or six, probably because of how sad she is. Ray wishes he could help in some way. Wishes he would have found her dog for her, before he caused the avalanche and everyone spent their time worrying about him.

'We could go down in the sand and look for his tire tracks,' he says. 'I'll walk with you. He probably didn't get too far. I bet we can find him.'

'Okay, maybe later. My daddy says we'll go in the truck after dinner.'

'How come those wheels? Did he get hit by a car?'

Megan shakes her head. 'He was born with a hurt back so he couldn't feel his legs. Sometimes he had to potty in the house and Mommy said it wasn't right. He'd take a long time to heal and maybe never. She said we should put him asleep. But I wouldn't let them. I told 'em Rusty was gonna sleep with me until he was all better. For Christmas, Daddy made him the bicycle, so he could take all the time he needed. This summer is his first vacation. He loves the beach. That's how come he can run now.'

Raymond looks at her while she waits for any sign. 'He knows you love him a lot. That's why he'll come back, I bet.'

'What if he forgets?' Megan says, looking up at him again.

'You saved his life. Dogs never forget someone who does that.'

She studies him, decides he is telling the truth. She smiles.

They watch over the beach, across the bay, and farther out, to the other side of the lake. The clouds over there look different. Not dark gray or black like the ones during the storm. These are white, lower and softer, forming a wide spiral that seems to be moving in all directions at once. Strange. The sky above and behind the camp site is blue, almost totally clear. Down by the dam, the last of the really dark gray storm

439

clouds are drifting away. This new formation doesn't seem related to the rest of the sky, and it keeps changing.

Raymond looks to Megan, to see if she notices it too. She does, her expression curious and remote, but no longer watching the beach for her dog.

Now several thin cones of white cloud hang from the spiral mass like icicles. Raymond begins to count them, and when he reaches eight, he sees that some of them are being sucked back up into the blanket cover while new ones drop lower, almost to the ground on the other side of the lake. He is about to point them out for her when a really big one spills down like yarn and touches the lake.

Beside him, Megan stiffens and reaches out, squeezing his arm.

They stand side by side as the wide spiral presses down, sliding closer to the lake. It must be miles across, and the whole thing is drifting toward them like a giant saucer. Ray counts the yarn-icicles again and this time reaches eleven. Eleven different strands swaying and curving, not all low enough to touch the ground, but at least three touch the lake. When they do, the waves around each stem flatten into a bowl and a spume of water leaps up.

'Should we tell?' Megan asks, still squeezing his arm.

'Prolly.' Raymond looks back over his shoulder, to the camp site.

Megan's parents are walking back with a small cooler and a bottle of wine. Raymond's dad scrubs the grill. Leonard crouches beside his motorcycle, and Colt calls something to Mom before stepping into the camper. Their voices are quiet. They don't see it. The sky above them is blue, but he doesn't think it will stay that way for long.

'We better go,' he says, but Megan won't let go of his arm.

'Look,' she says. 'Playground slide.'

Raymond looks out again as six or seven of the thin white cones rotate into each other, the spiral above sucking them into a single wide funnel. He knows what she means. It looks just like a huge white playground slide, and he can almost picture the ladder on the other side. The slide's bottom lip is wider, flat on the water. It's already in the middle of the lake and coming for the point.

'Come on!' Raymond shouts, leading her away.

The air fills with a buzzing noise like he has never heard, the sound of ten thousand bees drilling the air.

Megan clings to his arm as they run. He starts to shout but he doesn't have to this time. His mother jumps from the camper, eyes huge, running toward them. His father notices her blur past, then turns in confusion, the grill scraper in one hand. Megan's parents drop the cooler and the wine and shout their children's names. Colette leans out the camper door, not understanding. Leonard stands, holding the grip of his Honda, mouth falling open.

An explosive rumble shakes the point under their feet. Ray looks back once more to see a bowl the size of a football stadium opening at the edge of the cove, the pure white tornado becoming the most beautiful blue as it fills itself with lake.

They all see it.

They are all together as it reaches the point and carves a canyon into the beach. The screaming is his mother's and

441

Megan's mother's and then only the howl of the great slide, rapturous, engulfing.

Raymond Mercer is still holding Megan Overton's hand under the Bronco when the tires lift off the point and the slide carries her away.

Her small hand is warm and fits inside his larger hand as though it was meant to grow there. He holds it awhile, long enough for the two of them to wake up in the field of wild grasses and yellow flowers.

She sits up first, leading him across the field until they reach the cove made smooth by dawn. She tows him down the beach, running toward the point where they set off all the fireworks, and he remembers all the colors arcing over the black mirror of the night-time lake. It was the most beautiful thing he ever saw, until her.

They swim, dunking under the cool green water in the cove, taking turns holding their breath and counting to see who can do it the longest. Longer and longer, each one winning until the next one tries again. She is ecstatic to have someone to play with, leaping into his arms without warning, filling her mouth with water to spit in his face. He holds her and spins her around, throwing her over the tiny ripples to watch her splash down. She always comes paddling back for more, and they find new games to play until they are calm and familiar.

Kneeling in the rigid sand, lake up to their chins, they stare at one another, faces close, her small lips the color of peach skin, the ones that turn from red to gold. He cradles her, wondering what it would be like to kiss her and thinks she wouldn't mind. But he is at least two or three years older and, though he has never kissed a girl, he knows now is not the time. She is probably not the girl he will kiss, he probably will never have the chance, for when they are old enough she will be back to wherever she lives, and they will be strangers for the rest of their lives. The thought makes it hard to look at her, and so he looks away. Out across the water like a crocodile, trying to see the distant shore.

Her arms bring him back, small but strong around his neck.

The sun-darkened nub of her little nose. She pulls herself forward with a small splash and presses her lips to his, making a loud smooch when she lets go.

He feels embarrassed and strange but other ways too. Something more than happiness washes through him, making him warm, and he can't put a name to it yet but in his mind it is shaped like a little blue crystal filled with sunlight.

She laughs at what she's done.

On the beach around the point where the even the softest wind can't reach them, they huddle under a blanket she found in one of the abandoned tents. He is not cold, but it's better being under with her.

She leans against his shoulder while they watch the trees stir across the cove and talk about their favorite things, foods and candy for a start. Zero bar, he says, and describes it for her. He asks if she is hungry, realizing he's not either only once she answers no.

Where did everybody go? he wonders with her.

They have seen no one and no one has seen them.

I think they all got lost in the storm, she says.

How long have you been here? he asks. All alone?

I don't know, she answers, after a long silence. I haven't learned how to tell the time.

They open the blanket and lie back, holding hands under the sun. He is tempted to nap, but he's not tired yet and doesn't want to miss anything before her family comes back and she has to leave.

A distant sound makes her sit up suddenly, one hand over her eyes. Far up the beach is a dark surging spot, coming toward them, faster and faster, kicking up sand and soon they hear the crazy barking.

She pats his leg three times in excitement. She opens her arms, leaping to her feet. Rusty, she screams. Rusty, here, here here here!

The dog comes to her, a freight train of wet cinnamon fur and slobber and muscles like smooth pounding machines. His tail wagging so fast it blurs. Bunching up his shoulders and lowering his round head in the last furious strides, the dog launches himself and soars, crashing over the blanket with a delirious roll. He flops and leaps and twists like bucking bronco, slapping them with his sand-crusted tail. He tackles her and licks and licks and licks her face and she laughs and laughs and laughs.

Daddy was right, she tells him later, after the bulldog has settled in the sand beside her. The dog sniffs at him, and then at the lake every so often, but mostly he keeps his head

444

pressed to her, reminding her to keep scratching his ears.

Time heals all wounds, Daddy said, and it's true. Rusty can run.

I told you he wouldn't forget, he says.

They walk the woods, following the broken trail as best they can. The dog races ahead, through the ripped-out trees, through bushes and over the fields to sniff the messes and pale-skinned things out in the grass. Rusty whines over them, pushing his nose at them to wake them up, but they never do and he always comes back to walk at her side.

All the plants and trees are covered with sand, even the ones left standing, which are covered up to the top. The leaves are caked brown, heavy and drying in the sun. Back up through the fields they walk, through blades of grass coated with sand, passing spilled coolers and torn sleeping bags and upside down lawn chairs and trash, all the things scattered by the storm.

Her family's big green tent is gone, she says it turned into a giant kite. The white truck is not far from where her daddy parked, but it is flipped over on one side. Down the dirt road, past the iron water pump with the orange handle, the ranger truck is flat on its roof like a clumsy turtle. It is pale green with a brown badge on the door and all the glass from the windows is spread across the field like jewels.

Up the road a ways, as far as they care to walk, the ranger station still stands.

They don't like the swollen shape inside, the shadow it makes on the window, so they leave it alone.

445

What is it? she asks. What's inside there?

I think he was sad, he tells her. Because he didn't get here in time to warn them.

It wasn't his fault, she says. Poor ranger.

Going to be dark soon, he tells her. We should find a good place to stay the night.

She agrees, and they walk back to the point.

But most of that is gone, and what's left is a deep hole in the earth.

Their camper is shaped like the beer cans his dad sometimes crushed between his hands. The Bronco is sideways in the trees across the field. All the glass is gone and the seats and all the insides are coated with wet sand.

He points out their things all spread around, showing her the stick his brother used to catch snakes and his sister's favorite rainbow hair band. He finds his dad's blue Timex watch under a package of hot dog buns and tries to see what time it is, but the glass face is foggy and the hands are not moving only stuck at 7:26. He tries to remember where he was when the hands stopped but he can't.

He shows her one of his Incredible Hulk sandals stuck in a crop of wet grass. It is green with a red stripe down the middle, and the green is how he remembers it but the red is something else.

Rusty barks and runs the other way, so they follow him down the boat ramp to the beach and over to the blanket. He starts to sit, but she tells him not here.

The dog watches them from the end of the sand bar, past where all the fireworks went off. He barks but they don't listen. He barks at the lake and steps into it, but they won't listen. They carry the blanket around the point, to the other beach facing the sun.

The sun is setting and she wants to watch it go down.

It was always her favorite part of the day, the most beautiful thing in it.

They find a spot in soft sand and wrap the blanket over their bare backs. Sometimes she shivers and he pulls her closer, close as they can go. Soon they figure it would be easier to watch the sun if she was sitting in front, between his legs, and he lets her make a chair of his chest, his legs for the arms, and the blanket around them keeps the wind off better but he can still smell her hair in it, soft as it blows.

Her dog comes back, sniffing around them but no longer wagging his tail. He crouches beside them, licks her once, and rests his chin in the sand between his paws.

One time I dreamed I was really old, she says, relaxing into him.

What was it like?

I don't know. I think it was just lots of days. All of the other days.

What were they like?

I can't remember, she says, and he feels her laugh softly.

I can't remember mine either, he says. Only what was before this, the other vacations and a few things from home.

What were they like?

He thinks about it for a while. The far end of the lake pulls the sun down, bringing it closer and closer.

447

I don't know, he decides. You should have asked me before. Then I could tell you lots of things. I'm sorry. I wish I could.

That's okay, she says. Remember today? Swimming together?

Always.

The great orange is only half, the bottom under, the top floating.

She looks up, trying to find his eyes. Are you scared?

Earlier. Not now. Are you?

She turns her head, rubbing her ears between his arms.

He can't remember the dog's name when the dog stands up, licking her arm and giving a final soft whimper. The dog walks a few steps, looking back at her, then away to the reddening curve at the end of the lake. The dog barks at it, tail wagging, and he sprints off, hurling himself up the beach, hind legs throwing sand in a high rhythmic spray. He becomes a cinnamon spot running, running, until they see him no more.

She sits still inside his arms as the sky drains of color and the sand turns gray, first like the clouds from yesterday, then darker, burned to ash.

The blanket no longer holds them and he knows it was never here. The things they used to touch can't come with them.

Her name becomes like the dog's name and so is his own. He used to know it like he knew all the rest, the pale ones left in the field, but there is no more room for the names and the things and the days, only for her.

The roof of the sun becomes a single thinning arch of

blood orange, and then a last golden thread before sinking all the way. The lake has it now. Full night has come.

The wind is gone but still they shiver, pressing closer, but it's never close enough and her skin is too cold.

He waits, and she waits with him.

In the dark of the beach turned black around her feet, something moves. Brightly pale and timid, a baby toad crosses the dark ridges, kicking his way over the soft dunes. He hesitates in young but knowing caution, then scoots along, finding his way to the water by instinct alone.

She goes forth, pulling him up, leading him the way the toad knew. She always waited for him and now, in the last steps, he waits for her. She can't move her feet or anything else and he stops to lift her up, cradling her into his arms and down into the water as he did just before they kissed, weightless under the tallest part of the day.

The lake is a black mirror stretching beyond Nebraska, bottomless and longer than he ever dreamed. If you try hard enough, you can read the curvature of the earth across its surface, and somewhere beneath it the swallowed sun.

The two of them learn to swim the great bend of it as one, all.

Unbound.

When Conrad and Jo move into the historic Victorian house, it seems like a new start for them. With its fairytale porch, wooden floorboards and perfect garden, it feels as though they have finally come home.

But when Conrad is given an old photo album, he begins to discover what dark secrets the house is harbouring. Looking through the cracked, hundred-year-old pages, he finds a photo of a group of Victorian women standing outside his house.

And his heart nearly stops when he sees that one of the women – raven-haired and staring at him with hatred in her eyes – is his wife . . .

CHRISTOPHER RANSOM

THE
PEOPLE
NEXT DOOR

You will never guess their secret.
You will never forget the twist.

A PERFECT FAMILY

Mick and Amy Nash are an ordinary couple leading
ordinary lives. And then, into the house next door
move the Renders – beautiful, charming, perfect . . .
and not at all what they pretend to be.

AN EVIL SECRET

Too late, Mick learns that something is deeply, darkly
wrong with the neighbours. Who are these people?
Where did they come from? And what are
they hiding in the basement?

A SHOCKING TWIST

As death and darkness descend on the neighbourhood,
only Mick can save his family and expose the
horrifying truth about the people next door . . .

What would you do if you could become invisible?

A GIFT
Since childhood, Noel Shaker has been able to
disappear, without warning or explanation.

A CURSE
But his gift leaves Noel alone and afraid – and the more
he tries to control it, the nearer he comes to madness.

A DISCOVERY
When Noel learns that some people can see him –
and that his power has unleashed an otherworldly
evil – he must discover the source of his 'fading'.
But the truth is dark and dangerous …